PSYCHOTRON

For the martyred witches of our dark past,
and the female philosophers of the future.

PSYCHOTRON

JASON REZA JORJANI

ARKTOS
LONDON 2023

ΛRKTOS

🌐 Arktos.com 👍 fb.com/Arktos ✖ @arktosmedia 📷 arktosmedia

ISBN
978-1-915755-27-8 (Paperback)
978-1-915755-28-5 (Hardback)
978-1-915755-29-2 (Ebook)

Cover Design
Jason Reza Jorjani

Editing
Constantin von Hoffmeister

Layout
Tor Westman

CONTENTS

"The Aion is a child at play,
moving pieces in a game."
– Heraclitus

CHAPTER 1

STOLEN CHILD

They said they were my aunt and uncle. I always had my doubts. You see, my mother was the black sheep of her family. They more or less disowned her after she married my father. (At least, that is the story they later told me.) So by the age of five, when it happened, I had never met her twin sister. She and my mother were identical twins, and that was a real mind fuck when they came to pick me up. There was a much older man with her, and this was supposed to be my uncle. He was heavyset and expensively dressed, but in the gaudy style of a gangster. My mother's doppelganger wore more elegant attire, including a fur coat that she wrapped me up in as she carried me to the car. This 'uncle' had tried to pick me up, but I looked at him mistrustfully and he backed off with an expression on his face that hinted that my mistrust was more than justified and would be longstanding. In fact, I was so ill at ease with him that I almost wanted to stay with the police. But my aunt, Nikita, knelt down and implored me to come with them.

They drove me from Brighton Beach to their apartment in Manhattan. It was a luxurious penthouse in a high-rise building on the Upper East Side, which had a guestroom that was slowly converted into my new bedroom. That fall night, as I lay in a strange bed stiff as a log, with the lights on and my eyes wide open, all I could see were the horrific images playing themselves out over and over again. My mother pleading with my father to stop beating her. My little hand reaching for the steak knife on the kitchen counter to threaten him with it, so that I could protect her. His calloused hand easily twisting the knife out of mine, and then carving her up with it.

I was so hysterical with a tangle of overpowering fear, shock, and rage that it is hard to know how long I was screaming and weeping over my mother's mangled and bloody corpse while he paced the room frantically — cursing under his breath, pounding his forehead, and occasionally shouting at me. The next thing I remember is that wiry man in his blood-smeared wife-beater disappearing into their bedroom and then coming back with a pistol, which he proceeded to put in his mouth so that he could blow his brains out onto the stained and cracking wallpaper of our little living room.

They say that after suffering trauma a person sometimes succumbs to a deep sleep and then awakes with amnesia, both of the incident and of events leading up to it. That is not what happened to me. Nothing of my last day with my mother was lost to me. She had taken me to the local Orthodox church, where I always loved seeing her light the red glass candles under the glowing gold-leaf of the Russian icons. Then we walked along the beach from Brighton to Coney Island, where she took me to ride on the Wonder Wheel. I'll never forget her face, looking out over the heaving Atlantic Ocean, on that cold, gray day. There was an impenetrably profound sadness in her eyes, especially when she looked at me. For someone who was only 33 years of age, there was so much guilt and regret in that gaze. It was as if she was apologizing to me from the depth of her being for who knows what.

Perhaps I was staying so wide awake because, on some unconscious level, I was protecting myself from forgetting — guarding myself against the possibility that I might protect myself *by* forgetting. Or maybe that is exactly what would have happened if I had just lain there long enough into the morning to be exhausted. But not long after the sun started pouring in through the blinds, I heard my uncle grumble a few words to my aunt in Russian and then slam the door shut on his way to work. Never in all the years that I lived with them did it become clear to me exactly what this 'work' consisted of. It was only much later (relative to my brief life) that I was able to make a few educated guesses.

In any case, I might have finally fallen asleep after he left, but my aunt came into what was then still the guestroom and could tell that I had been awake all through the night. First she laid down next to me, and ran her fingernails through my hair in that hypnotic way that would become customary. But when this did not put me to sleep either, and she noticed that my clothes stank of the dried sweat with which they were saturated, she took my hand and brought me over to the bathroom in the master bedroom. It had a window facing the rising sun and I vividly recall the morning light illuminating the white tile floor.

She explained that there was no need to go back for my clothes, or for that matter, any of my things "in that awful house." Uncle would get me new clothes and whatever else I wanted. He was going to bring some back 'home' with him after work today. Meanwhile, I could wear one of his t-shirts after I got out of the bath. She explained this to me as she filled the tub and pulled the clothes off my listless body. Then my aunt, who acted as if she did not want to let me out of her sight, slipped her silk pajamas off before stepping into the bathtub with me.

Her body was also like my mother's, but without all the bruises and somehow less worn down. Her breasts were just as small, but they seemed more firm, and the nipples were larger — or maybe I just never remember having seen my mother with hard nipples. She wasn't as thin. In fact, although she was quite muscular and strong in her arms and legs, my aunt had a bit of a potbelly. As she stepped in over me, I could also tell that Nikita's hair was naturally the same dark brown color as my mother's; she had just dyed it platinum blond — I mean on her head. It was striking when taken together with her green eyes. She shampooed and soaped me, and then sat there quietly in the sunlight for a long while, holding my body between her strong thighs with her arms wrapped around me and her elbows resting on her bent knees. The sunlight streamed through the steam from the warm water. It was unreal. Mesmerizing. She would occasionally whisper into my ear in a tongue that sounded similar to the Russian that I was familiar with, but not enough to really understand it.

It was only years later, after the death of my uncle, that she confessed that the language (which she never spoke in front of him) was Ukrainian. She admitted that my mother was not really a Russian, but a Ukrainian, and that they had been born near Crimea in a coastal town on the Black Sea. It was only then that I grasped why I could not make out my mother's words in that last terrible fight as she yelled imploringly at my father. I had assumed that the traumatic shock of the event occulted their meaning, but she was actually speaking Ukrainian. Was my father, then, also a Ukrainian?

My aunt did not want to talk about my father, but once, when she was even more drunk than usual and we were alone together, she told me that what uncle had said all of these years about my father being a Russian communist was a lie. It was true that he had been investigated by McCarthy and the FBI, whose men in black suits I vaguely remember showing up to our home. But, my aunt explained, father misled them into suspecting him. He was indeed Ukrainian, and most certainly not a communist, let alone a KGB agent. There was an enigmatically fierce pride in her eyes when she said this.

Let me not get ahead of myself. When my uncle came home that evening and saw me in his shirt, which went down to my knees, he laughed. It was one of the few times I would ever hear him laugh, except for when he was drinking vodka with his friends and they would all burst out loudly laughing together. He brought me back some new clothes, and these were eventually replaced with ones that fit better. I remember the awkward experience of shopping with my aunt. Everyone assumed that she was my mother, and then wondered about how strange our interactions were. Neither of us ever corrected them.

School was another matter. The teachers and the principal treated me differently from the other children. I suppose they had been told what happened. It was difficult to make friends. The bus rides from Manhattan up to Horace Mann in Riverdale were long and lonely.

My room started to fill up and really become mine, rather than a guestroom. I remember lying on the carpeted floor and reading comic books. My favorites were the Batman comics. I especially identified with Bruce Wayne, for obvious reasons. The noir crime atmosphere of the *Detective Comics* in which Batman was featured also appealed to me. You see, after a while, my aunt started letting me watch *The Naked City* with her on television. It was a film-noir-style crime and detective series set right here in New York City. I think she realized that instead of triggering traumatic memories in a debilitating way, watching a show like that, even at such a young age, would help me to process what happened and make me feel like such terrible crimes were a part of life and I wasn't so singled out. Well, at any rate, that's what I told myself about why she let me watch it. As a kid, I wanted to be a detective. Our school's motto appealed to me, *Magna est veritas et praevalet* — "Great is the truth and it prevails."

For a long time, I also thought that hunger for truth was what motivated my intense interest in mathematics and science. I excelled in those subjects. To be frank, I was an all-around excellent student, and my near-photographic memory made History and Literature easy for me, but at a young age I was especially enthusiastic about math, chemistry, and biology. No one who knew me as a child would have been surprised that I eventually got an undergraduate degree in Physics. I wrote that I *thought* truth-seeking was what motivated me. Eventually, I realized that my enthusiasm for the stable and hard certainties of math and of the more mathematical sciences was a psychological defense against the almost overwhelming chaos of the uncanny and downright bizarre experiences that filled my life.

It started with the recurring dreams. No, these were not night-mares rehashing the death of my parents. I had surprisingly few of those. I am talking about a series of dreams that I started having around the age of six, where I was an old man living out of suitcases in hotel rooms. Although I couldn't call them nightmares, they were extremely disturbing. I would wake up from them filled with the most profound sadness, a feeling of being forlorn that did not belong to the consciousness of a six-year-old (however tragic his life had been thus far). No, the inner life of that old man would bleed over into my wak-ing consciousness for a while after each dream.

He had been abandoned and forgotten by the world. I saw him in a place that I later identified as Bryant Park, feeding pigeons, who were his only friends. How is it possible for a six-year-old to know what it feels like for an old man to pull the loose skin tighter on his face as he shaves in his bathroom mirror? Or what it feels like to pull your suit pants up too high, and buckle them too tight with your belt, because you're starving yourself to death, and although your clothes are all too loose you can't afford to buy new ones. How does a six- or seven-year-old know what that feels like? I did. The lobby of the hotel he was living in had high ceilings, and I remember him sitting there in a chair, with a filthy spittoon next to it. What little he ate, he ate in the diner that was connected to that lobby. He couldn't walk far and had a limp. You see, he had been hit by the front grills of one of those old New York checkered cabs, and it had fractured his leg. But when bystanders rushed to the old man's aid, he refused treatment. He was too embarrassed to wind up in a hospital and have the doctors leak to the press that the great man he once was had fallen on such hard times that he couldn't pay the hospital bill. Later in life, I recognized the hotel. It was the New Yorker.

My strange childhood experiences were by no means limited to these recurring dreams. Some of them are *so* strange that I cannot for the life of me put them into any sensible context. I am sure that, given my history, most psychologists would consider them false memories. But they are not. These things happened, and they were as 'real' as anything that happens. Let me give you just a few examples.

Once, my aunt took me to a house that had been decorated to look like the North Pole — you know, the way a place might be done up like that around Christmas. Except it wasn't Christmas, and the snow in the yard was fake. In fact, it was summer! She told me that we were going to see Santa Claus. We went up this narrow stairway in the house, which was full of dolls of elves and lit-up candy canes and the like. One of the doors in the hallway upstairs was marked with a sign that read "Santa Claus" in childlike handwriting. It was creaked open, and I can't remember a thing that happened after we walked into it, other than that I had every intention of sitting on Santa's lap. Oh, one more thing. There was an ice cream truck parked in the lot out front. I recognized it as the same one from our neighborhood, because even though no one seemed to be inside, its music was going, and this truck was broken and had a peculiar glitch in its tune.

Then there was this Greyhound bus ride that we took. It was just my aunt and me. We were headed back from Shoreham, Long Island, where for some reason she had taken me to see a run-down brick building that she said had been a mad scientist's laboratory. I guess I had become obsessed with the Frankenstein films, and she told me this man, who shared my name, "Nikolai," would create artificial lightning inside the lab, like the lightning that brought the monster to life in the movies. Or maybe she had another reason for taking me there, as I later came to suspect. But the building was practically a ruin, and being inside it, I was suddenly plunged into the densest depression that I have ever felt. But that is not what I wanted to recount.

We were headed back from this place, and just before we got on the bus, a shudder ran through my spine as I noticed a freakishly tall and very peculiar-looking man in a black suit and black tie, wearing a fedora hat. In retrospect, I would say he looked a bit like Lurch from the Addams Family. He was essentially Nordic in appearance, with buzz-cut platinum blond hair, but his facial features were extremely chiseled with high cheekbones and preternaturally large, mesmerizing blue eyes, sunken into deep sockets that surrounded them with dark shadows. The brim of his black hat appeared to conceal an unusually high forehead. He was loading what appeared to be a violin case into the luggage compartment under the bus. He hurled it with such force that the case popped open, and there inside it was the exsanguinated cadaver of a black dog, crushed in such a manner as to make it fit into the case. The man in black gave me a hard stare, one that silently said, "Yeah? What are you going to do about it?" At this point my aunt, who appeared not to have noticed, was pulling me by the arm up the stairs of the bus. What is at least as odd is that this man did not join us as a passenger.

We had a ski house at Hunter Mountain, a couple of hours north of the city. My uncle had taught me to ski. Despite his weight and his age, he was pretty damn good at skiing. One Friday evening, we were supposed to go up to the chalet for the weekend, but my uncle had some 'business' in the city that came up at the last minute. I was terribly disappointed. So instead of cancelling the trip, my aunt drove the two of us up there herself. I used to love watching her when she would drive. Bobby Darin's "Dream Lover" was playing on the radio as we wound our way through those narrow, wooded mountain passes with frozen waterfalls. Anyway, it was really late by the time we arrived. She quickly cooked us a little dinner from groceries that had been packed in the back of the car. Then we went to bed.

In the middle of the night, probably somewhere around 2 am if I had to guess, my aunt came into my room and woke me up. She was crouched down by the side of the bed, fully dressed in her ski outfit, and put her long bony finger across her lips as if to say: "Shhh." She got me out of bed, dressed me warmly, and then took me out into the cold to hike up into the woods of the hillside overlooking the ski resort, under the crisp starry night sky. She held me with one arm around my shoulders, with my head pressing into her jacket, as the snow crunched under our boots.

We got to a little clearing on the wooded hillside where the snow was slightly brushed off of what appeared to be a wooden trap door. Like a cellar door, with a black metal handle. She brushed some of the dusting of the freshest snow off it and then threw it open. Her green eyes were sparkling at me mischievously, as if she were also a child and we were on an adventure together. The moonlight made the platinum hair falling over her shoulders shine so steely. She took my hand and we descended into the darkness, down some creaky old wooden steps until we felt packed earth beneath our feet. I could hear glass and metal clinking, and then the blue flame of the lamp that she had reached for in the darkness flickered on.

The walls were covered in embossed designs, as if they were pressed into the earth but baked hard. My child's mind could hardly make out what these depicted, but in retrospect I hazard that they were Gorgons and owls. The place smelled of something between sulfur and cinnamon. I could feel goosebumps on the back of my neck as I got the impression that we were being watched from out of the dark corners. You might imagine that at this point I would have been terrified. Perhaps, and there was certainly something of terror in the emotions that seized my whole body with a visceral intensity beyond the mind's feeble comprehension. But that terror was overpowered by an awful fascination and excitement as my aunt proceeded to take her clothes off. All of her clothes. She took mine off too, and she pulled me down onto the cold packed earth with her. Her nipples were so hard, and so was I. She was dripping wet when I slipped into her.

The next thing I remember is her making breakfast in the morning. Now and then she cast me penetrating glances as I sat at the table while she was cooking in the kitchen. It was as if she was wondering whether I would let myself believe that it was just a dream. But I wouldn't, and at the first opportunity that I had to go out hiking into the woods alone — near sunset on some late afternoon a couple of years later — I went looking for the clearing and the trap door. What a feeling of dread and anticipation filled me as I finally scraped the snow off the wood and found it. When I mustered the courage to pull the black metal handle, it broke off from being so badly rusted. I resolved to come back with a shovel, perhaps in the spring, and pry it open. But my uncle died of a heart attack before the end of the ski season, and my aunt sold the Hunter Mountain house.

By now, I am sure that you see what I mean, and I have not even mentioned that sometimes I could hear people's thoughts in my head. It could easily have become debilitating. This also gave me a very early insight into how hypocritical most people are. It was especially bad when my uncle would invite people over for his boisterous parties. His macho friends contemptuously thought that I was an introvert crippled by shyness, but they did not realize that it sickened me to hear their thoughts — or feel their desires — inside my mind, especially since they all wanted to fuck my aunt. Well, she was beautiful, and so much younger than my uncle and most of his 'associates.' They wouldn't dare slight him by addressing her vulgarly around the dining table, but they were all imagining that they could show her a better time in bed. This 'ability' also got me into a lot of trouble at school. Kids are cruel enough to each other out loud, let alone in their heads.

Consequently, math and science really did become my salvation. I relished the reliability of equations and the elemental stability of nature's laws as I (falsely) imagined them. When I discovered Asimov's *Foundation* series and read it voraciously, I realized to my delight that it might be possible to take the same approach toward Psychology and History. I started psychoanalyzing the literature we were assigned, trying to categorize the behavior of the protagonists under certain definite patterns of personality that would have predictive power. Far more troublesome, at least for my teachers, was an increasing insistence that there had to be laws of history as there were laws of nature. My memory was excellent, so none of my history teachers could fault me for having forgotten any of the names and dates that we were forced to mindlessly 'learn.' That made them all the more frustrated in the face of my incessant challenges to them to *explain* the history that we were being taught. In other words, to convey some understanding of *why* things happened where and when they did, what the logic, interconnection, and developmental trajectory of these events was supposed to be.

Given my Russian background, some of the faculty at posh Horace Mann started to suspect that I was raised and indoctrinated by Marxists. At the time, I had no idea that Karl Marx had sought to develop a science of history, not altogether unlike the Galactic "Psychohistorians" that Asimov had imagined in *Foundation*. Their casting of aspersions was a catalyst for my discovering Marx. It is a good thing that my uncle was dead, because I think if he had seen me come home with the school library's *Communist Manifesto* in hand, he would have given me an unforgettable beating. "Like father, like son," he'd have said. Nikita was knowingly amused, and even bought me my own copy of the book. She always encouraged my intellectual development.

My serious interest in Marx, and then more generally in the claim of Communism to be a comprehensive science, served to enliven the connection that I had with my Russian heritage. Sputnik and the Soviet dominance in space only strengthened my pride in the Promethean spirit of the Communist commitment to science and technological innovation as the spearhead of human empowerment and liberation from every manner of backwardness and oppression. Senator McCarthy was, to my adolescent eyes, a modern-day American inquisitor comparable to those who ordered witches to be burned alive at Salem. By the time that the Cuban Missile Crisis took place in the weeks before Halloween of 1962, I had already developed a strange sense of the

Soviet Union as my motherland. I say "strange" because, although I did feel that natal and organic tie to Russia, it was the universality — even the *cosmic* destiny — of the Soviet idea that really appealed to me.

The 1964 release of *Dr. Strangelove* only intensified this feeling, and it probably triggered what would become an obsession with nuclear war. I remember reading Herman Kahn's book *Thinking About the Unthinkable* at the age of seventeen, only a couple of years after it came out. Kahn was a futurist and military strategist for the RAND Corporation think tank, and one of the founders of the Hudson Institute. He applied systems theory and game theory to thermo-nuclear warfare in what was the first and what remains to this day the most chilling and hair-raising analysis of how a nuclear war could be fought and 'won.' Kahn was one of several figures that inspired Stanley Kubrick's character of "Dr. Strangelove," specifically his earlier book *On Thermonuclear War*, and I admit that articles that noted this fact led me to *Thinking About the Unthinkable* and subsequent futurist writings of his, such as his visionary speculations on *The Year 2000*.

As fueled by news, films, and books my concern with nuclear war may have been, it was much more personal and profound than any morbid intellectual curiosity. I had nightmares. Literally. I would wake up in the middle of the night drenched in sweat, and then go out onto the wrap-around terrace of our penthouse apartment, with its spherical lights, breathing the night air with such urgency that it was as if I had just been exhumed from a mass grave. I would survey the expansive panorama of the city lights framing the primal darkness of Central Park and superimpose upon it the horrific sight witnessed in these recurring nightmares. They would begin with me in bed, waking suddenly from a blinding flash of light. Then I would go out onto the terrace through the shards of the glass doors shattered by a shockwave, only to see New York City burst into flames. The sensation of my body burning as if from within is what would wake me up. There were other thoughts in the dream, but these remained indistinct. It was as if they were the memories I had at the moment when I was awakened by the Soviet strike, memories of things that haven't happened yet. It would be a few years before I could tease apart what these 'memories' of the future consisted of and what picture they painted of the events leading to the war.

My aunt was in her mid-forties at the time, sleeping alone in the master bedroom, about a decade after my uncle's fatal heart attack and just before she died of her overdose. On one of the first occasions that I was visited by this nightmare of a nuclear holocaust, she heard me go out onto the terrace and joined me there. It was a hot summer night and she poured chilled Stolichnaya for us as she sat on the cushioned chairs in her silk robe, encouraging me to confide in her. I did, and she said some very strange things to me about atomic bombs and the aftermath of the Second World War that I did not understand until much later in my life. These things had to do with the Germans having built nuclear weapons *before* the Americans. She said that people, both Americans and Russians, had been told many lies about the war with Germany. This was the same night that she let it slip that my father was really Ukrainian, like herself and my mother, and that he was the furthest thing from a Communist, although he had behaved in such a manner as to deliberately come under the suspicion of having been one.

We got really drunk together that night. When I braced her as she eventually stumbled through the living room and the hallway back to bed, I was not of a mind to resist as she undid her robe and pulled me in with her by my hair. "*Pavuk plete,*" she whispered as her nails ran across my scalp and dug into the back of my neck, "*Pryyde pavuk.*" The spider is weaving. The spider will come.

I didn't know why at the time, but those cryptic words in my mother's tongue made me think of the Mabuse movies that my aunt had taken me to see with her. It was a trilogy of Fritz Lang, the last installment of which had come out in 1960, when she caught me up on re-releases of the first two films so that I could appreciate it. My mother's name, Marianna, was the Russian iteration of the name of the female lead, and the super-villain's lover, in *The Thousand Eyes of Dr. Mabuse*. That stuck with me. So did the concept of "The Empire of Crime" masterminded by the parapsychological terrorist whose specter defies death and prosecution by any earthly law and order. Something about the way my aunt whispered "spider" in Ukrainian that night made me think of Mabuse and his invisible *Reich*.

CHAPTER 2

MAGIC THEATER
OF CRUELTY

The sun had just risen when, on an early September morning of 1965, I arrived on the campus of Columbia University well in advance of my first college class. The steps around Athena were still empty, so no one saw me kneel to "Alma Mater" before I ascended the grand stairway up to the Rotunda. Strolling back and forth along the colonnade, I looked over the shoulders of the goddess of wisdom and war and surveyed the august names engraved above its Ionic columns, with Plato, Milton, and Goethe among them. Philosophy fascinated me, and I was drawn to Luciferian or Faustian literature, but I had already decided to exploit my aptitude for mathematics and exact sciences by majoring in Physics.

The fact that I did not live on campus meant that I was less distracted from my studies. I would commute daily from 77th and Cherokee, essentially spanning Manhattan every morning in a pilgrimage from the East River to the Hudson. I would often take the time to walk to the bank of each of them, so that I could overlook both on the same day. After my aunt died of a drug overdose (no doubt exacerbated by her consumption of alcohol), I decided to stay in our apartment. Somewhat morbidly, I even moved into the master bedroom and slept in the bed that I found her lifeless body sprawled across one morning in the late summer before my first year of college. The doormen, handymen, and the management were a bit unnerved by this, and there were undoubt-edly unkind rumors circulating about me. But my aunt had left me the apartment in her will, together with everything that she inherited after my uncle died. This inheritance amounted to a small fortune.

One might imagine that being independently wealthy, I would have used my penthouse apartment for wild college parties. Actually, the wealth somehow served to increase my isolation. So did the fact that everything in our building was self-contained. We had our own bank, post office, grocery store, shopping mall, full dry-cleaning service, and other amenities catering to shut-ins who liked to pretend to be "too busy" to see to all these things by themselves. Truth be told, this is one of the reasons that I stayed. There was even a regularly scheduled private bus to shuttle residents to midtown Manhattan and back home, so that we could avoid crowds on the subway. I would often walk to and from Columbia across Central Park. That helped to keep me in shape, with little other exercise left in my life. After my aunt died, the thought of going skiing alone in the winters was depressing to me. The two of us had continued to go up to Hunter Mountain together even after she sold the ski house. We would stay at Scribner Hollow, and would often be the last ones soaking in the underground grotto at night. It was almost inconceivable for me to go back there without her. Besides, I had never learned to drive and that would make it hard to stay overnight.

For my first few years at Columbia, that is, before the events that transpired on the campus during my senior year in 1968, the closest rapport that I had with anyone was not with a fellow student but with a teacher. After taking several classes with him, I became the protégé of Professor Gerald Feinberg of the Physics department. Gary was a dynamic lecturer with a dazzling ability to convey complex theoreti-cal knowledge in a way that could even be compelling to laymen. He would go on to make a career out of writing books that popularized the promise of science and technology for transforming the human future. Gary had penetrating and mischievous eyes that reflected his visionary genius, but for such a farsighted man he was also exceptionally kind and patient. By the time I was writing my senior thesis paper on the Many-Worlds Interpretation of Quantum Mechanics under his advisement, he had become my friend and not just my teacher. Gary had me over for dinner at his home on more than one occasion. We would often have coffee together around Morningside Heights, especially at his favorite Hungarian pastry shop across from the Cathedral of St. John.

My thesis already marked a transition from Physics into Philosophy, and if a less philosophically minded Professor than Gary Feinberg had been my adviser, I doubt that it would have been approved. Not only did Gary approve my thesis, but he also urged me to take a few more philosophy courses, stay an extra year at Columbia — a decision that would prove fateful — and secure a second major, in Philosophy, before graduating in 1969. My thesis argued that the MWI of Hugh Everett was incoherent because it denied free will, which is the precondition of even the most basic intentionality required to frame *any* testable theoretical model of physical phenomena.

Basically, the idea was that if the quantum uncertainty of probability functions was resolved *in every way that it could possibly be*, but that this was hidden from us because each resolution of a wave into a discrete and measurable particle took place in one of infinitely many parallel universes that are *isolated from one another*, then no 'person' in any one of these universes — including ours — ever really made a choice about anything. If our brains are made up of quantum particles, then what seem to be our trains of thought, let alone our decisions, are actually just the random outcome of wave function collapses. In every one of the parallel universes where there is a version of us, each of us thinks everything imaginable and makes every 'decision' leading to every action that we do not 'choose' to do in the other universes — including this one.

The moral implications of this are monstrous, but even just on an intellectual level, it makes nonsense out of rational thought. The kind of reasoning involved in developing a scientific theory, which must be testable in practice — in other words, through meaningful action — is a cognitive process that is intrinsically intentional. It requires some basic level of free will, even if this will is massively conditioned by all kinds of contingencies — physical, biological, psychological — beyond our control. It still has to be the case that the scientist has some cohesive agency, which is impossible unless he has an individual character defined by a coherent trajectory of meaningful choices that reflect *his* persona, aims, and interests. That kind of agency is precluded by the MWI of Quantum Mechanics, and so the theory itself is incoherent because it denies the ontological or epistemological preconditions of *any* meaningful scientific thought *as such*.

Far more interesting than this thesis is what came out of it in terms of my relationship with Gary. Feinberg found the paper fascinating for two reasons that were very relevant to his own work. The first was that it considered the scientist as a *type* of person and science as an *activity* in humanistic terms or from a perspective that I later realized was "existential." Feinberg was hardly an existentialist, but at just that time he had been developing a Promethean vision of the social task of the scientist to expand and explore the horizon of the human potential for future evolution. The second thing about my senior thesis that appealed to him was its implicitly non-reductionist view of the relationship between consciousness and physical phenomena. My argument at least implied that we needed a new Physics that, even if it did not abandon materialism altogether, would allow for an account of human thought and intentional action that described the mind as something more than an epiphenomenon of physical mechanisms. Gary was also looking for this and had been so bold as to seriously consider Parapsychology research as a domain wherein he might find evidence for it.

Before coming to Columbia, Gary had been a member of the Institute of Advanced Study at Princeton University and garnered a security clearance at Brookhaven National Laboratory on Long Island. Only those closest to him knew that this had brought him within the orbit of private think tanks and secret policy advisement groups with access to classified projects. Later, these groups would also grant him entrée to Rockefeller University, where he worked part-time in addition to his teaching responsibilities at Columbia. This nexus of clandestine connections was the matrix for Gary's monumental 1967 paper in *Physical Review* on the "Possibility of Faster-Than-Light Particles" and his monumental 1969 book *The Prometheus Project: Mankind's Search for Long-Range Goals*. The 1967 paper postulated the existence of a type of quantum particles that Feinberg named "tachyons," which he proposed were the physical basis for the hitherto anomalous mental abilities of precognition and psychokinesis. The 1969 book was nothing less than a proposal for a techno-scientific elite to take control of the world and guide a unified humanity into the achievement of Promethean goals such as radical life-extension (including by means of cryonics), the development of superhuman intelligence (by means of both genetic engineering and computational cybernetics), and colonization of the entire solar system. During the whole period in which Gary developed this vision, from 1966 through 1969, I was his protégé and confidant. Though I admit that in 1968 and 1969, my attention was more than a little divided.

Shortly before the spring of 1968, after I had begun seriously pursuing my second major, in Philosophy, I met a woman studying at Barnard (which was Columbia University's girls' college until coed integration in 1983). At that point I was almost 21. Anna was only 19. We met at the Hungarian pastry shop, where she was reading Dostoyevsky *in the original Russian*. This, together with her extraordinarily Eurasian beauty, was striking enough for me to overcome my characteristic introversion and address her *in Russian*. I asked, "Was

Raskolnikov wrong to think he sinned by aspiring to be a superman?"
She was toward the end of *Crime and Punishment,* and by the looks
of it she had read the beat-up volume several times already. To my
extremely inappropriate question, forwarded without any pleasantries
or personal introduction, she replied in a slow and deliberate manner,
after only a brief silence during the course of which she looked un-
flinchingly into my eyes, I dare say even trying to pry into my soul. "He
was mistaken about what it means to be a superman. Wrong about it
when he aspired to be one, and even more so, when he repented of it."

Within days of that first encounter, Anna and I were taking the subway from her dorm at the top of the hill on Morningside Heights down
to the Village to see late night screenings of Russian cinema together.
One of our favorite places became the Nicholas Roerich Museum on
West 107th Street, across from Riverside Drive. She introduced me to
the writings of a subversive group of Russian thinkers, who had been
exiled, mostly to Paris, after the 1917 revolution. My aunt had mentioned some of these intellectuals, but it was only after I met Anna that
I read them. The two with whom I felt the greatest affinity were Nikolai
Berdyaev and Konstantin Tsiolkovsky. The former was an existentialist whose fundamental concern was with the idea of freedom and its
realization as a divine destiny. The latter, who was the only one of this
group of dissidents to evade exile, was a rocket scientist and futurist.
He advocated our eugenic evolution into psychic cosmonauts who
would leave Earth behind as a womb while colonizing the universe;
the Soviets overlooked his ideological deviation, especially his eugenicist views, so that he could set up their rocketry program.

Anna's interest in Tsiolkovsky was somewhat outside the scope of
the subjects that she was most captivated by. She was studying both
Theater and Literature at Barnard, in the context of which she had al-
ready begun writing a book of her own titled *Magic Theater of Cruelty.*
It was a study of the idea of "the Magic Theater" in Herman Hesse's
Steppenwolf from the standpoint of Antonin Artaud's concept of the

"Theater of Cruelty." Actually, I would characterize Anna's argument in this book as a philosophical thesis, and I tried to encourage her to formally study Philosophy.

Anna's manuscript began by noting the centrality of the theme of suicide in Hesse's *Steppenwolf*. She showed how it was intricately woven into the narrative and served as a reflection of the protagonist's existential struggles and his search for meaning and identity. Throughout the book, suicide is explored as a profound existential dilemma and a potential solution to the protagonist's inner turmoil. Harry Haller is depicted as a deeply troubled individual, plagued by a sense of alienation and a feeling of not belonging to the world. He is a self-proclaimed "Steppenwolf," a lone wolf figure who feels disconnected from society and finds solace in his own inner world. Haller's intense existential crisis leads him to contemplate suicide as a way to escape the pain and disillusionment he experiences. He despairs and yearns for a release from his inner conflicts. But as he delves deeper into his existential crisis, Haller encounters Hermine, a woman who becomes a catalyst for his transformative evolution. Hermine challenges Haller's nihilistic perspective and encourages him to engage more actively with life, thus providing him with an alternative to his contemplation of suicide. Through their relationship, Haller begins to question his own assumptions and beliefs.

The key turning point is when Hermine invites Harry to visit some place called "the Magic Theater." This occurs in the second part of Hesse's novel, titled "Treatise on the Steppenwolf." After some initial skepticism, Harry decides to accept the invitation and ventures into the world of the Magic Theater. He enters the theater, which is described as a place of mystery and enchantment, where reality and imagination intertwine and the distinction between them is eventually deconstructed. The Magic Theater serves as a transformative space where Haller undergoes a series of encounters and experiences that challenge his perceptions and lead him towards self-discovery.

Inside the Magic Theater, Haller encounters a series of rooms or performances, each representing a different facet of human existence. These rooms offer a range of experiences, from sensual and erotic encounters to philosophical discussions and confrontations with his own inner demons. Each room exposes Harry to a different aspect of his psyche, forcing him to confront his fragmented identity and grapple with his existential struggles. One notable encounter within the Magic Theater is Haller's interaction with the jazz band and the young man Pablo, whom he is romantically attracted to. This encounter represents a passionate and sensual experience that awakens Harry's suppressed desires and challenges his rigid self-image as a repressed and detached Steppenwolf. Another significant episode takes place in the "Harry Haller's Records" room. Here, Haller confronts his own biography and the limitations of his self-perception. The room contains recorded narratives of his life, forcing him to examine his past, his relationships, and the choices that have led him to his current state of alienation. Additionally, the room of the "Immortals" presents Haller with an allegorical play that addresses the universal struggle between the Apollonian and Dionysian forces within the human soul. This performance encourages Harry to embrace the dualistic nature of his being and find harmony between the opposing aspects of his personality. The culmination of Haller's experiences within the Magic Theater is a climactic confrontation with a figure called "the Treatise Writer," who reveals himself to be an older version of Harry Haller. This encounter symbolizes Harry's confrontation with his own mortality and serves as a catalyst for his final transformation.

As Anna argued in *Magic Theater of Cruelty*, the Magic Theater described by Hesse is a realm beyond conventional reality, inviting exploration of the depths of one's psyche and the transcendent aspects of our existence. It is a mysterious and enigmatic place that, by offering us a series of surreal and symbolic experiences with archetypal power, serves as a space where the boundaries between imagination and reality are effaced, and one is left to confront one's fragmented identity on an existential level by diving into the depths of one's subconscious. Hesse was, in Anna's view, making the point that there are dimensions of existence that outstrip the so-called "reality" that our ordinary senses perceive, and hidden forces at play beyond the cognitive grasp of conventional thinking and that defy our attempts at rational explanation. Anna argued that this defiance is violent, in the sense of violation. Without the cruelty of this violation, the Magic Theater could not offer a transformation of alienation.

This argument in Anna's manuscript marked the turn to a focus on the work of Antonin Artaud, particularly his concept of the "Theater of Cruelty." Artaud most fully formulated this idea in *The Theater and Its Double* (1938), but he had been developing examples of the idea long before that. As early as 1925, in *Jet of Blood*, Artaud aimed to disturb the audience by presenting a series of disjointed and grotesque scenes. The play included shocking imagery, irrational dialogues, and a fragmented narrative that defied conventional storytelling. All in all, this created an experience that overwhelmed and disoriented the audience, confronting them with the absurdity and irrationality of existence. His 1935 adaptation of Percy Shelly's play *The Cenci* sought to intensify the emotional impact of the play by creating an atmosphere of visceral brutality. Artaud used harsh lighting, dissonant sounds, and exaggerated gestures to unsettle the audience. He also introduced elements of physical violence, including a scene where one of the characters is beaten with a mallet. The intention was to challenge the audience's notions of comfort and conventional theatrical boundaries.

Artaud believed that the traditional theater had become stagnant and divorced from the potential depths of genuine human experience. He sought to create a new form of theater that would use intense emotional and even physical responses from the audience to break down the barriers between the performer and the audience, and challenge societal norms, by engaging the spectators on a visceral level. Artaud saw art as a means to break free from oppressive social structures and to reconnect with a more authentic and primal existence. He criticized the limitations imposed by rationality and the societal norms that stifled individual expression. Artaud's work aimed to disrupt these constraints and create spaces for liberation and transformation.

As Anna explicated it, Artaud's "Theater of Cruelty" was an idea for a revolution in the nature of theater along these lines. Seeking to break free from the limits of representational language and to reconnect with the primal and irrational forces of existence, Artaud argued that theater should not merely entertain or provide escapism, but rather should be a visceral and transformative experience, which confronts and challenges the audience. The audience should be engaged and violated, not entertained as spectators. The purpose of this "cruelty" is to awaken dormant emotions through a relentless confrontation that shakes the audience out of their complacency and confronts them with the harsh realities of life and the contradictions of human existence.

Artaud's attempt to create an intensely immersive theatrical experience that bypassed rationality involved a radical rethinking of elements such as language, gesture, movement, sound, and space. Artaud argued that words had become empty and divorced from their primal and emotional origins, so he advocated for a language of gestures, cries, and sounds that would tap into the collective unconscious and bypass the limitations of rational discourse. He called for a theater that would tap into the primal energies of the body, unleashing its raw and irrational forces on stage. Furthermore, as Anna explained, the spatial arrangement of the theater was crucial in Artaud's concept. He rejected the classic proscenium stage with its clear separation between performers and audience. Instead, he proposed a more immersive and dynamic space, where the audience would be surrounded by the performance, engulfed in sound, light, and movement. Artaud aimed to break down the barriers between the performers and spectators with a view to imploding the dichotomous distinction between art and life.

After explicating the ideas of the Magic Theater in Hesse and Artaud's revolutionary proposals for redefining dramatic art, Anna analyzed and interpreted Hesse's Magic Theater in *Steppenwolf* as an example of Artaud's Theater of Cruelty. From the foregoing it is easy to see how that case could be made. What was far more interesting, though, was the end to which it was being made. The conclusion of Anna's study was that the ultimate "Magic Theater of Cruelty" would totally encompass human life, utterly obliterating the distinction between performers and spectators. While she did not go into great detail regarding the technology and techniques whereby this might be brought about, she did go some ways in exploring the motivations for bringing it about.

Here the side of her that appreciated futurist thinkers, whose writings verged on science fiction, such as the aforementioned Tsiolkovsky, was actually very relevant to her terrifying power of speculative imagination. Anna theorized that a sufficiently advanced superhuman form of life, whether that of a singular consciousness or of a super-intelligent society, might face existential despair through the exhaustion of a spectator's view and techno-scientific grasp of the cosmos. Such a life form (again, including a potentially social organism) would address this increasingly suicidal nihilism by contriving something akin to Hesse's Magic Theater, albeit on a grander scale, and losing itself within that arena through the kind of irrational immersion that Artaud was advocating with his Theater of Cruelty. I suggested to Anna that *Psychotron* would be a good name for this constructed domain of the psyche, an arena for forestalling entropy through transformative occultation and violent revitalization.

Despite her intense metaphysical idealism and romantic orientation toward life, or perhaps *because* of it, Anna was also radically political. She belonged to the Students for a Democratic Society (SDS) on campus, although she often clashed with the other members over their materialism. She envisioned a convergence of two future revolutions, one in America toward sociopolitical Communism, and one in Russia away from putatively 'scientific' materialism and back to the eclectic mysticism so characteristic of the Eurasian soul. Anna believed that catalyzing and alchemically fusing these two revolutions was the only way to save the world from nuclear Armageddon.

This idea resonated deeply with me and, for the tragically brief time that we were together, I embraced it as my own mission. What I brought to this mission was my scientific mind. I prevailed upon her that the problem with the Soviet Union was not its valorization of science, but a false reduction of scientific exploration to a materialist and mechanistic dogma that was at least equally entrenched in America and the West at large. The 1970 publication of *Psychic Discoveries Behind the Iron Curtain* went a long way toward convincing her of this. As it turned out, the Soviet Union was more open to Parapsychology, or "Psychotronics" research as they called it, than the American scientific establishment. The United States was forced to catch up. I will come, momentarily, to the significant role that I secretly played in this through my connection with Gary. But first, let me finish recounting how things unfolded with Anna, especially in those tumultuous years of 1968 and 1969 on the campus of Columbia University.

Anna introduced me to Mark Rudd and his inner circle, just before they led the student takeover of Columbia in late April of 1968. This group also included Ted Gold, who, as it turned out, would not have long to live. Anna and I visited Gold a number of times at his apartment on West 94th Street, where I also met David Gilbert and Bob Feldman, who were living there as well. By the time the Communist red flag was raised over the Mathematics building on the student-occupied campus, I was recognizable to most of the core members of SDS who would go on to form the Weatherman underground cell in New York City. The one exception was Terry Robbins, who I did not get to know until the "collective" (as they liked to call it) relocated to the townhouse at 18 West 11th Street, which belonged to Cathy Wilkerson's father. You see, Cathy and a number of other young white people who belonged to this group actually came from money and were rebels against their rich parents. That fact put me somewhat at ease about dealing with them, although I *tried* to never invite any of these individuals back to my luxurious apartment on the Upper East Side.

In any case, Anna and I were there on campus during the seven-day occupation of Columbia at the end of April of '68. Gary had only a vague sense that I was somehow involved with the SDS leaders of the takeover, but it was clear enough to him that he expressed his concern. When the NYPD stormed the campus with tear gas and cleared out the occupied buildings in the early morning of April 30th, Anna and I managed to slip out through a hidden tunnel system under the Physics building that Gary had told me about. It led to a sealed off part of the campus that was still radioactive from the research that had been done there in the early 1940s in order to develop the atomic bomb as part of the Manhattan Project. It was Columbia University's continuing relationship with the military-industrial complex (and its war in Vietnam) that had triggered the student uprising in 1968. The "Gym Crow" plan to build a segregated gymnasium only acted as an accelerant.

It was after we lost Columbia that SDS began to transform into the Weatherman organization. A lot of the restructuring took place in Chicago, under the leadership of Bernadine Dohrn and Bill Ayers. I only met Dohrn on a couple of occasions, although I admit that was quite enough for her to have been seared into my mind. She was a fiery raven and quite unforgettable. Anna was not so deeply involved in SDS as to have been privy to any of the infighting that led to the splintering of the original broad-based student movement and to the formation of Weatherman as the strongest of the breakaway groups. All we knew was that after whatever went down in Chicago, and following the failed occupation of the Columbia campus, the New York members of the group relocated their base of operations from Morningside Heights to

Greenwich Village, a kind of shared campus for New York University and the New School for Social Research.

That is where my involvement with these terrorists intensified, partly on account of the fact that after I graduated from Columbia, I took my second major and used it to gain admittance to the New School in pursuit of a master's degree in philosophy. I was a graduate student there when, on March 6, 1970, the Greenwich Village townhouse exploded because the nail bomb that Terry was building had faulty wiring. Ted Gold and Diana Oughton were killed together with Terry in the blast. The two Cathys, Boudin and Wilkerson made it out of the wreckage alive. Dustin Hoffman, who lived next door, was there surveying the smoking ruins of the townhouse as I got the two of them into a taxi and fled from the crime scene to my apartment on 77th and Cherokee. It was the first time that I had let any Weather 'men' in there.

Kathy Boudin and Catherine Wilkerson were not unattractive women, Boudin especially so, with her dark hair and handsome features. Cathy Wilkerson's light brown, at times almost dirty blonde, hair was less to my taste, but there was a beauty to the Nordic determination often seen in her face and I liked the bookish look that her glasses gave her. Of course, these had been broken in the blast that day. I took the two women in through the side entrance (the one toward Cherokee, not York Avenue) so that the doormen would be less likely to notice the dust covering their clothes and put two and two together when they watched the nightly news. All I needed was to lose this apartment, or likely much worse, for harboring fugitives caught in the act of preparing for a terrorist attack.

Anna met us there. I told her to bring some of her clothes for the two women to change into, including underwear. Both had soaked theirs through. By the time Anna let herself in with her set of keys, they were standing in the bathtub of the master bedroom together, still dazed and in shock, using the removable shower head and my sponge to scrub the paste of piss and pulverized red brick off each other's thighs, with their soiled panties strewn across the tile floor. Anna quickly snatched these up and threw them into the trash bin next to the toilet whose lid I was sitting on, talking to the two fugitives. I got up and motioned for her to sit in my place, but she declined and said she was going to go make a pot of coffee for the girls. I had an extra bathrobe that Anna would wear on the nights that we slept together here rather than at her cozy dorm in Morningside Heights. So one of the women was in my bathrobe and the other wore Anna's while they sat cross-legged sipping coffee on the king-sized bed, propped up by the bigger pillows on it. Anna and I sat on the two chairs that were in the bedroom, one of them belonging to my aunt's old makeup table.

That night was the only time that Anna and I ever participated in any of the habitual orgies of the Weather Underground. It was hardly a typical example of these loveless fuck-fests, which were meant to bond "comrades" together with the glue of erotic energy and sexual intimacy. From what I gathered, there was hardly anything truly erotic or intimate about the so-called "free love" in the "collective" whose Village love nest (and bomb factory) was now in smoldering ruins. It was all about proving oneself. I wonder how often the women involved were even able to climax.

That wasn't what it was like that night, though, when Anna and the two Cathys were in my bed. I had been in the living room. Anna, who was planning to sleep with me in my childhood bedroom, went in to check on the two of them, who we had given the master bedroom. When she didn't come back for a while, I went to see what was going on. I expected to find her comforting the two shell-shocked women, but instead I saw that they had pulled Anna into bed with them after she discovered them fondling and kissing one another. Anna gave me a look and nodded her head so as to ask me to join them. After I hesitantly looked into the eyes of Kathy and Catherine only to meet with a strikingly open and, for them, exceptionally vulnerable gaze, I took off my clothes and climbed in. The four of us fucked for hours. Both of the fugitives came on my cock before I let go inside Anna as she had her third orgasm of the night with the two Cathys sucking her tits.

There was blowback from that night. Not in terms of romantic entanglement, or any jealousy having to do with our foursome. The unintended consequence of rescuing the fugitives was that the "collective" figured out just how wealthy I was. They put pressure on me to fund them, and I did. It may be unwise for me to admit to this crime, but for a brief period from late March of 1970 until early June of that year, I funded the Weather Underground organization as it planned for a violent revolutionary overthrow of the United States government. I cut my funding after their June 9th bombing of the New York City Police headquarters. Anna agreed with me that SDS had lost its way and, while we continued to respect their radicalism, their vision of revolution — or rather, their lack of vision — began to sharply diverge from our more mystical and utopian ideas.

In the end, all I had to do to get Rudd and Flannigan off our backs was to give them a long lecture about how Parapsychology had to be integral to the worldwide Communist revolution. I argued that its scientific approach to understanding and explaining "miracles," which had been used by theocrats in order to manipulate people, would wind up being lethal to organized religion. I sat there, in my living room, Bible-thumping my copy of *Psychic Discoveries Behind the Iron Curtain* and praising the Soviet Psychotronics program as exemplary of the Communist vision of a comprehensively scientific approach to all phenomena. Anna was amused but tried to hide it. By the time they left, Mark and Brian looked flabbergasted and crestfallen. They wrote me off as an eccentric millionaire and one-time fellow traveler.

After Anna and I distanced ourselves from the Weather Underground, I delved deeper into both existential philosophy and mystical literature under her influence. I preferred Albert Camus, Franz Kafka, and Hermann Hesse to Jean-Paul Sartre and Søren Kierkegaard. I had a love/hate relationship with Nietzsche and Dostoyevsky, one that mirrored my own inner conflict between Luciferian and Christly inclinations. How Camus had chosen to open *The Myth of Sisyphus* struck a disturbingly deep chord with me:

> There is but one truly serious philosophical problem, and that is suicide. Judging whether life is or is not worth living amounts to answering the fundamental question of philosophy. All the rest — whether or not the world has three dimensions, whether the mind has nine or twelve categories — comes afterwards. These are games; one must first answer. And if it is true... that a philosopher, to deserve our respect, must preach by example, you can appreciate the importance of that reply, for it will precede the definitive act... An act like this is prepared within the silence of the heart, as is a great work of art.

In large part on account of Anna's treatment of the work in her unpublished manuscript, *Magic Theater of Cruelty*, Hesse's *Steppenwolf* became my favorite novel. I deeply identified with Harry Haller, even more profoundly than I had been able to see myself in any protagonist of Russian fiction. I had naively hoped, at that time, that Anna would become my Hermine, not realizing that her manuscript was a valiant endeavor on her part to save herself because she was even more like Harry Haller than I was.

For all that, I remained scientifically minded. That is not quite the right way to put it. Rather, like the narrator of Dostoyevsky's *Notes from Underground*, I saw scientific determinism as a vacuum of meaning that threatened to eviscerate my will to live in its event horizon unless an escape velocity could somehow be achieved. Whereas the certitude of mathematics once gave me solace, now the fatalism of physical laws appeared to my mind in their aspect as the unbending bars of a black iron prison of cosmic scale. The focus of my graduate work in Philosophy at the New School became deconstructing putatively 'scientific' arguments in favor of determinism — or for that matter, in defense of probabilistic randomness — with a view to reaffirming our existential freedom. I saw the empirical evidence for mind over matter that had been martialed by Parapsychology as the key to taking apart both the mechanistic determinism and sheer randomness (at a quantum level) that, taken together, characterized the predominant view of nature in modern Physics. This brought me back to Gary, who by now had a position at Rockefeller University. He enlisted me as his research assistant. I would walk from home down the East River promenade to join him there on the days that I was not at the New School.

It was mid-October of 1971 when Gary called me into his office at Rockefeller University to divulge what was then a closely guarded secret. I had spent that day, and the several days before it, watching coverage of the 2,500th anniversary of the Persian Empire, which was being broadcast from Persepolis by the Shah of Iran. The Shah's speech at the tomb of Cyrus the Great during the greatest of all gatherings of the world's heads of state was hair-raising and became seared in my memory:

> Cyrus: Great King, King of Kings, King of the Achaemenids, King of this Aryan Land, from my person, King of Kings of Iran, and on behalf of my folk, hail unto you!
>
> In this splendorous moment of Iranian history, I and all Iranians, all children of this ancient Empire, that 2,500 years ago was founded by your hand, stand worshipfully before your tomb and honor your immortal memory. All of us are gathered here at this time, wherein a new Iran endowed by honorable ancient virtues establishes a fresh covenant.
>
> ...We promise that the standard you raised 2,500 years ago will remain proudly in view. We promise that the greatness and glory of this nation shall be safeguarded with an iron will, as a sacred consignment from our ancestors, and that this national heritage — more victorious than ever — will be handed down to future generations. We promise to remain true to the tradition of humanitarianism and pure contemplation that you established as the foundation of the Imperium of Iran.
>
> In these 2,500 years, your country and mine was subjected to the most burdensome catastrophes, but in all that, this nation never surrendered its soul in the face of grave misfortunes... Many people showed their faces in this land with a view to upending it, but all of them left and Iran has

remained in place. And during all that time, Iran endured as a beacon of the cultivation of virtue and profound contemplation.

We, now, have come here to tell you, proudly: that after the passing of 25 centuries, today, like unto your honorable epoch, the flag of the Aryan Imperium flies triumphantly; that today, like unto your honorable epoch, the name of Iran is spoken around the globe with reverential praise; that today, as in your day, Iran is — in this troubled and chaotic world — a messenger of free-spiritedness and humanitarianism, and a guardian of the highest ideals of human existence. That torch which you lit, and which in these 2,500 years has never been blown out by the whirlwinds of calamity, burns more steadily and brightly than ever before in this land — and the aura of that fire, like in your time, has shone well beyond the borders of this Aryan land.

Cyrus — great king, king over all kings, the most free-spirited man amongst free men, and the champion of Iranian and world history: sleep soundly, for we are awake and shall remain vigilant!

For some reason that had not been clear to me at the time, this Fascist spectacle gave me goosebumps and made my hair stand on end. Frankly, at times, I even got heart palpitations watching it. So, I remember clearly when the phone rang during the televised broadcast of the military parade at Persepolis, showcasing Persian soldiers from every epoch of Iran's long history. It was Gary, asking me to come down and see him at his office.

Our usual work at Rockefeller University consisted of developing theoretical Physics models that could accommodate parapsychological phenomena such as precognition and psychokinesis. In addition to his proposal of tachyons as a causal mechanism for these uncanny abilities, Feinberg was also developing a model of the universe with eight dimensions rather than the standard four-dimensional space-time. I was working with him on the formulation of this hyper-dimensional Physics, the equations of which were supposed to accommodate clairvoyance of future times and places. But that day he had not called me in to talk about theoretical matters.

When I arrived at his office, I found that Gary's manner was even more excited than usual. The professor's eyes sparkled and there was an almost boyish mischievousness about his evident inability to keep some colossal secret that had been revealed to him by his government contacts. He had to tell me, but only after swearing me to secrecy. First, he closed the door of his office, then he paced almost frantically back and forth, before deciding that he didn't feel safe discussing these matters with me there. So we went out and sat on a secluded bench near the geodesic dome on campus.

Professor Feinberg looked around nervously. Then he leaned in and whispered, "They've decided to catch up with the Russians in Psychotronics. Not just to catch up, but to beat them as badly as we have in the space race and the arms race." I gave him a penetrating, wide-eyed look. In the past year, we had often discussed what *Psychic Discoveries* had disclosed about Psi research in the USSR and its Eastern bloc satellite states. "This is no joke, Nick, they're going to do it." I asked, "Who, exactly?" His eyes darted around again in a paranoiac fashion. "It's being funded by the CIA, but the pilot research and development will be done at the Stanford Research Institute in Palo Alto. Two physicists with security clearances are running the program. That's how I heard about it. They called me to help them figure out what to tell the senators when they ask *how* this weird stuff *works*, you know, theoretically. They need to tell some kind of story convincing enough to laymen so that the senate intelligence committee rubber stamps the classified budget for the program. They're calling it 'remote viewing' to make it sound more technical."

I sat back, sinking into the bench and into a staggering train of thought. Gary was leaning forward with his elbows on his knees. When I next opened my mouth, still struggling to decide which of the many questions racing through my mind to ask first, he cocked his neck to look at me. "And they're going to use this for *what*?" Gary had a positively devilish look on his face. "Everything," he said.

"Operationally?" He nodded affirmatively in reply. "There's a psychic here in New York who is already working with them to develop the protocol. He's an artist. Ingo Swann. I want you to come with me to see him before he leaves for Palo Alto, where he's going to be living for a while to help Puthoff and Targ develop the program. They're the physicists. Hal Puthoff, who I know from other classified work that we've done together, and some guy called Russell Targ. The CIA has its doubts about whether Targ has the stomach for everything they plan to do with these 'abilities' once they've rendered them reliable." I took a long, deep breath. The most dangerous and deadly chapter of my life was about to begin. I got the sense that everything else had been preparation.

CHAPTER 3

ARYAN APOCALYPSE

Gary and I went to see Swann, the psychic artist, who was living at an apartment in the Bowery. He was a flaming faggot, not that I minded much. What bothered me more than his annoying mannerisms was that a cursory look through his bookshelf made it clear that Ingo was a member of the Church of Scientology. Parts of his relatively small library looked like the L. Ron Hubbard required reading list. His paintings were technically impressive but had the same lurid and garish quality characteristic of *Battlefield Earth* and Hubbard's even lesser works. I looked over at Gary silently, with an expression that he had no trouble interpreting as some cross between dismay and contemptuous skepticism. Feinberg looked back in such a manner as to reassure me and urge me to be patient. The professor turned out to be right.

Ingo Swann's abilities as a psychic were truly remarkable. He picked up on my cynical attitude and was so affronted by it that he reached right into my mind, or as he might put it, reached out into past places and times, to confront me with information about my life that he could hardly have known. Some of this concerned my aunt, and I had to stop Ingo before he embarrassed me in front of Gary who was starting to look very uncomfortable. He had the decency never to ask me to elaborate on what Swann was getting at that day when I cut him off.

What Professor Feinberg did ask me about was the following exchange. Late into our visit to his apartment, the artist leaned back into his armchair and looked arrogantly at me while Gary and I sat across from him on the sofa. He stopped sipping his coffee, and blurted out, "He doesn't know, does he? You never told him — about your abilities." I gave him a curt look and a nod that wordlessly said, "Shut up." Ingo hissed while smirking. He knew that I would never disrespect him again. As for Gary, I had to explain to him that my interest in psychic phenomena was not purely intellectual, and that I had experienced more than the odd incident or two of telepathy or precognition that I confessed to when he shared similar trivialities with me as if they were unspeakably marvelous. Given the project at SRI that Gary was unofficially leading me into, the time was right for this confession. I admitted to a lifetime of intense psychic experiences, uncanny abilities that were strongest in my childhood but that had persisted in some measure all the way to the present. Ingo could see it — I don't know, in my 'aura' or something. I guess it takes one to know one. Later, he would tell Puthoff and Targ at SRI that when we first met it was like an incandescent light bulb of psychic energy had walked into his studio.

By the time I finished my master's degree at the New School in May of 1972, I had been extended an invitation to join Ingo at SRI to undergo the "remote viewing" training protocol. Officially, the invitation came from Gary's colleague, Hal Puthoff. Or rather, I should say that "unofficially" and on the face of it, Hal invited me. However, I knew full well that being invited to participate in such a project meant that I had already undergone a thorough background check and received security clearance by the CIA. When I thought back to the intense interest I had in Communism during my teenage years, and then *my involvement with the Weathermen* only a couple of years earlier, I found this whole situation to be astonishingly ironic. It was hard to imagine that they hadn't dug these things up, especially considering the fact that they were working with psychics — including a certain Pat Price, who had done clairvoyant work for police departments. But then it occurred to me: *they were working with psychics.* Clairvoyants and other occult adepts are notoriously eccentric and volatile people. My shady past was par for the course. Apparently, they had also grasped the connection between especially strong psychic ability and a history of trauma. So, what I suffered in childhood was also of interest to them. It was seen as a qualification, not to say, an initiation that cracked my mind open to exceptional perceptions.

Anna did not want me to travel to California, even if the training program was supposed to take only six months — or less, if I proved to have the aptitude that they were anticipating. It wasn't as if I was giving up my apartment, and I insisted that she make it her own home while I was away. She had been hoping that I would go straight into doctoral studies at the New School, where she had just entered the Philosophy department to pursue her MA after having graduated from Barnard. We fought about it, and then she felt ashamed for trying to hold me back from fulfilling my potential. Anna was full of trepidation, but she feigned a stiff upper lip and let me go. When I was about to part with her at the airport to get onto my Pan Am flight to San Francisco, she almost fell apart. It was painful to see.

That first night in California, I stayed at a hotel in San Francisco with a spectacular view of the Transamerica Pyramid amidst the downtown skyline. A driver in a black limousine picked me up in the morning and drove me down to Palo Alto, where I met Harold Puthoff in person for the first time. He introduced me to his associate, Russell Targ. Ingo was also there, and despite his typical freshness, he seemed genuinely delighted to see me (maybe he thought, or hoped, that I was a closeted homosexual). My first "target" turned out to be another building on the Stanford University campus. Of course, I did not know that until after the session was over.

It was chosen because of the distinctive pattern carved into its stucco walls. This consisted of repeating squares that were made up of four rectangular cutouts in the orientation of a swastika, with another smaller square in the middle of the four 'arms.' There were also trees and dense shrubbery beneath the walkway that stretched around the rectilinear atrium inside the building, and this was supposed to give me a material that would starkly contrast with the stucco and concrete, both in texture and color. Beginning with the swastika pattern, which I sketched out right away, I either visually depicted or verbally described all of these features in a degree of detail that stunned Dr. Puthoff and even made Ingo envious. There were also lamps hanging down from the tall ceilings, which my sketch and notes portrayed as "something like flying saucers... metallic, copper." I even picked up on these spherical bands of intersecting metal that reminded me of "gyroscopes." They turned out to be another kind of lights, or rather an open mesh casing for single light bulbs, suspended from the ceiling of a hallway on the second floor, whose windows without glass looked out onto the aforementioned atrium.

Finally, Russell Targ took me to see the building, squinting at it all the while through the thick glasses that only moderately improved his poor eyesight. It was the "Oakes Laboratories of Radiology and Biophysics." That I was allowed to tour the site meant that Targ and Puthoff were opening up the possibility that the information in my "remote viewing" session was actually obtained through precognition (whatever that means). I may have described *what I was going to see*. In any case, the confirmation was literally breathtaking. It really boosted my confidence, and so I learned *fast*.

The core of the training was to learn how to separate your interpretation of an unknown "target" placed inside of an envelope from the elemental impressions of it that you received through Extrasensory Perception (ESP). This was like learning disciplined meditation, quieting the mind's analytical faculties so that analysis could be left to the intelligence agents who would receive the "data" from any given session. One was never supposed to come into contact with these analysts, since they had knowledge of the target, or would have such knowledge, when doing their analysis. Impressions received were recorded both visually and verbally. An almost hieroglyphic visual language had been developed for quickly indicating the presence of flowing water, trees, or manmade structures in a few quick strokes without the mind interfering with interpretive overlay as one struggled to draw one's indistinct impressions. But this was designed for future recruits who were not expected to have any artistic ability. Although I was not as skilled as Ingo, I actually had considerable artistic talent despite my focus on mathematics and science. I excelled at drawing in high school, and my aunt had often offered herself as a nude model to encourage me to develop my talent. Consequently, I quickly dispensed with SRI's symbolic system.

There was also a checklist that had to be filled, which broke up and classified impressions in terms of a long series of predefined characteristics. This was meant to help determine whether a site was artificial or manmade, whether it was indoors or outdoors, whether there was water, if it was light or dark or alternating at various times. These are only a few examples; the list was very long and by analyzing the checkmarks that were supposed to be made without conscious reflection, an analyst would be able to form a composite image of the site. The aim here was to be able to 'look inside' clandestine Soviet facilities that were, say, masked by a seemingly natural landscape, like a weapons manufacturing facility deep inside a large hillside. If the checklist showed "artificial," "concrete," "electricity," etc. where there was only supposed to be a hill, that would tend to confirm other intelligence that indicated to the CIA that the Soviets had a secret facility at this locale.

When trying to focus on such a site, sometimes one would receive impressions of that place at a time in the past *or in the future*. It became clear that the mind would often be magnetically drawn to the target site at that time when it was giving off the most psychic energy, in effect, when the most intensely interesting things were going on there. At first, this was a distraction from gathering intelligence in real time, but it did not take long for the CIA to recognize the tremendous value of such a capability. Soon Ingo Swann, Pat Price, and I were being trained to move backwards and forwards in time as well as clairvoyantly view places remote in space.

I learned all this and more, but becoming a master of any art or craft means letting go of studied discipline and allowing it to become a fully internalized skill that effortlessly channels what had been raw talent. That was just as true in the case of "remote viewing." After a couple of months of intensive training, I was allowed to let go of the guardrails. In fact, Hal Puthoff encouraged me to do so. We conducted these relatively unstructured sessions privately — well, even more privately than the rest of the program. He instructed me not to inform Targ of what we were doing together. It turned out that both Pat Price and Ingo Swann were also doing sessions like this "off the record." I would do mine back at the furnished rental apartment on the Stanford campus that had been cleared for the duration of my stay.

The target for these sessions was 'chosen' by me, albeit unconsciously. It was not long after I began recording the impressions that I realized what had come together from out of my subconscious in order to select the target. For some reason, which was about to become clear to me, the recurring nightmares of nuclear war that I was afflicted with during my late teens interlocked with the terrible foreboding, even panic, that I felt while watching media coverage of the 2,500th anniversary of the Persian Empire that day that Gary called and had me come down to Rockefeller University, where he read me into *this* SRI program that I was in right now.

Three flashes of light in the desert, and the Shah of Iran's proudly determined face — as if he had seized lightning within his grasp, like Zeus or Indra. That was the first image that I got. With my history of morbid fascination with nuclear war, it hardly required much "analytical overlay" to conclude that I was watching Iran's first atomic bomb test. Later, the details of the terrain that I noted even allowed me to identify which desert this was. The Persians have two vast deserts

sweeping across the east of Iran. This was the Lot Desert, rather omi-
nously named after the prophet from the story of Sodom's destruction.

It took countless hours, over many days, to nail down the date — at
least to the year. I did that in part by focusing on one of the other individuals whose image kept prominently appearing in these sessions.
Our President, Richard Nixon. Despite deep concerns and some harsh
criticisms of the Shah being voiced by international media, Nixon had
put in a private phone call to congratulate his friend on bringing Iran
into the club of nuclear-armed nations. I saw this phone call and heard
Nixon assuring Pahlavi that the bad press would blow over. I also telepathically picked up on the fact that, despite his reassurances to the
Shah, in the back of his mind Nixon was concerned that his refusal to
punish Iran for violating the Nuclear Non-Proliferation Treaty (NPT)
would become a campaign issue over the coming year, especially
against a rival like Jimmy Carter, who was so critical of Pahlavi's human rights record. Now I knew that Iran's successful nuclear weapons
test would take place sometime around the fall of 1975.

The King of Kings would not bask in the glory of those lightning
bolts for long. I saw his country shaken, and then shattered, by a
violent Communist revolution. Nixon was now in his third term as
President. I saw him offering the Shah his full support, morally and
materially, to confront the mass of demonstrators and the cadres of
armed insurgents with brutal force. The Imperial Iranian military was
deployed in the streets of Tehran and other Persian cities. It seemed
our President had his own share of similar troubles at home, which
made him more than empathetic to Pahlavi. America appeared to me
to have become a police state.

The Shah believed, with good reason, that the leftist protesters and
guerrilla fighters rebelling against his rule represented an orchestrated
attempt by the Soviet Union to seize Iran, together with the warm
water ports and vast petroleum resources of the Persian Gulf. Such
an economic boon would almost certainly secure a Russian victory

in the Cold War. I write "with good reason" because the Shah had, some months prior to the uprising in Iran, witnessed a Soviet invasion of Afghanistan—a country whose northern half still spoke Persian, and which was an artificial state carved out of eastern Iran by British colonialists in the mid-19th century. In Afghanistan, a leftwing revolution, which was hardly organic, had established a Communist regime. When this nascent Soviet Republic was threatened by radical Islamic insurgents and feudal landlords, its Prime Minister, a man whose name I could discern as Amin, invited "assistance" from the Russians, who sent troops across the border. By the time the Communist uprising against the Shah began, Soviet troops were occupying Afghanistan and the USSR had lengthened its already long border with Iran.

Mohammad Reza Pahlavi had been traumatized in his youth by helplessly watching as his father, Reza Shah "the Great," was forcibly exiled from Iran in 1941 by both Allied *and Soviet occupying troops*. While British and American forces agreed to leave at the conclusion of the Second World War, the Russians tried to stay. They stoked secessionist insurgencies in several parts of northern Iran and, for a brief time, succeeded in setting up Soviet Socialist Republics in occupied Iranian Kurdistan and Azerbaijan — amalgamating the latter to the northern part of Azerbaijan that the Russian Empire had already seized from Iran in the Russo-Persian Wars of the 1800s. These 19th-century wars were a disaster wherein the Persians lost about a third of their territory, some of the "stans" of Central Asia (*ostan* means "province" in Persian), to the Russian Czar. The Shah had repeatedly gone on record, in interviews with the international media, that he would sooner see Iran destroyed than humiliatingly occupied once more by foreign forces. He had warned, "If you think you can come here again, you should know that there will only be ruins for you to occupy."

Moreover, anyone with half a brain, let alone someone as intelligent as Pahlavi, could see that the Russians had no intrinsic interest whatsoever in a godforsaken country like Afghanistan. What they had done there was a dry run and staging ground for the planned Soviet invasion of Iran. The CIA concurred with this analysis and Langley was already coordinating with SAVAK to turn Iran into the bastion of resistance against Soviet expansion into the Islamic world. The Shah was tasked with funneling funding and arms to the *Mojaheddin*, led by Ahmad Shah Masoud, in Persian-speaking northern Afghanistan.

As best as I could piece it together from my precognitive clairvoyance and telepathic penetration of the intentions of the various players involved, what happened next would be worthy of the annals of martial hubris. You see, few people knew that the Shah was dying of cancer and that he did not have years to sustain a drawn-out resistance against the Russians in Afghanistan, especially now that his own regime was in danger of being overthrown by Soviet-backed leftists. Believing that his friend Richard Nixon, however upset, would still back him after the fact, the Shah ordered the Imperial Iranian Air Force to attack Soviet positions in Afghanistan.

From what I could tell, it was the summer of 1980, because a lot of psychic energy was focused on the fact that many countries, including America, had to boycott the Olympic Games being held in Moscow in order to demonstrate their disapproval of the Soviet aggression in Afghanistan. There was also dismay over the fact that the 1984 Winter Olympic Games were scheduled to be held in Iran, where the Shah had invested in building massive ski resorts and other winter sports facilities. People were concerned about whether another round of the Olympics would be ruined by unrest. That ought to have been the least of their concerns.

The Iranian airstrikes against Russian positions in Afghanistan were devastating. Within 48 hours, the Shah had pulverized Soviet forces, especially those positioned closest to the Afghan border with Iran. At the close of this operation, he carried out his second nuclear weapons test, this time in the Kavir Desert, close enough to the Afghan border for the atomic flash to be seen by Soviet troops. He intended it as a warning flare. Then he declared the protesters and insurgents on the streets of Iran's cities to be the fifth column of a foreign enemy, namely the Soviet Union. Imperial Iranian Air Force helicopters were ordered to strafe strongholds of guerrilla fighters, and even large gatherings of unarmed protesters who refused to disperse.

Never has there been a grander and more costly strategic miscalculation. After taking a few days to absorb the initial shock of the Shah's preemptive strike, the politburo in Moscow ordered the Red Army to mass along the entire Soviet border with Iran, all the way from Azerbaijan in the Caucasus, around the Caspian Sea, through Turkmenistan and down into the new Afghan extension of this border. Under the pretext of protecting "the People's Soviet Revolution" in Iran from a "brutal American-backed dictator," the Soviet Union invaded Iran. Numbers, including specific dates, are very hard to nail down in remote viewing, but I was able to narrow the timeframe to mid-July of 1980, in part because the Olympic games in Moscow were prematurely suspended by a declared state of emergency.

The Shah engaged the Soviet troops with his own massive army, his often-criticized purchase of hundreds of tanks now having been more than justified by the turn of events. Pahlavi waited for foreign civilians attending the Olympics to be cleared out of Moscow by emergency flights before the Russians closed their airports in the capital as they had elsewhere in the USSR. Then, sometime in August of 1980, Soviet troops who had already occupied Tabriz finally converged on Tehran and entered the Persian capital from three directions — the west, coming from already occupied Iranian Kurdistan, the northwest, from occupied Azerbaijan, and the east, from occupied Khorasan.

Shâhanshâh Âryâmehr, the "King of Kings and Light of the Aryans," gave his final command from a bunker deep inside the Alborz Mountains. Three heavy payload long-range bombers were prepared for a kamikaze strike, which it was hoped that at least one of them would succeed in carrying out. Each was carrying an atomic bomb spray-painted with Persian calligraphy that read, "Never Again. Death to Russia! Long live Iran! Long live the Emperor!" (*Dobâreh hargez. Marg bar Roussiye! Pâyandeh Irân! Jâvid Shâh!*) To my horror, I watched with my mind's eye as one of them did get through Soviet air defenses to deliver its payload.

Moscow was obliterated. It all happened so fast that most of a ruined world would never be able to piece together who struck first or why. Within minutes of the attack on Moscow, the Soviet high command declared martial law and determined that the Shah of Iran had acted as a proxy of his close ally, the United States. Before Pahlavi could even broadcast his planned emergency address announcing his nuclear response to the Russian invasion of Iran, he and his staff watched from their bunker as every television station in the United States went dark. The Soviet Union had let loose their rain of ICBMs in what they considered a retaliatory strike on America, one so severe that its intention was to prevent a counterstrike. But Nixon, who was warned by NORAD of the incoming missiles, did manage to get America's own arsenal out of the silos so as to rain fire down on Russia. The Light of the Aryans had brought our world to a fiery end, one worthy of the ancient Zoroastrian prophecies of a global firestorm at the Apocalypse.

Hal Puthoff was almost as appalled by what came out of these sessions as I was. Anna was unnerved that I could not tell her over the phone why it was that I sounded so exhausted and on edge, why I wasn't getting more than a few hours of erratic sleep each night. The nightmares from my teenage years had come back, but now, instead of just being a vision of the thermonuclear incineration of New York, they were filled in with the details of this Aryan Apocalypse unleashed by the self-styled King of Kings.

One sleepless night, Hal came by exceptionally late and asked me to pour us a couple of drinks. (I had a minibar.) He sat in an armchair across from me as I leaned back into the sofa with my drink, eager to hear something that he was obviously itching to say. It turned out that the "data" from my freeform sessions on the Soviet invasion of Iran had struck a nerve somewhere high up in the CIA. I said, cynically, "Let me guess, the CIA wants to hire me fulltime?" He shook his head. Hal had a guarded manner of speaking but, by the way he was bending his neck down and looking up at me, I could tell that he wanted to share something with me but was only allowed to tell me as much as I "need to know."

After reiterating the extreme confidentiality of this conversation, he confessed that another psychic espionage unit was being set up. It wasn't only going to be involved in "remote viewing" but also in "remote influencing." It would even attempt *to change a pre-cognized future*. Targ would never be read into this other operation, which was not being run by the CIA but by Naval Intelligence. He could see me struggling to understand why the Navy would be developing a program parallel to the one being set up by the CIA, and even penetrating the CIA program in order to mine it for data and, as I was about to discover, harvest it for the top talent.

Hal asked me, "Nick, has it ever occurred to you that 70% of this planet's surface is covered by the oceans?" Then he continued, "Well, Naval Intelligence wants to know *what is going on down there*." I stared at him somewhat incredulously, as if to say, "Going on *under* the oceans?", while I wondered why the hell Naval Intelligence officers would be interested in the marine biology of squids and sperm whales. Then, as if tiring of the charade, he blurted out, "More than fifty percent of UFOs are seen entering or exiting the Earth's oceans." I almost dropped my drink when I tried to set it down on the table. A chill ran through my body, all the way up my spine, making the back of my neck break out into a cold sweat. I tried to suppress a shudder, but Hal saw it.

After an awkward silence, I looked dead into his eyes and said, "I understand, sir." It was the first time that I called Dr. Puthoff "sir."

It was also the first time I realized who *or what* I was dealing with. "I knew you would," he said, and nodded his head. "We want *you* — for the *other* unit." From the shit-eating grin on his face, he seemed to relish that he knew what my next question was going to be. "Where's it going to be based?" I asked. "New York City," he said, with a diabolical smile. "We've acquired a floor in the North Tower of the new World Trade Center. Well, technically, it belongs to the NSA, but we're leasing it from them."

I did not recognize the acronym. "NSA? You mean NASA?" He was annoyed with himself at having said somewhat more than he was supposed to say, and then, after taking a gulp of scotch, grumbled almost under his breath, "National Security Agency. You've never heard of it because as far as the public is concerned, it doesn't exist." It was interesting that he said "we're" when he shared that Naval Intelligence was leasing one of the floors that this "National Security Agency" had apparently bought in the Twin Towers, the construction of which was just barely being completed at the time. So, Puthoff was Naval Intelligence. *Interesting*, I thought to myself.

"One last thing, Nikolai. When you get back to New York and start working at the facility, don't mention any of this to Gary. I know you'll be tempted. But he doesn't have clearance." That really awed me. I know that intelligence is compartmentalized, but I couldn't believe that, with all Feinberg's government and think tank connections, which informed his writing of *The Prometheus Project*, I was being let in on something that he had no "need to know." How was I supposed to explain to him that I was not going to go straight into a PhD program? What was I supposed to tell Anna? I suppose Hal didn't mention her, not because she evaded the CIA's background check, but because he knew all too well that I could never lie to her. Of course, that also meant that she would become a liability for them.

Anna was ecstatic to hear that I was heading home early, especially since it was almost Christmas. She had tried to sound strong over the

phone when we would talk at night, but I could tell that she was straining to steel herself against nearly uncontrollable emotions having to
do with issues of abandonment and separation anxiety that had roots
in her childhood, which was almost as troubled as mine. She surprised
me by showing up at La Guardia airport when my flight arrived. I suddenly saw her running toward me at the gate in the black fur coat that
I had gotten her, and the next thing I knew she had thrown her arms
around me and was practically weeping as she tightened her grip. I
kissed the tears off her face.

When we got back to my apartment, I saw that, as soon as she
heard I was coming home ahead of schedule, she had gone out and
gotten a Christmas tree. She had already strung the lights on it and
was waiting to do the rest of the decorations together. Some of my
ornaments were ornately painted Russian Orthodox eggs, with icons
framed by sparkling gold and silver patterns. I remember that night as
one of the happiest in my life. Maybe the happiest of all. I could hardly
have imagined that I was about to look into the cold, dark depths of
hell.

CHAPTER 4

ATLANTIS RESURFACING

The view over New York City from the Naval Intelligence offices hidden on the 79th floor of the World Trade Center's North Tower was breathtakingly spectacular. Unfortunately, remote viewers like me had to do their sessions in a windowless room that was uniformly painted battleship gray. The reduction of sensory stimuli was part of the protocol for enhancing the data that we obtained through clairvoyance and precognition. When I walked off the elevator on the first morning at my new job, I had hardly cleared the false façade of the front hallway where I was given my badge by the secretary, when I heard someone shout, "So, you're the philosopher!" An overly self-confident, not to say arrogant, man wearing a loosened necktie, and a blue-gray suit that was a little too tight for him, got up from his desk and came over to shake my hand. Somewhat defensively, I replied, "I also have a degree in Physics." Jack nodded jovially as he patted my shoulder. "That's one of the reasons Hal sent you. He's a good friend of mine." Jack was to be my handler and guide for our work in the gray room.

By the end of the first day on the job, my life would never be the same. Granted, it felt as if I was only half-remembering things that I had once known but was made to forget. Still, breaking the locks on that part of my mind meant opening a floodgate that would eventually lead to my drowning. Within the first two hours of our remote viewing sessions together, Jack had me describing UFOs to him as they dove into the Atlantic Ocean off the coast of Antarctica. Some of these craft were polished and shining silvery discs; others were more dull-gray wingless cigar-shaped vehicles with windows that glowed blue at night.

When I was tasked with looking into these windows and following the occupants of the UFOs down into the dark ocean depths, I experienced something that my training had not prepared me for. I was blocked. They knew that I was spying on them, and they tried their best to block me. I reported this to Jack. He nodded wearily but gave me a glance of appreciation as well, as if to signal both that they had been having this problem for a long time and also that I was clearly on target. I persisted and, by the end of my first week of sessions, I was delivering clearer data about the targets than anyone who had worked them before me.

At that point, I was fully briefed by Jack regarding the intelligence already gathered through this project. This information was not limited to the vast submarine city built into the continental shelf of Antarctica, or the one beneath Lake Vostok. In addition to these sites, the remote viewers here at Naval Intelligence had discovered extensive structures on the dark side of the Moon and on Mars. I say "structures" because these far exceeded the scale and complexity of bases. They were the size of cities, and some of them were vastly ancient. Clairvoyantly following some of the saucer- and cigar-shaped craft lifting off from Antarctica had led my fellow psychic spies to these other locations.

On the dark side of the Moon, there was at least one large city, the remote viewing of which had been confirmed by feedback in the form of classified National Reconnaissance Office satellites positioned in the lunar orbit. Jack laid the photographs out in front of me. There were various polygonal structures, and some spherical ones as well, with one monolithic tower or obelisk of staggering height. All of these buildings were titanic in scale and appeared to be built (or carved?) out of something like stone (perhaps it was concrete). In any case, they were not metallic. There were also photographs of tread marks from tractors that appeared to be involved in mining operations.

By far the most disturbing discovery on the Moon was that these structures on the lunar surface were like the tip of an iceberg that extended deep beneath the moon dust, down into *a vast artificial structure!* As described by those on the project before my arrival, the Moon was largely hollow. Its interior surface was honeycombed with constructions of dazzling complexity and varying antiquity. The remote viewers who had been tasked with describing the cavernous lunar interior all had the impression that the Moon was actually older than the Earth and that it had been parked in Earth's orbit. Moreover, those who had piloted this cloaked space station were responsible for some gargantuan geo-engineering project on Earth, a sort of remaking of the ecological and biological matrix of the planet in such a manner as would be conducive to the guided evolution of humanoid life in place of the dinosaurs then dominant here. These engineers appeared to be from Mars, and their urgency to reshape Earth had to do with some horrifically unnatural catastrophe that they had suffered attendant to the deliberate and total destruction of a gigantic Earth-like home world that had been located between Mars and Jupiter. The asteroid belt that is there today consists of its remaining fragments.

Jack explained that there was as yet no feedback for what was remotely viewed on Mars. However, the psychically gathered data had been sent up the chain of command and had succeeded in convincing those who represented the national security establishment within NASA to target this region of Mars, namely Cydonia, as a focus of photography that would be sent back from the Viking probe within a year or two. The problem would then be to prevent this photographic confirmation, should it be forthcoming, from entering the public domain. "If the masses — of any society on Earth — were to learn of what we had already psychically spied on the surface of Cydonia, let alone beneath the surface of Mars," Jack explained as I nodded gravely, "the psychological, economic, and political consequences would be catastrophic."

Jack showed me the sketches and notes from remote-viewing sessions regarding Mars. By far the most impressive structure was a pentagonal pyramid that seemed to be several times larger than the Great Pyramid of Giza. Not far from it was a sort of Sphinx. Well, a Sphinx-like head at any rate, whose face was carved out of a huge rocky outcrop so that it stared up at the remote viewers looking down at the surface. Sphinx-like because it appeared to have a headdress. There was something vaguely 'Egyptian' about it. Although it was badly eroded, blasted and almost pulverized, a hauntingly foreboding expression of regret seemed etched into the face, together with a single teardrop.

There was one place, within a crater, where a geometrically regular checkerboard-type pattern could be seen, which was suspected to be the remnant of ruined buildings. These were vastly ancient, primordial. By contrast, there was a newer metallic structure — a tall antenna-type device that was bent. Those who focused on this structure were led, by association, down some air vents into a labyrinthine maze of subterranean tunnels that showed signs of having been damaged by explosions. Only a few of these were still intact, and they provided access to a city deep beneath the surface of Cydonia. Attempts to view the goings-on in this city were, however, repeatedly blocked by those who lived and worked there, and who apparently have psychic powers that dwarf our own.

I'll never forget how my heart sank the first time that I managed to follow these people piloting their craft into one of their lairs back here on Earth. Yes, they were *people* — more or less like us. They were as tall as professional basketball players and had the build of Olympic swimmers. Their faces looked like those of Nordic supermodels, except with more chiseled features and sunken eye sockets that made their almond-shaped brilliant blue or green eyes look preternaturally large. Their skulls were slightly tapered and a little taller than the cranium of your average Scandinavian, but in the men and women alike this was largely concealed by shoulder-length hair. This platinum blond, red, or jet-black hair was straight and very thick, combining qualities that we associate with Caucasian, Asian, and Semitic hair. The men were beardless and longhaired, so that the main feature distinguishing the women from the men were the full breasts of the former. All were wearing skintight uniforms of a pale grayish-blue color.

They disembarked from their craft in long tubular docks cut into the rock of the continental shelf. There was something mesmeric about the way they walked. No small talk or jesting or gestures expressing individual personality. They hardly even looked at each other, and yet it was as if they were moved by a single mind — or a single-mindedness inconceivable to us. A group of grayish humanoids that were very short (by comparison) trailed along behind them. Their heads kind of looked like those of overgrown fetuses, bald with huge black almond-shaped eyes, a vestigial nose over a slit for a mouth, beneath which was a pointy chin. Their bodies were slim and sleek and almost seemed to float off the ground. They had very long, thin arms ending in four slender digits. When briefing me on Antarctica, the Moon, and Mars, Jack had informed me that these things were biomechanical robots, which were manufactured to carry out various complex tasks and to function in high-risk situations, such as handling abductees.

I followed the Nordic types into their abode, and this is where what I saw made me succumb to a terrible sinking feeling that I was never really able to shake. The place was carved out of solid rock, in some places very smoothly, such as the polished floor, whereas in others the jagged walls had been left in a more natural state. It was very dark, lit only by the eerie greenish glow of phosphorescent stones of spherical and rectangular shapes that had been set into the walls and in certain places along the floor, especially the sides of stairways. These stairways had very broad steps that fit together with the titanic scale of everything else in this place, including high ceilings that contributed to an atmosphere of cathedral gloom. Along some of the walkways, including the very first one that I saw, were immense floor-to-ceiling windows. Seeing the ocean like that, with a jagged rock wall on the other side of me, was almost heart-stopping. My blood ran cold from fright, especially when I was able to make out the contours of a sperm whale with a giant squid locked into its jaws, not far from the glass. It reminded me of a diorama at the Museum of Natural History, but these were *alive*. In fact, I could feel their vital force behind the windows before I was able to see them.

After this experience, I went back to the museum to see this diorama. It was one of the dioramas on the bottom floor of the gigantic atrium that was the Millstein Hall for Ocean Life, with a gray whale suspended from its ceiling. What I did that night at the Museum of Natural History was a reflection of the state of mind that I found myself in after only a couple of weeks of remote viewing these submarine targets for Naval Intelligence. Near closing time, I found a restroom in an obscure wing of the museum, one that showcased small tribal artifacts that were part of ritual shamanism. With my feet up on the lid of a toilet, inside a locked stall, I hid until my watch read that it was a full two hours after the building had been cleared out. In those days, there were no motion sensors to sound an alarm. Just a few night guards spread far between, mainly at the entrances and exits.

I wound my way through the wooden hallways full of gigantically more-than-life-sized models of earth-boring worms and insects, until I was back at the Hall of Ocean Life. It was even darker than usual, but that is what I wanted. I was seeking a shamanic experience of sorts, an initiatory ordeal that would help me to overcome the terror that I felt in those occulted places that I had been remote viewing, so that I could more perspicaciously perceive what their denizens were doing. It upset me that Anna would be worried sick when I did not come home. Overcoming that binding tie to this life and this world was, however, to my mind part of the ordeal. Little did I know that I would find her again on another level altogether that night in the dark heart of the museum's oceanic simulacrum.

I slowly descended the steps, and then laid down under the whale with my initial trial being to overcome the uneasy feeling that it might fall on me. After hours of meditatively following flashbacks of what I had seen from that gray room atop the Twin Towers, and gleaning a few more glimpses into those underwater lairs, I either fell asleep or entered an altered state of consciousness that made the museum disappear into the ambient darkness. How long I remained in that state I do not know, but I awakened from out of it quite suddenly — not into the Hall of Ocean Life, but into a nightmare so terrible that many of us have chosen to collectively forget it.

The stars were brighter than I had ever seen in this life, especially in the sky over a city, and they were falling. It was as if the heavens had been unhinged. There, suspended high above us against the writhing Milky Way, was a ghostly white sperm whale tossed out of the depths by the tsunami whose mile-high tidal wave was closing in on us fast. We could feel the ocean spray in our faces. Despite her changed features, I recognized Anna at once. We were holding hands, tightening our grip as we braced ourselves to sink together with this world lost in a storm of dark wisdom.

After I snuck out of the museum the next morning and finally made it home to her, before she could rebuke me for going missing, I burst out weeping in her arms. Frankly, I can't even clearly remember how I got home. New York seemed utterly alien to me. What I *do* remember, and what I lamentably shared with her, was the flood of memories that pounded the battlements of my soul that night on the floor of the Hall of Ocean Life.

The city that I saw destroyed by the tsunami, and by whatever ungodly upheaval of the earth made the stars appear to fall, was like no city in recorded history. It was a vast metropolis, of a scale to rival Manhattan, but built in precisely-cut megalithic stone instead of steel and concrete. Rather than skyscrapers, there were multi-tiered pyramidal and polygonal structures with colossal stairways leading up them from the broad streets. Some of the buildings were interlinked by elevated walkways with colonnades in certain places. The stars could be seen so clearly at night because there was no electric lighting.

There was certainly electricity. In fact, the sky was full of it. A hexagonal stone tower that tapered toward the top, where it terminated in a bulbous dome overhanging the structure's edges, was shooting fearsome bolts of artificial lightning into the night's sky in every direction. It also produced something like the aurora borealis, which looked spectacularly ethereal as it radiated over the city. This system was used to wirelessly broadcast electric power to machines and vehicles of various kinds, including wingless cigar-shaped airships streaking through the sky, but it was *not* used to illuminate light bulbs.

Instead of electric lighting, phosphorescent stone spheres on pillars lit the major squares, and much smaller ones set into the curbside illuminated the path ahead on those avenues that were more peripheral. The quality of this lighting made the city's denizens look creepy by sucking the color out of them and whatever they were wearing, in exactly the same way as I had seen in the submarine facilities. In fact, these were *the same* Nordic-looking people. Their clothes were different, though. Instead of the skintight uniforms, they were wearing flowing robes or coats long enough to reach their ankles, with a kind of hieroglyphics or hieratic writing running along the edge of them from where they closed around the neck all the way down to the hem.

These were not the only people in the city, and the others looked nothing like them. There were armor-clad and helmet-wearing guards whose features were similar to the Nubians of today, except that they were so black that their skin had a blue corn chip hue when it was in the sunshine. My impression was that these were policemen or were being used as such. The whole place felt as if it was under martial law, and one was not supposed to be on the streets past certain hours without traveling papers. Then there were slaves of various kinds. Some of these hardly looked human. Perhaps they were Neanderthals or some other kind of primitive hominid. Their hair had been shaved and their hulking naked bodies were covered in a grayish paste of chalk mixed with sweat from working at the stone quarries, where they would be led in chain gangs.

I saw these slave laborers being brutalized by the black overseers. Starved, naked, broken, they stood in chain gangs all across the mountainside and farmlands. One might have known that they were Semitic in appearance, if their heads had not been completely shaven, and their faces and bodies painted in a paste of chalk and sweat. Fear, black fear, pierced their flesh and bones like a substance, pervading every organ and aching cavity with a tender trembling. Time, for them, existed only in breaths. In, out. In, out. A struggle between survival and despair.

It would be a stretch to call these *things* 'human beings.' Not an ounce of dignity was left to them. Their lives were an incomprehensible rush of grueling labor, followed in turn by a black coma of exhaustion that for some slipped seamlessly into death — which simply meant *freedom* — freedom from fear of miserable suffering, from fear of that dreaded and empty word "tomorrow."

Once in a while, there were nightmares, usually a single paralyzing image: fallen beneath the shadow of that wrinkled countenance darker than death, staring down harder than an angry gorilla… the blinding flash of the harsh sun on the point of a descending spear… a blood-spattered, black leather boot on the chalky earth of the stone quarries.

The chains rattled to the ball when they fell, to the left and to the right. The black overseers walked up and down the lines vigilantly, pulling on the chains here and there, pealing this one and that one up off the face of the earth to be battered across the skull with the butt of a spear. Still, so many lay writhing like maggots. Some of them half alive, the corpses of others already rotting in the oppressive heat.

Glimpsing the sight of the guardsmen as they moved among the corpses, skewering them, and clearing them to the side, would leave one with no doubt that these warriors were the most fearsome creatures that ever walked the face of the Earth. Proud and noble Africans with skin so purely black, blacker than black, that in the merciless sunshine of this bleached land they took on the indigo hue of blue corn. They had the features of their Nubian descendants, but they were colossally built, broad enough to bear the burden of their heaving muscles. It was almost as if their faces were incapable of showing joy, boredom, or anxiety. Rather, their rugged features were locked in absolutely fearless determination. One pitiless gaze from their small, darting eyes, set beneath an ever-wincing brow and forehead wrinkled with anger, was enough to turn the hot beating heart of the common man to solid ice.

At the end of the line, just as all throughout it, there stood such a man. One of his herd. His nose broken and his ears boxed in. His head hung down, utterly demoralized, as his naked body flexed to heave the pick over his head and into the face of the stone cliff. Once, twice... Then it happened. He seemed to forget where he was, to forget the guardsman towering over him. He seemed unable to remember for the life of him who he was, or what he was doing here. It was hot. That's all he knew. The sun beat down. He stopped and time slurred as he forgot to keep breathing. Sinking to his knees, slowly, he raised his eyes... A herd of mammoths thundered across the distant plains slothfully, oblivious.

A kick in the head and he was back down in the dust. He could see the guardsmen looming over him. The sun shone across their armor. Their fearsome countenances were framed, it seemed almost inseparably encased, in a crème-colored metallic helmet that was rounded over the top of the head and overset with a raised "U"-shaped symbol. It widened as it descended beneath a ridge in sharp, angular planes to cover the back of the head and the ears, and it ended in a rigid protrusion (like the lower half of an octagon) around the jaw. Their shoulders, from the upper arms to their sunken and strained necks, were covered in massive iron pads, angular on the sides facing the chest, curved around the outward-facing shoulder, and embossed in two layers. Their chests were brutally bare. Beneath their sculpted abs, they wore a thick metal belt lined with a single firearm holster and other small weapons, like knives or grenades. Under the belt hung sheets of armor in tiers that covered the groin, buttocks, thighs and went all the way down to the knees, but was open at the sides, up to the hips.

Their gruff voices could bark orders and their spears could point until doomsday, but he would not get up this time. He just stared straight into the pure blue sky, as if he were trying to say with his eyes the words that he could not form with his mouth. As if he were trying to testify to its emptiness. He had forgotten that he was alive. Dust sprinkled down into his parched mouth as a boot crushed the odd number of teeth in his gaping jaws, stamping out a human face with the seal of eternity.

The guardsmen seemed to know when it was time to head back toward the cyclopean walls of Atlantis. That is, the first ring of walls. There were three. Slaves were not even allowed past the first, except for domestic servants — who needed permits. On the treacherous mountain path, as far as their eyes could see, lining the way before them and behind, were planted the spears of guardsmen crowned by human skulls. The miserable souls had to stare them in the face as they walked to the quarries every 'morning.' An affirmation of destiny, it would seem.

Spears moved among spears as the guardsmen marched alongside the chain-gang, prodding it forward. Despite all the sophisticated gadgetry of their helmets and utility belts, each guardsman carried without fail at his side a tall spear with a massive iron point and used it most efficiently of all his weapons — especially to gesture directions as he barked orders while keeping an imposing distance. It was better to keep one's distance from a guardsman. For all but the slave, proximity was equated with certain death. The slave, who hobbled about amidst their boots, was already dead. Only the Nordic-looking Olympian lords and ladies who ruled over Atlantis could lock eyes with them, as a ringmaster gazes into the eyes of a mesmerized panther.

The guardsmen coldly studied the lines of skulls, as if they read in them a symbolic revelation regarding mortality. Some of these skulls — spiked at an angle — seemed to look up defiantly through the hollows of their eye sockets, cursing the Sun as it circumnavigated the pole so as to mark out a great symbol of futility.

Back in the city there were also domestic slaves, who, frankly, looked most like people do now. They were not as tall as the Nordic types that they served, nor were they as ethereal. But their skulls were shaped more normally, basically indistinguishable from those of a Mediterranean or Semitic type today. They were dark-haired and had brown or black eyes. Most of them were clothed simply, but there were exceptions. Certain women in particular were more exotically and extravagantly dressed than their masters, albeit also much more scantily clad, and ensconced in jewelry. They had the bodies and gait of dancers. As I knew all too well, these were courtesans.

That is putting it politely. To be honest, they were sex slaves. A great controversy surrounded their function in our society. Certain hardcore traditionalists believed that the use of these "things" — as the slaves in general were called — would corrupt us. Others contended that, since they were not conscious and did not really have souls, the sex slaves could be used just the same way as the other "things" were. They simply needed to be made more refined and skilled to carry out their tasks, which also included a variety of other work as domestic servants. A very small circle of us knew that both of these views were wrong. We had secretly committed the sin of falling in love with one or another of these women, who we found to actually be possessed of their own inner world and a character-building horizon of experience different from that of their masters. We had even removed the birth control mechanism so as to be able to interbreed with them, with a view to hybridizing their population and thereby strengthening it for a future rebellion.

The woman that I saw in the first image that came to me, the one that I was holding hands with under the falling stars and that I had recognized as a previous incarnation of Anna, was one of these courtesans. She looked much the same as in this life, with sharp features that were a cross between Eurasian and Mediterranean, with dark brown hair and amber eyes. She was just as thin and graceful, with small pointy breasts. Her bangle-studded ankles were strikingly beautiful, and so were her hands, which from fingertip to wrist, evinced a wisdom much older than her years and that it should not have been possible for one of her "kind" to have attained. These "things" were not supposed to have names, but I had given her one: *Marjâna*.

Each time she would come to me, I could tell that she was distressed from the anxiety of having passed through the several sets of guarded cyclopean walls and presenting her papers to the sentries. There was nothing inherently unlawful about her coming here, but our being in love was certainly forbidden and she was afraid that those two-legged guard dogs would almost smell it on her. Or, more likely, that it would be noticed by another citizen. You see, this was a telepathic society. Our thoughts were supposed to be open to one another. It is almost impossible to explain to a modern man what a suffocating reinforcement of conformity this was. Not for most people, since they were not really independent-minded individuals with any distinct personality that would even be capable of feeling smothered. But a few of us were different. We were secret rebels, and we had to work hard to compartmentalize our psyche so that we would not be identified and called out as "deviants." This mental compartmentalization only served to intensify and deepen our subversive individuality.

Anna — I mean Marjâna — took me back to her village with her. Now, visiting such a place was highly questionable for a citizen. They lived like troglodytes, in a honeycomb of dimly lit chambers roughly

hewn out of a mountainside. It is there that I beheld the living conditions of those who worked deep in the mines, including the ones
where radium was mined to paint our phosphorescent stone lights and
the dials inside our submarines and aerospace craft. They had cancer
from routinely inhaling and handling radioactive dust. Of course, they
didn't know what cancer was. Neither did Marjâna, until I explained
it to her. Some of them were frail, with their hair falling out. I'll never
forget her holding one man's bald and weary head in her hands as his
face twisted in agony while looking up at me as he lay in her lap. It was
as if he was trying to form a question to which no one in his benighted
world would ever be given an answer. There was something about her
posture as she held him that reminded me of a deer, or maybe a gazelle.
Marjâna would get a look in her eyes sometimes that made me worry
that she would bolt — from me, from this whole unbearable life.

So, I tried to expand her horizon. Once, I misappropriated an
aerospace craft to give her a view of the Earth from orbit. I can't say
that I stole it, because it was 'mine' — to the limited extent that anyone
had personal property in this society. But it was strictly forbidden
for anyone but full-blooded citizens to leave the surface of the Earth,
or, for that matter, to travel beneath the surface of the oceans in our
submarines. Her wide eyes were unforgettable. She looked down, astonished, then looked back at me with the wonder of a little girl, and
then out the cockpit window again, and then back at me. I smiled, with
tears in my eyes. "This is *your* world," I said.

As we descended toward the city again, others like it could be
seen amidst the dense forests of the vast continental island with its
soaring snow-capped mountains — the Transantarctic Mountains of
today. The cities were few and far between, encircled by a wilderness
teeming with beasts like saber-tooth tigers and mammoths grazing on
the plains. Each of the cities was heavily fortified against the savage
world outside its high walls. The polygonal megalithic construction
of these walls went back to the days when such a fortification had

to be strong enough to keep out small bands of surviving dinosaurs. These "dragons" had by and large been hunted to extinction by now, especially the ones who could fly over the walls to threaten the city's livestock from above. The few that endured had been cowered into keeping their distance from civilization. It was becoming increasingly difficult to maintain the heroic tradition of going into the wilderness to slay a dragon as an initiatory rite of passage.

Now, what was most menacing in the woodlands were the ape men. They were dimwitted and could be easily mesmerized, but when, occasionally, we failed to bring them under our hypnotic control, these beasts were capable of a kind of willfully homicidal violence unseen from any other predatory animal. This life form had been the basis for the genetic modification, hybridization, and eugenic breeding that eventually yielded the various quasi-human or humanoid races constituting the castes of any city's ethno-social pyramid. Producing these humanoid castes from the wild hominids of the woodlands was the first major project that preoccupied our ancestors when they arrived as refugees after the cosmic war that rendered the surface of Mars nearly uninhabitable and evaporated the oceans of our now desiccated home world.

The more Marjâna saw of our world and the more I gleaned of hers, we began to feel as if anything would be preferable to a continuation of this state of affairs. I remember being high up in the stone tower of my apartment with her, looking out the balcony as the sun set over the city, and kneeling together in the most profound and focused prayer. It wasn't just the two of us. Other secret "deviants" were doing the same. We prayed for a force of nature strong enough to bring the vampiric immortality of this godforsaken civilization to an end. We implored nature to turn on the undead master race, wipe clean the memory of their heavenly heritage and break the chains of history that destined everyone else to serve them. We begged for Poseidon or Typhon to baptize the world with a new beginning. But God helps those who help themselves, so we also began conspiring to use a system of directed energy and telluric resonance amplification for the purpose of triggering volcanic eruptions, massive earthquakes, and attendant tsunamis. We hardly expected that this would be so spectacularly successful that the tremors would cause the Earth's entire crust to slip over its mantle, tossing the oceans out of their basins and presenting us with the horrific illusion that the stars were suddenly falling in a defiance and derangement of celestial fate.

This made it considerably more difficult to execute the plans that we had made for bringing about a renaissance after the engineered catastrophes. The sites that we had chosen for educating the primitive population were battered by the worldwide flood, and we had to wait for the waters to recede before we could repair the damage and round up enough survivors to begin the process of reconstructing civilization — a new *human* civilization. There were twelve principal sites: two of them in what is now Egypt, at Giza and Abydos, one in contemporary Mexico, one in Bolivia, one in Peru, one in China, one in the part of the Gobi (at that time not yet a desert) that is currently within Mongolia, a couple in Northern India, and several in the Middle East (one each inside the present borders of Iran, Iraq, and Turkey). Megalithic buildings had been constructed at each of these sites in advance of the artificial cataclysm, and extensive measurements had been made, and ground plans drawn, for many more structures to be built afterwards — including gargantuan pyramids and massive temples aligned with stellar patterns and built in such a way as to mark the equinoxes and solstices.

We had a superbly high-precision, long-count zodiacal calendar that had been designed to keep time over the hundreds of years that it took for journeys back and forth between the various inhabited planets of the solar system and beyond. After the cosmic war, the remaineders of these worlds were largely cut off from each other, but the calendar endured as a legacy of that age when the once verdant surface of Mars was still our homeland. Those cities were tombs now, literally. Some of the leaders were still there on Mars in cryogenic suspension sarcophaguses that had been set up inside the largest pyramids. Little did they know that their side had lost the war, and no one would be coming to their titanic bunker to resurrect them. In a sense, they were the silent guardians of the vast archives that had been left behind on that planet. Once, I participated in one of the very few interplanetary missions that were launched with great difficulty in order to retrieve information from these Martian archives. We arrived in the midst of a terrible sandstorm, and all of us were killed. I had to astral-project back into one of the clone bodies in my chamber. Marjâna was repulsed by the slight differences in my physiognomy the next time we saw each other, even if the reincarnation also meant a significant increase in my vitality.

You might imagine that when I recounted these memories to Anna, she would think that I had gone insane. But something worse than that happened. She began to have her own recollections of that place. What place? We concurred that it had to be the lost civilization that, in both Russia and the West, has been referred to as "Atlantis" since the time of Plato. We went to the Strand and also a metaphysical bookstore in the village, where we bought numerous volumes on the subject, from the classic *Atlantis, the Antediluvian World* by Ignatius Donnelly to *Atlantis Rising*, which had just been published by a certain Brad Steiger. We scoured the books of Madame Blavatsky, Rudolf Steiner, and Edgar Casey for their references to Atlantis. Anna described her surfacing memories having the quality of something that one struggles to remember from a dream or from the forgotten parts of our early childhood, with no aid from photographs.

Some of her memories were very painful. They were of her life as a courtesan before she met me. When she recounted these to me, I could see why certain members of the governing elite were concerned that having sex slaves would corrupt us. Since I never engaged in such acts as she described, I could not have imagined what they meant by the corruption that these conservatives were concerned about precisely because *they were the ones* being corrupted. Apparently, having absolute power over the body of a woman who was not his own wife brought out the worst in more than one Atlantean man. This was why when she had met me in that life, she was so surprised that I did not treat her how she had, by then, expected to be treated. It is also why, after Marjâna got to know me, and we fell in love, she rarely wanted to have sex. That was fine with me, and truth be told, it felt more erotic to share subversive and mind-expanding secrets with her. But I did not realize how much trauma was behind the fact that she would get uncomfortable if I tried to do anything more than tenderly kiss or hold her. To her, sex had come to mean perverse humiliation and terrifying violence. Not something you do with someone that you love — or see as an angel of redemption.

Anna described how in her life as Marjâna, well, actually, before I gave her that name and she served namelessly, a number of different Atlantean men had badly abused her. The abuse consisted of various forms of sexual perversion, sadism, and occasional masochism — although, after the heat of passion, the latter would always end with a terribly sadistic reassertion of authority and a punishment for having witnessed the man being humiliated (or humiliating himself).

Sometimes this was followed up by torture from the 'proper' wives of these men. Once, one of the wives beat her with a rod, and then, as she lay on the stone floor unable to move, the woman pulled her dress up, squatted over Marjâna's face, and relieved herself. While she was still writhing in the piss and shit, this Atlantean 'lady' grabbed her hair and dragged her out of the room by it with Nordic brutality. Women like that resented her for bearing witness to their husbands shamelessly expressing themselves and indulging desires that were too crude for them to be allowed to experience.

On numerous occasions, she was chained, bound, whipped, and gagged, sometimes by several men at a time, men she believed were simply using her as a prop and an excuse to secretly explore their own deviant homosexuality. For example, when they would rub their cocks together as two or three of them made her give them oral sex simultaneously, or when one fucked her ass while she rode another and sucked the cock of a third man, who stood there overlooking the two men — occasionally grabbing them by their hair, when he wasn't slapping her. Like all sex slaves, she had been fitted with a device that prevented her from getting pregnant from all of the sperm that was shot into her, almost as much as she was forced to drink from one cock after another.

Marjâna — I mean Anna — was often in tears telling me these things. She was hardly a prude, but she found it hard to look into my eyes when she shared these surfacing memories. I think what really made her ashamed was that, on some level, reliving these experiences really turned her on. She did not tell me this, but when she would get in the bath, I would notice that her discarded panties were soaked through right where her lips were hugging them. She had never gotten that dripping wet with me before, I mean without even being touched or kissed. This was disturbing enough, but before long she stopped wanting to have sex with me. I never felt comfortable pushing her, especially since she had gone from being capable of multiple orgasms in all the years that we made love to not being able to climax no matter how hard I fucked her or how long I went down on her. She started getting really drunk at night before we would go to bed together. Then there would be days when I'd come home from the World Trade Center, and she would still be out — long after her day classes were over at the New School. Sometimes, when she would get home, Anna would go straight into the shower. She liked to soak in baths, but on these occasions, she would take a quick shower.

Finally, I confronted her. Passionate Russians that we were, we had our share of heated arguments through the years, but this fight was the worst. While she was in the shower, I had discovered cocaine dusted all over the inside of her handbag, together with a pair of panties that she had taken off because they were full of sperm. I wondered why she hadn't just thrown them out on the way home. It was as if she had wanted to get caught. Maybe she wished that I would punish her. She threw her high-heeled shoes at me. Then, although she was evidently already drunk, Anna poured herself vodka on the rocks with a lit cigarette dangling from her pursed lips. A half hour and two drinks later, she hurled that glass across the room at me. I ducked and it shattered on the wall.

I ran after her as she went toward the terrace, threatening to throw herself off the edge of the building. I tackled her to the carpeted floor of the living room, and then she tried hard to choke me. After grabbing her wrists to release her grip on my neck, I finally smacked her once across the face. She screamed through her tears: "Hit me! Hit me again!" I slapped her one more time, fairly lightly, but horrified at myself, nonetheless. "Harder! Please!" she cried. Then she reached for my pants and tried frantically to open them. Her bathrobe had already slipped open from the struggle. "Fuck me!" she screamed. "Can't you just fuck me?"

I pulled her hands off the crotch of my pants and slipped down to embrace her body with my head on her abdomen. "Please, please," she whimpered. From the way her stomach muscles reverberated, I could tell that she was silently weeping. Then, it was not so silent. I pulled myself back up over her and looked down into the most tortured and despairing expression that I've ever seen on a human face. That was with her eyes closed. When she opened them to look at me, so briefly before she turned away, I could see searing shame.

"You don't have to be ashamed," I said softly, "just talk to me. It's okay, you can tell me anything. Please, tell me what's been going on."

She responded to my reassuring voice by weeping uncontrollably, tilting her head back and looking at the terrace again, toward the ledge of which she also reached with each of her arms before I took her hands into mine and caressed them. "Just kill me," she pleaded.

It was a long time before Anna calmed down enough to talk coherently. She sat next to me in our bed and confessed everything. Before finding what ultimately forced me to confront her, I feared that maybe she had been having an affair, but no. It wasn't like that. Anna hadn't been passionately seduced into infidelity by some dream lover or fallen in love with a man other than me. She had become a prostitute.

Now, understand, at that time I still had considerable inherited wealth, and not only did I support her, I lavishly spent my money getting her everything that she even showed the slightest hint of desiring. No, she was not prostituting herself for want of money. She wanted to be degraded, abused, humiliated, and made filthy by the men who fucked her. One of the reasons she wouldn't let me have sex with her anymore is that she was having unprotected sex with them. She had an IUD, so she didn't need to worry about pregnancy, but she let herself be exposed to any disease that they might have. With her head buried in her hands, pulling away as I tried to put my arm around her, she admitted that on some days, instead of going to class, she would try to find three or four different men to cum in her. She didn't care much whether it was in her pussy, her mouth, or her ass. She just wanted to be defiled.

I asked her whether she enjoyed any of this masochism, if she got pleasure out of it or was just torturing herself. She crumpled down into a fetal position and turned away from me. I pulled her onto my lap and wiped the tears from her cheeks. "It's okay. Tell me." She admitted to having the most intense orgasms of her life. Sometimes several of them at a time. If some pathetic man prematurely ejaculated and left her unsatisfied, she would be sure to find another to fuck her brains out the same day.

It was not hard to understand what had happened. Marjâna's memories had been integrated by Anna to the point that they became her own, thereby deeply restructuring her personality from out of parts of her that had been locked in her subconscious. They hadn't been fully integrated, though. She was only half conscious when she prostituted herself. It was clear to me, from what she was describing, that Anna was in a quasi-mesmeric state when she did these things. It was almost as if Marjâna was doing them, with Anna's body. But there was more to it than a sense of not being able to help herself. She had come to deeply resent me, at least on a subconscious level. I was no longer just Nikolai to her. Now, I was also Dârâ-El, the Atlantean.

This man had been her master, in a society where she was a slave — a sex slave. It is true that he — rather, I — never abused her and was so determined to liberate her, and others like her, that I was will-ing to commit the highest treason imaginable by collaborating in the deliberate destruction of Atlantis. Still, I had been her *master* and heir to a civilization that was not even of this world, one transplanted from the dead planet Mars — a civilization that not only enslaved her kind, but that *created* her kind, humankind, as a race of biological robots who were never supposed to evolve into conscious and conscientious individuals.

Now that she was reintegrating her memories of having been Marjâna, Anna held my Atlantean heritage against me. She didn't mean to, but she did. On the one hand, her having sex with these ran-dom men rather than me was a sign of reverence, of seeing me as too sacred to defile, and, on the other hand, it was a punishment driven by vengeful resentment over implicit oppression — implicit in the sense that even my benevolence as a rebel Atlantean was a tacit reaffirma-tion of her inferiority, of her being at my mercy. These two convoluted motivations for her prostitution were inextricably conflated.

What made things a lot worse was the fact that my day job con-sisted of remote viewing what appeared to be *survivors from Atlantis*, and *not* ones aligned with those of us who went around the world on a mission of consciousness-raising and the enlightenment of humanity (really, in a sense, the creation of true "humanity"). Rather, the occulted undersea and subterranean civilization that I had described to Anna from the beginning of my work for Naval Intelligence (yes, in viola-tion of my secrecy oath) was clearly constituted by the Atlantean old guard. Or, rather, what I suppose you could call the Olympians — the self-styled "gods" who set up and ruled Atlantis before its rebellion against "Olympus." Their mission was to *restore* as much as they could of the Olympian society that we had sought to destroy with our Atlantean rebellion. They would never be able to regress the major-ity of contemporary humanity back into the mesmerized slaves that they had once been, but they could come as close as possible by us-ing new technologies and techniques of control to force people back into a caste system with themselves at the top of it. One thing that I had learned during my sessions atop the World Trade Center was that this Atlantean Underworld had created European Fascism and, especially, German National Socialism as a vehicle for a restoration of the Olympian Imperium. They saw the Nazis, particularly the SS, as *Kshatriyas* who would build a pyramid for them to ascend as the *Brahmins* of a New World Order.

This meant that Anna could not even take comfort in the trauma of her life as Marjâna being something that suffered in the distant past. The 'people' who had visited that suffering upon her were alive and well, planning their reemergence with the patience of titans, whose lives span thousands of our years and who have total recall from one incarnation to the next. She resented me for just watching them, day in and day out, without doing anything to stop them. Anna even suspect-ed that the purpose of the sessions was really to seduce me into col-laborating with this underworld, or with the post-war Fascist shadow government that is facilitating their machinations. It is not as if that thought had never occurred to me. I had suppressed this suspicion, but when Anna confessed that it was one of the factors motivating her extremely destructive behavior, I had to face it forthrightly. I needed to know. Was I being used? By whom? For how long? To what end? Tragically, Anna would not live to see me answer those agonizing questions.

One day, I came back home from work to find Anna missing. She had stopped prostituting herself for some time, so I was really worried. My intuition was that she was in real danger. In just the past couple of days, she had finally been able to surrender to total intimacy with me again. The first time that she climaxed with me since being overcome by memories of our life in Atlantis, her moans of ecstasy quickly turned into hysterical weeping. She could barely look at me, and when I gently compelled her to do so I saw overwhelming sadness, shame, and regret in her eyes. The next day we were closer than we had ever been.

I try to console myself with the thought that when I wrapped my arms around her from behind, breathing her hair, as she stood in the kitchen stirring her coffee with downcast eyes, she could feel my un-equivocal forgiveness and renewed adoration of her. That night, when we made love again, I implored her to keep looking into my eyes. She did, although I had to keep wiping the tears off her cheeks, which were covered with smeared mascara by the time she came. Then, looking up at me as if she would not see me again for a long time, she held my head in her hands as I let go. I wish I had understood that expression then, and I'll never forgive myself for going to work the next morning.

Throughout the evening and into the night, as I paced frantically while waiting for her to come home, I kept getting terrible flashes of her alone on a beach, crying and playing chicken at the ocean's edge with waves crashing from out of the darkness. I felt like I was suffocat-ing. My every impulse was to go out looking for Anna, to follow these impressions to Coney Island and scour the beach in search of her. But I was held back by the fear that she would finally come home, already so deeply distressed, and find me gone. It was possible that the images coming to me were only symbolic. How would I know where to look for her?

The next morning, I went to the police. They told me that she hadn't been missing for long enough to justify their doing anything about it. So I asked Jack for a favor. I knew I was too involved to trust the objectivity of any clairvoyant impressions of my own, so I explained as much of the situation to him as he needed to know before requesting that two other remote viewers be tasked — off the record — to find my Anna. As per usual protocol, they wouldn't need to know what or who the target was. Only Jack would know when he analyzed their independently obtained data. He agreed. Aware of the urgency of the situation, Jack had both of these men do sessions on the same day, and by early evening he was grimly comparing the notes and sketches made by them. After making the request in person that morning, I had gone back home to be there in case Anna returned, even though, in the pit of my stomach, I knew that she wasn't coming back.

Jack called me around sunset and asked if he could come over. I met him in the long hallway of the lobby. He had the gravest look that I'd ever seen on his face. Considering his personality, it was quite startling. He had a leather dossier holder under his arm. We didn't exchange a word in the elevator, and he tried to avoid eye contact. Without his needing to request it, I poured him a glass of scotch and made another one for myself. My hands were shaking as I tried to get the ice cubes out of the tray. He sat on the sofa in my living room sipping his scotch a few times before opening the leather portfolio. Jack sighed as he laid the papers inside it across my sofa. Then he sat back and glanced across at me. I was leaning forward in my armchair. "She's dead, Nick. She drowned herself. Brighton Beach."

Silence. Dead silence. I'd say I could hear my heartbeat, but I felt like my heart had stopped. I couldn't breathe. I didn't even bother to look at the papers. When I managed to form words again, I asked, "Where's her body?" Jack pressed his fingers into his forehead, covering his eyes with his hand, with his head downcast. "It'll wash up on the beach," he said.

What if she had no identification on her? How was I supposed to go to the police and ask them to keep an eye out for the corpse of a "Jane Doe" to wash up on the beach? Jack said that he would take care of it, and that he would also make the funeral arrangements for me. I explained to him that Anna was totally alienated from her family, and that she had few friends who would show up to any funeral. I wanted her cremated, and to keep her urn by my side, but only after I got to see her body one last time.

Jack came through. He had a Navy Seal team retrieve Anna's corpse from Brighton Beach before it was even discovered by the police, and before the seagulls could disfigure her too badly. Part of me died forever when I stood over her lifeless body at the morgue. The morticians had been instructed by Naval Intelligence not to ask too many questions. She was cremated, and the urn of her ashes became my most cherished possession. It was not gaudy gold, but black and embossed with the Trident of Poseidon.

CHAPTER 5

FAUSTIAN FUTURIST

A fter Anna's suicide, answering the question that she had forced me to formulate in full consciousness became an all-consuming quest. Despite how helpful Jack was in dealing with her death, I could not put him above the suspicion of being party to a vast conspiracy to manipulate me. There was the danger that indulging such conspiratorial suspicions was a sign of encroaching paranoia, which from a psychoanalytic standpoint would be considered an "understandable" reaction to all that I had been through in the mere 27 years of my life. But I knew better. Archontic forces were at work weaving this tangled web, whose strands included the gruesome death of my parents, trauma-induced paranormal ability, recruitment into the intelligence field as a psychic spy, and the suicide of my beloved. It was the spring of 1974 when I began investigating the misfortunes of my life. In hindsight, it was like being a detective endeavoring to discover *in advance* who and what *would be* responsible for the crime of one's own untimely demise.

I decided to start at the beginning. Nostalgic and sentimental as I am, I had carefully kept almost all of my aunt's personal belongings boxed up in my closets or in the storage of our building. I went through all of these things looking for some clue. It was not long before I happened upon a set of old photographs of what, on the face of it, was my father and mother. One might assume that it was my mother, because the body language between her and my father attested to an intimacy that is exclusive to longtime lovers. Also, my 'uncle' supposedly hated my father "the communist" to the extent that he forbade my aunt from visiting her own sister who was so contemptible as to marry such a man. (That's what I was told about why I had never met my aunt and uncle while my parents were still alive.)

This set of photographs showed my father from long after my uncle married my aunt. He was standing in a wooded area, apparently target practicing, but also mischievously engaging in horseplay with the woman in the photograph. Here is the problem. The woman is brandishing weapons. Proudly holding a sniper rifle, aiming a pistol, and holding a hunting knife to my father's throat with a darkly playful look on her face. I recognized that look. My mother, Marianna, would *never* even have gone *near* any of these weapons. I can't even imagine her firing a gun. This woman *was her identical twin*, namely my aunt Nikita!

What was she doing with my father? Well, obviously, paramilitary training of some kind. They were wearing camouflage outfits, and in some of the pictures a patch with an insignia could be made out on them: a sun wheel whose twelve spokes each extended out to become a bolt of lightning. There was also a pin fastened to each side of the fabric epaulettes of these fatigues, with one star on either side of the pin. But, I mean, what was she *doing* with him, especially given the story I had been told by my uncle? No wonder my aunt implied that she knew hidden truths about my father. It was obvious from these photographs that they had been comrades and lovers. I shuddered. For years, I had been fucked by my father's lover.

As I mentioned earlier, I was fairly talented at drawing. So I carefully reproduced the symbol on the patch of their gray uniforms, together with the design of the pin on the shoulder bands. I took these drawings to a military historian whose antique shop in Midtown Manhattan I had visited with Anna a few times. He remembered and asked about her. I did not get into details but told him that she had died tragically. I could have just lied and made small talk, but it was a good thing that I said this much because it put him in a more caring and concerned mindset. Otherwise, he might have thrown me out of his store or alerted the authorities after looking at my drawings.

When I set them in front of him, he stared wide-eyed at them for a moment with a look of consternation in his face. You see, he was a Ukrainian Jew. He breathed deeply as he took his spectacles off and laid them on the table with a poise that suggested he was struggling to suppress an angry outburst. Then, he looked penetratingly into my eyes, and asked, "Why have you drawn neo-Nazi symbols?" I said, "What?!" He explained, "These symbols, one is wolf's hook, the other is clever combination of Black Sun with SS lightning bolts."

The anger in his face disappeared and was replaced by bewildered concern, when he realized that I had no idea what he was talking about. "Where did you see these, young man? Where you draw this from?" When I remained silent, he added, "These symbols today are only used by neo-Nazis. The *wolfsangel*, this was runic symbol of insurgency against American and Russian occupation of Germany in 1945. The werewolves. This other one, it is invented. But I recognize elements. It is Black Sun, symbol on floor of Wewelsburg Castle of Himmler's knights, but the sun rays, you see, have been drawn like the lightning bolts of SS insignia. You know, SS lightning bolts?" He got up and brought over a black *sig*-rune emblazoned SS flag from his collection of World War II memorabilia. As I was staring at it, dazed, trying to contemplate the implications of all this, he also brought over a wolf's hook pin from one of his glass cases.

I had to quickly think of a constructive lie. "Mr. Lubetkin," I started. He interrupted, "Please, Yuri." I claimed that I had seen these symbols spraypainted on walls here in the city. Leaning in and whispering, I told part of the truth (enough of it to get fired), "I work for the government now. We are secretly investigating the people who made these graffiti. Do you know where I could find them?" He sat back in his chair and looked me over with curiosity and skepticism. "You have badge, young man?" I reached for my wallet, "I'm not supposed to show you this, so please, don't mention to *anybody* that I was here asking questions." I pulled out my access badge for the facility in the World Trade Center. "You are Navy Intelligence?!"

I motioned for him to lower his voice as I nervously looked around the large store from the desk in the back where we were sitting. There was only one other person in there, toward the front. He nodded affirmatively, then motioned for me to wait a minute while he got up and fetched something. It was a contact and address book, crammed with receipts. "These scum, they come here and buy paraphernalia from me. They pretend just interested in make collection from war history. But *I know*. They are neo-Nazi. Haircut, military style. Never they make small talk with me. Never eye contact." He opened the book up to a certain page and pulled out a few receipts, setting them to the side of it.

"You mean, like skinheads?" He shook his head violently. "No, more serious. Always they wear three-piece suit. Impeccably dressed, with silk scarf, you know. Look like old-style Italian Fascists." The pages that he had opened to, and that he now turned toward me, were full of handwritten addresses. Now, *he* leaned in to whisper to *me*, with a twinkle in his eyes. "I have — I had — them followed. *This* one apartment house. This one *coffee shop*, where they meet. *That* one bookstore." This old antique dealer and amateur buff of military history turned out to be a Nazi hunter. "My brother," he said with downcast eyes, "he died in Treblinka." Then he pulled up the sleeve of his sweater and unbuttoned the wrist of his shirt, exposing the number tattooed on his forearm. "I survived, in Auschwitz."

I tried the coffee shop first, because it was the easiest place to linger in on a regular basis. Then I started frequenting the bookstore. I considered staking out the apartment house, keeping my eye out for especially well-dressed men with fascistic haircuts. But before I had to resort to the latter, they showed up in the coffee shop. After they left, I asked to have a word with the manager. I pulled my badge out again, in total disregard of the consequences for my position with Naval Intelligence. Sufficiently impressed, he asked the waitress who had been serving their table to come talk to me. She very uncomfortably informed me that they were regulars, and, when pressed, gave me an idea of what days and times they tended to frequent the establishment. After a couple of misses, at one of these indicated times I arrived to find them there and got a booth next to theirs. Overhearing their conversation, I was able to conclude that the most senior member of the group of three or four men who would get together there was a corporate executive who also did work as a publisher or publicist.

Shortly thereafter, I saw the same man check one of the shelves in the bookstore, and then go into its backroom to talk to the store's owner. I did not linger long enough for him to notice me, but I came back and carefully looked through the particular bookshelf that he had been searching. That section of this obscure bookshop featured books from the Traditionalist school of Philosophy, with which I was only vaguely familiar at the time. Most of the writings of René Guénon and Julius Evola were there. But what was most interesting was the tome that I had noticed that man pull out before going into the backroom. It had a very dramatic red, white, and black cover, with hands clasped over a downward pointing sword, which made me think of Arthur's Excalibur. The title was *Imperium* and the spine identified it as the work of "Ulick Varange." The back cover, however, clarified that this was a pen name used by one Francis Parker Yockey, whose photograph was printed above a brief biography ending with his death in prison in 1960. The picture on the back cover showed him in handcuffs. I bought the book.

Imperium was a shocking read. In this self-described sequel to Oswald Spengler's *Decline of the West*, Yockey (aka "Varange") argued that, after the defeat suffered by Fascism in 1945, the decline of "Faustian civilization" that Spengler analyzed in the 1920s had entered a terminal phase. An even more unapologetically imperial form of totalitarianism would now be necessary to resurrect the dying European world. What was most startling about the thesis of *Imperium* was its valorization of the Soviet Union over the United States. One would think that Fascists would see Communist Russia as their ultimate enemy, and, especially given how many Nazi scientists were imported by America, and how racist the South had remained despite attempted desegregation, the United States would be viewed more favorably by them. But that is not how Yockey saw things. He preferred Stalinism to democratic American "degeneracy" and hoped for the Russians to defeat the United States in its current form as a capitalist liberal democracy, if only to catalyze the rise of a Fourth Reich — a pan-European "Imperium" — from out of the ruins of the postwar Anglo-American order.

After wrapping my mind around this thesis, I went back to that bookstore and my eye was drawn toward *Men Among the Ruins* by Julius Evola, which forwarded a similar argument. Then I read his *Revolt Against the Modern World*, and Evola's references in that magnum opus led me to the works of Réne Guénon, especially *Crisis of the Modern World* and *The Reign of Quantity*. I took extensive notes on these books. While reading them over, a diabolical idea occurred to me. I would write a book in the vein of these works, so that I could have an excuse to approach the publisher and others in his circle here in New York. But I needed to be able to devote my time to this project in a serious way. So, I contrived to disguise my work as research for a doctoral thesis that would critique Traditionalist Fascism.

For the last two years, I had held up my plans to further my graduate studies in Philosophy beyond an MA and in pursuit of a PhD. Before being sent to Jack's office by Hal, I had been thinking to expand my MA thesis into a dissertation. I set this aside now and decided that after receiving my doctorate I could publish a slightly expanded version of the MA thesis as my second book. My first book would be written under a pen name, as Yockey had written his, and it would be written parallel to a doctoral dissertation that afforded me the time to research it. My angle for proposing the PhD thesis would be to argue that 1920s and 30s European Fascism was internally incoherent, strained between opposed polarities of Traditionalism (Guénon, Evola, and Hitler) and Futurism (Nietzsche, Jünger, Marinetti, and, to an extent, Mussolini). Secretly, the research for this thesis would fuel the writing of a treatise that I planned to title *Faustian Futurism*.

An Iranian-born professor at the New School would be integral to helping me develop the project. Fereidoun M. Esfandiary had by then conceptualized the characteristics of a new type of Futurists, people who he called "Up-Wingers." These were visionary individuals who defied the typical Left/Right political binary, but not by being centrist. Up-Wingers recognized that the radical transformation of human society, toward something that Esfandiary liked to call a "Transhuman" (rather than Superhuman) condition, required social and political structures that could not be neatly categorized as entirely left-wing or right-wing.

Despite working on what he called "A Futurist Manifesto," Esfandiary did not seem that keen on the history of Futurism or of Faustian European philosophy in general. He had only a superficial familiarity with Nietzsche, and, as far as I could tell, had not read Heidegger. But what I wanted to appropriate from Esfandiary, who envisioned a world very much like that depicted in the concept drawings of Syd Mead, was the idea of a radical, revolutionary socio-political vision that was 180 degrees opposite to centrism. Rather than being a compromise between Socialism and Conservatism or Democracy and Totalitarianism, it represented a convergence of opposed polarities at a point beyond their extremes.

On this view, the socio-political spectrum was not just a shoehorn but actually a circle, and there was a position on it diametrically opposite to the moderate center, a position to the left of Marx and to the right of Mussolini. Of course, Esfandiary would never have put it this way himself. But my argument was going to be that such a position was not only implicit to *his* "Transhuman" Neo-Futurism, but it was also already there in the Fascist Futurism of 1909–1945. This kind of Fascism was in as much tension with 'Fascist' Traditionalism as it was with Liberal Democracy, or a Social Democracy headed toward Communism. In fact, in some ways, it had more in common with the Promethean aspects of Soviet Communism than it did with Traditionalism.

At the core of *Faustian Futurism*, there was to be a contemplation of the bargain that Goethe has his tragic figure of Faust strike with Mephistopheles. Faust makes this promise to the devil, "*Werd ich zum Augenblicke sagen: Verweile doch! Du bist so schön! Dann magst du mich in Fesseln schlagen, Dann will ich gern zugrunde gehn!*" "If I should say to the moment: But tarry! You are so beautiful! Then you might as well bind me in chains, then I will gladly go to my demise!" As Spengler understood when he characterized the West as a "Faustian Civilization," this devil's pact is meant to symbolize an ethos of unappeasable striving. Goethe grasped this well, from within himself.

> Mephistopheles:
> Who could divine toward what you aspire?
> It must have been sublimely bold, in truth,
> Toward the moon you'd soar and ever higher;
> Did your mad quest allure you there forsooth?
>
> Faust:
> By no means! For this earthly sphere
> Affords a place for great deeds ever.
> Astounding things shall happen here,
> I feel the strength for bold endeavor.
>
> Mephistopheles [still jeering and skeptical]:
> So you'd earn glory? One can see
> You've been in heroines' company.

Faust:
Lordship, possession, are my aim and thought!

The will to reach the Moon, already intuited here by the devil, is only another expression of Faustian man's uniquely exploratory spirit. For the sake of writing *Faustian Futurism*, I researched the history of exploration. What I found, and presented in the manuscript, was shocking. But it was sure to appeal to Thompson and his circle. As it turns out, when one defines "the explorer" as a distinct category that is not to be confused with conquerors who crossed vast swathes of land, such as Genghis Khan (or Alexander), one finds that there are only about 15 non-European men out of a total number of approximately 300 explorers in recorded human history. These explorers include naval navigators who sailed previously uncharted seas, and thereby discovered new lands, mountain climbers who scaled peaks, the vistas of which had never been beheld by anyone before them, as well as those individuals who led expeditions to conquer the poles of the Earth, both in the Arctic and Antarctica. Whether these men were ancient Greeks, with their extraordinary maritime culture, or the Vikings who made it to America long before Christopher Columbus, or Renaissance Italians such as Amerigo Vespucci, after whom "America" was named, Portuguese and Spanish merchants, British mountain climbers in Africa and India, Germans in the jungles of the Amazons or the Himalaya mountains, or their Germanic kindred in Scandinavia who braved Antarctica and named large swaths of the frozen continent — they were almost all white men.

What I argued in *Faustian Futurism* was that this was entirely inextricable from the incomparable accomplishment of whites — European and American — in the arts, literature, the sciences and technological innovation. For example, from out of painters and other visual artists of which we have any historical records, whether in Western, Islamic, Indian, or Asian histories, 479 were Westerners as compared to a total of 293 from all non-Western cultures combined (the total population of which far exceeds that of the West, meaning that the 479 Western artists represent a much larger percentage of the population of their own civilization and not just of the world at large). When it comes to great works of literature, 835 Western writers penned works that became historic whereas East Asia, India, and the Muslim world taken together only produced 293 notable authors (again, despite having a much larger combined population than Europe and its colonial territories in the Americas). The imbalance is even more significant in music, although harder to compare with any precision since non-Western cultures do not even have a tradition of music composition with identifiable individual composers (at least not until they were Westernized very late into modernity).

Finally, as far as science and technology are concerned, "white supremacy" is undisputed. Even when taking the considerable accom-plishments of the "Islamic Golden Age" into account, where it must be admitted that 90% of the scientists and inventors were Persians who at that time (800–1100) were still genetically (and not just linguistically) Indo-European, we still arrive at the conclusion that 97% of techno-scientific achievements in history are by white men — whether in Europe, North America, or Russia. This does not include the negligible number of Jews, whose contributions, especially in late modernity, are always overstated.

What is also evident from this statistical analysis, which was laid out in detail in *Faustian Futurism* and which I am only summariz-ing here, is that IQ is only one part of this puzzle when it comes to comprehending the excellence of Faustian man. It should go without saying that, with an IQ that is in some cases 20 to 30 points below that of Westerners, the native peoples of Africa, Arabia, and India (as com-pared to the small Aryan minority who brought higher culture there) could not possibly hope to compete with Faustian man in any area of human achievement. However, the Chinese have a very high average

IQ, comparable to the most intelligent Western populations, but as can be seen most clearly in their attempts at exploration, they lack all of the other personality traits that account for Faustian achievement. What one gleans from the chronicles of the voyages of Cheng Ho, and the burning of the Chinese ships that may have made it to the Americas, is a terror in the face of the unknown and its potential for destabilization of society. "May you live in interesting times," is a Chinese curse.

The Chinese fear of change, which is bound up with their ancestor worship, filial piety, collectivism, and conformism, precluded Chinese greatness in every domain of human achievement dominated by Westerners — including scientific discovery and technological innovation — *despite their comparable* mathematical and spatial reasoning capacity. *Faustian Futurism* argued that while the Chinese do not suffer from some of the genetic deficits that prevented other ethnic groups from rivaling the West in achievement, such as the poor impulse control of Africans or the undisciplined and unfocused laziness of Arabs in the Islamic World and the Dravidian majority in India, on a population-wide level, the Chinese — despite their discipline and focus — lack the genetic predisposition to bold inquisitiveness, curiosity to the point of dangerous risk-taking, iconoclastic individuality, wondrous enjoyment of pure creativity, and a horizon-expanding will to transcend all apparent limitations.

Every moment in the life of a Faustian man is felt to be incomplete as compared to an imagined moment of greater fulfillment. Heidegger is only reiterating this when, in *Being and Time*, he offers an analysis of temporality that describes existence as ever incomplete and always oriented toward a future from out of which the present secondarily takes shape, through an appropriation (or misappropriation) of the past. Western man is ceaselessly driven beyond himself, as restless as a vampire in the night of time.

The Heideggerian "homelessness of *Dasein*" is also an ethnolinguistic echo of the fact that Goethe's Faust feels as if he is a vagabond and an unsettled person — a "homeless person" — incapable of ever happily abiding in the world or belonging to any place that would be his own. This is the reason why the fifth and final act of Part II of *Faust* ends with the protagonist ordering Mephistopheles and his gang of devils to immolate Philemon and Baucis together with their home that, in the original telling of their tale by Ovid, had become a temple for Jupiter and Mercury. This elderly couple, who refuse forced resettlement, stood in the way of the completion of Faust's vast techno-scientific, political, and economic engineering project. Philemon and Baucis represent gratitude to the gods for the blessedness of the present moment. The transformation of their home into a temple signifies a sanctification of hospitality that presupposes this world can be hospitable — albeit under the roof of reverence for the God-Father and his errand boy. In league with the devil, Faust incinerates the house of this world's hospitality.

I had no trouble being admitted to the PhD program in the Philosophy department at the New School, especially since I was not asking for funding. What was more challenging was resigning from Naval Intelligence. When I broke it to Jack, I laid emphasis on my psychological distress over Anna's suicide. In fact, I had missed many days at work, and it was no lie that my mental state was deteriorating, and I was increasingly unable to focus on the task at hand there, especially since what I was remote viewing had a direct bearing on Anna's having drowned in our shared memories of Atlantis.

Jack agreed to grant me a "temporary leave." His insistence that I maintain my security clearance seemed to me to be a way of keeping a fishhook in me — or maybe it was a wolf's hook. After all, that's what I was out to find out. Who really wanted me immersed, on a daily basis, in a clairvoyance of the Atlantean Underworld, and *why*? Was I being initiated into a Traditionalist cabal that had managed to infiltrate parts of the American intelligence community? Before going back to work at the Twin Towers, I needed to know. Anna was intensely intuitive. Had she been onto some unbearable secret about me? A secret about my tortured life that even I had no *conscious* access to.

Within nine months of leaving Naval Intelligence and beginning my doctoral studies in Philosophy at the New School, I had a working draft of *Faustian Futurism*. I wrote that draft like a madman in Frankenstein's laboratory, hammering away on my typewriter through many long nights. I had enough to approach the publisher. Meanwhile, I also managed to follow him to his corporate office at 16 East 52nd Street. I had a word with the security guard, who proved to be easier to prevail upon than I could have imagined. He assumed that I was from the FBI, since apparently the feds were also carrying out clandestine surveillance of this man. His name was Harold Keith Thompson, and one wintery day in early 1975 I was headed up to his office, typed and bound manuscript in hand, dressed in the same impeccable manner as was customary for him and his Fascist associates.

When I stepped out of the elevator, I saw that Thompson was well-protected. There was a secretary up front, and the place was walled off in a way that offered no direct access to his office. An envelope with a letter in it was paper-clipped to the manuscript, which I left with his secretary. She asked, "Is he expecting it?" I lied, "Yes, miss." I also gave her my phone number and my real name, as opposed to the pen name, "Nick Griffin," which appeared on the manuscript's title page. Within five days I got a phone call from the same secretary, who set up an appointment for one week from the evening that she contacted me. I assumed, rightly as it turned out, that this meant Thompson had started reading the draft of *Faustian Futurism* with interest and wanted to finish it before meeting with me.

What I could not have been prepared for is the reception I was given when I walked into Thompson's office. He was a hard man, of stoic Northern European demeanor, with a clean-cut long face and closely trimmed dark hair. I had hardly seen a smile when I spied on the conversations that he had with his associates at the coffee shop.

But the icy stoicism of his full lips broke into an irrepressible smile as he saw me appear in the open doorway across from his desk. He did not get up, but he gestured for me to sit in the chair across from him. I smiled back and extended my hand to shake his as I took my seat, hoping to feign a calm confidence. He had a wicked look in his eyes as he shook my hand, and then grabbed it for a moment longer as I attempted to release my grip.

"Welcome home, Nick." He saw how speechlessly disconcerted I was by this greeting, wondering whether he meant it only metaphorically, as an indication of how much he identified with what I had written in the manuscript. "You don't remember me, do you? Of course, you don't. You were just a boy. A very shy boy, as I recall." Then, slowly, terribly as fate, it started to come back to me. Yes, I *had* seen this man before. He was one of the 'gentlemen' sitting around our dining table at one of the soirées that I witnessed in the first year, or maybe even the first few months, after I had moved in with my aunt and uncle. He was about 20 years younger then, but he hadn't changed all that much.

"My god," I couldn't stop myself from mumbling under my breath. "Did you know my aunt?" I asked. He sneered. "Did I *know* her?! We called her *mother*. She *led* us, Nick. Until she was burdened with the responsibility of actually being a mother to you. She took that very seriously, and we stopped seeing much of her." He picked up the manuscript of *Faustian Futurism*, "I see she raised you well." Now he got up to pour us drinks from the decanter of scotch to the side of his desk. "Let's drink to that."

What was I going to do? I felt like I had stumbled into a den of wolves, and that the only way I was going to survive was to pretend to be one of them. Moreover, I now knew beyond denial that the woman who had raised me, the sorceress who had initiated me, was the she-wolf at the head of this pack. I proposed a toast to Nikita, and we sipped scotch together.

"You know what happened to my aunt?" He nodded gravely. "She could never get over the death of your father," he said. "He was good friends with Yockey, your father was." While trying to process the shock of learning that the author of *Imperium* had been a personal friend of my father, I retained enough mental focus to pointedly ask, "Over the death of *my father*? What about the murder of *her sister*?" He gave me a hard stare while swirling the whiskey in his glass.

There was a long silence. "My mother..." I started to say again. Thompson looked at me a little bit like one looks pitifully at a witless man. I felt 'reality' giving way under my feet right there in that office. He cut in before I could embarrass myself, "Listen, kid, I know you had a hard life. But what doesn't kill you, makes you stronger, and judging by what you've written here, you've become very strong indeed."

"So, you'll publish it," I said, a little too hesitantly. "You better believe it, kid! Not only am I going to publish it, I want to introduce you to someone who will ensure that this masterpiece makes it to all the right people." I strained to keep a poker face. "Michel d'Obrenovic. But you wouldn't know him under that name, because we asked him to write all of his books under a pen name. Ever heard of George Hunt Williamson?" I nodded that I had. Williamson had been a member of the infamous contactee George Adamski's inner circle, before the two had a falling out and Williamson formed his own flying saucer cult with a group of fellow occultists. He was best known for *The Saucers Speak*. I had happened upon his books back when I was digging up everything I could about Atlantis. A number of his books, such as *Secret Places of the Lion* and *Secret of the Andes* had archeological themes involving ancient Egypt and Peru, alleging that these civilizations had been established by the "Space Brothers." In 1961, Williamson disappeared and no one, including his numerous followers, had heard a thing from him since then.

Williamson went around calling himself "Doctor," which is how Adamski had referred to him, but it later turned out that his academic credentials were fraudulent. I raised this point with Thompson. He replied, "They weren't faked. His degrees were under his real name, Michel d'Obrenovic, which he's gone back to using now. His doctoral dissertation was on Mayan hieroglyphics. The guy's military credentials were also legitimate, by the way. Again, just not under the name Williamson. D'Obrenovic worked for both the Army and the Navy."

"Why did he pull a disappearing act?" I asked. Thompson smiled smugly as he leaned back in his chair, swirling his scotch again. "Well, he hasn't exactly disappeared. He's just done playing his part as George Hunt Williamson. Good actor, that guy. Figures that he's been involved with so many dramatists — playwrights, actors, actresses. His second wife, Jennifer Holt, who he just married a couple of years ago, is an actress who's starred in tens of Westerns. They live in Santa Barbara. I want you to go down there and meet with him, after he's had a chance to read this manuscript of yours."

Somehow, I muddled through an hour of awkward conversation with Thompson, before hailing the first checkered cab I could find to take me back home. My head was pounding the whole time. I had to roll the windows down. The taxi driver looked at me in the rear-view mirror a few times, concerned that I was going to puke all over his back seat. When I finally got home, I collapsed onto that bed that my aunt had seduced me into for all those years after my uncle died. The bed that she had overdosed in, the one that I had bedded Anna in before she was driven to prostitution and suicide.

CHAPTER 6

HOTEL CALIFORNIA

When I finally woke up, rather than wondering if the whole thing had been a bad dream, it was as if I had awakened from out of life and into an inescapable nightmare. I began to feel like Number 6 when he woke up inside that apartment that was a simulacrum of his own but built inside the Village. *The Prisoner*, starring Patrick McGoohan, was one of my favorite shows. I was now convinced that whoever wrote this series knew that there was in fact an occulted third power in the world, an international cabal coveting futuristic technology that allowed it to pursue its own objectives above and beyond the exoteric opposition between the American and Soviet camps. There was even an allusion to UFOs in the form of the "rover" spheres that are launched from out of the water around the secret island, acting as vigilant warders of its prison population consisting of former intelligence agents from both sides of the Cold War.

I began obsessively researching Williamson and his connection with the more infamous Adamski. If I was going to fly out to California to meet this shady character, I figured that I had better know as much as possible about what I was getting myself into. I began with what was publicly available about Adamski before I paid a few visits back to the joint NSA and Naval Intelligence facility at the World Trade Center, with my still intact security clearance, to unearth some information that is not publicly available — especially about D'Obrenovic.

The first thing that is noteworthy about Adamski, who emigrated with his parents from Poland to New York at two years of age, is that prior to becoming the leader of a contactee cult, he was the founder of the Royal Order of Tibet in Laguna Beach, California. Here is what the *Los Angeles Times* had to say about the self-styled "Professor" as early as April of 1934. The article is titled "Shamanistic Order to be Established Here" and includes an interview with the guru, who claimed to have studied secret doctrines from the lamas in Tibet:

> The 10-foot trumpets of far away Lhasa, perched among perpetual snows in the Himalayan Mountains in Tibet, will shortly have their echo on the sedate hills of Southern California's Laguna Beach. Already the Royal Order of Tibet has acquired acreage on the placid hills that bathe their Sunkist feet in the purling Pacific and before long, the walls, temples, turrets and dungeons of a Lama monastery will serrate the skyline. It will be the first Tibetan monastery in America and in course of time, the trained disciples of the cult will filter through its glittering gates to spread 'the ancient truths' among all who care to listen. The central figure in the new movement is Professor George Adamski...
>
> "I learned great truths up there on the roof of the world," says Adamski, "or rather the trick of applying age-old knowledge to daily life, to cure the body and the mind, and to win mastery over self and soul. I do not bring to Laguna the weird rites and bestial superstition in which the old Lamaism is steeped, but the scientific portions of the religion."

Six years later, Adamski had moved from Laguna Beach to Palomar Mountain, California, the site of what was then one of the greatest observatories in the world. The Polish immigrant was apparently already wealthy enough to have purchased twenty acres of land on the mountain, which he called Palomar Gardens, where he opened up a restaurant. It is here at the Palomar Gardens Café that, in 1946, Adamski was approached by a group of military officers who told him that the UFOs he had recently observed in the area were "not of this world." Interestingly, this was not Adamski's own initial impression. In his first book, *Flying Saucers Have Landed*, published in 1953, Adamski wrote of the first cigar-shaped UFO that he saw in California, "I figured that during the war some new type of aircraft had been developed and that this was one of them." In his second book, *Inside the Spaceships*, which came out two years later in 1955, Adamski offers a cryptic and deeply disturbing remark that suggests this "new type of aircraft" developed during the Second World War was a product of Nazi German engineering:

> National security has many facets and the powers that be are themselves pushing out in the direction of space and of anti-gravity. Also, they know they have an enemy. And they do not know how far the enemy may have gone in this general field of a new form of power and propulsion. They do know that at the close of the war all the German scientists with knowledge did not come to this country.

Adamski is clearly referring to Operation Paperclip here, and letting it be known that he is privy to American military awareness of fugitive Nazi scientists with knowledge of anti-gravity who went elsewhere than to America and who are still considered "an enemy" of the United States. This is just the rim of the rabbit hole. Adamski demonstrates detailed knowledge of a flying saucer's propulsion system, which, as I was able to piece together from the information that I had access to at Naval Intelligence, was a system achieved by the Germans at a research facility in Prague in 1944 as part of a "Project Chronos" that was being run by the SS in quest of a "wonder weapon" that was expected to be so "decisive for the war" that it was given the highest classification above top secret, higher even than the Nazi atom bomb project.

In *Flying Saucers Have Landed*, Adamski describes the saucer's technology as "magnetic," relating that he "noticed two rings under the flange around the center disk. This inner ring between the outer one appeared to be revolving clockwise, while the ring between these two moved in a counter clockwise motion." This kind of electro-magnetic counter-rotation was used by Nazi scientists to spin an isotope of mercury-thorium inside a prototype free-energy and anti-gravity device that they had called "the Bell" (*die Glocke*) on account of the acorn-like shape of its casing. Adamski goes on to describe a "rod of power" with each of its ends anchored to the ceiling and floor by two "great lenses" at the dead center of any one of the flying saucers, which his blond-haired Nordic-looking "Space Brothers" allowed him to board. They explained to Adamski that this was the "magnetic pole" of the craft and that it could interact with the Earth's magnetic field.

Adamski elaborates on this electro-magnetic anti-gravity technology in *Inside the Spaceships*, where he writes that he "was aware of a very slight hum that seemed to come equally from beneath the floor and from a heavy coil that appeared to be built into the top of the circular wall. The moment the hum started, this coil began to glow bright red but emitted no heat." Soon after it began to glow, Adamski heard a sound that he describes as a "soft hum as of a swarm of bees." The Nazi Bell was also called *der Bienenstock,* or "the Beehive," on account of exactly this sound that it made as it began to levitate, pulling on the chains that were used to tether the prototype inside a research rig. Adamski's putatively faked photographs of flying saucers happen to be dead ringers for the designs depicted in SS papers that outline Mark I, II, and III Haunebu saucer-shaped craft that the Bell was going to be installed into as a power source and propulsion device.

Adamski claimed that the Space Brothers told him that they would share the technology of gravity control, were it not for the fact that they feared that terrestrial humanity would weaponize it into a kind of electro-magnetic gravity bomb that would produce an implosion far more powerful than a hydrogen bomb explosion. Only they were wise enough to wield this power. In fact, Adamski claimed that they were so wise that they would be capable of solving all of Earth's problems. He told the coterie of cult followers that flocked to him that the beautiful Nordic-looking cigar and saucer pilots had a system of government far more futuristic than that of the United States, one wherein warring nation-states had been done away with, and churches, educational institutions, scientific research, economy and industry had all been centralized under a single government with a spiritual mission, which bound their telepathic society together through a common purpose involving perpetual reincarnation and "spiritual growth through service."

The psychic powers of these Supermen were so great, claimed Adamski, that should they wish to do so, they could produce miracles that would awe humanity into submission. For now, they were attempting to use more modest means to persuade the United States to give up its nuclear weapons — which they claimed were harmful to the ecosystem. They had even sent an emissary to the Pentagon to make this demand. Adamski claimed that he was told that they already had 40,000,000 of their people living here on Earth, men and women who could pass for very tall Scandinavians. These were not just Venusians, but people from numerous populated planets or planetary satellites in this solar system. One Martian allegedly said the following to Adamski:

> We live and work here... We have lived on your planet now for several years. At first we did have a slight accent. But that has been overcome and, as you can see, we are unrecognized as other than Earth men.
> At our work and in our leisure we mingle with people here on Earth, never betraying the secret that we are inhabitants of other worlds. That would be dangerous, as you well know. We understand you people better than most of you know yourselves and can plainly see the reasons for many of the unhappy conditions that surround you.

When I looked into Adamski back at Naval Intelligence in the Twin Towers, I was able to pull the file that the FBI apparently had put together about him. It included testimony from individuals who claimed that the "Professor" had told them that the United States of America was comparable to the Roman Empire in its last stage of degenerative decline and that seekers of higher wisdom should welcome the impending conquest of its ruins. He had also admitted to these associates that his wartime sympathies had been with Nazi Germany. One wonders whether Adamski did actually travel to Tibet, and whether he perhaps met men from the SS *Ahnenerbe* that Himmler had sent there around the same time to investigate Tibetan esoteric knowledge about the lost world empire of the Aryan race. The file made much of Adamski's connection to "George Hunt Williamson," or as Thompson unmasked him, Michel d'Obrenovic.

Like Adamski, d'Obrenovic was of Eastern European ancestry — *and what an ancestry!* It turned out that the guy was a direct descendant of Prince Lazar I, who ruled Serbia from 1371 to 1389. More immediately, he was the grandson of H.R.H. Prince Wilhelm Maximilian Obrenovic Obelitz von Lazar of Serbia. This prince, being the sole survivor of an insurrection in which his royal family was eradicated, was taken in by Antoine I, the King of Saxony, and thereby entered Germanic aristocracy.

In his youth, d'Obrenovic joined an American Fascist group founded by William Dudley Pelley (1890–1965). After a near-death experience in 1928, Pelley became an evangelist for an esoteric form of Fascism. He named his group the Silver Legion and they were informally known as the Silver Shirts, on account of the silver-colored shirts that they wore as a play on Mussolini's Black Shirts. Pelley was able to establish branches of the Legion in almost every American state. The most significant of all of these places, the headquarters of the movement, was set up on a Western ranch near Los Angeles donated by a wealthy heiress — a ranch which, not incidentally, would be reclaimed by Charles Manson and his "family" in the 1960s.

In 1936, Pelley stood as a third-party candidate in the race for President of the United States. His open support for Adolf Hitler and the Nazi Party throughout the 1930s became such a bane to the administration of FDR that he was summoned before the House Un-American Activities Committee in 1940, which ordered federal marshals to shut down every branch of his organization across the country.

Despite receiving this stern reprimand, Pelley continued to attack FDR and to oppose war with Germany until he was charged with sedition and high treason in April of 1942. The sedition charge was dropped, but Pelley was convicted and sentenced to 15 years of imprisonment on other charges. Prior to his arrest, Pelley's portrait had appeared on "Wanted" posters throughout the United States.

It is during his imprisonment that Pelley wrote *Star Guests*, which was published in 1950 and laid out his religious philosophy of "Soulcraft." In this opus, Pelley claimed that truly human beings journeyed to Earth from outer space in vast geological antiquity. Darwinian evolution is rejected in favor of an interpretation of the biblical story of the fallen angels, wherein, according to Pelley, the "sons of Heaven" that interbred with mortal women were those members of a cosmic white race who basically committed bestiality by spawning offspring with subhuman apes to produce the various inferior races of the Earth. Pelley was paroled in 1952, the year that Adamski had his second major contact experience, on November 20th, which became the basis for *Inside the Spaceships*. Before joining Adamski's inner circle, as a witness to his earliest contactee experiences, d'Obrenovic was the editor for Pelley's Silver Legion magazine, *Valor*.

It turned out that Thompson's contact information for Williamson—I mean d'Obrenovic—was a bit outdated. *Faustian Futurism* had been forwarded to him, but by the time I arrived in California to meet the man, he was living in Los Angeles, not in Santa Barbara. It appeared that he was already having marital difficulties with Holt, and as I gathered from my time with him, he had a mistress who was a psychic working with the Los Angeles police department. When he had me meet him at the really swank Biltmore hotel on Grand, I was not offended that he hadn't invited me to his home. Rather, I assumed that he was staying there with his mistress. She didn't join us, though.

He was waiting for me in the somewhat baroquely ornate Renaissance-style Gallery Bar and Cognac Room. Whereas Adamski had died in the mid-sixties, d'Obrenovic was, at this time, still only 49 years old. He looked even younger. There was something about him that reminded me of a cunning bandit, despite the fact that he was dressed in a suit. I could easily imagine him hunting ancient mysteries in the Andes, and maybe keeping his eye out for hidden treasure that he could pocket along the way. He had the manuscript of *Faustian Futurism* with him, and although Thompson had probably told him my real name, he addressed me as "Nick" or as "Griffin." He had the air of a man who is not easily impressed, trying to conceal how impressed he was.

"You've somehow perfectly reconstructed the rationale of our project," he said. "Although I would call it Archeo-Futurism, rather than just Futurism. But *Faustian Futurism* has a nice ring to it as a title — and I suppose the Faustian element suggests the cultural-historical dimension of the project, although you could have gone for something more archaic and primordial. Perhaps, *Promethean Futurism*. Doesn't roll off the tongue as melodiously, but it would have been more apt. Maybe just *Prometheism*." This remark steered us into a conversation about Piłsudski, who had already used that term, and from there into a discussion of the Intermarium project and our common Southeastern European ancestral roots in countries that had fallen within the Soviet Eastern bloc. I took the opportunity to turn toward a discussion of his involvement with Adamski, who I pointed out was also from the same besieged easternmost frontier of the Faustian West.

D'Obrenovic motioned for the bartender to bring us a second round of drinks. Then he explained that Adamski was someone who wound up believing his own propaganda, or rather the propaganda that he was selected to disseminate. He confirmed for me that Adamski was a military-intelligence operative, which he knew better than anyone else because his purpose in that contactee circle was to be Adamski's handler. "The writings of someone involved in psyops always contain some of the hidden truth. It's intrinsic to disinformation that there's quite a bit of authentic information in it, which is revealed together with falsities rather than simply being hidden." I nodded affirmatively, before going on to complete his thought.

"The rationale is that pure concealment may not be effective *especially in the case of what's behind UFOs*," I said, eager to convey to him how clearly I understood what he was telling me, "so the perception of what people might glimpse is distorted by providing some background information that is true as context for it, while at the same time mixing this information with lies." Then, as a rejoinder to this, d'Obrenovic concluded, "Lies that are often of a preposterous or absurd nature, which are intended to discredit this embedded information in advance of any potential, accidental leakage of it into the public domain."

This had been the kind of operation that Adamski was supposed to carry out, but being a cult leader got to his head. His background in Tibetan mysticism rendered him prone to getting lost in delusions and thought forms projected from his own subconscious mind. He probably really believed that he had been given a tour of a giant mothership orbiting the Earth, when in fact Adamski had only been allowed inside small flying saucers on a couple of occasions and had certainly never left the Earth's atmosphere in them. It was once Adamski suffered this psychological breakdown that "Williamson" broke away from Adamski to salvage the contactee project under his own direction.

"Where are you staying?" d'Obrenovic asked. "At the Cecil Hotel," I answered. He winced with disgust and looked at me like I had brain damage. "*You know* that place is *haunted*, right? Do you have *any idea* how many people have been raped, mugged, and murdered in that hotel?" After a moment's silence, with somewhat downcast eyes and a slight shrug to accompany my smirk, I said, "I guess I tend to go looking for trouble."

"Well, there's someone I want you to meet, and I'm not asking her to visit you at that godforsaken place. Although, come to think of it, she'd probably be into that." I looked at d'Obrenovic questioningly and somewhat intrigued. "I'll book you a room here at the Biltmore. That way, we can also spend some more time together. Go check out of the Cecil and collect your suitcase. By the time you get back, I'll have a room prepared for you." It was an offer that, out of sheer curiosity, I wasn't going to refuse.

A few hours later, in the early evening, I had settled into what was an embarrassingly luxurious room at the Biltmore. The room featured antique gilded armchairs, the bathtub was made of solid marble, and every sheet and pillowcase on the canopy bed felt like it was woven from the finest silk. Granted, after I was adopted by my aunt, I had been raised in quite a comfortable environment, but this opulence was really over the top and made me slightly uncomfortable — especially since someone else, who I had barely just met, was paying for it. I hated being in anyone's debt.

After shaving for the second time in the day and changing into the most elegant clothes that I had brought with me (including a vest and silk tie), I went down to the "Music Room" where d'Obrenovic had asked me to rendezvous with him and the mysterious woman who I was supposed to meet. They were sitting at a table near the fountain, under one of the Venetian glass chandeliers suspended from the awe-inspiringly ornate ceiling with a fin de siècle wrought-iron skylight as its centerpiece.

The woman had hardly extended her hand when chills ran through my spine and my hair stood on end just looking at her. To begin with, her height put me ill at ease. I don't want to sound like a chauvinist, but having to look up into the eyes of a woman who is a foot taller than you is disconcerting — especially when you are used to being one of the taller people in any group. I was 5'10 and this woman must have been at least 6'9. On that account alone, she attracted quite a bit of attention when she stood up. A number of men sitting at other tables turned their heads to gawk, much to the chagrin of their wives. She had a freakishly high forehead, to the point where it was almost uncanny enough to mar otherwise beautiful features that were as chiseled as a classical sculpture. Her hair was sandy blonde and she had a deep tan, as if she'd spent a lot of her time here in the sun.

What was most unsettling were her eyes. They were more deeply set above her prominent cheekbones than is normal, and they were piercingly blue-green — almost the color of turquoise waters in the Mediterranean. You had to see them to believe that someone could actually have eyes that color. But it wasn't the color of her eyes that gave me shivers. It was the look in them, or rather, the way that they were able to look *into me.* Those were the most soul-piercing and at the same time mesmerizing eyes that I've ever looked into in my life. Even as someone who is used to staring people straight in the eyes, it was hard for me not to look away. It was as if she made me naked before her with that gaze and, at the same time as seeing right through me, offered some kind of entrancing sense of acceptance that was even more disarming.

She didn't let d'Obrenovic introduce her, and now that I think about it, that rogue who had seemed so sharp at the bar earlier today looked like a sheepish lapdog next to this lady. "Pleasure to meet you, Nikolaus. You may call me Cybele." I bowed and kissed her hand, which was jarringly masculine in its size and strength. She could tell that a shudder ran through my spine when I did, even if she couldn't see the hairs standing up on the back of my neck. Fortunately, we sat down right away, because that wasn't the only involuntary physiological response that I had. I felt my face flushed, and hurriedly drank some of the ice water in my glass. "Do you stay here often?" I asked, nervously.

"I find this hotel charming, partly because it is haunted," she said, "Paramhansa Yogananda dropped dead in this very room, you know." I looked at d'Obrenovic with a mixture of annoyance and astonishment. Not because I minded staying at a haunted hotel, but because he had said that I needed to get out of the Cecil since *it* was haunted. He knew just what I was thinking and quick-wittedly came back with,

"The difference is that we only have high-class ghosts here." "Or in his case, high-caste," she added. So she had a sense of humor. "He was an extraordinary man to have known, truly marvelous." I was taken aback by this. As best as I could recall, Yogananda died here in 1952, the same year as Adamski's second most significant encounter. This woman did not look more than — well, come to think of it, there was something ageless about her — but, on the face of it, one might take her to be 30 years old at most. She read my mind, and was amused.

"Your proposal is quite revolutionary." I was surprised by this statement. "You've read my manuscript?" With a wicked smile on her face, and her eyes locked onto me with an implacable stare, she replied, "*He* read it, and I read him. Isn't that right, my dear George?" D'Obrenovic played with the Caesar salad that we had just been served in such a manner as to avoid eye contact. I heard him crunch a crouton with his fork, then another. "I wonder if you realize what you're demanding of people, Nikolaus." She did it again, calling me by the ancient Greek or Roman form of my name. "What would you say to those — and I *assure* you that they have a *clear majority* among my people — who believe that it would be more compassionate to simply de-industrialize the planet, reestablishing more traditional types of societies that are not in any imminent danger of catastrophic misuses of the technologies and techniques that, at this rate, will be openly and ubiquitously developed by no later than the middle of the next century?"

It was now clear to me, without any shadow of a doubt, just who I was dealing with and what the stakes were. She read my mind, again, and cautioned me. "Don't overestimate my importance or influence." She smiled, "I'm what you might call a public relations liaison. That's all. Someone who has a unique perspective, with one foot in this world, where I was mostly raised, and the other foot... well... you know." Still staggered by the implications, and wanting to diffuse the tension before launching into defending a doctrine that I had only contrived to gain access to people who could help me make sense out of my own life, I endeavored to change the subject for a moment. "So, you were raised *here*?" She gave me the breathing room that I needed. "Not *here*, exactly. Colorado. We have extensive property in the Rockies. *We even* pay taxes," she said with a certain jovial cynicism as she raised an eyebrow and twirled her fork. "Ski much?" I asked, trying to be clever. "I'm an expert," she retorted as she attacked the steak that had just been placed in front of us (she had ordered hers rare).

Throughout dinner, the two of us were in deep discussion about the vision of *Faustian Futurism*. It was an odd discussion, because I often didn't need to complete my thoughts out loud or even finish all of my sentences. Her rejoinders to the things that I would say implied her having raced five steps ahead and processed all of the implications of a line of thought that I was just embarking on with one or another statement. Having once been intensely telepathic myself, and still retaining a measure of this ability on account of exercising it in the psychic espionage program at the World Trade Center, I was also able to read some of her thoughts and emotions.

So it was not as surprising to me as it ought to have been when, after we were through with dinner, d'Obrenovic, who had said very little this whole time, got up and almost disdainfully threw his white napkin back on the table before bidding us goodnight. "Don't mind him," she said. "His mistress is upstairs and will make him all better." I looked at her, wondering why the mistress hadn't joined us for dinner. "She's a psychic, like you. We didn't want her getting inside your mind — or mine, for that matter. She's not a part of the project."

We lingered only long enough to let d'Obrenovic head up before us, and then, without any need for words to be exchanged about it, we got up from the table, and "Cybele," or whatever her name really was, followed me into the elevator and did not press any button other than the one I had pressed for my floor. The hairs were standing up on the back of my neck again. I let her feel that I felt that. She took one of those strong hands and put it on the back of my head, at which point I felt something like a rush of cool air in my crown chakra, followed by a warm sensation slowly filling the rest of my body with an especially intense heat building up along the length of my spine. I walked off the elevator and down the hallway in an almost trance-like state, and by the time she followed me into my room, I was extremely aroused. Our rapport was magnetic.

As I looked into her eyes while she removed her dress, I saw that all of the disarming pleasantries she brought to bear at the table had slipped away like a velvet veil. Those were the eyes, and that was the expression, of a ferociously intelligent predatory animal — *not* a human being as *we* understand what it means to be "human." She stood there before me brazenly, stark naked. I knew that if I didn't take my clothes off at once, she would tear them off my body with such force that she might also tear through my skin. Once I disrobed, with both of our clothes strewn on the carpet, she literally tackled me. So much for the satin sheets. As I lay there on the floor, I felt as if a panther had mounted me. I tried to hold her waist, but she pinned my arms back with an iron grip as she ground down on my cock. I was relieved at how wet she was, and I psychologically surrendered to being taken by a woman far more powerful than myself. Fortunately, there was something contagious about her magnetic energy that electrified my own body and made me harder, for longer, than I had ever been before. When she came, she let out a cry so primal that it lacerated my heart and reverberated in my blood.

I was still rock-hard when Cybele got up off of me, with a wickedly playful look on her face. Her expression had changed to that of a terribly mischievous child. "You wanna go back down and have some dessert?" she asked. "Where I come from, we never get to have dessert." I looked down at how stiff I still was, with my body spellbound by her preternatural magnetism. "Is that *stuck*?" she said as she chuckled tauntingly. I was astonished at the rudeness of her manner of expression now, as compared to the way she carried herself at dinner. Actually, it was really refreshing and got me even more excited. I was standing at the side of the bed, and she pushed me down onto it. Finally, the satin sheets and pillows. "Let's fix that, so we can go back down together."

She lunged into the huge bed with me, and rolled my body on top of her perfectly sculpted form. "Fuck me however you like, and fill me." Astonishing. I did as she asked. Although, judging by her attitude, I was not expecting her to have another orgasm, she got inside my head such that she could experience herself through my body in a way that I could tell really aroused her again. So, when I let go into her full bush, which was the same sandy blond color as her hair, with her hands gripping my head and her turquoise eyes piercing mine, she came hard — as if she was coming through me and into herself. Then we sloppily slipped our clothes on and, with unkempt hair, went downstairs to have that dessert that she was so childishly insistent on getting, together with another round of drinks. She told me that among her "people" this kind of behavior (indulging in the decadent dessert and hard drinking, not the primal sex) was considered degenerate. It was one of the perks of her position that she could bend, or even break, some of their rules.

When we came back upstairs again, this time she brought me to her room — which, if you can believe it, was even more opulent than mine. I noticed a few odd things there as we took our clothes off, but I was too drunk to think much about them before we staggered into bed together. For example, there was something that looked sort of like a briefcase-sized telegraph machine, but it was wireless. There was also a pale green glowing phosphorescent sphere about the size of a crystal ball. When we entered the room, it was the only light source. She rather hastily covered it with a nearby piece of cloth. At some point, it must have been shortly before dawn, I just barely became conscious enough to notice that Cybele's place in the bed was empty and I wearily fluttered my eyes open to see her sitting in a perfect meditation posture in the middle of the room. Maybe I was dreaming, but I could almost swear that she was glowing blue and floating slightly off the carpeted floor. Then, as I felt something like a cold hand gently brushing against my forehead, I heard her voice in my mind saying "sleep," and so I did.

The next morning, we had breakfast in bed together — another decadent luxury that she seemed to relish indulging in as if it were some abuse of power. Cybele was still naked, having only put on her bathrobe to retrieve our tray when room service brought it to the door. In the morning light, I noticed how her tan was totally even across her whole body, with no bikini lines. When she saw me marveling at her, marveling in fact at being in this situation with her, she said, "We're just *people*, you know. *You* remember what it was like to be one of us, don't you?" I did, and I also recalled what had happened to Anna when I remembered being one of *them*. Cybele heard me go through these thoughts, then looked at me somewhat pitifully and said, "I'm sorry." Then, after a moment's silence, she went back to devouring the crispy bacon that she held in her greasy fingers.

When she was done with her breakfast, she looked over at me with a bit of a foreboding glance. "I knew Nikki." This caught me so off guard that it took me a moment to even understand what she meant. "You mean Nikita, *my aunt*?!" "Sure," said Cybele, "your aunt." It should not have been that much of a surprise; after all, Thompson had said that my aunt was the leader of the group that both he and d'Obrenovic were part of. Cybele realized that I was looking at her with a slightly reproachful expression. "I wasn't about to tell you that before we fucked." This made me wonder whether she knew about the nature of my relationship with my aunt. Given the way that she looked at me next, I think she discerned that thought. Then she said, "We worked together some years before you were born." Now I knew for a fact that, despite appearances, this woman was old enough to be my mother.

I was going to ask Cybele to elaborate, but d'Obrenovic called the room and arranged things for the day. We met him in the driveway. He was behind the wheel of a stunning retro late 50s black car with tailfins. "Get in," he said to me curtly. I opened the car door for Cybele. These gestures were always rather odd when it came to her, since I knew that I was dealing with a woman who, if she wanted or needed to, could literally tear me apart with her bare hands. I tried to get into the front passenger seat next to d'Obrenovic, but Cybele pulled me into the back seat with her like I was her pet. "I'm glad to see the two *of you* are getting along," he quipped. "Nice car!" When I said this, he winced at me in the rearview mirror. "It's *my* car," said Cybele, "I only let him drive it." Wow. George Hunt Williamson, heir to Serbian royalty, contactee cult leader, and now... chauffeur? Who *was* this woman?

We drove to the north for about an hour, at which point Cybele gracefully removed the scarf on her neck and tied it around my face to cover my eyes. I knew not to demand an explanation. The car made some erratic turns after that. I could tell we were off the highway and onto some rocky dirt road, and that we were climbing in altitude pretty precipitously. It would have wrecked my nerves if it weren't for the fact that rubbing against Cybele's body had a strangely tranquilizing effect on me. Finally, the car stopped, and she removed the blindfold. D'Obrenovic had already gotten out and opened the door for us.

As I stepped out behind Cybele, I was awestruck at the breathtaking vista of giant sequoia trees and waterfalls pouring down over steep cliffs, which we beheld from atop the rocky canyon that we were now standing on. I guessed that we were in the San Gabriel Mountains. She took my hand and we followed d'Obrenovic as he led us into a crevice in the rocks that was just barely wide enough to walk through. There was a camouflaged door carved into the rock, with a concealed panel next to it that was revealed by turning a fake outcrop of rock. He typed in an access code and the door slid open. We were met with a rush of cool, damp air and a phosphorescent green glow lit the way ahead as the automatic door slid closed behind us.

Now Cybele took the lead, as d'Obrenovic and I descended rapidly behind her. We were walking fast down broad steps cut into the rock. The steps were illuminated by phosphorescent spheres about the size of a soccer ball embedded into the sheer stone wall to our left side at regular intervals. She led us down to a platform with another door, this one with a shiny metallic surface. After placing her palm on a reader next to the door, it slid open to reveal a decent-sized room, maybe about thirty by twenty feet with a fifteen-foot-tall ceiling. There was another door across the room, on the opposite side as the one through which we had entered. In the room were a row of suits hanging from hooks that came down from the ceiling. Some were black, others medium blue. There were also several glass cylinders large enough to easily accommodate a person.

"Get undressed and go in there," Cybele said to me, as d'Obrenovic, who seemed to already know the routine, was stripping and placing his discarded clothes onto empty hooks that were on the opposite side of the room as the ones with the suits hanging down from them. "After you step inside, hold your arms up, spread your legs apart, and keep your eyes closed until it opens again." I hesitated, partly transfixed once more by the sight of Cybele's nude body as she stepped into one of the cylinders after hanging her dress up. I finally stepped inside one of these devices, which seemed to zap my body with some kind of radiation that I supposed was meant to be decontaminating in nature. Afterwards, I rushed to catch up with the two of them, who were already suited up — Cybele in a blue, skintight suit that was made of something like spandex and showed off every curve and crevice of her sculpted body, and d'Obrenovic in a more loose-fitting black suit, also of one piece. "Put the black one on," he told me. There were accompanying boots, which were not as sleek and pointy as the ones Cybele was wearing. Once I was ready, we all went through the other sliding door together, at which point I stopped again to marvel at where I was.

We were on the platform of what appeared to be a vast subterranean monorail station, cut right into the rock. This place was also lit
by the phosphorescent spheres, with their eerie pale green glow, but
these ones were larger and mounted on the top of stone pillars that
tapered upwards. I had hardly been able to take all this in, before a
sleek and windowless bullet train slid into the station, magnetically
levitating on the rail that led to and from a tubular tunnel bored into
the mountain. D'Obrenovic and I followed Cybele onto the train
through a curved door that opened upwards like the trunk of a car.
Once we were seated in the sterile white, featureless interior of the
cabin, this thing *flew* at a speed that I could barely imagine and that
was hard to estimate, but in the pit of my stomach I could sense how
fast it must have been — despite the fact that there was no turbulence
at all. Clearly, this magnetically levitating train had been placed inside
a vacuum. There was a barely perceptible pop every now and then,
when, I imagined, the air was being sucked out of one section of tunnel
after another, each with its own airlock.

At the next station, a man and a woman boarded our compartment. After casting a fleeting glance at us, they seemed to put as much
distance between themselves and us as possible. Both were wearing
the same blue suits as Cybele, except they were not tan and they had
platinum blond hair. They also shared the same oddities of her facial
features. The man must have been at least 7'5. I got the distinct sense
that he saw d'Obrenovic and I as beneath contempt. As for the woman,
who occasionally glared at Cybele out of the corners of her eyes, my
psychic impression was that she saw Cybele in much the same way as
a proper lady would look down on a prostitute. The words "Sister of
Mercy" flashed into my mind, at which point Cybele turned her neck
and gave me a hard stare before smirking and then staring straight
ahead again.

Maybe fifteen minutes had gone by before we reached a station
where Cybele got up and motioned for us to follow. She seemed too

self-conscious to take my hand in front of the two others, but she did cast a spiteful glance at them on the way out of the train. This station was even larger than the one we had embarked at, and there were other people on the platform. Once we walked through the sliding door, we entered an enormous cavern full of stalactites, some of which were quite frightening because in the phosphorescent light they looked like monstrous creatures. In addition to the dampness that one would expect at this subterranean depth, there was a faint smell of sulfur and cinnamon mixed with the scent of something like cardboard that had been burnt and then gotten wet. I thought I saw some hideous shapes of subhuman stature slinking between distant stalagmites, but when I tried to stare hard at one of them, what I saw was an impossibly large owl — so I just put it out of my mind.

As we walked through a roughly hewn tunnel, we came face to face with a man of gigantic stature — maybe 8 or even 9 feet tall — with features like those of the butler from the Addams Family. He had to pass close to us, because the tunnel was just barely wide enough for two of these large people to stand side by side within it. As he approached Cybele, he muttered something to her in a strange language, and I got the impression that he had no need to say it because she could read his mind and vice versa. But he said it just to make a point, as a gesture of rebuke. Cybele talked back to him defiantly. He stopped and turned around to give d'Obrenovic and I a hard stare before continuing on his way toward the tube station that we had just come from.

It was a tongue that sounded something like Sanskrit, but softer in the way that Persian is, and with a melodious quality to it, somewhat like Swedish. D'Obrenovic, the linguist and amateur archeologist, could tell what I was thinking, and he said, "These days, academics call it Proto-Indo-European." He meant the Aryan root language, but this was no hypothetical reconstruction. They were still speaking it here, fluently, as a living mother tongue. I also noticed that there were inscriptions in this language, written on some of the doors that we walked past as we took several turns through this tunnel network. The script looked like a cross between Mongolian (except oriented horizontally), Tibetan, and hieratic ancient Egyptian. We finally went through one of these doors.

It opened onto a walkway around a vast atrium, lit by a skylight that was presumably providing artificial UV rays because it felt like the sun was pouring in, but we were too far underground for that to be possible. The rocky interior of the cavern had been largely covered by perfect megalithic stonework, with water flowing over it in certain places and covered by verdant shrubbery and vines in other places. (That these would grow here added to my suspicion that the artificial sunlight had UV properties.) At the bottom of the atrium was a plaza or the nexus of a mall, with people converging on it and passing through it from multiple directions. There were geometric sculptures on pedestals, and pools where the water flowing down the stone slabs would collect. The only designs were repetitive geometric patterns, and the only colors were different colored stone. Just a few of the people were wearing the type of skintight bodysuit that Cybele had on. Most wore clothes that looked like something between a robe and a very long jacket, and all of these garments were in drab colors like beige, olive, tan, and ivory.

We took a glass elevator down the side of the atrium to the ground level. Then Cybele led us through the crowd, which wasn't hard considering the fact that these people cleared away from d'Obrenovic and I as if they were Puritans under orders to shun us. We walked at some length down one of the hallways extending out from the plaza. I suppose you could call it a subterranean avenue of sorts. The further we got from the skylight, the more we relied on the illumination of the phosphorescent spheres which were, here as in the tube station, set on pillars like streetlights. In this lane, I stopped dead, startled at the sight of little children playing with one another as they walked down the street with what were presumably their parents. They also stopped when they saw us, and they appeared to be intensely curious about d'Obrenovic and I in our black jumpsuits. But their parents grabbed them by the hand and hurried them away from us. Cybele looked at me and smiled, but there was also a profound sadness in her expression, and I thought I even saw tears welling up in her eyes.

She led us through a large stone doorframe that looked like polished black granite, and up a series of steps made of what I imagined was a poured stone — like concrete. At the top of the stairs was the interior of an extremely austere apartment, with its own small artificial skylight. There were no decorative flourishes on its cold stone walls and very little furniture. There was, however, a dining table, where a meal had already been laid out — presumably for us — by a downtrodden woman who I could see shuffling things in a back room off to the side, and who gave me the impression that she was a maidservant. Perhaps even a *slave* — but one incapable of forming any notion of rebellion.

We sat down together at the table. I was quite thirsty by this point and gulped down the water that Cybele poured for us into metal cups that kept it cool. It tasted like it had minerals in it. I took my cues on how to eat this food from Cybele. Some of it was similar to Mediterranean food and some to the kind of seafood served in Scandinavia, but other things were quite unfamiliar, and I tasted them hesitantly, after watching Cybele eat them. One of these was comparable to honeycomb. We ate in silence, so that the peace and tranquility of this place settled from its stone walls into my bones. Looking back on it, I suppose that this supper was meant to be a kind of communion.

Before we headed back, d'Obrenovic asked to use the restroom and I got the impression that he was doing that just to let me know that there *was* one in case I wanted to go. I followed him, and after he came out, he said, "Just sit there, it'll do the rest." I was relieved to discover that he was right, since there was no toilet paper in the room. The toilet had some system whereby it would crystalize waste matter before blowing it away as a fine powder and then using jets of water and blasts of hot air to clean you off. It ended with a puff of mild perfume. I was amused by this novelty, which was a welcome relief to the intense emotions that I had felt since entering this subterranean city. I almost had the feeling that if I stayed here long enough, my life — rather, my lives — on the surface of the Earth would feel like the frantic wanderings of a runaway child are remembered by him once he has been brought back home.

We headed back to the maglev train station, along the same route as we had come. This time there was no one on the train with us, so I asked Cybele, "How far do these tunnels extend?" "On *this* continent? Across the entire United States, both down into Mexico and up into Canada in two directions — toward Alaska, and also toward Greenland, where there are bases for submarine routes that cross the North Atlantic." I looked at her astonished. Then d'Obrenovic broke in, "Yeah, we could even take you back home to New York right now — if your luggage weren't back at the Biltmore. One of the maglev tunnels connects to an abandoned station in the oldest, deepest levels of Grand Central Terminal. We could be there in less than an hour."

After passing through the changing room again, we emerged from out of the hidden doorway at the top of the canyon to see that it was night. We were far enough to the north of Los Angeles that the stars could be seen pretty clearly, and I took a moment to stare up at them in wonder before getting back into Cybele's black car. This time she didn't stop me from sitting in the front beside d'Obrenovic, and I saw that it was because she wanted to sprawl across the back seat by herself and nap until we got back to LA. The two of us looked back at her in the rearview mirror, and then at each other with an unspoken understanding that could have become the beginning of a real bond.

The overnight concierge was on duty when we returned to the Biltmore, and, since it was a weekday, its opulent hallways were quiet. "I'll take you to the airport tomorrow myself," said d'Obrenovic when bidding us goodnight. My flight from LAX back to JFK was around noon the next day. When we got off on the second floor, I immediately noticed a little girl running down the hallways and playing by herself. It was well after midnight. Cybele registered that I was perplexed and explained, "Don't mind her. She's a ghost." Indeed, when we got to the fork in the hallway that she turned down, the girl was nowhere to be seen in either direction. Cybele looked at me like I was being ridiculous as I kept looking down one hallway and then the other. "After *all* you've seen today, *that* perplexes you?" She grabbed my arm and pulled me into the room with her.

As we walked in, she noticed that a message was being typed out on that machine that I glimpsed last night — the one that looked like a wireless telegraph device. She sat down at the table that it was on, uncovering the small phosphorescent sphere for lighting instead of turning up the room's dimmer switch. I watched her glowing face and fingers as she typed out a reply, walking up to her slowly. She turned slightly toward me in acknowledgement, at which point I dared to place my hands on her shoulders and look over her head down at the machine. I could now see that the letters on its keyboard were in the same script that had been inscribed on the doors in the subterranean city. Another couple of lines came through on the machine before she got quite annoyed and flipped a switch that shut it off. "They're reprimanding me for having brought you there today." She slipped her arm around my waist, still sitting at the table while I stood next to her. "I wanted to give you a taste of my world — or to remind you of the world that was once your own. You need to know — you need to remember — before you threaten the Olympian Order with your *Faustian Futurism*. Not that you *shouldn't* do it!"

Cybele got up and filled the spacious marble bathtub. We threw our clothes onto the bed and slipped into the water together. It was a strange feeling to be held by her. I guess it should have been the other way around, but I gave into it because by know I was sure that this woman, despite her youthful appearance and the vulgarity of her occasional, brazenly adolescent manner of expression, was more than old enough to be my mother.

"You know, I have a son" she whispered, after hearing my thoughts. "What's his name?" I asked. "Apollyon," she said. "Nikki met him. Nikita, your… aunt. She tried to help him understand this world better. I don't want him growing up in hiding. He's so creative and could shine in *this* world." Then, with an unexpected tinge of desperation in her voice, she asked, "Can you make us young again?" When she said that, a series of images flashed through my mind: Friedrich Nietzsche, James Joyce, John Coltrane, Frank Lloyd Wright, Jackson Pollock, Elvis, David Bowie, Jim Morrison, and Jimi Hendrix.

Their science and technology were in some ways far more advanced than ours. There was hardly anything that our physicists, biologists, or engineers would be able to teach them. But when it came to art, literature, and philosophy — they had reached a creative dead end, suffering stasis and stagnation for millennia. "Sing a song to make us young again, Nick. Be a brother to my son."

CHAPTER 7

MASTERING LIGHTNING

My experience with Cybele was so intimate that "close encounter" doesn't come close to doing it justice. Our time together came back to me in vivid detail as I watched the rather sensationalist media coverage of Travis Walton's abduction. On November 5, 1975, a group of seven loggers from Snowflake, Arizona, who were working in the Sitgreaves National Forest, witnessed a flying saucer in those woods at the outset of their evening drive back home. It had all of the typical features of close encounters. For example, the object was deathly silent and seemed to just hang in the air. Once it started moving again, it wobbled like a top — as UFOs typically do. One of the men, Travis Walton, got out of the truck that they were all riding in and approached the object, despite the vehement protests and warnings of the other terrified loggers. When Walton got very close, he was struck by a beam of light that lifted him off the ground and then threw him back down hard onto the forest floor. The other men, to their later embarrassment, drove away as fast as possible — leaving Walton for dead. Shortly thereafter, out of a sense of guilt, they drove back but his body was missing. After notifying the authorities, including local Sheriff Marlin Gillespie, a massive search and rescue operation was organized.

Over the course of the next 48 hours, the Navajo County Search and Rescue Team, the Heber Forest Service, and a number of other volunteer groups canvassed the entire forest, not just on the ground, but also including men using high-powered binoculars to search the thinned forest from out of helicopters and private planes. There was no sign of Travis Walton anywhere. The men began to come under suspicion of having murdered their associate and hidden his body. Consequently, they were compelled to submit to polygraph testing. On November 10, Michael Rogers, Steve Pierce, Allen Dalis, Kenneth Peterson, Dwayne Smith, and John Goulette were all hooked up to lie detectors at the Holbrook County Courthouse. The only test that proved inconclusive was that of Allen Dalis, who was known for his hot temper and was being extremely combative and uncooperative, to the point where his polygraph readings were all over the place. As for the others, Cy Gilson, the Arizona Department of Public Safety officer who administered the tests, was grudgingly forced to conclude, "These polygraph examinations prove that these five men did see some object they believe to be a UFO." That statement was all over the news, and it certainly caught my attention.

Still, it was nothing compared to what happened that night at 12:05 am, exactly five days and six hours after Travis Walton's abduction. Walton's brother-in-law Grant Neff received a call from an obviously distressed Travis, who had made it to a phone booth at a service station after being deposited on a deserted highway by a flying saucer that he saw shoot straight up into the sky as it departed. Travis thought that only a few hours had gone by. In other words, he had *five days* of what UFO researchers call "missing time." His few hours of memories from the abduction are, however, quite fascinating. Walton remembered these things spontaneously but was able to process and recount them with less anxiety and stress after undergoing a regression hypnosis performed by Dr. James Harder. This hypnosis was witnessed by a number of other professionals as well, including Dr. Howard Kandell, Dr. Joseph Saults, Dr. Robert Ganelin, Dr. Jean Rosenbaum, and Dr. Beryl Rosenbaum. They became the first people to hear the astonishing story that the media would widely report, and often misreport, over the coming days and months.

Travis Walton's first memory after being knocked unconscious by the UFO was waking up on some kind of operating table inside the flying saucer. He was surrounded by short, bulbous-headed beings with large almond-shaped eyes and very thin limbs covered by a kind of ivory-colored material that was more like marshmallow than human flesh. After struggling to get free from these beings, an extremely panicked Walton ran through the craft's hallways like a caged animal until he found his way into an empty room with a chair that had buttons on its console and that afforded a view of the stars *through its curved walls that seemed to become transparent* — although he wondered if this was actually a kind of projection, as in a planetarium. Finally, a man came to retrieve Walton, who was very relieved to encounter what appeared to him to be another human being — rather than the monstrous "aliens" that he had dealt with earlier. Upon reflection, Walton realized that these "aliens" may have been very sophisticated android robots.

The man took Walton out of the saucer into what appeared to be a hanger or perhaps a shuttle bay inside of a much larger craft. A number of flying saucers like the one that he had been inside of were parked here. The man then led Walton into another smaller-sized room, where he was even more relieved to encounter three other *people* — two men and one woman — all of whom were also blonds. Walton has had an artist carefully render his description of these people, and the paintings produced depict individuals that have a vaguely Nordic look to them. They had sandy blond hair, were tan as if they had been in the sun, and what especially struck Walton was how perfect their features and skin were — with the men having faces as smooth as that of the woman. Her hair was longer than theirs, which was (by our standards) already long for men. They all wore skintight blue bodysuits, which revealed their exquisite physiques. None of them would answer any of Walton's questions, and they responded to him only with a slightly empathetic smile that suggested they were being tolerant. They put him on another table, holding him down gently after he began to resist, at which point the woman placed something like a wireless oxygen mask over his face and he became unconscious. The next thing Travis knew, he was laying on that cold highway around midnight.

In the late fall of 1975, when the Travis Walton abduction was all over the news, I started watching a new series called *Space 1999*, which was a British production. The first episode of *Space 1999* was titled "Breakaway" and after watching it, with *The Prisoner* in mind, I began to formulate the idea of a "Breakaway Civilization." The show depicted a relatively near future where the Moon had been colonized. I marveled at how no one seemed to realize that the aesthetics in shows like this, the way that people in the futuristic Moon facilities were dressed, the architecture of their living and working places, and even their mannerisms, were all deeply Fascist — albeit in a modernist sense that represented a kind of extension of Italian Futurism into the space age.

In any case, this opening episode was about how certain "magnetic" anomalies on — or within — the Moon cause it to break away from Earth's orbit and essentially become a spaceship. It occurred to me that the writers of this show had access to classified information about the Moon being a hollow, artificial construction that is quite possibly capable of propulsion — since it was brought from elsewhere and parked in Earth's orbit to begin with. The "breakaway" seemed to me to be a metaphor for the breakaway of a futuristic Fascist elite from the civilizations of Earth and their becoming a space-faring civilization in their own right. At one point, the lead character, played by Martin Landau, exclaims that "we're sitting on the biggest bomb ever invented." Given the episode's focus on lethal magnetic "radiation," which is explicitly contrasted with nuclear radiation, this seemed to me to be a reference to the magnetic bomb that Adamski's Space Brothers were worried that we would create if they shared the technology of gravity control with us.

In a subsequent episode, titled "Black Sun," which aired the day after Walton's abduction, the crew of this spaceship Moon confronts the danger of a black hole. It could hardly have been lost on the writers that the "Black Sun" was an esoteric Nazi symbol. I suspected that they even knew that it was what Project Chronos was attempting to create, namely an artificial singularity or space-time vortex that could both be tapped for unlimited energy and also serve as an anti-gravity propulsion system.

I thought back to something that Williamson had told me in the course of our final conversation as he drove me to the airport in Los Angeles. "It's about power," he said. "As in Nietzsche, *The Will to Power*?" I had replied somewhat naively. He smirked and said, "Sure. But I mean literally. Power." I looked at him searchingly, "Like electricity?" His eyes lit up. "Yes — and magnetism. Mastering lightning and wielding magnetic power. Controlling the motor of the world."

I had to disappear. I knew too much, and I wanted out of this nightmare. *Could* I disappear? I would have to figure out how. Meanwhile, I couldn't bear to stay in my aunt's apartment. I still had the elegant wooden dining table that Thompson had sat around in the living room, when I had just been taken in as an orphaned child. I remembered my recurring childhood dream of the old man who lived out of suitcases in hotel rooms, the last of which I had identified as a room in the Hotel New Yorker based on what I recalled of its lobby from those dreams.

One cold day in December of 1975, I had a false identification manufactured at a place in the East Village. Then I packed my suitcases and checked into the New Yorker under an assumed name, paying cash for a stay that I explained I might want to extend — indefinitely. The chandeliers that hung over the lobby were so eerily familiar that they gave me goosebumps. I requested a room with a clear view of the Empire State Building. They said they had a few rooms with that view available, on the 28th, the 30th, and 33rd floors. With my penchant for occult symbolism, I obviously chose the one on the 33rd floor. The clerk gave me a glance that I only understood later. It was room number 3327.

When I walked into the dark room, my eyes were immediately drawn to a spectacular view of the Empire State Building, already lit for the nighttime, as a blood orange sunset seared the skyline of downtown Manhattan through one of the windows. I set my suitcases down, and without flipping the light switch, I sat on the bed to take in the vista. The strangest sensation came over me as I sat there in the darkening room and watched the city lights start sparkling against the evening sky. In all my life, I never felt closer to being at home.

I laid down and fell asleep, in my clothes, without ever turning on the light. When I awoke, I was startled to find that the bed had shifted closer to the wall. The room was still dark, but I could tell right away that it was full of strange things. There were locked metal cabinets and filing drawers across from me. The walls were covered with large, framed drawings. There was a big wooden crate in the corner of the room. I was severely disoriented. In fact, for a few panicked moments that seemed like an eternity, I could not for the life of me remember who I was. My body felt extremely frail as I struggled to get up out of bed. I almost fell onto the floor, before remembering to reach for the cane by the bedside.

Then, I stumbled across the room, leaned on a cabinet, and looked over at one of the drawings. I could barely make it out in the indigo light of the predawn hour that was beginning to come in through the curtains. In a thick dark wooden frame, there was a horizontal drawing of a polygonal tower studded with illuminated windows, which tapered toward the top into a sphere that appeared to be radiating luminescent energy into the night sky. A more low-lying and broader rectangular building was immediately behind the tower. This structure was in the foreground, and it was separated by water from what appeared to be the distant skyline of Manhattan. Beams were emanating from the top of the tallest skyscraper. In the distance between them, sleek airships — a number of them wingless — streaked through the night, with rays extending out from them as if to suggest that, like the city itself, these were being powered wirelessly by the tower.

Before I could even remember who I was, this drawing triggered an associational image in my mind. It was of a tower similar to the one depicted, but out in the secluded countryside and built much more crudely. It was constructed of wooden beams and surmounted with a metallic mesh dome, which was shooting artificial lightning into the night and producing a radiant glow similar to the aurora borealis. The townspeople were terrified of it. No, they were terrified of *me*. Then it started to come back to me.

I looked at another one of the framed posters. There was a man sitting on a chair, as if calmly reading a book, inside a huge room — a veritable Frankenstein's laboratory. He was surrounded by high pillars on tripods. One of these, which was encircled by an iron cage, was topped off by a metallic sphere that was pouring artificial lightning bolts out into the room to be caught by the tall black cylinders. I recognized myself as the master of lightning in that photograph.

There was a blue glow in the room now, and in this dim light I could see that it was full of crates and boxes stamped "N.T." I went over to the window and pulled aside the transparent curtains to see how close it was to dawn. Snow was falling gently in the chasm between my window and the Empire State Building, which had been built on the ruins of the magnificent Astor Hotel, with its Peacock Alley, that I had called home for the best years of my life. They could at least have gone ahead with plans to use the top of the new skyscraper as a dock for airships arriving from Europe. If Morgan hadn't killed my plans to wirelessly power airships rather than filling them with flammable gas, the Hindenburg zeppelin would never have exploded and spooked Mayor La Guardia into forcing the owners of the Empire State Building to turn their proposed airship port into an "observation deck." There would, at this moment, be wirelessly powered airships gliding through the skies over the kind of Manhattan that Hugh Ferriss had dreamed of.

Instead, after having appropriated my patents, Morgan had secreted away the technology. From various contacts of mine throughout the intervening decades, I had learned that his Chase Bank was funding a private group of Prussian industrialists and engineers based in isolated parts of South America, wherefrom they were fielding an already large fleet of airships so fantastical in their design that they would put the imaginings of Jules Verne to shame. From what I was given to understand, the latest models of these craft were also capable of diving into the ocean like submarines. An immaculately dressed and brash young representative of this group even approached me at one point. This was at the bar of the Hotel Astor, my former 'home,' which stood right where the Empire State Building now rose up to crown the skyline. I rejected his offer to join them on account of it being conditional on my "disappearance" from the public world. You see, these men that Morgan was funding, or "supermen" as they saw themselves with their utter contempt for humanity at large, had broken away from society to form their own occulted civilization. When I refused to stop striving to raise up mankind as a whole, they warned that my Promethean hubris would break me. They called themselves the "Atlantis Society" or, in German, *Thule-Gesellschaft*.

As I contemplated the snow, I suddenly became deeply depressed at the realization that it was Christmas morning. Maybe that's why my memory had just failed so badly, that memory so extraordinary that, in my youth, I could memorize whole books and, later in life, afforded me the ability to work out any design in my mind without committing the invention to paper until it had been perfected and needed to be sent to the patent office. Maybe I *wanted* to forget why, yet again, I was alone on Christmas, the day of the saint of my namesake, at the age of 87.

The spirit of Christmas, of Saint Nikola, had defined my lifelong endeavor to empower and liberate mankind by dramatically increasing industrial energy, making the worldwide wireless communication of information possible, and laying the groundwork for automatons who would one day free men from all manner of drudgery. This Christmas of 1942, broken, abandoned, and nearly penniless, I was waiting for the world to receive one last gift from me — a weapon that could bring an end to this current war in Europe, stop Fascism, and render futile all future wars.

The patented design for a prototype of the Teleforce device was inside one of the two locked safes in my room, not the smaller green safe — the larger gray one. The press had hyped it up as a "Death Ray" that would burn enemy planes and ships out of the air and sea by hurling precisely directed lightning bolts, like Zeus striking his foes from Olympus by pointing his divine finger. In actuality, it was a particle beam weapon. Particles of a mercury isotope supercharged by electromagnetic rotation inside of a spherical container would be channeled out of a gun in the form of a plasma that could remain a co-herent ray over long distances. This ray could wreck any target almost instantaneously.

After the Nazis seized power in Germany, I tried to sell the Teleforce system to the United States. Then, when my adopted country was uninterested, I turned to the British. They also declined. I even tried to sell the designs for an array of seven of these devices to the government of Yugoslavia, to be placed at various strategic locations in my homeland in order to protect it from Nazi invasion. After all, the King visited me here and, embarrassed at my apparent poverty, he volunteered a stipend to support my most basic living expenses, so I thought he might accept the proposal. But the Yugoslav govern-ment dismissed old Tesla as a mad scientist suffering from delusional senility.

Finally, increasingly convinced of the danger of Nazi Germany's expansionist ambitions, in 1935 I made contact with representatives of the AMTORG Trading Corporation of the Soviet Union. They drew up a contract for Teleforce that was dated April 20th, not incidentally Hitler's birthday. I was never allowed to sign that contract. Instead, two G-men in black suits barged their way into my room at the New Yorker and explained to me that they were aware of my dealings with "the Reds." Apparently, they had been monitoring my phone calls from the switchboard at the top of the New Yorker, which was then the largest telephone communications facility in the world. The men, who threatened in no uncertain terms to revoke my citizenship and reclassify me as an "alien," identified themselves as agents of the Office of Strategic Services (OSS). They had been sent by a Dr. Vannevar Bush. It also turned out that Fitzgerald, my associate and assistant, was actually an OSS spy, whom they had tasked to pass on to them every piece of scientific and technical information that I shared with him. The two men in black moved into a room on my floor at the hotel, and from then on, I essentially resigned myself to living as a prisoner. This was when I started using carrier pigeons to secretly continue my communications with the Soviet agents who had been interested in using Teleforce to defend against Nazi German territorial expansion. The communist spies would wait in Bryant Park for my tagged pigeons to arrive with coded messages.

Despite the risk of slipping on the snow, I went for my habitual walk in Bryant Park that Christmas morning. Between the Hotel New Yorker and the park, I ran across a drunk dressed as Santa Claus, ringing his bell in an attempt to solicit donations to the Salvation Army from every passerby. I've never stopped believing in Santa and his elves. By comparison, Christ and his angels are a cruel joke. Santa runs a smaller but more trustworthy operation. What's hardest for him is to keep up that jolly public face, because the truth is that he's usually thinking of all the good little children that he just didn't have it in his power to help even though he's tried his best. He cries so desperately into that long white beard from out of his whole soul. That big stomach of his is all cotton stuffing, you know. Part of the public image. The truth is that he's cried himself damn near down to a skeleton all the while he works around the clock. St. Nick knows that no one will be left to help him in his old age. All the little elves will be put away in cupboards then, and winter will only bring a howling wind to dry the children's tears.

When I arrived at the park, I leaned on my cane with both hands for a few moments, marveling at the rainbow-colored lights on the brightly lit Christmas tree standing tall against the white marble of the rear façade of the New York Public Library. As I struggled not to fall while opening my bag of breadcrumbs for the pigeons, I was reminded of how Mephistopheles restored Faust to youth and I wondered whether, at this point, I would accept such a devil's bargain if it meant living long enough to ensure that my inventions would save the world from a Fascist victory in the current war.

It was Goethe's *Faust* that, at the zenith of my youth, had inspired me to invent the alternating current. I had been studying at the University of Prague in Bohemia. During a stroll through the city park of Prague with my good friend at that time, who often recited poetry with me on such walks, I was suddenly reminded of a passage from Goethe's masterwork, the entirety of which I had committed to memory. You see, the sun was just setting, and when I beheld the glowing solar disk, these verses from *Faust* came to mind:

The glow retreats, done is the day of toil;
It yonder hastes, new fields of life exploring;
Ah, that no wing can lift me from the soil,
Upon its track to follow, follow soaring!

A glorious dream! Though now the glories fade.
Alas! The wings that lift the mind no aid
Of wings to lift the body can bequeath me.

Just as soon as I recited these lines to my companion, a flash of light filled my mind of the kind that often preceded my intensely precise visualizations. What was revealed in that flash was the design of a motor powered by alternating current, essentially the same diagram that I would present to the American Institute of Electrical Engineers six years later. At once, I broke a stick off one of the park's trees and drew this wonder wheel in the sand for my friend. Four coils arranged in a cross around a motor's circular frame were alternately activated using electromagnets in order to reverse the direction of an electric current running through the circuit. The whole contraption looked a bit like a solar wheel, or Swastika, which I presume is why the idea happened upon me while contemplating the setting sun.

The prospect of seeing through the industrial manufacture and implementation of the so-called "death ray", albeit for the sake of world peace, would not be my only temptation to accept a Faustian bargain that could restore my youth and vitality. Nor would the other tempting prospects be restricted to the realization of uncompleted or suppressed technological projects, such as the World Wireless system that was buried when my tower at Shoreham on Long Island was dynamited some years after Morgan defunded it. Rather, my greatest regret is not pursuing the romance offered to me by the Divine Sarah.

Of all the women who attempted to seduce me away from my single-minded devotion to technological invention and scientific innovation, Sarah Bernhardt was in a class of her own. It was at one of her parties that I had met Swami Vivekananda, and we began conversations on *prânâ* and *akâshâ* that were indispensable to my formulation of an etheric Physics model at odds with that of Einstein. Far from being a mere actress, Sarah was a brilliant woman with a penchant for mystical contemplation and she relished participating in these dialogues.

One of these conversations was particularly memorable. It was my only heated argument with Vivekananda. First of all, don't let anyone tell you that the Swami was a vegetarian — as he sometimes claimed to be. This particular conversation of ours took place in a back room at Delmonico's, my favorite restaurant in New York. Not only did Vivekananda enjoy his steak, but he was also quite a connoisseur of whisky — to the point where he sent back an Old Fashioned *at Delmonico's!* Sarah was amused by this. I was not, especially given that I was a regular, so I looked at the waiter rather apologetically.

We were arguing over the socio-political structure of the *varnas*, or "caste system," and its relationship to the cosmology of the *Yugas*, or "world ages," in Sanatana Dharma. The Swami took the standard view that the castes were a way for souls to practice various forms of Yoga or disciplined devotion appropriate to their level of respective devolution, all the way from the *Bhakti* Yoga of low caste people to the *Jnana* and *Raja* Yoga of the highest caste people, and thereby evolve back toward union with *Brahman* over the course of many successive lifetimes. The color-coding of the caste system, the name of which, *Varna*, literally meant "color", had originated as a way to segregate people of vastly different levels of ability and understanding, so that disembodied souls in the transitional state between one incarnation and the next would not get mixed and be born into the wrong caste. It was, he explained, a means of establishing psychical distance and differentiation, so that people could be born into conditions that resonate with their own spiritual state and are most suitable for the further development of their *atman*.

Vivekananda knew that I was no egalitarian, but he was somewhat taken aback at the vehemence with which I attacked Hindu theology for the integral role that the caste system plays in any authentic version of it. I pursued three lines of argument against this system. Firstly, it conceived of human beings as *types* rather than as individuals and thereby reaffirmed unreflective collectivism. Secondly, given that human beings are in fact individuals, at least to one or another degree, in any actual caste society it is quite possible and even likely that certain brilliant individuals will wind up being born into the wrong caste and consequently be subjected to treatment that is detrimental to their spiritual development and that deprives them of an opportunity to benefit others. Thirdly, this entire caste hierarchy, I argued, is stratified upwards in the direction of the *daevas* — so that not only are the *Kshatriyas,* or knightly warrior caste, reduced to servants of the *Brahmins* (which in itself I did not find all that objectionable, since it subjugates military power to spiritual refinement) but the *Brahmins* themselves are turned into mere servants of, or attendants to, the *daevas.*

If one were to mistakenly believe that the "gods" are only mythical beings and objects of superstitious faith, that would be one thing. There would still be a question about the content of these myths and how the *Brahmins* were using them to control this caste society. However, once one recognizes that the *daevas* are really existing beings — as real as you and I — *and that they are often manipulative, deceptive, power-hungry, and even tyrannically sadistic,* then the entire caste system has to be called into question from the top down. By the time we had this conversation, *Gospel of the Buddha* had become one of my favorite books and so I reminded Vivekananda that this rejection of the *daevas* as paragons of enlightenment, and even a recognition that there is more opportunity for enlightenment in the human realm than on the planets of these *daevas* deluded by their luxury and power, had been one of the Buddha's key insights.

Closely connected to my rejection of the caste system was an equally impassioned opposition to the *Yuga* cosmology, which, unfortunately, even the Buddhists seem to have unthinkingly adopted from the Hindus. By the time I launched into this, the Swami's eyes were bugging out and he was looking around nervously for the waiter so that he could order himself another scotch on the rocks. Sarah was looking at me with the kind of admiration that one has for some predatory beast, like a Bengal tiger. She knew that Vivekananda, who was now being schooled, was used to being treated like a guru.

I told him that I thought the Hindu conception of world ages was regressive. I believe that I even characterized it as "retarded." Two main problems were the focus of my critique of this conception. The first was that a view of declining world ages, with each epoch more degenerate than the one preceding it, leading up — or rather, down — to the present *Kali Yuga,* or "Dark Age," (associated with the goddess Kali) is profoundly inimical to fostering human progress. My entire life's work was to power the engine of progress on this planet, with all of my scientific research and technological inventions being merely a means to transform human society, on a planetary scale, in a utopian direction. Ever since I arrived as an immigrant here, I had accepted the motto of New York, *Excelsior* or "Ever Upwards", as my personal mantra, one reflected in this city's skyscrapers, such as the Woolworth Building, where I was proud to have had an office. Then, there was a second, related problem. When contemplated within the context of cosmic eternity, any cyclical view of time ultimately implicates a repetition of all events — not necessarily after only one complete cycle, but ultimately. Cyclical time denies the possibility of infinite creativity in the same way as that thought experiment of Nietzsche's which I always found so contradictory to the rest of his Promethean ideas, namely "the Eternal Return of the Same."

These problems with the *Yuga* cosmology were inextricable from my objections to the *Varna* system insofar as putatively "proper" social organization in terms of the castes is supposed to decline together with the world ages, such that in the Kali Yuga many of those who ought to be Brahmins and Kshatriyas fall through the cracks and are crushed at the bottom of a debased materialistic society dominated by merchants, thieves, and thugs. I granted to Vivekananda that it is certainly the case that in a world dominated by industrialists and financiers — such as Morgan, and his associate Rockefeller — many undeserving and avaricious people, who are ruthlessly driven by the basest passions, thrive while certain brilliant individuals have their light snuffed out to the detriment of humanity. Had this conversation taken place later in my life, especially now on this cold Christmas day, so many years after being defunded by Morgan and reduced to humiliating destitution, I would have conceded this even more readily. Nevertheless, I argued — and would still maintain — that a caste system will never function as a true meritocracy that rewards the most visionary and creative individuals. This is precisely because creativity, when seen through the lens of the *Yuga* cosmology, can only appear to be subversive deviance.

We are not living in the most decadent and degenerate age of the world. Rather, we are fortunate to live in the epoch of the greatest degree of creativity and innovation known to human history. Even Atlantis, I argued, was no evidence against this. I explained to Vivekananda that the bygone antediluvian world empire had collapsed precisely because, despite possessing certain types of relatively advanced technology, it was locked within a caste system — actually within the very socio-political order that was the model for the Hindu *Varna* conception. On the whole, the people of Atlantis were not somewhat more enlightened denizens of a world age less degenerate than our own, namely that of the *Treta Yuga*. Rather, they were almost subhuman in their relative unconsciousness as compared to the modern individual — let alone geniuses of our time.

I concluded by saying that it all came down to a faith in energy. The Hindu socio-political and cosmological conceptions were radically conservative in the literal sense. Their felt need for conservation came from a lack of faith in infinite energy, or unlimited potential. Here, Sarah closed the conversation by adding, "Life engenders life. Energy creates energy. It is by spending oneself that one becomes rich." I smiled and got the check.

Certainly, I was being hounded by wealthier and more influential socialites than Sarah. These were women who could have secured funding for my projects, but who also would have wanted to cage me in the domestic life of a dutiful husband. That was out of the question.

Sarah was nothing like that. She was not looking for a husband, nor could I have expected fidelity even if I had agreed to become a long-term lover of hers.

She had many lovers, some of whom she brought along on her travels bound into coffins. Her practice was to die herself in a coffin and reemerge from it as the tragic character she was contracted to play on the stage. When she was not using a coffin for this purpose, it sometimes became a suitcase to carry one or another man who had fallen under her spell. It was probably also her ironic way of suggesting that, after a while, such men became baggage.

Sarah loved me because I was nothing like them. She confessed that I was the first man that she could really be friends with. What she proposed, on so many visits to my old laboratory, was an intimate friendship, one without boundaries, and which would never become binding. My old pal Sam Clemens, better known by his pen name "Mark Twain", had met Sarah on a couple of occasions, and thought I was crazy for not taking her up on it.

The truth is that my various complexes, including an aversion to women's jewelry and an antipathy to touching hair, were crippling obstacles in the way of any attempt to develop this kind of intimate rapport. I would be lying if I said that it was simply my single-minded determination not to be distracted from my work. One time, when I met her at Penn Station, I was struck dumb by the sight of her without any jewelry and with her dark wavy hair tightly bound by a crimson turban. I was flattered to the point of embarrassment that she had done this in an effort to get closer to me. This was one occasion when instead of taking her to my laboratory at 8 West 40th Street, I brought Sarah back to the Astor Hotel where I lived.

Oh, the warmth of the steam that rose from the hot bath that she took in my room, wearing only the crimson turban, and the cold of the snow crunching beneath my beat up shoes now! The unpretentious frankness and searing honesty of how she expressed her erotic attraction to me that night, her ardent but patient desire to know her enigmatic friend better, was the most polished mirror that anyone has ever held up to my own inadequacy and limitations.

If I could change one thing in my overly long life, it would be to have had a more ecstatically open and enduring relationship with Sarah. Now, to the great annoyance of the maid and other hotel staff, my closest female companion was one of my two carrier pigeons — the one that the manager had briefly seized when she got disoriented and crash-landed onto another floor of the New Yorker. But then I thought of what Faust says to Helen of Troy in Part II of Goethe's magnum opus: "The mind looks neither back nor beyond. This present time alone, Helen, is purest bliss." I would no more have meant this, had I ever been able to say it to Sarah, than Faust means it when he says it to Helen, who is supposed to be the embodiment of Beauty.

I became so absorbed in the old man's reminiscences that, when I awoke again in his deathbed the next morning, I had total recall not only of this lucid dream reliving his lonely last days, but of many experiences from earlier in his life. The disjointed images of my recurring dreams in childhood now fit into a deeper and much broader context. It was so uncanny walking out into Bryant Park that morning and standing where he — I mean where I — had stood toward the end of my dream, seeing how things had changed since then and how much had stayed the same. The darkly magnificent Radiator Building towered over the park in the same menacingly Gothic way that it had then. Only its gilded details had faded, having been caked in soot.

One thing was certainly different. On the way into the park, on the corner of West 40th street, I looked up at the yellow street sign that said, "Nikola Tesla Corner." This corner had been chosen, not because of its proximity to the New Yorker, but because one of the last offices that I could afford to have was at 8 West 40th Street. I walked over to the New York Public Library and spent the day there reading *My Inventions and Other Writings*. What had not come back to me spontaneously flooded into my mind as I sat there absorbed in the pages of a relatively slim autobiography written by Tesla around the age of 60. By the time I finished, they were getting ready to close the main reading room for the night. On my way out, I looked with changed eyes at the lights of the Empire State Building through the semi-circular windows cut into the high ceilings. It was almost as if I was giving *him* the eyes of a time traveler. Tesla, the ardent Eugenicist, would have been terribly disappointed by this most un-Faustian future.

After I went to bed back at the New Yorker, I had a horrific nightmare. My withered and emaciated corpse — I mean, Tesla's dead body — was lying there beneath me. I was hovering toward the ceiling and looking down on it, as a whole group of men in black suits moved rapidly around the room, opening crates and boxes and sifting through papers. It seemed to me that it was the middle of the night on the day after I had died. They moved a whole bunch of the crates and boxes down the hallway to the room that they had, for years now, occupied on my floor. They also took the safe with the patent papers of the Teleforce device design in it, which three of the men struggled together to move. That backstabbing bastard, Fitzgerald, was with them and he kept saying something to the other men about how the materials that were left in my room, the ones that they didn't "need to bother with" were going to go to someone named "Trump." But what really made this a nightmare is that amongst these men was *a woman* who I recognized. It was my aunt, Nikita. She was young, maybe in her mid-twenties, sporting her natural hair color. She also looked very fit and had the demeanor of a soldier.

Moreover, as I stared down at her, partly through Tesla's disembodied eyes, and partly with my own consciousness and memories as Nikolai, I realized that this putatively "Russian" woman was involved with the supposed "Soviet" agents who had presented themselves as negotiators on behalf of the AMTORG Trading Corporation. No wonder they had chosen Hitler's birthday to date their fake contract! These people were not communist spies — they were *Nazi spies* who had entrapped me into a supposedly "Un-American" act of "communist collaboration" so that they could imprison me here. The OSS agents who had been assigned as my wardens at the New Yorker were *double agents*, American Fascists aligned with the Third Reich from within the US government. Who knows how long they had been spying on me and whether they had interfered to make sure that my offer of Teleforce to the US Department of the Navy was not accepted, because *they didn't want America* to be able to use this "Death Ray" to defend against a Nazi aerial invasion or naval armada from across the Atlantic.

After the men cleared out of my room, and Fitzgerald left with them, making sure to replace the "Do Not Disturb" sign that would prevent the hotel staff from discovering my body for another day or two, Nikita stayed behind with my dead body. I watched as she stripped stark naked, draping her clothes over the chair at my desk, before getting into the bed with my already rotting corpse. She held my head — I mean, Tesla's skull — running the fingers of one hand through his hair and those of the other, backhandedly, down his gaunt cheek. "Come to me, Nikolai," she whispered. "Be mine." I felt like a boa constrictor was tightening its grip on my soul — then I woke up, drenched in sweat.

CHAPTER 8

WONDER WHEEL

It took about a week's stay at the Hotel New Yorker for me to clear everything that I planned to take with me out of the apartment at 77th and Cherokee that had been my home since I was orphaned. It was another month before I was able to get rid of it on the real estate market, thereby replenishing the small fortune in my bank account before it had been much depleted by my living expenses.

If I had really been wise about choosing where to disappear to, I would not have moved to Coney Island. Nostalgia has always been an Achilles' heel for me. Not only did I grow up down the shore, at Brighton Beach, Anna also drowned herself there. Besides, the neighborhood was becoming so decrepit, crime-infested, and rife with gang violence that no one would think to look for me in this godforsaken ghetto, let alone in a low-income housing project. I had rented a two-bedroom unit under a false name, and with the offer of a deposit large enough that it could not be refused. By the end of the five years that I would live there, the second half of the 1970s, Coney Island would become nothing less than a post-apocalyptic wasteland, almost as bad as the South Bronx. In some ways, worse.

The run-down beachfront amusement park certainly contributed to the perversity of the place. Unlike the South Bronx, which had become a racially homogenous black ghetto, where one knew exactly what to expect, Coney Island was still pretending to be a place for working class white families to come for "fun in the sun." That made it much more twisted than the South Bronx or certain similarly devastated and crime-ridden neighborhoods in Harlem and Brooklyn. Then there were the Brighton Beach Russians, just one neighborhood over, who often strolled to Coney along the coastline. They were their own kind of gangsters, much more ruthless than the Russians I remembered from my childhood there.

I confess that the amusement park was also one of the most alluring aspects of the locale for me. Without its being there, an odyssey to the place of my childhood and of my beloved's suicide would not have sufficed to seduce me into self-exile here. The cheap thrills, freakish curiosities, and lurid colored lights all conspired to turn the Wonder Wheel into a metaphor for the absurdity, not just of *this* life, but of *any* and *every existence* bound to the wheel of rebirth, without any edifying law of karma.

As if Coney Island wasn't dangerous enough during the day, within short order of having moved there, I became a creature of the night. My "days" generally began in the early afternoon. Over the course of several cups of coffee, the first of which was accompanied by eggs to soak up the previous night's liquor, I did a couple of hours research reading and several hours of writing each day. Then, in the late afternoons, I would take a stroll along the boardwalk, smoking one cigarette after another. I was becoming a chain smoker. There was a bar there named "Atlantis" that I liked to stop at for drinks, despite the rough clientele. I never ceased to appreciate it as a commentary on how much like a simulacrum this entire, decaying modern world appeared to be when viewed against the backdrop of the Neptunian realm beneath the waves that I had been tasked to spy on. The whole of it appeared to be a reflection in a funhouse mirror.

In the early evening, during or just after sunset (depending on the season), I would listen to my favorite records. These included *In the Court of the Crimson King*, the debut album of King Crimson, *Agents of Fortune* by the Blue Oyster Cult, Pink Floyd's *Dark Side of the Moon*, and numerous albums of The Doors. My favorite song, from out of all of these albums, was "Epitaph" by King Crimson:

> The wall on which the prophets wrote
> Is cracking at the seams
> Upon the instruments of death
> The sunlight brightly gleams
> When every man is torn apart
> With nightmares and with dreams
> Will no one lay the laurel wreath
> When silence drowns the screams
>
> Confusion will be my epitaph
> As I crawl a cracked and broken path
> If we make it, we can all sit back and laugh
> But I fear, tomorrow, I'll be crying
> Yes, I fear, tomorrow, I'll be crying
> Yes, I fear, tomorrow, I'll be crying
>
> Between the iron gates of fate
> The seeds of time were sown
> And watered by the deeds of those
> Who know and who are known
> Knowledge is a deadly friend
> If no one sets the rules
> The fate of all mankind, I see
> Is in the hands of fools

By that time in my life, at the not-so-tender age of 28, every line of this song spoke to me. I listened to its lyrics religiously.

At night I would get on the subway at Stillwell Avenue and disembark in Greenwich Village. I had so little contact with fellow students and faculty at the New School that the chance anyone would recognize me as a fugitive PhD student was slim to none. Obviously, what I was more concerned about was being apprehended as a fugitive Naval Intelligence operative. But I doubted very much that Hal would frequent the restaurants and nightclubs that became my refuge. My favorite of these was a certain *Darvish*, which served Persian food and featured live bands playing both Western and Persian popular music for the clientele on their dance floor. They were especially fond of disco, including some fairly impressive disco music that was apparently being made in Iran.

I had been following the Shah of Iran closely, for obvious reasons. If I ever saw him on television, I would stop to listen carefully. By the year's end of 1975, I was extremely disturbed by two things — although I suppose I ought to have been relieved by them. First, the Shah had not publicly tested nuclear weapons in the way that I had envisioned during my off-the-record remote viewing sessions at Stanford, the ones that had supposedly proven me worthy of recruitment by Naval Intelligence. Second, Richard Nixon had been forced to resign the presidency on the brink of impeachment over the Watergate scandal.

These two events seemed connected to me. I could not help but wonder who those men were that convinced Nixon, about a year after my remote viewing session, to trust them to break into the Democratic National Committee headquarters in the Watergate building. I suspected that they were CIA agents, and that their purpose was to remove Nixon from office before he could encourage the Shah to turn Iran into a military nuclear power. If that was where the changes to history ended, one might be forgiven for imagining that I had given way to paranoia. Subsequent events in Iran, at the very close of the decade would, however, confirm that I had in fact changed the course of events. But let me not get ahead of myself.

Sometimes instead of spending most of the night at Darvish or some other club, I would go to see films at a couple of the more artistically inclined cinemas in the village. The one that made the deepest impression on me, and which I went back to view more than once, was *World on a Wire* by Rainer Werner Fassbinder. It had originally been made for German television, but one of these art house theaters had gotten hold of a copy that they were screening for small audiences.

After the screening, I secured a bootleg VHS tape of the movie and re-watched it repeatedly at home. The film was based on a sci-fi novel called *Simulacron-3* by Daniel F. Galouye. I picked up a mass market paperback of the book at the Strand, and I quickly read it cover to cover — twice. The book was also available in an edition with the alternate title *Counterfeit World*. I eventually bought a copy of that one as well.

This film, together with the novel that it was based on, did not help my state of mind. I became increasingly convinced that we were, indeed, living in some kind of artificial, programmed, and re-programmable construct. I don't say, "rather than in reality," because what was worst about my reflections on the movie and book was the deeply unsettling, even vertiginous, suspicion that it is simulations all the way down and archons all the way up. *World on a Wire* and *Simulacron-3* intensified my interest in the paranormal, even the most lurid forms of it such as the efficacy of Astrology, not because they were evidence of a "spiritual world" but very much to the contrary, because they were clues to the fact that we are living in some kind of computer-programmed construct run by an Artificial Intelligence akin to that depicted in *Colossus: The Forbin Project*.

When I read a transcript of Philip K. Dick's speech on this subject at a conference in Metz, France, which had been printed in a sci-fi magazine in 1977, I took his remarks regarding the "reality" of the over-written timelines depicted in his novels as confirmation of my own suspicions. His claims that, in particular, both *Man in the High Castle* and *Flow My Tears the Policeman Said* were based on his residual memories of a timeline overwritten by the programmers of our simulation struck a deep chord with me. After all, I myself had seen the world in which Nixon remained in office and, as for the Nazis having won the Second World War, I knew that Dick was also onto something in that regard as well. There was a terrible kernel of truth to that nightmarish vision, not in an alternate or defunct world but, as

I had discovered by investigating my aunt's life and her various connections, it was something true on an occulted level in our own world.

After my nights in downtown Manhattan, I would get on the subway and head back to Coney Island. The trains were appalling in those days. Covered with graffiti and filled with dangerous delinquents. I was already tempting death. Not just on the trains, but when I would arrive back at my ghetto housing project after drunkenly walking along the dark beach to get there, with my shoes in hand and my feet in the sand. Every now and then, I would be confronted by some murderous black hoodlum in the stairwell of the high-rise. But before he could pull a knife or gun on me, his eyes would recognize the thousand-yard stare in mine. When they saw that, they would leave me alone — some out of fear and others out of pity. Maybe they imagined that I had served in Vietnam and was, consequently, a psychotically hardened killer.

Oh, that was the other thing. In the future that I had seen, Nixon crushed the North Vietnamese. He burned them out of their jungles, not just with napalm, but ultimately with tactical nuclear weapons. Instead, on this timeline, he had withdrawn US forces from Vietnam in the most humiliating defeat suffered by this country since Korea. Soon, as the North Vietnamese invaded South Vietnam, and President Ford refused to resume American intervention, that war became the worst defeat in the history of the United States. There were other consequences of this that I found personally demoralizing. Rather than building up into a powerful revolutionary force, the Weather Underground, with which I still had some sympathy, lost their *raison d'être* and broad-based ideological appeal in society, such that they withered into a fringe terrorist group even more marginal than the New Age cults that had sprung up contemporaneously, in 1968 or 1969. In the four years between 1976 and 1980, each time another member of the Weather Underground turned him or herself in, I became more depressed and demoralized. It is not as if I identified with their ideology, I never really had — despite briefly funding them. However, I did see them as rebels against the intolerable status quo and shooting stars that portended a true revolution.

That revolution would never come, and the Communist revolution that I had foreseen in Iran was somehow subverted into the most bizarre theocratic Islamic 'revolution' — if one can even call something so regressive "revolutionary." Events with the Soviets in Afghanistan played out exactly as I had foreseen, with the same timeframe of 1978 to 1980. But in Iran, instead of Marxist proxies of the Soviet Union rising up against the Shah, these groups were marginalized and eventually co-opted by a much more virulent theocratic opposition committed to the Islamic fundamentalism of the Ayatollah Khomeini. When I saw Khomeini in Paris, surrounded by the international media, and read the disparaging CIA assessment of the Shah leaked to the press, then watched the Carter administration repeatedly undermine Pahlavi, it was clear to me that I was neither paranoid nor narcissistic to believe that I had changed the course of history.

The data that Hal had passed onto the CIA from our sessions on the Soviet invasion of Iran had evidently inspired a plan to replace the Pahlavi regime with a so-called "Islamic Republic" that would contain Soviet Communism without risking a nuclear confrontation with the Shah who, not incidentally, never completed construction of the nukes that Nixon would have encouraged him to build. I was sickened by watching women forced under black veils, homosexuals being executed, and the sophisticated forward-looking Pahlavi regime replaced by draconian medieval laws against the sinful consumption of alcohol and erotic relations outside of marriage (which was now legal for nine-year-old girls, following the exemplar of Muhammad).

That I had a hand in this was appalling to me, and having saved the world from nuclear Armageddon was little consolation. I felt as if a world this absurdly warped ought to be set on fire. It broke my heart to see the Shah of Iran in exile, wasting away from cancer, less than a decade after that monumental pageantry at Persepolis — especially his unforgettable speech about Persian imperial resurgence at the tomb of Cyrus the Great. By 1979, when the CIA was at work destroying Iran, and what little remained of the radical left in America was surrendering to the state, I could barely tolerate watching the news. Instead, my television consumption turned into a cocktail of paranormal programs, both fictional and purportedly factual.

Since I moved to Coney Island, I had been watching reruns of *The Twilight Zone* late at night. To this was added the sequel of that TV series, *Night Gallery*, where Rod Serling would step into an art gallery full of creepy paintings and focus in on one as he delivered the opening narration for the night's episode. By the time I started viewing the *Night Gallery*, the early 1970s series *The Sixth Sense*, featuring Gary Collins as the Parapsychologist Dr. Lucas Darrow, had been repurposed and integrated into the show, with Rod Serling delivering introductions to what had once been episodes of this separate series. Paintings were produced to reflect the repurposed material. Then there was *The Outer Limits*, which, with its harder science edge to its science fiction, appealed to what was left of the Physicist in me, as compared to the uncanny fantasy of *The Twilight Zone* and *Night Gallery*. I also began religiously watching the non-fiction show *In Search Of*, where Leonard Nimoy hosted an exploration of various paranormal phenomena and mysteries of history, from ESP to Reincarnation, UFOs, Atlantis, and the Loch Ness monster.

Somehow this visual carnival contributed to the atmosphere of living in Coney Island. It was as much an immersion into the carnivalesque atmosphere of the place, as it was an escape from reality. There was something comforting about these four television shows, or five if you count *The Sixth Sense* as separate from other episodes of the *Night Gallery*. As limited as their audience may have been, they still served to relatively normalize the bizarre horrors that were actually the element of my increasingly ethereal existence. They were also an antidote to the brooding seriousness of what would be my final writing project. *Invisible Imperium* was my working title for it.

Within the first year of becoming a fugitive, I had transformed my MA thesis on the Physics and Metaphysics of Free Will into a book called *Being Bound for Freedom*. Then there was *Faustian Futurism*. The third project, which I had spent most of my time on since relocating to Coney Island, was something like a dialectical product of the tension between the first two books. *Faustian Futurism* had been critical of Traditionalist Fascism in order to develop the concept of an alternative, Fascist Futurism. I had intended it as a tool in an attempt to infiltrate a hidden Fascist network that I believed may have been manipulating me, from my early childhood onwards. By contrast, *Invisible Imperium* was an exposé of the genealogy and structure of this Fascist shadow government, and a critique of its ideology and aims on the basis of the metaphysics, epistemology, and implicit ethics of *Being Bound for Freedom*.

Invisible Imperium was also meant to be a cathartic confrontation with the reality of my own life, or as much of it as I could piece together. When my research revealed that the CIA was constituted in 1947 from out of an OSS assimilation of General Reinhardt Gehlen's Nazi spy network in Eastern Europe, which was spearheaded by Ukrainians, I also unveiled the true identity and allegiance of both my aunt and my father. Thompson had told me that Otto Skorzeny was my aunt's commanding officer. He meant *after* the war. While Gehlen was busy helping the Americans build the CIA as a cold war weapon against Soviet Russia, Skorzeny had set up an organization of former SS officers, which was officially called ODESSA, but unofficially known by its code name, *die Spinne* or "the Spider."

In addition to Gehlen Org assets in Eastern Europe, in 1946 ODESSA absorbed the remnants of the Intermarium organization masterminded by the Polish military tactician and statesman Józef Pilsudski. Also known as "Prometheism," in homage to the rebel titan Prometheus who was chained in the Caucasus mountains, the Promethean spirit of the movement can best be seen in the archeo-futuristic art of the Polish painter and sculptor Stanisław Szukalski. These advocates of the formation of a super-state stretching between the Baltic Sea, the Black Sea, and across the Caucasus to the Caspian Sea, were initially opposed to both the Germans and the Russians and were intent on defending their independence from both major powers. However, when Nazi Germany collapsed in 1945 and the Soviet Union invaded Eastern Europe and extended its territory in the Caucasus into northwestern Iran in 1946, even if it was over Pilsudski's dead body (he died in 1935), the partisans of Prometheism agreed to be integrated into the Spider's web of anti-Soviet resistance. This delivered even more assets into the hands of ODESSA, from anti-communist Ukrainian and Polish patriots all the way to Persian nationalists in the Soviet-occupied Iranian province of Azerbaijan, who, as heirs of Zarathustra, had been the southeastern-most frontiersmen of the Prometheism project. Almost no one realized it was because of the network Pilsudski's Prometheism project had already established extending to the Caspian that so many Poles fleeing, first Nazism and then Communism, were able to take refuge in Iran in the late 1940s.

The Spider played a significant role in planning and executing Operation Paperclip, the OSS and then CIA repatriation of thousands of Nazi scientists from various fields to the United States. They would become the bedrock of the American military-industrial complex. The most prominent of these men, Dr. Wernher von Braun, was put in charge of the Apollo program that successfully took America to the Moon based on project designs that he had originally drafted for Hitler. "Paperclip" referred to the fake dossiers manufactured to sanitize the record of repatriated Germans such as von Braun, or the majority of his handpicked team at NASA who, like Kurt Debus, were also hard-core Nazis. For example, it was hidden from the American public that von Braun was an SS major who used slave labor inside hollowed-out mountains to build V-2 rockets for the purpose of targeting civilians in cities like London.

The men imported into the United States were at least as bad, if not worse, than the ones tried for war crimes at Nuremberg. Those who were prosecuted, and in some cases executed, were simply more dispensable than the brilliantly wicked ones worthy of being recruited by the USA. Certain very valuable Nazi scientists, such as Josef Mengele, were simply too blood-soaked to even attempt to sanitize with false dossiers. ODESSA arranged for these men to be resettled in Latin America rather than in North America. This was done with the full knowledge of the Nazi operatives who held key positions in the CIA from its inception. The Vatican also facilitated this relocation. Most went to Argentina, some to Chile, and a few to Mexico.

When I learned of this, it brought back a couple of childhood memories that were so disturbing that they had been totally buried in my subconscious. My aunt and uncle had taken me to Southern California, supposedly for a summer vacation. I think this was between second and third grade. We stayed in Los Angeles for about a week, where they took me to Disneyland and some of the Hollywood studios. But then, and this is the part of the memory that I had totally repressed, we drove down past San Diego and across the border to a coastal part of Baja, Mexico.

My uncle was very silent in the car, but my aunt told me that they were taking me to a "school for special children." Even now, it is a struggle to hold onto a few fragmentary memories of what happened there. What I *can* tell you is that the place was run by Germans. In fact, I don't remember a single Mexican from that brief excursion into Mexico. This "school" was a creepy old mansion that looked like a cross between an elegant chateau and a hunting lodge. It had lush, verdant gardens full of monarch butterflies. There were large, circular wood chandeliers inside the mansion. It was built atop a rocky promontory with steep cliffs diving into the waves of the Pacific Ocean.

I vaguely recall being corralled into a dungeon with other children there, and being forced to listen to the most horrific screams in the pitch dark before the stone cellar was shot through with artificial lightning that intermittently illuminated severed limbs and mangled corpses all around us. One of these other children, a little girl, huddled close to me throughout this and other similarly horrific experiences that we shared for what must have been several days. In retrospect, I realize that she looked an awful lot like Anna. I couldn't know for sure, because Anna never showed me pictures of her as a little girl. In fact, having cut off her family for reasons that were never clear to me, she refused to say very much at all about her childhood.

Rome was the locale of the other memory that came back to me through this research on Skorzeny's Spider and Gehlen's Organization. It was about a year after my uncle had died, so I was 11. My aunt, who was by then 39 years old, had brought me with her to Rome, where we stayed at a hotel that was more like a rented apartment in a building with a courtyard where we would have breakfast. Over the arched gateway into the courtyard and the apartment complex as a whole, there was a frieze of Romulus and Remus sucking at the tits of the She-Wolf. One day, after walking around the ruins of Capitoline Hill, where my aunt was able to tell me the most obscure and yet fascinating details about some of the monuments, we went to the Vatican to meet a man who had arranged to take us on a private tour of the catacombs.

He was a very intimidating dark-haired gentlemen with a mustache and fencing scar, who had a knowing look on his face as he spoke with my aunt *in fluent German*, and a wicked glimmer in his eye when he looked at me. My aunt had saluted him — Roman style — when he arrived, but he quickly motioned for her to cut that out and gave her a warm hug with a kiss on both cheeks.

We descended into the dark underbelly of the Vatican, stepping over chains and warning signs that blocked off certain paths, and winding our way through rocky passages that became narrower with each turn. Our guide had a flashlight, which he would occasionally put under his chin when he looked at me. Man, did he look creepy like that, especially with the scar. After doing the research for *Invisible Imperium*, I recognized that face. It was Otto Skorzeny, Hitler's master of Psychological Operations.

Skorzeny would point the light at various tombs cut into the rock, and full of the bones of ancient Romans. I clung closer and closer to my aunt, with my head pressing into her breasts, smelling her perfume mixed with the dense mildew of this place. There were cobwebs everywhere. At a certain point, Skorzeny turned off his flashlight. All I remember about the impenetrable darkness of that moment is that the smell of the place changed. Now, mixed with the perfume and mildew, there was a scent that vacillated between sulfur and cinnamon. There was also a sound, which I can only compare to a croaking of cicadas that was, in its own way, as melodious as birdsong. It made my heart flutter and my stomach quiver.

The next thing I remember is being back in the hotel room with my aunt that night. I found it strange that no one else was staying at this 'hotel,' especially since it was the peak summer travel season. In any case, we had a furnished apartment with one bedroom and no neighbors. The maid who would serve us breakfast in the courtyard knew not to come to the apartment unless she was sure that we were out for the day. We were on the top floor, on a hilltop, with a spectacular view over Rome. I remember walking up to my aunt as she leaned out over the windowsill into the night air with the gauzy drapes blowing. Nikita drew me into her chest so that I could take in the night view of the ancient city with her.

I turned about between her and the window and looked up into her face, watching her gaze out over Rome before looking down into my eyes. She kissed my forehead, with the fingers of both hands wrapped around my head, as if she were drinking from a skull chalice. Then, with the window left open, she led me to the bed and sort of just fell into it while pulling my body down over hers. Nikita unbuttoned my shorts, and I bent my knees as she pulled my underwear off. My flushed cheek pressed against her face — almost as warm as my cock, which was burning up like a branding iron.

She flipped me over, so that I was under her, and removed my shirt after unzipping and pulling her own dress off. She wasn't wearing any undergarments. Then she reached over to one of the bedside tables and pulled a strange clear flask out of the drawer, laying this next to us on the crumpled blanket. With a mischievous look in her eye, she started going down on me. When I tried to pull her body up a few times by the shoulders, so that she could sit on me, she instead swung around and straddled my face with her thighs as she continued to suck my hairless tautballs and prepubescent cock. She would occasionally place her fingers gently on my stomach, carefully sensing the quivering muscles.

Finally, her sucking felt so intensely pleasurable that it hurt. She noticed that I suddenly stopped playing with her dripping wet vulva and gripped her thighs as I squirmed as if to pull my cock out of her mouth. Then she quickly slipped the head of my cock into the opening of the flask's neck, while she held the bulbous part of it against my stomach. I looked down and saw my own cum for the first time as it spurted into the flask over and over again, while my legs trembled. The liquid was so warm that I could feel it through the glass pressing against my stomach. As soon as my cock stopped spurting, my aunt twisted the flask away so as not to spill it.

She pulled me close to her naked body under the silk sheets and cozy blanket, stroking my head and neck hypnotically and whispering in my ears until I fell asleep. That night I dreamt that a large gray owl was sitting in the windowsill staring at me as I lay in bed. The next morning, before Nikita woke up, I looked everywhere for the flask. It wasn't on the bedside table and was nowhere to be found.

In any case, *Invisible Imperium* exposed the machinations of "the Spider" — a vast inter-continental Fascist network that was based in the deepest strata of the United States military-industrial and intelligence complex. I showed how their faction within the CIA was behind Charlie Manson, how he was a Frankenstein's monster that they were, at one point, planning to turn into a rock star and then into an American Hitler on a subsequently abandoned timeline that would have led to a race war by the 1980s. The whole Laurel Canyon phenomenon, and a lot of the psychedelic drug cults and ghetto drug dealing of the late 1960s, was manufactured to accelerate the decline of a decadently permissive society so as to drive the West toward what Spengler called "Caesarism" and what Yockey had elaborated on in *Imperium* (except that they did not share Yockey's view of the Russians). On the one hand, they were pouring accelerant on liberal-democratic America and giving the children matches to eventually set it on fire. On the other hand, they were working to defeat the Soviet Union and bring about its collapse. Once the latter was accomplished, they could finish the job of destroying American society from within by promoting identity politics and a radical leftist agenda that could only end with the violent disintegration of the United States.

The Spider hoped that something like the Confederacy would re-emerge from out of this collapse, the largest chunk of the Former USA, and that they would be in a position to govern this American rump state more or less directly. They would then interlink it, NATO-style, with Fascist states that they planned to carve out of the Eastern Bloc of the collapsed USSR, with Ukraine as the backbone of the Fourth Reich's European territories. All of this was merely stage-setting, a rolling out of the red carpet for the denizens of the Atlantean Underworld who planned to resurface as angelic saviors and act as the true founders of the "Thousand-Year Reich."

Around the time that I finished *Invisible Imperium*, a large black dog had started to follow me along the beach and the boardwalk at night. This bitch became so persistent that she eventually tailed me all the way to the door of my apartment. She did this several times before

I finally let her in late one night in the summer of 1980, after staggering home again along the beach drunk and barefoot, with my feet skirting the tide and the bitch running along beside me, imprinting her paws into the wet sand. When the initial liquor-induced slumber wore off, around 4 am, I noticed that she had gotten up and was walking toward the door to my apartment, repeatedly looking back at me. I had fallen asleep in my clothes. For some reason that I could not explain to myself, as I got up to walk the dog out of the building I grabbed the black metal urn of Anna's ashes, which, as you may recall, was embossed with the Trident of Poseidon.

The black bitch led me out of my building and back down to the beach. It was a couple of hours before dawn, and the only lights anywhere were those of the Wonder Wheel, which oddly enough, had been left on. This hound goaded me along the shoreline from Coney Island to Brighton Beach, and then she stopped dead almost exactly where Anna's body had been recovered. She looked up at me insistently, barking a few times. I took the lid off the urn, and carefully held it down at the edge of the tide, allowing a little bit of the ocean foam to wash into the ashes. Then, I dug my fingers into the urn and started smearing the wet ash all over my face and neck. I stripped stark naked, doing the same thing with the rest of my body until I was caked in Anna's remains. The black bitch watched, almost silently, but for occasional panting and muffled moaning. Then I walked into the water, and I kept walking. It felt cool compared to the warmth of the summer night. After swimming some ways out into the Atlantic, I turned around and looked back at the beach.

Perhaps I would have come to my senses and swum back, with all the force of a man who decides to cling to life at the last moment. But what I saw on the beach made me swim out even further. Two chalky white-faced tall men in black suits and black ties, wearing fedora hats, had walked up behind the now whimpering dog. One of them was carrying a knife that glistened in the full moon's light. The other seemed to be opening a violin case, which he laid down on the sand. Then he grabbed the black bitch and just as suddenly, the other man slit the dog's throat and I saw her legs buckle under her. She collapsed next to the discarded urn of Anna's ashes, which I had emptied onto my own body. Even though I was too far away to clearly make out their eyes, I could feel the two men in black staring at me menacingly. I swam out so far away from them that by the time I stopped I knew that I would never make it back.

CHAPTER 9

THE LUNATICS

My lungs burned when the water filled them, and I could feel my heart stop as I suffocated under the waves. Instead of rising up out of my body, I felt myself fall out of it through my feet with a sensation similar to that of falling dreams. I saw my corpse slowly sinking in the water above me, as I was pulled out into the Atlantic and down into the ocean depths with great speed and fluidity. Before long I saw the glowing blue window portals of a metallic, perfectly cigar-shaped vehicle with no fins or wings. I passed right through one of these windows and found myself haunting the inside of this vessel. It was speeding up through the ocean, surrounded by a membrane of some kind that eliminated any resistance from the water. The crew consisted of those tall, Nordic types. They were manning controls with glowing, multicolored lights that stood out against the relatively color-less gray and blue-gray surfaces inside the ship, which complemented the livid skin-tight uniforms and platinum blond hair of these men and women. I thought of Cybele.

The Earth could soon be seen out of the windows, first as a breath-takingly gigantic vista, and then as a shrinking blue planet. Meanwhile, the Moon kept getting larger. Eventually, the craters on the bright side of it could be seen in detail. Then we went over the top of the Moon and gracefully descended onto the dark side of it. As we approached the surface, I could see lights twinkling inside a large crater. When we got even closer, there was the stunning sight of a vast array of geometric buildings that appeared to be made out of some kind of poured stone. They gave me the impression of concrete bunkers, but on a titanic scale and built of something more like the precisely interlocked polygonal megaliths of ruins in Peru or Bolivia. Unlike the majority of these structures, a few of the most gigantic ones were spherical. There was also a very tall obelisk-shaped tower, like the Washington Monument, with blinking lights on top of it.

When the crew disembarked from the vessel inside a huge hangar, I followed several of them as they exited the spaceport and made their way down a long hallway with a ceiling that tapered in tiers, like a key pattern. This hallway terminated at what appeared to be a tube station, where they waited for a monorail, like the one that I had ridden with Cybele, levitating slightly above the track that it pulled up on. This train took them to a station that was connected to a gargantuan command center, with ceilings that were at least two hundred feet high, and walls that were covered in display screens apparently connected to hulking banks of machinery studded with colorfully lit control panels. It was clear that something was generating a local gravity field in this city, equal to the gravity of Earth.

The atmosphere and technology were essentially the same as what I had witnessed of the undersea world during my remote viewing work for Naval Intelligence at the World Trade Center. We had known that these 'people' were going up to the Moon and had glimpsed this city that I was now in, or at least one like it. However, it had been even harder to see anything clearly here than it was to clairvoyantly perceive the facilities built into the continental shelf and hollowed-out mountain ranges under the oceans. It was as if we had been psychically blocked from exploring the Moon, especially its dark side, where cities like this one were located inside large craters. We could only look through a glass darkly at what I was experiencing first-hand now. I recall that on one occasion I hesitated reporting to Jack that I had seen a group of these people practicing Yoga *asanas*. The men and women striking these poses in perfect synchronicity with one another were stark naked and didn't have an ounce of fat on their perfectly sculpted bodies. They moved as if they were the limbs of a single mind, with their gazes hypnotically fixed on something beyond the Moon, the Earth, or even the stars.

The most disturbing encounter that I had during one of these Naval Intelligence sessions took place when I was noticed by one of the Nordic supermen working here. He was psychically alerted to my presence, and even seemed to be looking at me as I remote viewed him and his surroundings. "You shouldn't be here," he 'said' *telepathically*. "What *is* this place?" I asked. "It is where we harvest the souls of people who have perished." I was appalled at this answer, and I asked, "*Harvest* them?" He replied, "Yes. Our perpetual motion machines run on souls."

When he said this, I got a mental image of all manner of 'intelligent' machines with the vital energy of what *had been* 'people' trapped inside them, powering them like batteries. "For *how long?*" I asked, exasperated. "Until they wear out," he said. "*Wear out*?!" I exclaimed. "Yes. The psychical constitution of a being can only sustain itself for so long under such conditions. It wears thin in isolation from sensuous reality, and under a pattern of activity that is so routinized." Deeply demoralized by this answer, I questioned him in dismay, "Then even souls die?" Despite the fact that I mumbled this more than half-rhetorically, the Nordic superman explained, "Everything can be torn apart in time. Nothing is eternal. Nothing and no one."

That conversation had been like a half-forgotten dream until I found myself here, in what Tibetans call the *bardo* state between death and rebirth, face to face with these self-appointed harvesters of souls. Fortunately, I had not gone "into the light." From what I was able to gather that is how they trap souls and successfully lure some of them into those machines. I was wary of getting too close to these contraptions, although I managed to get a good sense of some of their functions while I wandered in this place for what seemed to be days (given the lack of an atmosphere, it was a lot harder to keep time, especially in this disoriented postmortem state). The most burdensome task performed by these diabolical devices was the formulation of projected futures. These could be modeled in a high degree of detail, and then altered with a view to the adjustment of variables, back on Earth, with a magnitude sufficient to redirect the trajectory of human history. These *lunatics* were aiming to use this technology in order to resurrect their lost world over the ruins that they planned to make of modern terrestrial societies.

Even if I was terrified of looking directly into the quasi-sentient and inhuman intelligence of these devices that were dependent upon the repurposing of what had once been human souls, I could still form a fairly sophisticated picture of the future that was being projected. For that, all I needed to do was to telepathically penetrate the minds of those who were interacting with these unholy machines. This was easier said than done, because the 'people' up here had much more of a sense of when their minds were being probed than ordinary folks on Earth did. But I had practiced this when, at the behest of Naval Intelligence, I was trying to read the same people stationed in their submarine facilities or undersea cities.

The more I spied on the thoughts and emotions of those involved with the project of reemerging into the open on Earth, the more precognitive glimpses I began to get of this possible future. I was no longer simply reconstructing it analytically with my intellect. This future became something more like a remote viewing target. In the end, I was drawn there as if by a magnet. Instead of merely traversing vast distances of intra-lunar space in the astral state, I was projected many decades into the future. The intelligence that I had produced to foresee and prevent the Soviet invasion of Iran had not averted the apocalyptic return of the Olympians. Instead, it had only changed the conditions under which their occulted Leviathan would surface. I witnessed bizarre scenes of life on this planet from about the year 2048 until 2112, when the time barrier was broken so badly that chronological history became meaningless.

The first hair-raising image which I beheld in the bardo state was the inside of a boardroom in a skyscraper that was one of many buildings with an Art Deco aesthetic, but constructed on the titanic scale of the futuristic metropolitan architectural drafts of Hugh Ferriss. It was built on highlands that overlooked the skyscrapers of Manhattan, as they rose out of the waves of the Atlantic Ocean that pounded against the sides of them and washed through the channels that were once the streets of this city. In this boardroom, a group of businessmen were seated around a long rectangular table that shone like a slab of polished dark gray stone. Its surface reflected the sunlit, glinting gold in a metal sculpture of a chimerical cross between a dragon, a bird, and a dog. It stood out from the wall in relief and somehow periodically morphed its shape. The men all wore black suits and ties, and they had gaunt faces with high cheekbones and chiseled Nordic features. On the table in front of them was a feast that they were about to dig into — the crispy cooked carcass of a jet-black dog on her back, with her limbs in the air. The bitch's stomach was sliced open to reveal garnished stuffing. I was left with the distinct impression that this was not a typical business lunch of any kind. Rather, it was more akin to a ritual sacrifice intended to inaugurate some great undertaking.

The next image involved the attempt made by the tall Nordics to reshape the ruins of the modern world into an Olympian Imperium. The Olympians, the old-guard of Atlantis before the rebellion, wanted to replace the "degenerate" cult of the individual in the modern West, which they saw as definitive of its terminal decline, with a hierarchy of human *types* that would constitute an organic state in an integral and co-dependent fashion, the way that a brain, heart, and limbs are all integral to a single human organism. The social organism of their ideal society was held together by telepathic and telekinetic control, both from the top down and across the collective of each caste.

I saw them inside of a blue-gray marble building with awe-inspiringly tall ceilings. It reminded me of the interior of the front of the International Building, behind the statue of Atlas, at Rockefeller Center, but it was more titanic and had a waterfall. The building was an administrative center or base of operations embedded in an increasingly hostile urban landscape. I focused on one woman in particular, who was walking up a very broad stairway. She had the same beautiful brutality to her build as the rest of them did, but I noticed something else in her posture and expression. Her strong legs were almost trembling, and she looked overwhelmed.

I could see into her mind, which was uncharacteristically disarrayed for an Atlantean — perhaps even a bit frantic. What I saw were buildings exploding into shards of glass onto sidewalks emptied out by martial law and curfews. The terrorism was getting worse, and the insurgents responsible for it were as elusive as ghosts. The Atlanteans had wanted to be received as angels, but now they were losing the battle for hearts and minds. There was a shocking fragility to her. What happened next was truly startling. She *saw me*, there on those steps. She stopped dead and looked straight into my eyes like a startled predator. Then she went to grab my arm, and as her hand passed through my spectral form, I could hear her wordless, desperate plea inside my mind: "We're not demons! *You* can still save us."

No, they were not the ones who looked like demons. Although, appearances can certainly be deceiving. I *did see* creatures that looked like devils or demonic elves. These were the biomechanical robots that, back in my Naval Intelligence work, I had learned 'manned' the Atlantean vessels and dealt with the abductees. Cloaked inside a hollowed-out asteroid, there was a facility where, by means of some mad science that was more like alchemy, these artificial beings were gestating and growing in glowing incubators. They were hairless, with bulbous heads and pointy chins with hardly a trace of mouth or nose. They had slender torsos and freakishly long, skeletal limbs. The hands had only four fingers, ending in long black nails. Their feet were bird-like, and looked as if they could gut a man. Their eyes were almond-shaped and huge. The whole place was permeated with an awful smell that reminded me of sulfur and cinnamon, or smoldering cardboard that has gotten soaked. When I was up close to an incubator, wincing as I took in the shape of these hideous gray things, one of them opened its eyelids. The blackness therein was so deep and vast that it felt as if my soul had been captured by the event horizon of a singularity. This may have been because their bodies were shells or suits designed not only for navigating space but for penetrating past epochs.

In fact, the technology and techniques of time travel that I witnessed from the late 21st century and into the early 22nd century convinced me that history did not have to end this way. I vowed to go back, and to elaborate a vision that would preempt this horrific future. I began to be pulled back to New York in 1980.

...I raised my head from out of my hands. The sound of car horns had disturbed my weeping. As my eyes opened, I saw the taxis that were causing the commotion. Then, struggling with the disorientation of one who emerges from the deepest and longest of dreams, I realized that I was sitting on the steps of St. Patrick's Cathedral. Judging by the style of the checkered cabs, and by the attire of all the pedestrians, I seemed to have returned to New York — except that it was no longer summer. A light snow was falling, and the tears froze on my cheeks. Perhaps only six or seven months had gone by. It was early 1981. There were some discarded, partly crushed boxes that suggested Valentine's Day might have just gone by.

At first, I was ashamed to be sitting on these public steps in such a wretched condition, like one of the many homeless men huddled on them through most of the late 1970s. Then, when I went to cross the street, I realized that no one could see me. Almost no one. As I stood beneath the gaze of Atlas, the King of Atlantis, I had the most uncanny sense that the eyes set in that implacable black face were staring down hard at me with an expression between indignation and expectation.

I walked down Rockefeller Plaza and leaned against the wall over the ice-skating rink to contemplate the statue of Prometheus soaring through the ring of zodiacal constellations with his stolen flame in hand. The inscription from Aeschylus engraved above him read: "Prometheus, teacher in every art, brought the fire that hath proved to mortals a means to mighty ends." The ice was empty, but for a single woman practicing her figure skating with the grace of an Olympic gymnast. She was ice dancing to Jimi Hendrix's rendition of "All Along the Watchtower." As my eyes ran over the contours of her beautiful body, I knew that it was just about time to be born again.

CHAPTER 10

THE DEVIL'S PATH

I found myself on the Devil's Path. Once reputed to be "the most dangerous hiking trail" in America, it treacherously snakes its way across three or four mountains in the Catskills range with the highest summit being the peak of Hunter Mountain. One of the most closely guarded secrets of medieval European history was that in 1178, the Knights Templar led a naval expedition here to this land that they called "Onteora." They took the same northern route that had already been traveled by the Vikings, sailing down toward Hunter Mountain by way of the river that only centuries later would bear the name of Henry Hudson. The Templar Grand Master Odo de St. Amand planned the mission, and it was nominally captained by the Templar knight Ralph de Sudeley. But the real charismatic leader of the expedition was a pirate and pagan priestess by the name of Altomara De León. Though the rest of the explorers, having successfully carried out their mission of retrieving certain scrolls from an ancient Phoenician temple on Hunter Mountain, set sail back to Europe in 1180, Altomara alone remained, it is said, "because she saw the owl." Having been initiated by the High Priestess of what was now a Celtic sacred site, Altomara lived out the rest of her life treading these paths that the Dutch would brand as belonging to the Devil himself. Lady Altomara's ashes are buried in a hidden cave on Hunter Mountain. I have found the cave.

Local legends claim that it is the very same cave that henpecked Rip Van Winkle found his way into late one afternoon when he wandered far away from his overbearing wife, his rent-seeking hound of a land-lord, and the Dutch townsfolk who had made him the butt of many jokes. In the cave he happened upon faerie folk who offered him some witches' brew that put old Rip Van Winkle into what seemed to be a twenty-year slumber, during the course of which he did not age. Once he awakened and finally wandered back to his village, the town now known as Tannersville (the most high-altitude town in the old "Empire State" of New York), this time-traveling Dutchman found to his sur-prise that it was populated by a new generation of "Americans" whose recently "United States" had undergone a Republican revolution.

Now, long after the disintegration of those (formerly) United States, there is still a magic in these mountains that has power over time itself. Although I was born in the city-state of Gotham, I was raised as much in this province as in the metropolis to which it gave birth. Gotham was, after all, conceived here — in the architectural studio of the chalet that my parents built out of the ruins of the old Scribner Lodge on a hilltop across from Hunter Mountain. I remember that from earliest childhood I used to love to stamp my shoes hard on the stone floor in the vast entry hallway and vestibule of the lodge, so that I could listen to the echoes resonating in the wooden walls of the atrium with a ceiling that seemed so very high when I was still so little. I would also pound my way up and down the two wrought iron stairways flanking this vestibule, leading both up to the third floor, on one side, and also down a flight to our dining room on the other. (Since the structure was built on a sloped hill, the entryway to the chalet, with its grand hall and vestibule, was actually on the second of the three floors.) As an only child and daddy's little girl, my father couldn't help but to smile in his kindly way. However, I recall my mother repeatedly yelling at me to stop and also scolding her husband and warning him, in a threatening tone, that he would be responsible if I cracked my skull on the stairs. But I was too hard-headed for that to ever happen, and too nimble.

That came in handy when I started to become a serious hiker. I trained at the Kaaterskill Falls, which, dark pun intended, had actually killed more than a few hikers who came in the summers to bathe in the waterfalls, those falls that freeze over so beautifully when snow blankets the creek and ravines in the winter. Even in our relatively liberal enclave of Greater Gotham, outside the grasp of the Olympian Imperium, Dana Avalon became infamous for always swimming stark naked under the falls. This was still Tannersville, after all. When I was a little girl, other hikers didn't care all that much. They looked the other way, especially knowing who my parents were. When your father is the last great builder of a collapsing modern world, and your mother is the grand architect of Gotham City, you can get away with quite a bit. But when I kept doing it throughout my high school years (during summer break), my skinny-dipping at Kaaterskill came to be seen by the locals as if it were some ill-omened apparition.

One day in the late summer of 2087 — when I was eleven years old and had graduated to hiking the relatively less arduous parts of the Devil's Path — I snuck away from the rest of my hiking group, as had been my habit (much to the supervisor's aggravation). It had not been 15 minutes before I had the most uncanny sensation that something — or someone — was calling me up toward what appeared to be the mouth of a cave. All the sounds of the woods and the critters of the tall grass fell dead silent around me. I was suddenly, and very uncharacteristically, afraid. It was a visceral fear, more of the body than of the mind. To tell you the truth, I almost pissed myself on my way back to the hiking group — who gave me hell.

That night I had a "dream" or… I don't know what to call it. It didn't feel like a dream, but I found myself back in my bed in the morning, with no recollection of how I had returned. A "witch" came for me that night. She was quite beautiful for a witch, though. She did have a rather long and somewhat hooked nose. Her features looked like those of certain Kurdish women. Her piercing and enchanting green eyes were

unforgettable. So was her grin, which was as taunting as it was inviting. This woman took me into her arms like I was a rag doll, and the
next thing I knew she had somehow flown us up the mountain — all
the way up. But then we descended into some kind of subterranean
structure. On the way down into it, I vividly remember a cauldron set
in a place of distinction — as if it were an altar. The enclosure was full
of terrible sights that my conscious mind could barely recollect the
next morning. The flagellated and bound bodies of bleeding Indians.
Black dogs ravenously devouring half-dead men.

The "witch" took me to a stone opening in a wall, which, frankly,
looked like a crude representation of labia surmounted by a huge clitoris. I was stripped naked and made to crawl on my knees into the
narrow tunnel that this opened into and given to understand that I
was crawling into some kind of womb. There was something — somebody — in that "womb." Was it a womb, or a tomb? I have seen some
depictions of Scythian Kurgans. The atmosphere of that place was
similar. There was a certain smell of smoldering cardboard mixed
with sulfur and cinnamon. This *thing* or *person*, or whatever — it had
a distinctly feminine energy to it — extended a long arm with bony
fingers toward my pubic mound. I felt a pulsating electricity engorge
my clitoris to the point where the sudden pleasure quickly became
painful. The next thing I remember I was back in my bed, with the
morning light streaming through the fluttering blinds. My knees were
badly scraped.

For many weeks and months after that experience, I searched for
the cave again — intuiting that there was some connection between the
uncanny feeling I had when I saw it in the distance, and the "dream"
that I had that night. Finally, I found the cave. Or, rather, it found me,
as I was frantically trying to put some distance between myself and
a bear that I startled on the Devil's Path one day late in the following
spring. The trails were muddy, and Hunter Mountain was still snow-
capped. I must have been quite out of my mind, because for all I knew

this could have been the bear's own cave and other bears could have been slumbering in there. I always carried a flashlight in my backpack. When I cast its light across the walls of this cave, I had the eeriest feeling as what appeared to be European-style petroglyphs were revealed to have been carved into the rock.

After discovering the petroglyphs in this cave, I began to scour the whole region around Hunter and Tannersville for folklore that might hold the key to deciphering the dream, or vision, or — dare I say — abduction that I experienced that night the witch came to initiate me. I found the answer in the library of the grand old Field House of the Onteora Club in Tannersville. The club had been frequented by the likes of Mark Twain. As it turned out, Sam Clemens and other founding members of this aristocratic society of literati and artists also came to these mountains in search of the truth behind the same legend. Although it was a book that an eleven-year-old should not have been reading, my parents were both esteemed club members who, I might add, made large donations to the institution. So, I got away with it.

The book in the library was a tome written by Tracy Twyman, and donated to the Onteora Club in gratitude for her brief stay there in the last years before she was murdered in 2019. Well, "suicided" as they say. It was called *Baphomet: The Temple Mystery Unveiled*. Even though the Onteora library does not exactly loan out books, I brought the tome back with me to our chalet and I spent the later part of the winter season of 2088 poring over it. I even skipped a few days of skiing, which was at that time my favorite sport, to keep on reading from early in the morning until I was forced to go to bed at night. On some nights, I read on with a flashlight under my covers. Across hundreds of pages of careful scholarship, Twyman painstakingly demonstrates why it really was that the Knights Templar were declared heretical on Friday, October 13th of 1307 by King Philip IV of France with the support of Pope Clement V.

This is the infamous event that has since been memorialized by the "Curse of Friday the 13th" that eventually made its way into modern American popular culture. The Templars had previously been honored as the foremost among the Crusader knights. They were even rumored to have found the Ark of the Covenant beneath the Temple mount, where they were based and where they earned their name, during their crusade in Jerusalem. But on that Friday the 13th they were formally accused of heresy, blasphemy, including both cursing the name of Jesus Christ and spitting on the cross, homosexuality and other deviant sexual behavior. But Twyman argues effectively that these were not random aberrations. What Pope Clement had discovered was that the Knights Templar were actually Satanists — or to be more precise, Baphomet worshippers. They were forced to confess their "crimes," and many of the "sinners" were burned at the stake.

Baphomet eventually decodes the symbolism of the hermaphroditic goat-headed deity as an esoteric synthesis of the following elements. The primordial serpent, the one who offered us knowledge in Eden, was believed to have originally been a hermaphroditic entity who was split into two beings: Lilith, the first wife of Adam who proved insubordinate and became a child-murdering demon after she left him, and Samael, the demon who is the archenemy of the angel Michael. The Templars inherited an ancient belief that if Lilith and Samael were to manage to reunite through mystical intercourse, they would bring the prison world fashioned by the sadistic demiurge — namely Yahweh — to an end. This they could not do directly, but the goat demon Azazel was believed capable of serving as an intermediary for their reunification. This reunification into the primordial serpent, namely Typhon or Set, was taken to be a reversal of the current of creation that had been ossified into the cosmic order of Yahweh or Yaldabaoth, returning it to the "abyss" (*Bythos*) of eternal potentiality that is Chaos. The Templars further symbolized this in an image of the Phrygian primal nature goddess Cybele, who they called "Mete," pulling the sun, moon, and stars out of the sky with chains that she holds like reins.

In the name of their preeminent icon, this "Mete," meaning wisdom (as in the *methe* that forms part of the name of Prometheus), was combined with "Baph" for baptism because the Templars claimed that the true *gnosis* was taught by John the Baptist and passed down to his disciple, Simon Magus. The Hellenized Israelite Simon ("Shimon"), the magician who engaged in a rather public occult battle with the apostles and infamously went around with a harlot named Helen, who he claimed was an incarnation of the divine Sophia, was also known by his Latin title *Faustus*. The greatest alchemist of his time, Simon was the original "Faust." According to the Templars, Jesus the so-called Christ actually corrupted the teaching of John that was correctly transmitted to Simon. The Gnosticism that took shape in the shadow of Simon Magus was an adulterated and compromised *gnosis* insofar as it failed to reject Jesus, as the Templars did. The Templars reached back to the older, pre-Christian *gnosis* of the Ophites or Sethians who worshipped the knowledge-bringing serpent in Eden. Consequently, *Baphomet* means "baptism of wisdom."

The Templars used the severed head of John the Baptist as an occult object for prophesying, a practice rather common in the Middle East where the Templars had dealings with the Order of Assassins based in Iran — that radically antinomian Iranian order whose creed was "Nothing is true; everything is permitted." By their own account, the Templars attempted to create a synthesis of all historically persecuted beliefs with the symbol of Baphomet representing this deviant eclecticism. The sexual deviance and orgies to which they confessed when these formerly esteemed "Crusader knights" were subjected to inquisition by the Catholic Church were actually intended to ritually enact the reunion of Lilith and Samael through Azazel and the destruction of Yahweh's world by Cybele. This going against the grain of a natural order established and controlled by the demiurge included not simply the rejection of procreative sex but even the perverse use of it to engender fetuses that would be ritually aborted, devoured, and defecated out in order to essentially symbolize the fact that we live in a bloody fucking world of shit.

According to the inquisitors, the Templars went further than the ancient Carpocratians in this practice, just as they went further than the Carpocratians in their unapologetic denunciation of Jesus. Whereas Carpocratian orgies led to the sacrifice of fetuses, Church inquisitors claimed to have extracted confessions from Templars to the effect that they sacrificed infants as well. They were even accused of using the severed and embalmed heads of these infants for scrying, in the same vein as they used that of John the Baptist's for prophesying.

Once I discovered all this, the Templar naval expedition to a pagan goddess temple on Hunter Mountain made a lot more sense to me. As did the fact that it was unofficially led by a woman so charismatic that, as the sole female on the expedition, she was able to command the loyalty of a boatful of knights for a months-long journey. I remember being deeply impressed by this story when my father first recounted it to me as a little girl, paraphrasing from the pages of the now well-worn copy of *The Templar Mission to Oak Island and Beyond*, which quickly found its way from my parents' library to my own bookshelf. Was it Altomara herself who had come for me that night? Or was it the High Priestess of Hunter who had initiated her? Or perhaps the "goddess" herself—the one to whom the ancient stone temple was dedicated. Whoever the "witch" that carried me away was, I understood why, when they arrived here, the good Christian Dutchmen had hoisted an ancient megalith up into the likeness of a giant grave marker and named it "the Devil's tombstone" as if to bury the "evil" that they believed to be haunting the peaks along the trail that they likewise named "the Devil's Path." That megalith, immovable as ever, still sits in the valley between Hunter Mountain and Plateau Mountain, the very same area wherein the Templars first encountered both the native redskins of the region (who shot arrows into their armor in vain) and then the Celtic women and men who had taken over the much older Phoenician temple.

As far as medieval European men went, the Templars were, of course, freethinkers. That is the least that can be said of them if they were in fact Baphomet worshippers. But even these knights were taken aback to find on the slopes of Hunter Mountain a society in which women enjoyed full equality with men — except in the sanctum of the temple, wherein they were superior in status. The women were full partners in all decision-making and they fought alongside the men, so ferociously that the bravest of the Indians — who initially attacked the arriving Templars — were afraid of them. But only women were allowed to be initiated at the temple, originally dedicated to a Phoenician goddess, and later rededicated to a Celtic one by the subsequent wave of intrepid Old-World pioneers who made it from the Hudson River to the highest point in the Catskill Mountains. The Templar chronicles noted that some of these Celts clearly looked like they had absorbed the earlier Phoenician settlers, and some of them even bore traces of Indian blood in their features.

The goddess was known as "Astarte" to the Phoenicians, the figure called "Ishtar" by the Babylonians and "Setareh" by the Persians. The Celts called her "Artio" and associated her with bears, who also happened to be the dominant animal of the Catskills region. She was depicted either *as* a bear — in shamanic fashion — or as a woman astride a bear. Obviously, this is the very same goddess who is more widely known by her Greco-Roman names: Artemis, or Diana. The Huntress. Hence "Hunter Mountain." It sent shivers up my spine and gave me goosebumps when I realized that. Some Romans also identified her with Venus. Others, in an attempt to reconcile this with the syncretic identification of her as Diana, called her "Diana Lucifera," since Venus, when she appears as the morning star and bringer of the dawn from out of darkness, is known as "Lucifer."

The chronicles written by the Templars on the expedition, based on Altomara's testimony, described a stone temple, reinforced by mud, and partly subterranean, which had at its center a cauldron of the kind that I remember from my experience with the "witch." Another feature is also mentioned, the description of which made my skin crawl as I read it, since, as I said, I vividly remember having been there that night because I am slightly claustrophobic. A "stone vagina" that opened into a tunnel with a rather tight crawl space, leading into a subterranean chamber. Altomara had seen something in that chamber that made it so that she could not return to Europe together with the Templars. The chronicles refer to it simply, and most cryptically, as "the owl." She saw "the owl" and so she could not go back.

I had another "dream" around the same time, which I believe has something to do with this "owl" symbolism and is connected to the experience with that witch and the temple that she took me to. In this dream I found myself in a place that I remembered having frequented. You know, in those "dreams" of the type wherein you suddenly feel as if you are in a place that you remember having been many times before, but that your conscious mind forgets about entirely shortly after you "wake up" from being there. (I wonder which is the domain of the "sleeper" and which is the place of "awakening.") This place was a library or rather a large study, smaller than a library, but big enough to fit six or seven rows of chairs facing in the direction of an ornate desk or lectern behind which an authoritative woman was instructing those assembled. On each of the chairs was a woman, *only* women. I was one of them. Resting against a leg of every chair was the shield of each of the women. All of our shields were actually in the shape of a face. Although I had the impression that the function of this face was akin to that of the gorgons embossed on certain Greek shields, the face on all of the women's shields was the unmistakable and implacable countenance of a "gray." In the literature of "alien abductions," which

I've begun to delve deeply into, these grays often shapeshift into huge owls.

Was it a so-called "gray" that my father saw that night he came up to the chalet alone or, as he described it, "a demon"? Is there a difference? As he tells it, this was some night in December of 2076, just a few weeks before I was born. (I'm an Aquarius.) My mother was back in Gotham, with her friends hosting a "baby shower" for her. My father drove up to Hunter alone, but along the way, in the last stretch of narrow winding mountain road before Tannersville, right around Wildcat Ravine, his hovercar suddenly died. Its engine, lights, and dials all just went out. He remembers it being around 8 pm. Then, as my father was standing next to the grounded hovercar on the side of the empty road, everything turned back on again and he continued the drive to our chalet. Oddly, all of the lights were already off in Tannersville. When he walked into the house, it was as hot as an open oven. On his way over to check the thermostat, which oddly showed a normal room temperature, he noticed that it was after midnight. The last leg of road from Wildcat Ravine up to our Hunter chalet ought to have taken no more than twenty minutes to drive, and he cannot recall the car having been dead for more than a few moments. What would he have been doing on that roadside for nearly four hours? He opened all of the windows and doors to let the inexplicable and unbearable heat out of the house. Finally, he was able to go to sleep.

At some point in the middle of the night, he woke up to go to the bathroom. As he approached the bathroom door, he saw illumined by the dim nightlight that, to his horror, from out of the woodgrains of the door some "demonic" looking thing emerged and quickly slinked off into the darkness of the hallway outside the bedroom. My father described it as having very long thin arms, a twiggy body, and a bulbous head ending in a pointy chin. He could faintly see that it had huge almond-shaped eyes. There was something about its *gestalt* that reminded him of a cross between a featherless owl and a praying mantis. He was of a mind to go through the house with his shotgun and try to hunt the thing down, but before he knew it fatigue overcame him, and he collapsed back into bed.

The next morning, while looking in the bathroom mirror as he brushed his teeth, my father noticed that he had what looked like a healed scar cutting across most of his forehead. It diagonally crossed the horizontal wrinkles that had naturally formed over the years. As soon as he got back to Gotham and saw my mother, she was so startled by it that she blurted out, "What happened to your head?" The "scar" is still there. Considering what a prominent personality Richard Avalon is, it has even merited some speculation from the media in Gotham that perhaps he had undergone some kind of surgery. That would be a bizarre form of brain surgery, which would require an incision in someone's forehead.

Other strange things happened in our Hunter chalet around the time that I was born. My mother's jewelry would regularly disappear, including some of her most expensive pieces. My father had to replace his wallet, and everything in it, several times. The house had a sophisticated alarm system, so they could not figure out how a burglar could possibly have gained entry. Besides, some of the items disappeared while both of my parents were at home and wide awake. Most disturbingly, they would occasionally hear a clink or a thud and then find that one of these missing items — usually a piece of jewelry — had suddenly reappeared on the floor somewhere, as if it had been dropped there from out of thin air. Fine silverware also went missing from the kitchen, only to reappear in a cluttered mess in the snow outside the chalet with the sun glinting off of it.

After my experience with the witch, I also began collecting other research material relevant to what I discovered in the book on *Baphomet* and the Templars. Besides skiing, during my winter breaks from school, and hiking, during my summer vacations, this became my predominant preoccupation during my time spent in the Catskills.

My bedroom in the Hunter chalet eventually turned into something of a Gothic library.

The books that I filled my shelves with, and that were intended to broaden and deepen my understanding of what Twyman had set my mind ablaze with in her *Baphomet*, included such classics as the Bible, the apocryphal Book of Enoch, the *Malleus Maleficarum* ("The Witches' Hammer," 1486) penned by the German inquisitors Heinrich Kramer and Jakob Sprenger, Milton's *Paradise Lost*, Goethe's *Faust*, William Blake's *The Marriage of Heaven and Hell* (1793), Percy Shelley's *The Revolt of Islam* (1817), Lord Byron's *Cain: A Mystery* (1822), Sheridan Le Fanu's *Carmilla* (1872), Moncure Daniel Conway's *Demonology and Devil-lore* (1878), *Dieu et l'etat* ("God and the State," 1882) by Mikhail Bakunin, Ada Langworthy Collier's *Lilith: The Legend of the First Woman* (1885), Helena Blavatsky's *The Secret Doctrine* (1888), Bram Stoker's *Dracula* (1897), *La Révolte des anges* ("The Revolt of the Angels," 1914) by Anatole France, and Aino Kallas's *The Wolf's Bride* (1928). As I read these works during my late adolescence and early teenage years, a certain picture formed in my mind.

It appeared to me rather obvious that Romantic poets such as Blake, Shelley, and Byron were absolutely justified in their view of Satan as a rebel against injustice and an enlightening liberator of Man — and especially of *women* — from oppression. From the beginning of the Book of Genesis in the Bible, Yahweh shows his true colors as a tyrannical, sadistic, and jealous egomaniac. We are expelled from Eden out of his fear that, having listened to the serpent and eaten the fruit of a tree symbolizing knowledge in the sense of discernment, we will go on to eat from the tree of life the fruit of which symbolizes the immortality of the Elohim — "the gods" (plural) of which Yahweh is the chieftain. Our "sin" — the one for which so many Church fathers in their commentaries held Eve, and by extension womankind, as more responsible for than even the serpent — our "sin" simply consisted of threatening to break free from the control of Yahweh and his fellow gods by actualizing our potential to become their equals in terms of our capacities and capabilities. We were "naked" in Eden because in antiquity slaves worked naked, and slave labor is what is meant when the Bible describes us as "tillers in the field" of the garden of the gods.

This reading is clearly reaffirmed by two other episodes in Genesis. First, when 200 of the angels known as "watchers" revolt against the heavenly order by taking mortal wives and teaching these earthly women all of the crafts, arts, and sciences — from beautification and birth control to astronomy and metallurgy. As elaborated in the Book of Enoch, a civilization of hybrids is spawned from this eroti-cally charged seeding of secret knowledge to what had been a race of slaves. These demi-god "giants" who refuse to revere the Lord and who putatively "pervert" his Creation by modifying nature in all kinds of ways, presumably using the techniques and technologies disclosed to them by the "fallen angels," are punitively drowned by Yahweh in a global deluge. This is the so-called "flood of Noah," which obviously represents an Israelite parallel to the legend of Atlantis just as the gift of knowledge and technology both by the serpent in Eden and again by the fallen angels thereafter forms a clear Hebraic parallel to the Greek legend of Prometheus. Then, in the second episode, later in Genesis, an unrelenting mankind unifies to build the "tower of Babel" that reaches up as a stairway to Heaven. Yahweh angrily and, again, jealously laments that "if this is what they can do, as one people united with one language, then nothing will be impossible to them." So, in the oldest example of "divide and conquer," he destroys the tower, scatters humanity across the Earth, breaks us up into different tribes with divergent languages, and sets us at war with one another. What a great "God" this is!

Then, of course, there is the God Father's particular penchant for abusing and torturing women. The Bible served as a bedrock of misogynistic patriarchy throughout the medieval period, after the collapse of the classical world that can be specifically dated to Bishop Cyril's authorization of the public flaying and burning of the female scientist and academy leader Hypatia as a "witch" in 370 AD, and the attendant Christian burning of the Library of Alexandria, of which Hypatia had been the last guardian. According to the Church fathers, Eve "taught" Adam when she offered him the fruit (of knowledge) that the serpent supposedly "tempted" her into eating. From St. Paul himself onward, this served as the basis for a prohibition against teaching by women. As St. Paul writes in his Epistle to Timothy (2:12): "But I suffer not a woman to teach, nor to usurp authority over the man, but to be in silence." This, taken together with Exodus 22:18, which reads "Thou shalt not suffer a witch to live" (i.e., 'do not tolerate witches by letting them live'), was the scriptural basis for the burning at the stake of those women branded as "witches" from Hypatia onwards.

There were repeated waves of these persecutions of headstrong and supposedly insubordinate or otherwise non-conformist women, both in Europe and in the colonies of North America. It spread from France and Germany in the 1480s to Switzerland and England in the 1560s, to Flanders and Scotland around 1600, then again across many parts of Europe in the 1620s, with a final outbreak during the infamous witch trials of Salem in the Massachusetts colony of North America in 1692. Ironically, the invention of the printing press by Gutenberg in 1436 only fanned the flames of these persecutory outbreaks by allowing for mass publication and dissemination of books such as the *Malleus Maleficarum* ("The Witches' Hammer," 1486). These texts, written by Inquisitors, allowed local churchmen and judges to familiarize them-selves with the supposed telltale signs that a woman might be a witch. These included evidence that would be indicative of her receiving nighttime visits from demon lovers, in the male form of the incubus, or of themselves becoming a succubus or female demon who visits and corrupts men of the community in the dark of night. Such charges reached back to the aforementioned intercourse of "fallen angels" with mortal women, which is admitted in Genesis and elaborated on in the Book of Enoch.

The vampire and werewolf tales of Gothic horror pick up on this theme of women as the confederates of Satan. A figure like Stoker's *Dracula* is almost exclusively interested in sharing his vampiric power with women, even though he has many opportunities to transform men who are soft targets. The female vampire, as most powerfully exemplified in the five consorts of Count Dracula and also in *Carmilla*, is clearly a nineteenth-century literary reiteration of the medieval- and Renaissance-era conception of a coven of witches in league with Satan. As scientific rationalism rose within the realm of public discourse, and the legal system was secularized, this belief retreated into the realm of the Gothic literary imagination. As with Dracula himself, whose name *Dracul* means "the Dragon" as understood to be "the Devil" in the form in which he appears in the Apocalypse of St. John, vampires were taken to have the shamanic power of shapeshifting into wolves. In other words, they were also werewolves.

This is most strikingly expressed in stories wherein the werewolf is a woman, symbolizing the ultimate defiance of domesticity and liberation through return to the wilderness of the dark forest, such as in Aino Kallas's *The Wolf's Bride* (1928). Even the child murder attributed to female vampires, such as Lucy in *Dracula*, when set in the historical context of Victorian England with its puritanically patriarchal culture, is an act of defiance against the overwhelmingly overbearing and seemingly inescapable burden of the expectation of a life of submissive motherhood that has been the fate of women for most of recorded history. Interestingly, some of the earliest and most radical revolutionary movements to socio-politically challenge this predefined role for women, such as the anarchism of Mikhail Bakunin, explicitly took up the symbol of Satan as a positive icon of rebellion and human emancipation.

Besides books, I also began to collect printed images of certain historical works of art, both paintings and sculptures, wherein Satan is depicted as either fully female or at least as hermaphroditic. Much to the chagrin of my mother, I plastered my walls with the prints of these paintings and lined my desk and library with 3-d printed reproductions of the sculptures.

"The Devil as a woman" was a more common theme in medieval and Renaissance art than we have been led to believe. For example, all the way from the late twelfth century until the late sixteenth century, the most common depiction of the serpent in Eden featured a female face and breasts. Even Michelangelo painted one of these for the ceiling of the Sistine Chapel, namely his piece *Temptation and Expulsion* (1511). A sculptural form of the same image adorned the Portal of the Virgin at the Western entrance to Notre Dame Cathedral in Paris. In his marble sculpture of *Adam, Eve, and Satan*, Michelangelo also clearly depicted the serpent as female. This is one of the reproductions that sat on a shelf of my bookcase. Displayed prominently on the back of the door to my bedroom at our Hunter chalet was a poster-sized print of a caricature published in *Harper's Weekly* in 1872, wherein a rather handsome, strong, winged, and gothic-attired "Mrs. Satan" is holding a placard up that reads, "Be saved by free love." In the background, set against a brutal rocky mountainscape, is a housewife who is straining as she carries her three children and also her drunken husband on her back. At the bottom of the image is a printed caption, attributed to the burdened housewife, which reads, "Get thee behind me, (Mrs.) Satan! I'd rather travel the hardest path of matrimony than follow in your footsteps."

The most famous — or infamous — depiction of Satan as a hermaphrodite is of course the engraving of Baphomet by Éliphas Lévi that was first printed in his *Dogme et rituel de la haute magie* (1855). I got a hold of a copy of the book — in the original French, a language that I was already learning then — and I also enlarged this engraving into a huge poster that I nailed into the wall above my desk. Lévi's image starkly emphasizes the transcendence of all polarities, such as light and darkness, celestial spirit and earthly matter, good and evil, and of course male and female. He believed that all of these are refractions of a single "astral light" that he identified with the essence of "Lucifer," like the way in which white light that enters a prism emerges from out of it as the spectrum of seemingly distinct colors. This occulted spectral transcendence of all polarities was at the heart of Lévi's teaching and of what he meant to represent with the symbol of Baphomet.

CHAPTER 11

LITTLE DEVIL

I am a native of Gotham, and my parents played a significant role in building this city. My mother, Brenda Wells, was an architect, and my father, Richard Avalon, was what, in the last couple of centuries, would have been called a "real estate developer." To speak of "real estate" in the context of the pseudo-economy that we have in this enclave makes little sense. I suppose you could say that he was in "construction." Dick was already in his early sixties when I was born, in late January of 2077. (Yes, I'm an Aquarian.) Career-wise, he cut his teeth on Simulacra construction in the 2040s. This was a relatively short-lived trend of building habitats or "total environments" that were reconstructions of particular past eras. Imagine highly fortified gated communities with an entirely consistent and cohesive style. More authentic and less gaudy than simulacra of various places at the casino resort hotels of old Las Vegas.

By then the world had been completely devastated by convergent catastrophes, from pandemics to super-volcano eruptions and multiple mega-tsunamis produced by tremendous earthquakes. A coronal mass ejection had ravaged our hemisphere in particular. There had also been catastrophic climate change, resulting in droughts, deep-freezes, and mass starvation. Most of the severely diminished population was disease-ridden and desperate. Under these appalling conditions, many of the superrich retreated into micro-cities that were modeled on the aesthetic and lifestyle of one or another past epoch of relative peace and prosperity. The majority of those who could afford to live in such places opted for modern conveniences, so simulacra of the 1950s were more popular than reconstructions of the Wild West or Victorian Britain.

The *most popular* of all of the "total environments" were communities modeled on 1980s America, which is the type of construction that my father specialized in. It is how he met my mother, who was an architecture student researching her doctoral thesis by doing an on-site study of a small-scale urban reconstruction of an Eighties American cityscape that he was building (there were also suburban simulacra). She recruited him into Prometheism. She appealed to his practical sensibilities, motivated by her own opportunism. "The movement" (as she was fond of calling it) had always valorized "the Eighties" of the previous century as the zenith of social development and cultural innovation. In the 2040s, many of the wealthy individuals who opted to live in simulacra of that era were Prometheists. In fact, the dominant Traditionalist discourse had by then framed Prometheism as an ideological superstructure intended to morally justify the greed and deviance of reactionaries who wanted to salvage the evils of Capitalism, albeit by dealing in cryptocurrencies after the global abolition of "filthy" money. This, despite the strong Communist currents in the thought of Jorjani — but I am getting ahead of myself.

Richard Avalon "converted" to Prometheism because he saw construction opportunities and business deals with individuals who, at least implicitly, still believed in personal wealth over the putatively "greater good" of so-called "public welfare." Meanwhile, my mother became Brenda Avalon because my father (who was already twice divorced and too old for her) was an insurance policy that she wouldn't wind up a "paper architect" in a world where 99% of architecture firms had gone out of business and almost all construction projects were run by the state. They were both career-driven enough that they waited two decades into their marriage to decide to carry a pregnancy to term, and this was only because by then my mother was in her mid-forties and this was her last opportunity to give the great Dick Avalon a flesh and blood bearer of his legacy as the world's last great builder.

I was born in Gotham, only about a dozen years after the ground-breaking of the project — which was the crowning glory of my parents' collaborative enterprise. No mere micro-city or gated simulacrum, Gotham was the first new full-scale metropolis constructed since The Arrival in 2048. As such, the building project could not but be considered an act of insurrection on a titanic scale. That the construction was completed at all was, in truth, a testimony to the confidence of the Olympian Imperium, which decided to use it as a dark crystal-lization — a tumor, epitomizing everything that they considered wicked and depraved about what was fast becoming "the old world" of Modernity.

What can I say about my childhood? I was always a tomboy, but then so were most girls here in Gotham by the standards of gender norms that had been reimposed worldwide by Traditionalists under the paternalistic guidance of the Olympian Overlords. But my boyish-ness went above and beyond the average, even for Gothamite girls. I took up scuba diving by the time I was old enough to carry the weight of a sizeable oxygen tank on my back, and I abused the privilege of my parents' access to the restricted area of Manhattan to dive on the ruins of the old city.

The Avalon Corporation was cleared for entry into that part of New York Harbor so that its team could draw inspiration from studying, photographing, and modeling the details of the decaying skyscrapers. Their partly shattered hulls were being steadily worn away by the waves of the Atlantic Ocean, which broke around them before pressing on up the Harbor through the geometric grid of channels that had been the streets of Manhattan. After the last remnants of the Antarctic ice sheet melted, laying bare the ruins of Atlantis, the sea-level had risen up to about the 30th floor of the Empire State Building. Her spire, originally built as a zeppelin dock, still stood as a monolithic sentinel over the dead city that Gotham was modeled on.

One of the most unforgettable dives that I did, together with my mother, in the last year before my relationship with her fell apart, was on the Guggenheim. I had grown up surrounded by Frank Lloyd Wright designs, and blueprints for new buildings with decorative details that were partly inspired by the archeo-futuristic elements of his Deco period. Though my parents attempted to shelter me as much as possible from the world of the Olympian Imperium, outside the defense perimeter of Gotham, I knew that the Traditionalist state that had consolidated control over most of the planet branded Wright as one of the principal degenerates of the so-called "Kali Yuga." Children were taught that he was a "murderer" whose architectural designs were a product of his evident mental derangement. All of that was in the back of my mind when we dove through the shattered glass dome of the Guggenheim that day, casting our flashlights onto corroding Modernist sculptures that crouched inside the guardrail of the spiral walkway like demonic totems. The Guggenheim's atrium had become a kind of self-contained aquarium for slithering, shimmering fish, and a feeding tank for a couple of geriatric sharks who we had to put out of their misery.

I was also an avid skier. The plans for Gotham were actually first drawn up at our Hunter Mountain chalet. This area of the Catskills, about 120 miles north of Manhattan, had enough existing infrastructure that the Prometheist movement had chosen the Avalon Corporation to build an Eighties-style community at this location, and to reconstruct the ski lifts and lodges for the use of those who settled there. Our paramilitary forces filled the dense forest surrounding the designated area with fortifications capable of mounting significant anti-aircraft fire.

After a few skirmishes, on the level of partisan warfare, those locals in the Catskills who were loyal to the Olympian Imperium decided to put enough distance between themselves and our mountain enclave. The landing of a few armed electro-gravitic vessels and personnel transports at a makeshift spaceport that had been built on a peak adjacent to the Hunter Mountain summit was enough to spook them into believing that our "rebel" forces were considerably more formidable than was in fact the case. In point of fact, our connection to the Asteroid Belt colonies was tenuous, and we wondered if the Imperium would cut this Prometheist lifeline at any moment. But, meanwhile, we skied — mainly as a means of clearing and refreshing our minds.

My parents' chalet was the largest in the community, built from out of the deep infrastructure of an old, ruined hotel, on a hill diagonally across from the mountain. It was in the skylit and sunbathed studio on the upper floor of this chalet that, I am told, the blueprints for the construction of the first set of buildings in Gotham were drawn up by a small group of architects and engineers overseen by my parents. These were the towers furthest south along the Palisades Cliffs, with the clearest and most breathtaking views over the partly submerged skyscrapers of Manhattan. Prime real estate, which Imperium propaganda portrayed as belonging to the Devil himself. Funny to think that this had once been New Jersey. Maybe it was the Jersey Devil.

"You little devil" is a phrase that I often heard throughout my childhood and adolescence. I stopped hearing it only because at a certain point my mischievous antics and rebellious contrarianism were no longer amusing, especially to such scions of respectability as my parents were in "the movement." I was a talented artist and, around the age of eleven, the content of my drawings began to shock them. They wondered what prurient influence I had come under, and where all the spectacular violence in these images was coming from — as if we weren't living in a world that had just gone through a global holocaust ending in the brutal imposition of a totalitarian socio-political order.

A number of artists were a conscious influence on what took shape as my style of drawing: Philippe Druillet, Jean Giraud (aka "Moebius"), and Philippe Caza. All of them were from the late twentieth century and most of them were French or worked predominately in France. Their work is one reason that I was so motivated to learn the French language. They also had in common that they were all featured in *Métal Hurlant* ("Heavy Metal") magazine in the late 1970s and throughout the 1980s. I found an archive of vintage issues of this magazine, some of them water-damaged, when the content of an old storage unit near Hunter was being auctioned off at an antiques shop in Tannersville. The unit, and most of the others in the long-abandoned storage facility, had been used by native New Yorkers from the time before the Old City was destroyed by the Las Palmas tsunami and then again, later on, by a couple of hundred feet of rising sea levels attendant to the precipitous deglaciation of Antarctica. In other words, the time before Avalon Corporation began to build the skyscrapers of Gotham on the Palisades and Hudson Highlands, overlooking the partly submerged skyline of Manhattan.

I don't know what exactly my parents expected that I ought to be drawing, sunflowers and rainbows perhaps, in a world that had faced convergent catastrophes and wars so severe that Earth lost about three fourths of its population between 2025 and 2050. A world that, ever since then, has been almost entirely dominated by a regressive — I dare say *retarded* — Traditionalist Order whose reactionary destruction of everything that defined the Liberal and Progressive world of Modernity has spared not a single city or country besides ours. Even Greater Gotham is only still standing because the Traditionalists want to use it as a living example of the putative deviance, decadence, and degeneracy that they are proud of having stamped out everywhere else on Earth. (Well, on *land*. The outlaw oceans that Gothamites often traverse are a different story.) We Gothamites were to serve as the Sodomites who embodied everything that a Trad youth was brought up to revile and despise. When they were done with us, this Sodom, namely our Gotham, would also be turned into a fiery pillar "like the smoke of a kiln," as the author of Genesis puts it. Then, the Prometheist colonies in the hollowed-out asteroids in the belt between Mars and Jupiter would be our only reliable refuge. That is, if the Olympians and their Traditionalist minions didn't manage to cut the space transport and supply lines between the Belt and Greater Gotham either before or after they decide to destroy Earth's last true metropolis.

So, why shouldn't my drawings have been dark and violent? Or, for that matter, sexual? It is this last element that probably set off the alarm bells in my parents' censorious minds that were given over to daily self-delusion and willful blindness to realities of our world that even an eleven-year-old girl was capable of grasping. The sexuality in my drawings represented a defiance of all-pervasive and encroaching death by the primordial power of the Life Force. I suppose they were alarmed by seeing such imagery in the sketchbooks of a girl who hadn't even reached puberty yet, as if the erotic were circumscribed by the biological bounds of reproductive sex. It's not as if I threw these images in their faces either. My mother regularly rummaged through my stuff, and there didn't seem to be a closet or drawer either back in our apartment in the city or in the country where I could effectively hide my sketchbooks from her inquisitorial intrusiveness. She did things like shame me for the volumes of *The Diary of Anaïs Nin* that she found I was hiding under my bed, volumes that I "borrowed" from her bookcases.

Not incidentally, it was discovering Nin's captivating diaries that inspired me to begin writing my own, which I would never otherwise have done since diary writing is such a contemptibly girly thing to do. I mean, I was such a tomboy. At school, back in the city, I would never have been caught dead writing in a fucking "diary." It would have destroyed my image. Well, an image that, even then, rather authentically reflected who I really was. But reading Nin's journals, I realized what a so-called "diary" could be. Eventually, I decided to begin writing my own at the same age as she had made her first entries in what became a decades-long confessional contemplation of every aspect of her life as well as an earnest attempt to bring the contents of her subconscious into her reflective awareness. These memoirs are closely based on that diary. I also used my "diary" as a dream journal and a place to write down the poems that occasionally took shape in my mind, like this one, which came to me all at once while I was drawing melted steel buildings and mangled bodies immolated by nuclear explosions on August 6, 2088, the anniversary of the nuclear attack on Hiroshima:

> In the depths of history's darkened tome,
> Where shadows of anguish find their home,
>
> In the ruins of Hiroshima, Nagasaki's despair,
> A tale of devastation, heavy in the air.
>
> The atomic storms, unleashed with dread,
> Leveled cities, left countless souls for dead.
>
> Oh, the horror, the madness that did unfold,
> As mushroom clouds billowed, stories untold.
>
> The flesh disintegrated, bones turned to dust,
> In the wake of destruction, trust was lost.
>
> Japan's dreams shattered, its Empire torn,
> As fire and radiation transformed the morn.

Although nuclear weapons were used somewhat more extensively in the Third World War than in the Second, that first use of "the bomb" in anger against a civilian population has remained an unforgettable milestone in the history of human cruelty.

My mother finding Nin's diaries under my bed was also something like a boy being caught with pornography. Besides the book on *Baphomet* and some of the other related writings on Satan, witchcraft, and vampires that I had collected, Nin's diaries unlocked larval depths of my psyche that I imagined remain repressed even in many full-grown women — especially in the Trad world outside of Gotham. *Carmilla* wasn't bad either, I have to say, and I went to bed with the book more than a few times, but Sheridan Le Fanu was a fucking misogynist who intended his lesbian vampire to be seen as a monstrous aberration from proper womanhood. It was different with Nin. She was the kind of woman that I could deeply relate to. More than the specific erotic exploits — of all kinds — that she recounts in the pages of her diaries, it is the author herself who began to magnetically attract me with her ravishing prose. I wanted her. I wanted to know her from beyond the grave, especially when she was a young woman.

I remember asking myself whether this meant that I was "bisexual" or maybe even a "lesbian"? I didn't know, and I really didn't care. I figured that the Trads could keep the labels they use to categorize someone with the intent of more effectively persecuting them, once the hapless fool who buys into these labels has been boxed in. All I knew was that I'd go down on Anaïs Nin in a fucking heartbeat, and more than any man's cock I wanted those fingers that wielded her pen to be what took my virginity. Alas, for that, I'd have to be a time traveler, and it was long before I became one that someone else's fingers deflowered me.

I was fascinated by history and literature, which were my strongest subjects in middle school. Digging my claws into every book that I understood to be banned by the regime reigning outside my relatively sheltered environment became an obsessive mission. My rebellion never took the form of affirming the Traditionalism of the outside world, which was after all the ideology of the majority of sheeple on Earth. Rather, I was radicalized in the opposite direction. My reaction to living under the shadow of such prominent Prometheists was to become "holier than the Pope." I started to express contempt for their construction endeavors as a superficial and rootless misunderstanding of the Promethean ethos. Like most Prometheist households, our library included the complete works of Jorjani. I began by holding these up as mirrors to the shortcomings of the Prometheists of our time, but then I turned on the "canon" itself. By the end of my high school years, I was reading Jorjani against himself.

That's when the terrible break with my mother took place. My father was blessed to have already died of heart failure during my junior year, because otherwise I would probably bear the guilt of killing him with the stress that this scandal caused for our family. The worst that he had lived to see was my starting to date girls more often than boys, and it was hardly appropriate for someone so prominently associated with Prometheism to express any displeasure over his daughter turning out to be a lesbian, or at least bisexual. I can tell you that my mother wasn't all that pleased by it, even though she tried to keep that to herself and find other excuses for expressing her disapproval. Things were never the same after she caught me and my first girlfriend in an indecent state. It was a formative experience and is a story that is worth telling.

Hardly anyone had said anything on the hovercar ride back home. Least of all my mother, who made sure to glue herself to her holographic tablet so as to even avoid eye contact. It would have been easier in an old-style automobile, where everyone faces front, but with these hovercars, which drive themselves, all of the seats around the interior of the car face inwards. We had brought Cynthia up to Hunter with us for some early spring skiing over the weekend. Well, just barely spring. The equinox had been the day before. I guess that makes the catastrophe that happened all the more momentous and unforgettable.

Actually, to have the full context for this story, I have to back up and recount to you who Daren is and how I got involved with Cynthia. It was Halloween of 2088. Halloween is still my favorite holiday. What happened could *only* have happened *because* it was Halloween. My few pals from school and I were trick-or-treating as a group, hitting every apartment in my own posh building, and then traveling — unsupervised — to the high-rises immediately adjacent to mine. This was made possible by the fact that my father, the construction magnate responsible for building this apartment complex, and my mother, who architecturally designed them, together with most of the rest of the earliest stratum of Gotham, were so well known by the doormen and security personnel in the complex that even at age eleven (going on twelve, in January), I was allowed to run loose between these few buildings. At least on Halloween.

This holiday had been banned in the Olympian Imperium. Well, effectively banned. In some places it was rebranded as "All Hallows' Eve" or a very sanitized and Trad version of "Samhain." But *classic* American Halloween was considered to be degenerate devilry. That rendered it especially appealing to me, on top of my own somewhat Gothic sensibilities. But there was something else about Halloween that struck the deepest chord with me, and I suspect it is the real reason why Traditionalists have banned the form of it that became popular in modern America, especially in those parts of the country, like Gotham, that have such a spectacularly palpable fall season. The blaze of yellow, orange, and red that engulfs the trees here over the course of the season, leading up to this night, promises the chaos of decomposition. Like the fallen leaves underfoot in our parks, and further up in the Hudson highlands, the ordered expectations of society themselves seem to crack as the sun sets on October 31st. For those who honored this as a "day of the dead," there were more spirits than ever to be mindful of. The world's population had fallen by something on the order of 75% in the past 50 years. Billions were wandering in the bardo.

It was a hell of a night. I went out dressed as a witch. Of course, the group I went trick-or-treating with consisted entirely of boys. My parents already knew that my only "friends" at school, if they could even be called that, were the weirdest guys in our grade. My mother was a bit unnerved about that, but neither of my parents wanted me to be any more hermetic than I already was. They also knew that there were a few girls that I was trying to befriend. These boys didn't want them coming trick-or-treating with us, though. See, they considered me to be "one of the boys." But they did agree to come to my apartment complex, because the most well-to-do people lived here and that meant looting the best candy. What appealed more to me was that we *did* have the best decorations of any building in central Gotham. The residents in this complex of high-rises went all out. As Halloween approached, the home owners got together, floor by floor, to plan the design for the utility fog coating the hallways. This meant that, come Halloween, the halls of each floor, and the doors to the various apartments, would look and feel like something out of a horror movie. On top of that, our smart contact lenses would pick up Augmented Reality objects that were programmed to appear in these spooky spaces. Like moving spiders, and floating ghosts.

Daren was my favorite of the several boys that came over. He was lanky and tall for an eleven-year-old. He had really shot up in the past semester. Somehow, he had also gotten away with CRISPR-ing his shoulder-length hair *blue*. Though an underachiever of his own accord, Daren was smart. I think he'd managed to get into his sister's CRISPR kit. (Man, he could have really fucked himself up. I admire the balls it took for him to take the risk.) The blue hair was really striking with his green eyes. He was dressed as Ikuto Tsukiyomi from the old anime *Shugo Chara*, which had recently been adapted for immersive Cyberspace. The other two boys, namely Kevin and Jim, who were dressed up as Replicants from *Blade Runner*, made fun of him. I suspected that the hidden subtext of this might have been that, unlike them, and most of the other boys in our grade, Daren might have already started going through puberty. Besides his growth spurt, I noted that his voice was cracking a bit.

At some point, about halfway through the night, Daren had enough of their deprecating wisecracks and stormed off with the intention of going home. I followed him into the elevator and, whereas he was going to press the button for the lobby, I commanded the car to take us up to the floor beneath mine — the one under the Penthouse. (I didn't want to go straight to the roof because the doorman watching the cameras might get suspicious. This way he could just assume that our trick-or-treating party had broken into two groups.) Once we got out of the elevator, Daren who was silently surprised followed me to the stairs and then some ways up them, past the two floors of my apartment, and up to the access door to the roof. I wasn't supposed to have the override code for the optical scanner, but I did. After all, I was Dick Avalon's daughter. He built the fucking thing.

When we came out into the crisp fall air, we were immediately met with that vista of the skyline of the dark and decaying skyscrapers of Manhattan in the distance, silhouetted in the moonlight that also illumined the crests of the counter-currents between the Hudson River and old New York Harbor. Against the backdrop of the night, the blue in Daren's hair looked almost florescent in this light.

"Forget those jackasses," I said. "They're just jealous of you, Daren." He looked at me a bit wide-eyed with his head slightly downcast. "*Jealous* of me? For what, Dana?" I reached my hand up high to put my fingers on the top of his head. (He was a lot taller than me.) "For the fact that you're growing up much faster than them." Daren shrugged and looked a little embarrassed. If it wasn't so dark, I might have noticed him blush.

"Hey, I *like* you, you know," I said as I nudged him on the shoulder. "You're different from them. From all of the other boys." Daren looked at me somewhat skeptically, mostly out of insecurity. "Really? *How* am I different? I like you *too*, Dana. I mean… *you* really *are* different — from *everyone*. Isn't that *hard* for you?" Now I was looking up into his eyes, and he mustered the confidence to look straight down into mine.

"Yeah. Actually, you have no idea. I mean about the girls — they're especially horrible. I mean if you think the boys are bad…" Daren looked away shyly, casting his gaze down off the edge of the building and onto the flowing water in the span between the cliffside beneath us and the sunken city of Manhattan. "I… uh, yeah… I've heard some of the things they say about you… I'm sorry. They *are* a bunch of airhead *bitches*." My eyes widened when he said this, and I suppose now I was the one blushing. "What have you heard?" I blurted out. "Uh… you know, um… it's stupid," he muttered, swallowing his words. After a moment's awkward silence, our eyes locked again. I decided to dig myself out of undeserved shame with brazenness. Hell, it was Halloween after all — right?

"Do you want to know if they're telling the truth?" Daren couldn't believe his ears. "What?" he asked, looking confused. "Those lying bitches, do you want to know if they're telling the truth about *one* thing?" I almost started feeling bad for him when he came back with, "Uh… about what?" He knew full well what I was talking about, but maybe he just couldn't process how brazen I was being. I looked back at him mischievously, even naughtily, as I added, "*You know*, that *thing* they say." Although my heart was beating fast and my stomach was starting to knot from nervousness, at the same time I could feel my clit becoming totally engorged. "You mean that you're a *lesbian*? *Who cares* if you like girls, Dana." While looking down at myself, I replied, "I *hate* girls. …Well, *those* girls, anyhow. *No*. I meant the *other* thing they say." I think I heard him swallow hard. "*So*, do you want to know or *not*?" I chuckled nervously as I looked back up at Daren with what must have been both an impishly silly and a positively diabolical gaze. My eyebrow arched invitingly as I said, "I'll show you *mine*, if you show me *yours*."

For a minute I thought that he might run away, and then become my biggest problem at school yet. Then he stopped looking like a deer caught in headlights. "I'm sorry. Did you want me to kiss you first?" I asked in a way that was at once intended to be both disarming and taunting. After lowering his head for a moment, he raised it enough to meet my gaze as a grin started to break across his face and he nervously ran his fingers through his blue hair in a lame attempt to "be cool" about what was about to happen. "You first," he said. "Fine." I dropped the brim of my conical witch's hat that I had been holding, letting it fall onto the stone rooftop pavers, so that I could pull my dress up.

Within half an hour we were run off the roof by the building's security. It's not like I even had any tits for him to grope, so what else were we going to do? I guess I could have kissed him. I *did* kiss him when I caught Daren alone in the stairway at school the next day. It was a hell of a Monday morning after a night like that. My teachers noticed that I could hardly focus during my classes. I was especially on edge all morning, until I got a chance to be alone with him for a few moments. That was the beginning of a months-long "friendship."

The turning point of that rapport came on the Sunday morning after my twelfth birthday. It was January 24, 2089. My party went pretty late into the night. I got to have three boys and two girls come over, so we were three and three. In the several months since Daren was assumed to be my "boyfriend," Kevin and Jim had stopped picking on him so much. So, the three of them were there together, and my mother was very pleased to see that I had become friendly with two of the girls in my grade who weren't part of the pack of bitches that were always on my case. (Actually, truth be told, they had also toned it down a bit once the gossip got around that I was dating Daren. At least they stopped calling me a "lesbo.") Anyway, the two girls were Cynthia and Laura.

I was a little annoyed at Kevin and Jim because they kept trying to talk to my dad, who humored them by taking them on a tour of the restricted basement levels of our building. The area that connects, through hidden tunnels, to the subterranean maglev train lines of the metropolitan transportation system. I mean, I understood that he was a celebrity and all, and they probably thought it was pretty cool to interact with him when they came over to my place. At least they didn't dare call him "Dick." I've never seen those two punks be so respectful to anyone. "Mr. Avalon, sir," they kept saying. It was actually a bit sickening.

When they went downstairs to see what I had seen, and where I had roamed, many times during my childhood, Daren and the girls stayed upstairs at the party. The whole living room and my bedroom were decorated with silvery streamers and glow-in-the-dark balloons of every florescent and iridescent color. Real ones, not just AR projections for smart contacts. That was rare these days. My father had them delivered from a retro party store. My mother was busy in the pantry showing Laura how the robot that works in our kitchen (the same one who cleans our house) had "baked" the birthday cake. It was a huge, layered cake in the shape of an Atlantean pyramid, with smart frosting that would move around to make different designs of serpents and stuff in the "stonework" of the pyramid. The "candles" were torches set into the uppermost platform of the structure.

Anyway, while my mother was distracted, and my father was downstairs with the other two boys, I got to be alone with Daren and Cynthia for a while in my bedroom. I was showing them a few of my latest drawings, as well as some of the research material about Satan and witchcraft that I had brought back to the city with me from our country home in the Catskills. Daren had seen me draw before, but the content of these particular sketches seemed to really creep him out. So did the books that I was reading. For example, *La Sorcière* ("The Witch," 1862) by Jules Michelet, which argued that the witches who were burned at the stake in wave after wave of persecutions over the centuries were in many cases really women with occult power.

I asked Daren why this was hard to believe when a similar witch hunt had essentially broken out much closer to our own time, back in the 2040s, as mainstream science was forced to accept parapsychological phenomena and people began to train latent abilities that had previously been derisively branded as "paranormal." The mass hysteria that broke out then, and the strain it put on an already unraveling legal system, was one of the major factors that led to the terminal collapse of the modern world over the following couple of decades. Of course, the "Arrival" of the "Olympian" Nordics in 2048 didn't help, since the whole discourse of these paternalistic "Ancestors" dramatically strengthened the hand of the Traditionalists, who wanted this witch hunt to end with a prohibition on all "occult" practices that weren't circumscribed within some form of institutionalized (and always patriarchal) Orthodoxy.

In any case, Daren seemed to be scared by the idea that the earlier witch hunts were essentially precursors of the very same social phenomenon that was so much closer to our own time, and that played a large part in the demise of progressive civilization outside of Greater Gotham. He wanted to believe the liberal and secular myth that these women were persecuted simply because they were social pariahs for much more mundane reasons, like non-conformity to expected gender roles.

As for my latest drawings, they were of space amazons — you know, women warriors in space-faring armor — cutting down the Olympian overlords together with the Trad masses that follow them and feeding these "people" to Reptilians. In some of the sketches, I had depicted the amazons naked and astride the Reptilians as part of a hybridization program. I'd also drawn a few of the resultant hybrids. The scenes were from Jorjani's novella *Artemis Unveiled*. But Daren hadn't read that, and he was disturbed at the thought that I came up with these images myself, and I could see he was more than a bit taken aback by the violent savagery of the wrath in them.

Not Cynthia. She seemed fascinated both by my drawings and by what I was explaining about the history of witchcraft and its persecution as I showed off the most recent additions to my occult library. Cynthia was really into art history and music. She hadn't been privy to the bullying I endured in the locker room because she wasn't on the swim team or any other sports teams. Instead, she took music and dance classes as her electives. I had already been over to her place a couple of times and found that her equivalent to my occult library was a collection of art books. That is extremely rare — for someone to actually collect *physical* books with pictures of paintings and photographs in them. But her parents were art dealers who ran the biggest gallery in Gotham. They specialized in pieces salvaged from the great museums of Manhattan.

Cynthia was particularly interested in my training to be a diver because of this. Adept divers are used to find and retrieve sculptures and other non-perishable artworks from deep dive sites like the old Metropolitan Museum of Art, the Museum of Modern Art, the Whitney, and the Guggenheim. Her parents tried a bit too hard to befriend mine because my father's company, the Avalon Corporation, has special access to the restricted area of Manhattan. As I said earlier, my mother and father used this access to study the classic Deco and Modernist structures of Old New York, with a view to incorporating their styles into retro architectural designs for Gotham. But they would also afford deep dive access to art scavengers. Cynthia wanted to learn diving too. But between her dance and music classes she had enough on her plate. She was most interested in music from the 1970s and 1980s, as well as some techno from the '90s. She liked the darker stuff from this era. The Doors, King Crimson, Blue Oyster Cult, Depeche Mode, Massive Attack, and so forth. That was just the kind of music that I also loved.

Now, to go back to what I was recounting regarding the disaster that took place at our Hunter Mountain chalet in the spring of 2089; Daren and I had drifted apart over the past several months, and Cynthia was by that time fast becoming my closest friend and confidant. On the first night that she slept over at our chalet, Friday night, I showed her my occult library. Obviously, she could also see all the Satanic and witchy posters plastered on the walls of my bedroom, and the 3-d printed sculptures lining my bookcases and desk. With her penchant for art history, she loved it all. Her own room, back in the city, had reproductions of surrealist and futurist paintings all over the walls. Mostly Remedios Varo, Leonor Fini, Max Ernst, and Giacomo Balla. It's one of the reasons the other girls thought she was weird. Not your average twelve-year old's bedroom. (Her birthday was in February. She's a Pisces. My present to her was a book of Rosaleen Norton's artwork.) After we said goodnight to my parents, whose room was far away from mine — in the opposite wing of the chalet — across the atrium, Cynthia and I stayed up for a while talking about the Templar legend of the expedition led by Altomara, whose ashes, I explained to her, were buried on the mountain that could be seen right out my window.

"Will you take me there?" she asked, eager to see the cave with the petroglyphs. "The snow is still pretty deep around there, but we could try. It's on the Devil's Path, pretty far from the skiing trails. We'd have to pretend to be skiing somewhere my parents think is safe, then hike there and back as fast as possible." Cynthia looked at me with wide-eyed excitement, as she said, "Do you really think we could get away with it?" I thought introspectively for a moment, then nodded affirmatively. "Yeah, you're as nimble as I am, and you're fast too." She smiled and said, "Thanks." I added, "People don't think of dancers as strong, but they're so wrong. I've watched you practice your routines. They take as much strength as a gymnast has." Then I felt for the muscles in her calves and thighs. "Damn, your muscles are as big as mine." She said, "Let's see," as she pulled her pajama pants off.

I followed hesitantly, since we had both taken our panties off when we changed for bed, and Cynthia hadn't seen me naked yet. What I mean is that she hadn't seen what the girls in the locker room showers made fun of me for. I tried to hide it at first by leaning forward and tightly closing my thighs. But that only made my clit start to get hard. When Cynthia began feeling up the muscles in my leg, as I was gripping hers, I relented and sat with my thighs as open as hers were. She just kept feeling my muscles. Even though her labia were so tight that you couldn't see her clit at all, she either wasn't taken aback by my little monstrosity or she didn't want to embarrass me over it.

Instead, she impishly asked, "What about your arm muscles?" We pulled our pajama tops off over our heads, so that we were both sitting on her sleeping bag completely naked. My nipples had just started to bud a bit over the past few months, such that they'd become extremely sensitive. I still had no tits to speak of, though. Cynthia wasn't quite as flat-chested as me. Her breasts were just barely beginning to form, but her nipples were a lot smaller than mine. Actually, mine were getting pretty puffy. This she let herself notice as she was feeling the muscles in my flexed arm. She whispered, "Have you had your period yet?" I answered, "No, have you?" "Actually, yeah, it just happened a couple of weeks ago — *in dance class* of all times. It was *so* embarrassing. I had to run out when the other girls noticed *before I did*, and it ruined my leotard."

Cynthia's eyes were glowing in the light of the little fireplace that was still ablaze, keeping our bare bodies warm enough to be comfortable on this cold night. The moonlit snow on my room's terrace was just beginning to thaw. I smiled at her, and she smiled back. "*Yeah*, I guess that *would* be embarrassing, but it couldn't be worse than what I go through in the locker room on a regular basis." Cynthia looked at me quizzically. "What do you mean? *Why?*" "Haven't you heard?" I asked pointedly, wondering if she could possibly be clueless about what all those gossips bantered about me, even in the cafeteria. "Now that you mention it, I guess I did hear them talking shit once — about how you're a lesbian, but that was before you started going out with Daren." "I'm not going out with Daren anymore," I said. "But, anyway, I meant the other thing." "What other thing?" she asked, apparently sincerely. I looked down at my clit.

Cynthia burst out laughing, then caught herself and apologized for being insensitive. "I'm sorry. You know they probably just *envy* you.

I'll admit that *looking at that*, I *certainly* envy you." My face must have turned bright red because I felt how hot my cheeks got and it wasn't from the fireplace. I had to remind myself that I was dealing with a girl who was into Surrealism and had pulled out her well-hidden copy of Georges Bataille's *Story of the Eye* when I was in her bedroom last week. "Really, Dana, you shouldn't be embarrassed. You're gonna have a lot more fun with that than those cunts will ever be capable of. I bet half of them will wind up frigid."

We were already sitting very close to each other, but I leaned in to the point where our noses touched, and she could feel the heat of my cheek as it brushed past hers on my way to kissing her shoulder blade. I kept my head on her shoulder for an uncomfortably long moment, too shy to look her in the eyes again just yet. Then, as if she could discern what I felt, Cynthia put her arms around me, with one hand bracing me and the fingers of the other stroking the back of my neck and then running through my wavy brown hair. When I lifted my head and looked into her face again, she ran her fingertip along one of my eyebrows as she said, "I love how this one arches up a bit higher than the other one. It brings out the regal aspect of your personality."

The fire was starting to die down, and I didn't want us to get cold, nor was I ready to put my pajamas back on, so I got up and grabbed the black iron stoker. I gave the glowing logs a few hard pokes, until the embers flared up into full blaze again. When I turned around, I saw that Cynthia's head was tilted back and she was looking up at my body with the kind of languorous gaze that said she'd lost herself. Instead of sitting down, I came right up to her and gently wrapped my hands around the back of her head, digging my fingers into her short curly hair to draw her face into the warmth between my thighs.

Before either of us knew it, her tongue was slipping between my lips, and she was sucking softly on my clit. My legs started to go weak, and I came back down onto the sleeping bag with her. Cynthia was super flexible and so she bent into the perfect posture for us to go down on each other at the same time, 69-style, or you could say, like the astrological symbol of the Pisces fish. Soon enough, we were writhing together like electric eels. I'd love to have been able to see the fire's play of light and shadow on the trembling muscles of our bodies. We came almost at the same time. Finally, I brought Cynthia into my bed with me, and we kissed until we fell asleep with our fingers in each other's hair.

We woke up early the next morning because I had forgotten to close the blinds, so the rising sun streamed in through the glass of the terrace doors. We remarked to each other that it was probably a good thing, because we were still naked in my bed together and the last thing that we wanted was to be caught like that by my mother barging in to tell us that breakfast was ready. (Little did we know what was going to happen before the weekend was over.) I started up the fireplace for us. I always loved the smell of burning logs in the morning. I had my own bathroom, so Cynthia and I took a shower *together*. I was relieved that she was totally unashamed about what had happened the night before. That was abundantly obvious from how gleefully she lathered my body with the soap. I squealed when she slipped her soapy fingers into my butt crack. She jokingly grumbled, in a feigned demonic tone of voice, "Turn around so that I can sodomize you!" I shrieked and shook my head. Then we both laughed.

After we dried off and brushed our teeth together, we finally slipped the pajamas that were strewn on her sleeping bag back on, so that we could pretend to have been good little girls. Cynthia made it look like she'd actually slept in her sleeping bag. Then, while we waited for my parents to wake up, I jotted down this poem that our night together had inspired, and I read it aloud to Cynthia, who sat there cross-legged and biting on her fingertips:

Together they stand, in sisterhood and might,
Casting away the darkness, igniting the light.

Their souls aflame, their spirits unbound,
They reclaim their voices, with a vibrant sound.

In orgiastic revelry, they celebrate,
Their bodies intertwine, a symphony innate.
In the temple of pleasure, they find release,
An anthem of ecstasy, where judgments cease.

In this anarchic fusion, their desires entwine,
Unveiling truths that have been confined.
In the union of women, their strength is found,
A revolution of love, profound and unbound.

A little past 9 am, about two hours after we woke up, I heard my mother coming down the hallway. In her typically intrusive fashion, she creaked open my door *before* knocking on it. Breakfast was ready, she said. We had bacon and eggs to fortify us for what was supposed to be a day of skiing on Hunter Mountain. Little did my parents know what we were planning to do. I felt rather mischievous staring straight into my father's face and telling him what slopes we planned to ski. Twenty years my mother's senior, he was getting old enough that if he would ski at all, it would be a few leisurely runs in the afternoon. My mother promised to leave me and Cynthia to ourselves around lunch time, after making sure that we got off to a good start in the morning. She was worried that, expert skier that I already was, I would run Cynthia ragged on the slopes.

We were on the mountain by 10:30 am. After seeing Cynthia keep up with me on Hellgate and Racer's Edge, my mother felt confident to leave us alone for the afternoon. She just made me promise not to take Cynthia to K-27 or Hunter West. Since we had no intention of spending the afternoon skiing, that was an easy promise to make. It was around 12:30 when, deciding to skip lunch and make the most out of the little time we had, Cynthia and I snuck back to our locker, making sure not to run into my mother, and changed out of our ski boots into regular snow boots. We parked our skis on the racks in front of the old Hunter lodge, but we took our ski poles with us. Then, much to the chagrin of the lift attendant, who let it slide only because he recognized me as Dick Avalon's daughter, Cynthia and I got on one of the ski lifts without skis on. By 1 pm we were on top of the trail that was closest to the Devil's Path. I made sure that no one noticed it when we headed out of bounds and into the woods.

The hike to the cave was arduous and took well over an hour. I was worried that we wouldn't make it back to our chalet by the time the ski runs closed for the day. But I tried to put this out of my mind as I held Cynthia's hand and guided her into the cave where Altomara's ashes had been buried. Having brought a small flashlight with me in my ski jacket, I used it to show her the petroglyphs on the cave ceiling. She was wide-eyed with wonder. We didn't have long to linger there, but what little time we spent in the cave was positively magical. The snow was starting to melt over the mouth of the cave, with a steady stream of drops falling through the faint mist that extended into the forest. Cynthia and I stood face to face for a bit, right under the petroglyph carving, drinking the desire from each other's mouths.

Then we headed back to the marked ski trails. We made it just in time before the lifts closed, and I prevailed upon another attendant to let us ride down the lift without skis on. By the time we approached the ski lodge, my mother was calling on my wrist phone to find out where the hell we were. I told her that we were heading back home. She asked if she should come pick us up in the hover car, but I said that we'd walk back and be home in time for dinner. We were.

I should have known that things were going to go awry when my mother looked at us suspiciously while we dug into the wild boar, trying to stuff our mouths so as to be as unresponsive as possible in the face of her questions about what slopes we had skied. After dinner, while my mother wasn't looking, and we were sitting with my father in the main living room around its central fireplace, my father offered us a bit of cognac. Probably contrary to his intention, that gave me the idea of raiding his liquor cabinet that night, while he and my mother slept.

It was after midnight, and I was really quiet as I snuck a little bottle of brandy that I didn't think he'd miss back up to my room. Cynthia was sitting in front of the fireplace, waiting for me eagerly. As we drank the brandy from shot glasses, we rubbed heads and kissed in silence for a while. "Thank you for taking me to the cave with you, Dana. I have some sense of what that place means to you." I smiled back at her and said, "Now if only we could find the ruins of the Temple of the Goddess. I'd love to be able to take you *there*." That's when I told her about my experience with the "witch," including how my knees were scraped when I woke up from this "dream" of being initiated in that narrow tunnel that led from the stone vagina into the Kurgan-like womb of the long-lost temple.

Cynthia listened very attentively and then met my eyes with a look of profound vulnerability and trust. "I want you to initiate *me*, Dana." I ran my fingers through her curls, asking her with my eyes if she'd elaborate. She took my fingers into her hand and placed them between her thighs. "I want you inside me, before any man. I want you to open me up to my hidden depths." Then she kissed my fingertips, noticing how boyishly and closely trimmed my fingernails were. "Will you do it for me, Dana?"

"We'll do it for each other, Cynthia." I got up and pulled my pajamas off. She did the same. Then, before we slipped into my bed together, I had the presence of mind to grab a black towel from my bathroom and throw it under us. Before long, drunk on brandy, with the fire blazing in the background, we were devouring each other like savage animals. When we finally came up for air, our hands and faces were stained in each other's blood. Especially our fingers and around our mouths, chins, and noses. We looked like a couple of vampires.

The fucked-up thing is that we were so drunk that we fell asleep together looking like that. What is worse is that on account of the hangover the next morning, the first in my life (and surely in hers), I didn't hear my mother coming down the hallway or even creaking open my door. See, I *had* closed the blinds that night, so the sun didn't wake us up either. But my mother didn't need sunlight to see our naked bodies sprawled on my bed together, with our faces covered in each other's dried blood. I am glad that I didn't see her expression, although I can't seem to stop imagining what it must have looked like. Her slamming the door to my room shut is what woke me and Cynthia up. The traumatic shock was so severe that it took until we were under the shower water for us to fully process what had just happened. It was also in the shower that the two of us realized that we had left teeth marks on each other's bodies, especially around each other's necks and thighs.

A lesser girl might have died of shame to ever look at me again after that, and over the course of the most silent and awkward breakfast in my life, I was terribly anxious about the possibility that I might lose Cynthia over this. But when my mother left the house that morning, with great haste, supposedly to get in some ski runs before we had to head back to the city in the late afternoon, and we were left with my father, who clearly had been told, and who had the grace to slink off to his study without trying too hard to make polite conversation, Cynthia and I got to be alone again.

We went up into the woods behind the house. From the way she embraced me, and wouldn't let me go, kissing me all over my head and cheeks and neck, and then, most tellingly, kissing my fingers, I knew that we were going to be together for a long time. She was going to close ranks with me against both of our parents, mine and hers, assuming that my mother would tell her parents in what state she had found us. Although I doubted that, since my mother was the type who would cover up whatever might call her own responsibility into question. Besides, our parents already had a business relationship. The calculating bitch would factor that in too.

The breaking point in my tense relationship with my mother finally came when, like all young adults in the movement, I underwent the past life regression sessions that were expected of anyone between the ages of 18 and 22. The therapist and attendants involved in my regression hypnosis sessions violated their confidentiality oaths by gossiping about the content of the memories that had been unlocked from my subconscious. Rumors spread like wildfire, and scandal engulfed the "Avalon" name over my father's fresh corpse. Dana Avalon, it was said, claims to remember having been Jason Reza Jorjani — the movement's martyred founder. This, in turn, meant that she was also claiming to have been a number of other figures of historical significance, which were believed to be previous incarnations of Jorjani.

I will never forget the first of my past life regression sessions, at the age of 18. When I came back to my room that evening, I took a long hard look at myself in the mirror. Then, for the first time, I understood in much more tangible terms what Ian Stevenson had been on about when he pointed to morphological resonance across lifetimes. My face looks more than a little like Jason's countenance as I had seen it in historical photographs of him as a young man. My eyes are the same amber-tinged hazel color, and one of my eyebrows arches almost as high above the other as his did. I do have slight dimples to the sides of my mouth, which he didn't. My undyed hair is the same shade of brown as Jorjani's and even its natural texture is alike, just wavier as his would have been had it grown out longer.

I found the resemblance to be quite striking — accounting for the basic difference between typically male and female bone structure. My shoulders are actually broader than Jason's. (I guess I'd have made a better rugby player.) Overall, I have a somewhat androgynous look — but in a sleekly pretty way, not at all butch. I noticed that even my somewhat boyish body is similar to his at that time in his life when he was thinnest and most fit. I am somewhat more curvaceous — but not nearly as much as you would expect for a girl. I have really tiny tits — albeit with huge and aggravatingly excitable nipples, which, to-gether with my hypertrophied clitoris, became the butt of many cruel jokes made by mean-spirited girls in the school locker room (especially after I came out as more interested in girls than guys).

I'll never forget the first time that this happened. We were getting changed out of our wet swimsuits, and a whole pack of these hyenas were jeering at me. I guess, of all things, I shouldn't call them "hyenas" though, because female hyenas are notorious for having clitorises that are so large, they can be mistaken for male genitalia, and what these little bitches were mocking and shaming me for was the size of my clitoris. Even when I was little, it didn't escape my notice that it was a bit bigger than those of the other girls, which you really couldn't see at all. But ever since that night I "dreamt" of the witch, my already protruding nub grew into something more prodigious. It's especially noticeable if I'm stimulated or aroused by something, like I guess I must have been when we were stripping our wet swimsuits off in the air conditioning of the locker room. By the time I was under the shower water, almost all the other girls had hysterically cleared out from under the shower heads and were pointing and leering lewdly. A few of the grade A bitches accused me of getting turned on by looking at their naked bodies. Others rushed to wrap towels around themselves.

By the time the dismissal bell rang, I decided that instead of endur-ing more abuse on the school bus ride back home I would stroll the full length of the avenue that stretches all the way up to a promenade on the Palisades where you can look over the cliffs down onto the waves of the Atlantic Ocean beating against the rotting skyscrapers of Manhattan. The ones that were taller than thirty stories and formed the last vestiges of that majestic skyline. I knew that I would catch hell from my mother when I got home late, and I did. But I wouldn't trade the sight of that shattered skyline at sunset for anything. I've always felt as if I was out of my element, and *that* was my city. The one washed by the waves.

CHAPTER 12

THE FALL OF GOTHAM

The skyscrapers of Gotham were so massive that they looked like slabs of black granite as they exploded into a twilight cut through by lethal neon laser beams. That was the impression I had every time that the vibrations shook me out of the trance, and I slipped back into this time and place long enough for my gaze to fix itself on the view from the horizontal window cut out of this colossal bunker of a building. The architectural drafts of Hugh Ferriss had been a major inspiration for the design of our new city that stands atop the Palisades, from Englewood Cliffs all the way up into the Hudson Highlands, overlooking the storm-battered towers of Manhattan as they rise from out of the waves of the Atlantic Ocean.

These towers, growing like crystals from the cliffs and hillsides, seamlessly fused Neo-Deco with Brutalist and Modernist elements in a self-conscious embrace and synthesis of those features of New York's architectural heritage that stood most defiantly against the reimposition of Tradition in the world. Now the city's defense perimeter, which once extended for a couple of hundred miles in every direction, had been breached by soaring armadas of sleek Olympian attack ships, and these pillars of defiance were being brought down, one by one. I could hear a steady cascade of shattered glass pouring onto the empty streets. Empty because the city had already been almost completely evacuated.

A week ago, when the first Olympian stealth scouts were sighted inside the defense perimeter at night, Gotham's last holdouts began to reluctantly pack into transport ships headed for the Prometheist colonies carved out of large asteroids in the belt between Mars and Jupiter, where finding them would be like searching for a needle in a haystack. There, they were undoubtedly welcomed as tragically defeated heroes by off-world Prometheists who saw Gotham — the only living metropolis left on Earth — as the last bastion of terrestrial resistance against the so-called "Golden Dawn" of Tradition and the ultimate symbolic repudiation of the Olympian Imperium. As the transport ships dove beneath the waves of the Atlantic Ocean and illuminated the submerged streets of Manhattan in their searchlights, the fugitive Gothamites must have identified with the last denizens of Atlantis.

The attendant adjusted the electrodes fastened to my forehead as I focused on the commands of her hypnotic voice, and I went under again as my floating body relaxed back into the cathedral darkness of the Regression Room. It was an uncannily seamless transition to being in the womb, until I felt the umbilical cord strangling my neck like a noose. In retrospect, I wonder why the imminence of death did not abruptly catapult me back here — into the Gotham of the fall of 2112. Instead, I found myself floating high above Booth Memorial Hospital on a crisp late winter day in February of 1981, looking in the direction of the Terrace on the Park and the old World's Fair grounds in Flushing Meadows. Then, I focused downwards to see my father — or the man who would become my father — walk out of the hospital for a smoke, as my would-be mother entered her twentieth hour of labor.

This was the last of my regression sessions. That was the usual protocol, to end with one's birth in a previous life. But these sessions were much more intensively immersive than the standard past life regressions that every Prometheist went through in young adulthood. I had gone through that before, not without causing a scandal that subjected me to nearly shattering stress. This second round of regressions, which was drawing to a close, was intended to prepare me to operationally take charge of the mission that I had already initiated. My task was to flip from past life recall to an out-of-body experience of the world of my previous incarnation, astral projecting from out of static memories into a dynamic experience and exploration of New York City in the 1980s. This was preparation for a plan to actually time travel to our city in that era.

As the reincarnation of the founder of the Prometheist movement, I had grimly arrived at a fateful decision a few years ago. Before the close of the first decade of the 22nd century, it had become clear to me that the battle against the Olympian Imperium was lost in the present and that the only way to win the war would be in the past. Of course, I kept this information strictly classified, sharing it only with a small think tank, whose members unfortunately confirmed my analysis, and an elite cadre of the most superbly trained time travelers in the Prometheist Resistance. According to our analytical models and projections, the decade of the 1980s was the last possible historical moment wherein an alteration in the chain of events could probably avert something like the presently unfolding defeat of Prometheism by the tyrannical forces of Tradition. Specifically, we determined that the collapse of the Soviet Union from 1989–1991 was the fulcrum that, should it be prevented, could tip world history back into an ascendant trajectory for long enough to build a viable Prometheist Resistance against the mid-21st century Olympian re-conquest of Earth.

So, I developed an elaborate plan for a series of key alterations in the chain of events that would take place in the course of the 1980s. In order to provide a resource base for this operation, the elite cadre of Prometheist time travelers was deployed as a spearhead. I had them sent back to 1977, giving them several years of lead time to amass resources by building a pharmaceutical company on Long Island that would market at least a dozen breakthrough drugs whose chemical formulas I had sent back in time with them. These were phenomenally marketable drugs which, on our timeline, would not be invented until the 1990s or the early years of the 21st century. They were trained to set up insider trading as well, so as to make a secondary profit on the skyrocketing stock of the publicly traded drug company. I also set them to work forging false documentation to construct my supposed biography as a corporate executive woman of the late 20th century, a task for the accomplishment of which they drew extensively from the Soviet KGB playbook of placing deep cover spies in foreign countries, such as the United States.

My plan is to join them in 1980, with Manhattan as the international hub for my attempt to reshape the timeline. Of course, what this means is that the original timeline will be overwritten. The world that I have known in this lifetime as Dana Avalon, and for that matter much of my immediately preceding incarnation as I lived it, would melt into non-existence — except for in the personal memories of the time travelers sent on this mission. It is my prerogative to make the determination that the situation is so hopelessly desperate that such drastic measures are called for. The responsibility rests on my broad shoulders alone because I have Phenomenal Authorization.

My first session in a Regression Room was unforgettable. I was already familiar with the procedure, in theory, but nothing can really prepare you for the experience of surrendering your naked body to the saltwater of the tank in the middle of the dark room, with a ceiling so high that it makes your heart sink to look up into its pitch blackness.

As the psychoactive drugs were administered through water-resistant adhesive patches, which also fastened the pulsed neural recalibration electrodes to my forehead, the therapist guided me, with her hypnotic voice, into a vivid visualization of what my subconscious knew to be the most traumatically significant event in my immediately preceding incarnation. That was the established method. Not to begin with one's death, even if it was a traumatic or violent one (as I eventually discovered that mine had been), but to zero in on the single most significant nexus and trace its branches of longer-term effects and root causes out from there, like tracing the dendrites in neurons as they light up during a brain scan.

The first thing that appeared from out of the darkness while I floated in the Regression Room was the ethereal image of a jellyfish, glowing with shades of blue light. Specifically, it appeared to be a huge man o' war. At first, it was floating with its tentacles reaching down toward my head and its bell just under the ceiling, giving me the impression that I was under water.

Jellyfish predate the dinosaurs by hundreds of millions of years, and they may outlive man. A jellyfish can lay up to 45,000 eggs in a single night. The cells of the immortal jellyfish change identity under stress, shedding tentacles and transforming into a polyp that perfectly clones the creature. Jellyfish are thriving under the same ecological stresses that threaten the survival of other animals in Earth's oceans. In fact, research has revealed that they are the dark energy of the Oceans.

Wind and tides (influenced by the Moon) cannot account for the amount of energy required for the degree of water-mixing that we observe. Bioengineers have used fluorescent dyes and underwater cameras to film the interaction between fluid and the pressure differentials in front of and behind the body of a jellyfish. What they found is that when the fluid moves from the high-pressure field in front of the jellyfish to the low-pressure field behind it, the water is trapped at the rear end of the jellyfish and moves along with it. On a large enough scale, significant oceanic turbulence and water-mixing is caused by the interaction between this displaced water and the crosscurrents that eventually dislodge it. In other words, what appear to be miniscule forces that one imagines would be absorbed into the wind and tidal friction of the seas are actually capable of stirring up storms and possibly even climate change on a planetary level. It is relevant in this regard that some jellyfish are even longer than a blue whale, the largest surviving mammal on Earth.

Despite lacking a brain and spinal cord, the neural net around the inner margin of the jellyfish "bell" allows it to form images and see color through its 24 eyes, some of which are on stalks and capable of peering above the water. It is the only creature with a 360° field of vision. Jellyfish also afford us the ability to illuminate the invisible. The gene for the Green Florescent Protein (GFP) that makes them glow in the dark when they are agitated was isolated and used to develop florescent tracers for research on the progression of Alzheimer's disease and cancer.

They are deadly, and you usually cannot see them surrounding you. Harpoon-like cells lining the bell deliver their venom with a pressure hundreds of times stronger than the punch of a professional boxer. While some jellyfish stings only tingle, others can kill a person in under five minutes or leave their victim badly disfigured.

When the spectral jellyfish floating above me in the Regression Room wrapped its tentacles around my brain and body, a flood of memories came back to me. It was from a period in the life of Jason Reza Jorjani that extended between 2016 and 2018. I processed these disturbing and convoluted memories for several weeks by writing out extensive notes. The vivid recall, over many regression sessions, was augmented by a treasure trove of Jorjani's correspondences that I secured from a closely guarded archive maintained by loyalists.

Prior to my regression, I had never been afforded the opportunity to go through these. But once rumors of my being the reincarnation of Jason leaked out, one of these esoteric Prometheists who respected the Avalon family name let me go through them at my leisure. During my first year of college at Gotham University, I read and reread my notes based on the past life regressions and reconstructions from reams of Jorjani's private letters, until their basic elements were branded in my mind. Their lines acted as cyphers to bring scenes from my past life into a present recollection that was at least as vivid as reliving incidents from my childhood. I wrote these notes in the voice of Jason, as if I was still him, and I colorfully titled the document "Riding Satan's Ass."

CHAPTER 13

RIDING SATAN'S ASS

Like some accursed lair of the fairy folk, the inside of the majestic building seemed incomprehensibly vaster than the space it took up along the street of this posh neighborhood in London. It had a central atrium *surrounded by numerous libraries*. I do not remember seeing a single other person while we were there, besides the security at the imposing front door. The place reminded me of the Illuminati estate depicted in Stanley Kubrick's *Eyes Wide Shut*. It is in one of the many dimly lit libraries cavernously encircling this mansion's central atrium that I had my first extensive meeting with Frederick Boulder.

Incongruously dressed in a bow-tied shirt and black leather jacket, Frederick Boulder struck me as a lanky, long-limbed man with mischievously wild eyes that darted around intensely to follow the Monarch butterfly of his mind. His closely trimmed, pointy beard made him look a bit like the Devil. There was a third man at the meeting. Frederick had put me in touch with Darius Guppy some months earlier. Unlike Frederick, Darius was a polished letter writer and we kept up a considerable correspondence until I had the pleasure of meeting him in person when he attended my talk at the London Forum a day before we reconvened in this quiet and cavernous mansion.

When Darius walked into the London Forum meeting, I spotted him immediately, and after I made my way through the crowd, we embraced in Persian fashion with kisses on both cheeks. The man certainly stands out. In fact, I would say he is the most handsome man that I've ever met. His mother, Shusha Guppy, is an illustrious Persian singer and writer of Bakhtiari descent. The Bakhtiari are known for their height and robust stature. But it is not just his looks. Darius has an aura about him, penetratingly intelligent but also profoundly charismatic. During my lecture on Heidegger, his eyes were closed in deep concentration. Occasionally he would nod approvingly, with a bit of a smirk. "That was brilliant!" he remarked, as the police burst into the venue at the end of my talk and escorted us out of the building with choppers overhead.

Later that evening, when we were cramped into a sort of safe house and right-wing salon, I noticed that Shahin Nezhad, the leader of the Iranian Renaissance, was looking across the room intently at Darius, who was sitting next to me. Shahin said, "Jason dear, Darius looks awfully familiar. I think I've seen him somewhere before." I replied, "No, you're remembering him from James Bond movies. He looks exactly like Sean Connery playing 007." Shahin's eyes widened in surprise behind those thick bifocals, and, after a bit of stunned silence, he blurted out, "You're right!" Darius smiled. In that charming British accent of his, he said, "I think I'll not comment on that."

It had been the question of Iran's future that made me take Frederick Boulder seriously in the first place. He had contacted me in the summer of 2016, praising *Prometheus and Atlas* to high heaven — or perhaps he was shouting its praises up from the depths of hell. Frederick introduced himself to me as the head of the British branch of the Vril Society — the occult group in which esoteric German aerospace projects had their earliest origins. I found what he was writing to me hard to believe, and his atrocious spelling and poorly punctuated messages did not help me to take him seriously. So, I would rarely respond to him. Then he offered to concretely assist my work with the Iranian Renaissance movement by putting me in touch with Michael Bagley, the President of Jellyfish Inc., which Frederick described as a private security and intelligence agency working with the Trump team to prepare a new United States policy regarding Iran and the Islamic world. I was told that General Michael Flynn clandestinely worked for Jellyfish, and I appreciated Flynn's position on how to deal with the Islamic threat. In fact, one of the close associates of the Iranian Renaissance, Erfan Ghaneifard, had translated Flynn's book into Persian.

I figured that engaging with Bagley would be a way to find out whether Frederick was a crank or whether other things he was telling me might be true. It turned out that Michael's clients mostly consisted of the chief executives of Fortune 500 companies. I first met with him months before the 2016 presidential election and then again in the early days of the new administration. Michael claimed that he would see President Trump on a regular basis, and he introduced me to others with even more access, including Walid Phares, who Michael described as "the shadow Secretary of State." He said that Rex Tillerson was just supposed to be a front man, and that when I spoke to Phares I should assume that I am essentially speaking directly to President Trump. He also explicitly stated that Walid was "Deep State" and had built his reputation in the intelligence community during the Lebanese Civil War.

I met Walid Phares and discussed Iran policy with him. Later on, I wrote him a very substantive letter warning the Trump administration not to go down the pro-Saudi path that it wound up choosing to pursue with respect to regime change in Iran. This was the secret plan that Hillary Clinton had for dividing and conquering Iran, and the main reason that I and so many others within the Iranian Renaissance movement supported Donald Trump was to make sure that it never actually became US foreign policy. The one thing that could turn the largely pro-American Persian people against the United States was American support for a Saudi-led Arab war against Iran.

The hook that Michael reeled me in with was a proposal that I act as a liaison who provides media content produced by the Iranian

Renaissance for Jellyfish to broadcast into the Islamic Republic of Iran from a facility in Croatia. But Frederick and Michael's interest in me was not limited to what we called "the Iran project." Frederick's group was the hidden virtual audience for my October 2016 Identitarian Ideas conference speech in Stockholm, "Occult Science and the Organic State," which secured me the position of Editor-in-Chief of Arktos within a week of having delivered it (so quickly that by the time the video footage was processed, the title appeared next to my name). At a meeting we had in Washington in an annex of the Old Ebbitt Grill, just across the street from the White House, which Michael only half-jokingly described as his "office," Bagley proposed to "take Richard [Spencer] out" and install me as the leader of the Alt-Right.

By then, I had met and befriended Richard Spencer during the infamous NPI 2016 "Hailgate" conference. I naively counter-proposed that Spencer (who I still hadn't gotten to know well enough) was a reasonable guy who would accept direction from above if it meant that, through a figurehead other than himself, he could have access to the President. Steve Bannon was known to be a reader of Arktos books and Michael's plan was to send me into the White House to cultivate a relationship with Bannon, and through him, to influence President Trump.

At the time, my main reason for wanting to have such influence was to help determine Iran policy. Michael claimed to have gotten at least one of my letters on this subject into the hands of the President. I wrote the letter, but it was co-signed by Shahin Nezhad. In it, on behalf of the Iranian Renaissance, I explicitly warned Trump not to pursue a pro-Saudi or generally pro-Arab strategy for regime change in Iran. In retrospect, I suppose that through that letter the President and his policymakers also acquired some fairly substantive intelligence on the outlook, intentions, and capabilities of the Iranian Renaissance movement.

Together with Frederick and Michael, a plan was hammered out to secure my position as the leader of the Alt-Right by creating a corporate structure that unified the major institutions of the movement, in both North America and Europe, bringing Richard Spencer's National Policy Institute think tank together with Daniel Friberg's European Arktos publishing house, and the Red Ice Radio and Television network founded by Henrik Palmgren. A major investment would allow me to become a majority shareholder both in this new Alt-Right Corporation and in its would-be subsidiary, Arktos Media, replacing Daniel Friberg as its CEO. When I expressed concern to Michael about what this plan would mean for my academic career, he replied, "What do you need an academic job for? You've been there and done that. Now it's time for us to put some money in your pocket." When a man who routinely does work on contract for Fortune 500 executives says that, it certainly seems like an assurance that one will not be thrown under the bus. Unless, as I later realized, the whole thing was a set-up.

I was still very far from this realization when, in mid-December of 2016, Richard Spencer visited New York for a few days. His right-hand man, former *Radix* journal editor 'Hannibal Bateman', slept over in my Upper West Side apartment and Richard and I got to spend a lot of time together. Between a business lunch at Persepolis on one day, and a long evening that ended with a Dionysian, intoxicated hours-long conversation in my living room, I seeded into Richard's psyche the idea for a corporatist unification of the major institutions of the Alt-Right movement. But Richard did not know something about this act of inception, which I commemorated by leaving an Easter egg for the future in a picture that I suggested we take in front of a statue of Hermes, the Trickster, on that evening of December 17.

What Richard did not know I disclosed to him about a month later, during a late-night dinner at the Hamilton restaurant in DC. By then we had decided against renting an office in a Manhattan skyscraper, in favor of a more private shared workspace in a townhouse in Alexandria, just outside of Washington, which would also be Richard's apartment. I told him about my backers and that they were going to provide me with a startup capital investment for our proposed business venture as part of a larger black budget project to be implemented by the Trump administration. With the birds of the Hamilton's taxidermy aviary as the only eavesdroppers, I whispered to Richard that this project involved the construction of a vast constellation of "micro-cities" in North Africa and Western Anatolia to contain the flow of migrants from the Islamic world, and to act as resettlement areas for illegal migrants expelled from Europe.

I was fully aware of the catastrophic damage that these migrants were doing to the social fabric of European countries: increasingly frequent acts of terror, molestation of women and children, and the spread of no-go zones where *sharia* law is enforced in ghettos of cities like London, Paris, and Frankfurt. So, I would have had no problem sleeping at night knowing that I was profiting from a project that would relocate these mostly military-aged Muslim men to places where they cannot volunteer to act as a fifth column for the Islamic State (IS). This was especially the case since I had been forced to helplessly witness IS destruction of the irreplaceable Iranian heritage in regions of northern Iraq and Syria that were once cultural centers of the Persian Empire. Not to mention the rape, enslavement, and genocide of the Yezidis.

After listening to my explanation of who my potential backers were, and of what capabilities they had, Richard agreed that granted such an investment would be forthcoming I would be on point. What was especially compelling to him was the promise of engagement, through me, with people inside the White House, such as Steve Bannon. I explained to Richard that my backers suggested that I could do this but that it would not be possible with Richard at the helm. He said, "I get it. All I want is not to be cut out."

The next day, Monday, January 16, 2017, which happened to be Martin Luther King Day, at the then secret HQ on King Street in

Alexandria, with no furniture and Richard's belongings strewn across the upstairs bedroom in open suitcases, we co-founded the Alt-Right Corporation. The other partners had not signed on yet. We called Daniel Friberg and Henrik Palmgren while perched on a windowsill, with nowhere to sit. Rosie Gray's photograph of us for her piece in *The Atlantic* was taken late that afternoon. She's right that the only thing to drink in the kitchen was a half empty bottle of whiskey. Well, half empty by the time she showed up.

I went on to discuss the plan for the capital investment and my leadership of the corporate unification of the Alt-Right with every single core board member of our company, including Arktos CEO Daniel Friberg. Daniel and I even shook on the deal in February of 2017, as captured by a photograph that is really haunting in retrospect. We are in front of a huge sunken ship that was famously looted while it spent years partly exposed in Stockholm's harbor. I used the lead-in to my speech at the Identitarian Ideas IX conference to hint at my central role in forming the Alt-Right Corporation. That policy speech, in February of 2017, just weeks after the formation of the corporation in late January, was supposed to be a prelude to the investment that I was promised would come later the same month.

The startup capital for the Alt-Right Corporation did not come through, as promised, in February. Michael told me that the funds would be available by March. Then Frederick explained to me why there would have to be another delay until May. Allegedly, both Neo-Cons and Neo-Liberals at high levels conspired to ensure that President Trump never authorized the construction of what they considered glorified concentration camps, even though Michael and Frederick assured me that the funding for the "micro-cities" had already been allocated. Another excuse was that there was a sustained campaign to purge the Trump administration of everyone connected to Jellyfish and potentially open to a secret policy dialogue with the Alt-Right. This began, in February, with the dismissal and threatened prosecution of General Michael Flynn, included the ouster of Sebastian Gorka, and ended with the forced resignation of Steve Bannon in August — not coincidentally, the same month that I would leave the Alt-Right.

By then I was already under surveillance. As early as my October 2016 trip to Stockholm, I noticed I was being directly monitored by intelligence agents. One night when I came back to my hotel at 2 am, there was a man dressed in black sitting on a wheeled rotating chair in the hallway a few doors down from my room. Before scribbling some notes on his pad, he gave me a look like he was bored to death, and I was long overdue (the conference had started very late and ended hours later than expected). At first, I thought maybe he was a Swedish secret police agent who was tracking me because during this trip I visited the home of the notorious broadcaster Omid Dana, who is something like the Iranian Alex Jones. In retrospect, I changed my mind, because by the late summer of 2017, almost every time I would make a reservation at a restaurant in Manhattan using my telephone, someone who was all too obviously a spy would show up at the table next to mine. This was so evident, and so disturbing, that some of my friends stopped wanting to be seen with me in public out of a concern that these agents, usually sitting at the bar or at the next table over, would clandestinely photograph us together or record our conversation.

Months before my resignation from the Alt-Right I began writing letters to Frederick warning that I was losing control of my partners and influence over the direction of the corporation. I wrote that I would be forced to take drastic measures if he and Michael allowed me to be humiliated in front of them on account of hollow promises and repeated, false assurances that the obstacles had been cleared and the capital would finally reach us. That never happened before I was defamed in *The New York Times* on September 19th, 2017. I contacted both Frederick and Michael and gave them a final opportunity to do right by me. I would never have been in that pub being surreptitiously recorded by Patrik Hermansson (aka 'Erik Hellberg') if they had not set me up as an Alt-Right leader. Frederick later confessed that, although Hermansson was posing as a far-right student doing a dissertation on the suppression of free speech in academia, and although claiming that this was his cover for infiltration on behalf of an Antifa organization, the "Hope Not Hate" group that Hermansson supposedly worked for is a front for British intelligence.

Why did the promised funding for their plan never materialize? Is it because Michael really ran into trouble selling his North African concentration camps to the Trump administration, especially after Flynn and Bannon were purged? Perhaps motive can be reconstructed from consequences. What was the consequence of the investment not having come through? I became publicly identified as the unifier of the Alt-Right, a business partner of Richard Spencer, without being able to make a living out of it. At the same time, as Frederick and Michael made excuses and renewed their false promises, month after month, I was humiliated in front of my Alt-Right business partners and then sidelined by them. My association with the Alt-Right was also used to tar the reputation of the Iranian Renaissance.

Mr. Hermansson was sent my way by people closely connected with Frederick Boulder. It was Frederick who contacted the coordinators of the London Forum, Jez Turner and Stead Steadman, to set up that talk for me at the Forum on Saturday, February 4th, 2017, where Hermansson first set his sights on me. He also secured an invitation for Shahin Nezhad to give a speech as well. You see, Frederick Boulder co-founded the British New Right. It launched at a gathering with almost thirty people in Central London on January 16th, 2005.

By the time I spoke at the London Forum, twelve years later, Frederick's pedigree was impeccably established in British right-wing circles, including a leadership role in the Center for Anti-Marxist Studies at the London Club. This is remarkable, because in 2004, only a year before founding the British New Right, Frederick was writing letters to fellow "comrades" claiming to be a Communist who supports "the ideas of Stalin, Mao, Hoxha, Lenin." He would close these letters with the phrase, "All things Soviet." Unfortunately, I discovered this only after cutting ties with him.

Frederick was the London office head of Jellyfish Europe Limited, located at 4 Huntington House Street on Saint Paul's Avenue in Willesden Green. Although American journalists have described the founders of Jellyfish as the "sons of Blackwater," and it is true that Michael used to run intelligence operations for Blackwater founder Erik Prince, it seems that Jellyfish was more than the salvaged intelligence directorate of Blackwater. It is also relevant in this regard that at one of our meetings Michael told me that he had a bad falling out with Erik Prince, whose quasi-exile from the United States he considered well deserved.

So, Jellyfish was not, as some had assumed, a direct successor to Blackwater in the way that Xe was. It had another predecessor as well, a European group called g3i that was based in Rome and, at any given time, had 20 to 49 employees. Frederick was the UK representative of the g3i group, which he described as a "security company… with top level projects for oil and intelligence agencies." The company was particularly involved in "offshore" oil projects, which is interesting in light of the water element evoked by Jellyfish. Of course, "Blackwater" also suggests the blackness of oil mixed with the water surrounding offshore platforms — perhaps including platforms operating outside of the jurisdiction of any sovereign nation. From our earliest communications Frederick had emphasized Jellyfish's connections to offshore oil projects. He told me that OilPrice.com is a Jellyfish front.

On April 2nd of 2017, several months before the revolt against the Maduro government in Venezuela, Frederick sent me a nearly $1-billion itemized oil contract and business plan to pass on to Shahin Nezhad, whose day job was as a top-notch engineer at one of the world's largest oil companies. Frederick had confessed to me that his people were planning to overthrow the socialist government of Venezuela and that they needed to get into the oil industry there before doing so. Fortunately, Shahin came back and said that Occidental Petroleum was not capable of the project. This was fortunate because the attempted coup in Venezuela failed, and how curious that President Nicolás Maduro's primary target in successfully resisting his engineered ouster was to go after oil bosses in a graft purge.

Venezuela was not the only failed coup that Jellyfish was involved in. While devouring his favorite Persian food at a lunch we had during one of his Manhattan business trips, Michael hinted to me that Jellyfish was behind the July 2016 Gülenist coup d'état in Turkey. He was exasperated and outraged at President Obama for helping to restore Erdogan to power. Erdogan went on to unleash a bloodbath of reprisals against the coup plotters and every conceivable collaborator. Later on, I learned that Frederick was involved with Fetullah Gülen.

That was not Frederick's only high-level contact in the Islamic world. The Emir of Qatar, Hamad bin Khalifa Al-Thani, was also an associate of his. It is during this Emir's rule from 1995 to 2013 that, due to a drastic engineering expansion of the small emirate's offshore oil and gas industry, Qatar was able to rise from third world status to become the richest country on Earth. Al-Thani brought both the Asian Games and the World Cup to Qatar. He hosted the UN Climate Change Conference in 2012. By 2013 his international investments exceeded $100 billion, including in The Shard, Barclays Bank, Heathrow Airport, Harrods, Paris Saint-Germain F.C., Volkswagen, Siemens and Royal Dutch Shell. The Emir also founded Al Jazeera, the Arab world's most influential media group. He has been linked to the Islamic Republic of Iran and is a supporter of Hamas, which is why his son and successor came under pressure from Saudi Arabia. A man in Frederick's position who has business ties with the Emir of Qatar and deals in billion-dollar offshore oil projects should easily have been able to come through with the $1-million promised investment in the Alt-Right Corporation.

After bringing me to the London Forum, Frederick did not attend
the talk himself. He complained about the Antifa demonstrators who
surrounded the venue. To be fair, the protest was so large that there
were even police helicopters circling the high-rise building, oddly
enough, during my lecture on Heidegger and Technology. However, at
the start of the event, Frederick was actually in the lobby of the conference hotel, and he sent up a certain Kroptin Mehrzad. Mehrzad is well-
known as a leftist in London circles, who takes left-leaning positions
in television interviews. This troubled Shahin and me, as well as our
close associate Aria (Ali) Salehi Pamenari — a member of the board of
trustees of the Iranian Renaissance. That is because we had encountered Kroptin a day or two earlier at an Iranian Renaissance event in
London. He was not there as a sympathetic audience member but as a
person carrying out surveillance, sitting alone in the back of the room
with a disapproving look on his face. Kroptin did the same thing at the
London Forum event where Shahin and I spoke. He came in, checked
things out, reviewed the book stand, and then left grumbling about
how we were a bunch of "Mosleyite Fascists."

What was a leftist like Kroptin doing at either event? Why was he
an associate of Frederick, a scion of the British New Right and someone
seemingly interested in facilitating the aims of the right-wing Iranian
Renaissance? Frederick claimed to have left the conference hotel to
meet Darius and bring him back inside. Darius was coming straight
from the airport. He had flown in from South Africa, first-class, just to
meet me in person. When Darius arrived, he was able to walk straight
past Antifa and police into the hotel, "bold as brass" as he put it, like
any other hotel guest. Frederick refused to go back inside with him,
claiming that Kroptin had told him "it isn't safe." Why was a founder
of the British New Right using someone who is rumored to be an asset
of Scotland Yard to scope a place out? Kroptin also has connections
to the Mojaheddin-e-Khalq Organization, radical left-wing Maoist-
Islamists who are even worse than the Islamic Republic.

Where does the MEK (or MKO) get its money? Tel Aviv and the Israel Lobby in the United States. The Mossad trained the group's operatives to carry out assassinations of nuclear scientists in Iran and clandestinely gather intelligence on Iranian nuclear facilities. Meanwhile, the American Israeli Public Affairs Committee (AIPAC) successfully strong-armed Hillary Clinton's State Department to remove the Mojaheddin from its list of terrorist groups. Elie Wiesel and Alan Dershowitz were among the group's most prominent advocates.

Would it surprise you to learn that Frederick Boulder was also a Zionist? He put me in touch with Avi Churkin, an agent of the Mossad who divides his time between Jerusalem and Moscow and was a key liaison of the State of Israel to the government of South Africa. In a conversation we had late in the spring of 2017, Churkin, who was involved with the "micro-cities" project, nonchalantly mentioned to me that Frederick worked for British intelligence. He did not mean to reveal this. It was in the course of a conversation about something else that Churkin said, as if he assumed that I should already know it, "He's done some pretty impressive work for MI6." I made sure not to react with surprise, but I was deeply disturbed.

British intelligence had been involved in the occult since its inception. After all, Her Majesty's Secret Service was founded during the Renaissance by John Dee, Queen Elizabeth's court magician, who also set up the British Royal Navy. Satanist Aleister Crowley, the self-proclaimed "wickedest man in the world," waged an occult war against the Nazis for MI6. The motto of the secret intelligence service was "Semper Occultus."

At the age of 27, Frederick Boulder had been the director of the Association for the Scientific Study of Anomalous Phenomena located at Hatton Garden in London. It was founded in 1986 and he ran it from 11/27/1993 until 11/21/1994. About a year earlier, at the age of 26, Frederick had become chairman of the Rennes-le-Château research society. The society's activities at the mysterious village were the primary source for the book *The Templar Revelation*. Why did Frederick resign from the Association for the Scientific Study of Anomalous Phenomena only a year after assuming its directorship? He was subjected to investigation by MI6 for his connection to the French far-right and the Priory of Sion secret society at the heart of the mystery of Rennes-le-Château. MI6 suspected him of being involved in a plot to restore the Merovingian dynasty across all of Europe (an obvious danger to the British throne). At that point, he was caught up in this investigation and was probably either sincerely turned or coercively convinced to join British intelligence himself as an infiltrator of various groups with diverse ideological orientations. The only common denominator was that they were the most radical political groups, especially ones that defied clean-cut ideological definitions. They were those groups most threatening to the reigning Establishment.

It would be convenient to claim that my concern for the future of Iran was the only Achilles heel that Frederick aimed for when he set me up with the Alt-Right. But that would be a lie. As I've said, when he first introduced himself to me, it was in his capacity as the head of the London branch of the Vril Society. I would go on to discover, both through conversations with him and my own digging into his background, that the Vril was only one of many occult orders that Frederick belonged to. Just to give a few examples, he was a Freemason, a member of the Double Horizon Lodge of the United Grand Lodge of England, the Group of Thebes, the Osiridean Egyptian Orient, the Universal Grand Lodge of Argentina, and P2. (At one point, he wanted me to set up a New York branch of P2 for him by working together with members of Italians For Trump.) What I learned from Frederick, fairly early on in our communications, was that all of these esoteric societies were connected by an international network that transcended exoteric cultural, religious, and ideological boundaries, and that had been in place not for decades, but for centuries. Those who belonged to it were called "Illuminati."

In *Confessions of an Illuminati*, Leo Zagami came straight out and identified (by his real name) Frederick Boulder, his former associate and close friend, as a fellow member of the Illuminati. On at least a couple of occasions, Frederick told me that he was a member of the Illuminati and in one of these instances his remark suggested that he was recruiting me. Frederick publicly listed his profession as a "freelance librarian." Later, I learned that the term "librarian" has an esoteric meaning. Not long after Adam Weishaupt founded the Order of the Illuminati, in 1785 the Bavarian government outlawed the organization. The concern was that its members, who were also called "invisibles," were infiltrating numerous European regimes and institutions. When the Elector of Bavaria forced the Illuminati underground, they survived the ban on their activities by setting up libraries and disguising themselves as a network of book clubs. These "librarians" chose an owl above an open book as the seal of their secret society. A few years later they were implicated in catalyzing the bloodbath of the French Revolution, which dialectically led to the unification and modernization of Europe under the aegis of Emperor Napoleon Bonaparte. Later, they engineered the rise of Adolf Hitler. But they aren't Nazis. The owls are not what they seem.

The "esoteric projects" that Frederick invited me into were what was really irresistible. In retrospect, I realize that was undoubtedly by design. The most interesting of these was a clandestine exotic energy and propulsion project. This project was headed by a former NASA Jet Propulsion Laboratory scientist with an impressive resume who also had an interest in parapsychological phenomena. Frederick introduced me to this scientist because ever since *Prometheus and Atlas* won the 2016 Parapsychological Association (PA) book award, I had cultivated connections with prominent researchers in the PA and the related Society for Scientific Exploration (SSE).

Frederick had seen my personal photographs with men like Colonel John B. Alexander and Jacques Vallée, well-respected individuals with

PhDs who were not only involved with paranormal research but had worked on classified military intelligence projects. Dr. Alexander's dissertation, at Harvard, was on "Thanatology," or the science of death, knowledge he would apply as he went on to become an advocate for the development of non-lethal weapons. I befriended Dr. Alexander and his wife Victoria through Jeffrey Mishlove, the parapsychologist who hosts the *New Thinking Allowed* program that I appeared on many times. Frederick had probably seen the cheerful photograph I posted with John and Victoria Alexander during a visit to their home in July of 2016.

They had moved to Las Vegas around the same time as Mishlove to work on a paranormal research project funded by Robert Bigelow, the eccentric billionaire who would later award Mishlove half a million dollars for research that made the case for the soul's survival of bodily death. Bob Bigelow funded an interdisciplinary group of scientific researchers, including Colonel Alexander, to study the anomalous phenomena at the Skinwalker Ranch. In addition to his expertise in PsyOps and non-lethal weapons, in the 1980s John Alexander led an internal intelligence investigation into the alleged MJ–12 group. The conclusions of his investigation, and his view of the UFO phenomenon as a manifestation of the Trickster, can be found in the book *UFOs: Myths, Conspiracies, and Realities*. The book's foreword was written by John's close friend Dr. Jacques Vallée, who, despite decades of studying UFOs, is still a successful venture capitalist.

Jacques Vallée invited me to his San Francisco home on Saturday, April 8, 2017. Across from the sofa I sat on was a spectacular view of the skyline, with the Transamerica Pyramid right at the center of it. Jacques' second wife, Flamine, made us a delightful dinner. Frederick saw me post the photo that Flamine took of Jacques and I in his living room, and he wanted me to see if Vallée was interested in contributing to the project. Meanwhile, given the repeated funding delays, I was beginning to revert to my initial skepticism regarding Frederick despite his impressive connections. So, I was also interested in introducing Jacques to the ex-JPL engineer in order to get Jacques' advice on whether I was being manipulated by tricksters of the kind that he discusses at length in his book *Messengers of Deception*. Unfortunately, Jacques came down with an ear canal problem and he had scheduled surgery for later in the same week we had set the meeting with the project engineer. Jacques' daughter was staying at his apartment to look after him post-op, so we never got to regroup after the meeting to privately discuss his impressions of the project.

When I asked Frederick about the origins of this technology, he told me to read the works of Joseph P. Farrell on Project Chronos. He seemed to be amused by how close Dr. Farrell had gotten to the truth about *die Glocke*, the Nazi "Bell" device. That background research on my part culminated in the essay "Black Sunrise" published in *Lovers of Sophia* (Manticore 2017, republished by Arktos in 2019) and later expanded upon in *Closer Encounters* (2021). I think that the concept I first defined at the core of that essay, namely "destructive departure in worldview warfare" (*Abbauender Aufbruch im Weltanschauungskrieg*), adequately grasps the aims, motivation, and modus operandi of the Illuminati network that Frederick belongs to. It is not, as I suggested in "Black Sunrise," a strictly Fascist organization, but one that uses Fascism and many other ideologies that would appear to contradict each other.

The "Bell" was a Zero Point Energy (ZPE) and propulsion device based on electro-magnetically powered torsion of a Mercury-Thorium serum. Hal Puthoff, a physicist who did decades of classified research for Naval intelligence and the National Security Agency, and who worked on contract for the CIA at the Stanford Research Institute, went on to research ZPE at his Institute of Advanced Studies in Austin, Texas. He was the next person in the SSE that I was going to reach out to, through Jacques who knew him well, to see if he would consult on the project. Dr. Puthoff knew that ZPE devices could be miniaturized for use in a wide variety of vehicles, or even for installation in anyone's backyard. However, if such a ZPE system were to be weaponized there would be "enough energy in the volume of your coffee cup to evaporate all the world's oceans many times over."

Jacques and I met with the power and propulsion project engineer over brunch at the Fairmont Hotel on Nob Hill in San Francisco on Monday, August 14, 2017. He showed us the blueprints for what was allegedly a retrofitting update of the 1940s Nazi "Bell" design, reconstructed to contemporary technological standards and miniaturized to fit inside of a car. The project was a system for electron harvesting from a Mercury-Thorium "battery" for power and propulsion purposes. The presentation that was made to Vallée — in his guise as a venture capitalist — pitched it as a clean energy alternative to coal-burning plants, nuclear power, and other power generation systems that adversely impact the environment.

Unlike these systems, the device did not need to be connected to the power grid, thereby allowing for decentralized "off the grid" operation of electrically powered devices and vehicles, within homes and offices or traversing land, flying in the air, or navigating at sea. The device had a modular design that made it scalable for power generation at various levels, from a small automobile to the largest cargo ship. It could also power drones, provided that the casing of the drone incorporated ceramic insulation of the Mercury-Thorium power cell. This ceramic insulation had been a prominent part of the German design of the Bell in Project Chronos.

Finally, just as in the nuclear industry, where applications included electrical power, atomic weapons, and nuclear medicine, there were also potential medical applications of this technology. The Mercury-Thorium reactor could be used for treatment of cancers, since it generates electrical impulses of a type that are destructive to cancer cells (with less deleterious effects than in chemotherapy). For obvious reasons, this venture capital-oriented presentation did not get into the weapons application of the technology (which would not have been lost on Puthoff).

After the meeting with Dr. Jacques Vallée in San Francisco I flew to Newport Beach to visit with Dr. Fariborz Maseeh, an MIT-educated Iranian innovator whose breakthroughs in micro-electro-mechanical systems (MEMS), i.e. nanotechnology, allowed him to become a billionaire and "venture philanthropist" in the year 2000 at the age of 41. The previous summer Dr. Maseeh had flown me out to Newport Beach to privately teach him the *Gathas* of Zarathustra. We had met at the Pacific Club, next to the Duke Hotel where he put me up for several nights. This time his secret proposal was to fund me to write Iran's next constitution. When he contacted me, I was actually already in Los Angeles for the meetings where my colleagues in the Iranian Renaissance and I formed the Iranian United Front. Quite a synchronicity.

I told Fariborz that I had a date set to meet with Jacques Vallée in San Francisco but that I could return to the LA area after that if he wanted to meet while I was still on the West Coast. So, he flew me from San Francisco back to Newport Beach. I am mentioning the meeting with him in Newport Beach now because it figures in the other "esoteric project" that Frederick tried to involve me with. It was also based in Newport Beach and, given Fariborz's expertise in nanotechnology and his venture philanthropy, Frederick wanted me to see if he would be willing to get involved. As it turns out, I did not pitch it to him, partly because Maseeh's proposal that I become Iran's Thomas Jefferson stunned me and I did not want to divert him from this.

The Illuminati project at Newport Beach revolved around race and genetic modification. This pet project of theirs was actually based in India, but a Vedic institute in Newport Beach played an important R&D role. During my second set of face-to-face meetings with him in London, in the week of May 22, 2017, Frederick explained that this project involved the excavation and collection of remains of a group of very tall hominins with naturally elongated skulls. Frederick and his associates were obsessed with the idea of "Atlantis" and interpreted these finds as remains of the Atlantean engineers of the civilizations of Peru, Mexico, Egypt, Mesopotamia, and of equally titanic ruins as of yet unearthed in the Gobi Desert. The things that Frederick shared with me suggested that they were trying to redevelop this phenotype along with the psychical abilities that set these early humans apart from us. Their ultimate aim was a hybridization of that form of early humanity together with modern man, who has certain analytical and creative cognitive capacities that these giants lacked. After the hit pieces in *The New York Times*, *Newsweek*, and other mainstream media outlets in September, my letters to venture philanthropist Fariborz Maseeh went unanswered. Before the defamation, Maseeh had planned to bring me out to his ranch in the fall of 2017 to have in-depth discussions about my work on the proposed Persian Constitution. So much for becoming Iran's Thomas Jefferson.

Why was I continually encouraged to present policies to the shadow Secretary of State, in person, and to the President of the United States, in writing, which Michael had already told Frederick were unacceptable? How could this have been allowed to go on for so long that, on August 11 of 2017, we formed the Iranian United Front (*Jebheyé Irângarâyân*) in Los Angeles, unifying the most established patriotic political parties opposed to the Islamic Republic, including the Pan-Iranist Party, under the false assumption that the Trump administration would give us a serious hearing? Perhaps because certain agencies wanted the Iranian Renaissance to put all of its eggs in one basket, so that they could break them all at once. Perhaps they wanted to do the same thing to the Alt-Right.

As the youngest and most intellectual member of the new coalition, I was the one who named it *Jebheyé Irângarâyan* (literally "Iranist Front") during one of the several days and nights of meetings we had in Los Angeles from August 11 to 13, while my Alt-Right partners were making a mess in Charlottesville. My speech introduced the coalition to the English-speaking world. Tarring me could potentially be used to destroy the whole coalition. On September 28, 2017, the mainstream Persian media outlet *Radio Zamaneh* ran a hit piece on me even more libelous than that of *The New York Times*, titled "In America, an intellectual leader of Iranian Fascism has been dismissed from teaching." The Iranian (Persian) Renaissance Foundation is referred to as an imperialistic "fascist" organization, and its fate is explicitly and irrevocably tied to mine. This was done to take us out of the picture when the key moment arrived, sooner than some expected, in the winter of 2017–2018.

The Iranian uprising against the Islamic Republic began in late December of 2017. I had been staying at Shahin Nezhad's home during the *Yalda* (Mithraic Christmas) holiday, so I bore witness to some of his initial communications with people inside the country. By the time I was back in New York, the demonstrations had become much more fearsome and widespread. No one in the mainstream media seems to have noticed that the uprising in Iran took place six months after the most well-established Iranian opposition groups were unified for the first time in 38 years of theocratic tyranny. Or maybe they were told not to notice. I will never forget that late summer night in Los Angeles when we, the founders of the Iranian United Front, sat in a circle, with our faces illumined only by the light of a pool of fire in a dark courtyard. By the year's end, that fire spread to 70 Iranian cities.

For some time, a faction within the so-called "hardliners" of the Islamic Republic had been considering embracing the idea of an Iranian Renaissance in order to salvage some of the core structures of the Islamic Republic that protect Iran's banking system from globalist control and secure Iran's territorial integrity in the face of foreign-backed separatist agitators. This faction was centered around Esfandiar Rahim Mashaei, who briefly served as Mahmoud Ahmadinejad's Vice President and was unsuccessfully backed by

Ahmadinejad to run against Rouhani (because the Guardian Council deemed Mashaei a "deviationist" for his nationalism). Mashaei's circle had been reading Iranian Renaissance texts, such as *Aryan Imperial Political Thought* by Shahin Nezhad. As part of the core structure of the Islamic Republic themselves, these hardliners were able to secure permits for demonstrations against worsening economic conditions and corruption. Ahmadinejad gave a speech threatening the regime's corrupt establishment shortly before the protests began, and in very short order he was arrested by the Islamic Republic for provoking unrest. The slogans of the Ahmadinejad-associated protests condemned the so-called "reformist" Rouhani administration for its broken promise that Iran's concessions in the nuclear deal would raise living standards. These legal demonstrations were organized in the city of Mashhad, the hometown of Shahin Nezhad, which is also where the grand Shi'ite shrine of Imam Reza is located.

At the same time, the Iranian Renaissance planned a celebration for Ferdowsi's birthday. The event was originally scheduled for the 27th of *Âzar* (his actual birthday), but then Shahin rescheduled it for the 2nd of *Dây* (the date that he gives for his birth, not adjusted to changes in the calendar system), or December 23, 2017. The tomb of the author of the Persian national epic, the *Shâhnâmeh*, is in Tous, just outside of Mashhad. The idea was to replicate our Cyrus Day event, when hundreds of thousands gathered at the tomb of Cyrus the Great on October 29, 2016. Once busloads of ultra-nationalists arrived at the tomb, they were informed that their rally permit was revoked. These angry ultra-nationalists were diverted to Mashhad where they encountered the legal hardliner demonstrations, and joined them, shifting the slogans in a nationalist direction. Then they went back home to the smaller cities and towns where the Renaissance had its largest following, rather than in more Westernized major metropolitan areas. The rest is history.

The violent protests that engulfed more than 70 Iranian cities and towns from December of 2017 through January of 2018 were fundamentally different from the Green Movement of 2009. Back then I was a solidarity demonstration organizer and a human rights activist running the New York Chapter of *Iran Crime Watch*, an organization set up by Akbar Moarefy. My primary responsibility was lobbying the ambassadors of the member states of the United Nations Security Council. I also wrote a letter to then US Secretary of State Hillary Rodham Clinton. Unlike in 2009, no one was asking "where is my vote?" and not so much as a green handkerchief could be seen on the streets during this uprising. The slogans were not calling for democracy or demanding so-called 'free elections.' Instead, masses of protesters were yelling: "We are Aryans, we don't worship Arabs!" "Islam and the Quran, we sacrifice them both to Iran!" "Whether by cannons, guns, or tanks — the clergy have to go!" and "Reza Shah, may your soul rejoice!" By the first week of January 2018, the protesters chanting his name were burning down mosques and setting fire to the religious schools that train mullahs and produce the regime's reigning ayatollahs.

Reza Shah came from the rural working class, and contrary to the more peaceful nature of the upper-class 2009 protest movement, this working-class uprising was a violent insurrection spread across the countryside rather than concentrated in large cities. People in the streets were not demanding a chaotic 'democratic' revolution, one that would decimate the nation's industries and threaten its territorial integrity. Rather, they were inviting a military coup and removal of the ayatollahs under martial law conditions. It is safe to say that it resembled a "color revolution" in no way whatsoever. In fact, I knew from having discussed the situation at length with Avi Churkin that the Mossad was taken completely by surprise. Churkin informed me that the Mossad was tracking the uprising at more than 1,200 distinct flashpoints across the country (on a 'big board' that synthesizes data from various sources, including hacked CCTV cameras), but they had no hand in catalyzing the protests and were unable to control them. Meanwhile, the Trump administration had not yet even formulated, let alone implemented, a cohesive plan for how to effect regime change in Iran.

I know that because I played the largest single role in drafting the first such plan, and we were still in the process of conveying it to the President when the uprising began. After my defamation in September of 2017 resulted in a cutting of ties with Jellyfish, through which we had initially hoped to amplify our ability to organize the opposition within Iran, the secret triumvirate within the Iranian Renaissance decided to salvage our political project and use a different angle of approach to the Trump administration.

I call it a triumvirate because during the time we were dealing with Michael Bagley and Frederick Boulder, it consisted only of Shahin Nezhad, Aria Salehi Pamenari, and myself. Although Shahin and Aria participated in one video conference call with Michael and met Frederick in London on a couple of occasions during our February 2017 London Forum visit, I was the agreed upon point of contact with these operatives. Due to the charter of our 501c3 cultural organization, none of these political activities were approved by the board of trustees or the board of directors of the Persian (Iranian) Renaissance Foundation. They were secret.

In October of 2017, Siegfried Shahram Aryan, was brought into this secret group. Shahram was a rocket scientist with a PhD in theoretical Physics, and an advanced degree in biomedical science. He also knew six or seven languages, including Ancient Greek, Latin, Pahlavi, and Old Persian. The man was a polymath. He was the single largest contributor to the Iranian Renaissance think tank, regularly delivering erudite and captivating lectures on Iranian history. Much of what I learned about racial differences in IQ and genocidal miscegenation as a factor in the decline of Iranian Civilization came from his think tank lectures. S. S. Aryan would often joke that he himself was a descendent of the Turkic peoples most responsible for this decline.

Since Aria is not an ideas man, Shahram was brought in to collaborate with Shahin and me on drafting a proposal for regime change in Iran. The proposal would then be conveyed to Vice President Michael Pence via a certain Texas billionaire who was a business partner of Donald Trump. This man had told Aria that Pence, not Trump, was responsible for coming up with an Iran policy. Whatever Pence decided on would be approved by the President. This made some sense to me considering the fact that back in 2009, it was Pence who most sternly chastised Obama for not backing the protesters and gave a most rousing speech in Congress calling for America to help free Iran. We were assured, in no uncertain terms, that despite Trump's infamous "Arabian Gulf" speech, a definitive and detailed Trump Iran policy did not yet exist (in November).

During November and December of 2017, Shahin, Shahram, and I wrote a detailed proposal for US Vice President Michael Pence. The document is, without exaggeration, about 70% my work. In the draft stage Shahram was assigned with writing the "Historical Analysis," I wrote the "Analysis of the Regional Situation," and Shahin wrote the "Sociological and Demographic Analysis." However, given their poor English, their sections had to be reworked, and I was instructed to edit them into a stylistic harmony with each other and with my section. Most importantly, I wrote the "Executive Summary" (then we nitpicked it as a group and I repeatedly revised it accordingly). Although, of the four people who signed the document, only Aria's contact information is listed in the final draft, since he was, via the Texas billionaire, the point of contact with Vice President Pence, Aria played absolutely no role in formulating the contents of the proposal. I eventually presented this proposal to a member of the National Security Council at a bunker underneath Capitol Hill, in late February of 2018. Shahin Nezhad, Aria Salehi, and President Trump's business partner were all in attendance.

The Texan flew in and met us at Capitol Hill. In my first meeting with him, I clearly impressed this Davos summit core member. A man of few words, who is not easily impressed, he turned to Aria and Shahin and said, "I *like* this guy."

One night in early 2018, Shahin Nezhad called and asked me to replace Dr. Ali Akbar Jafarey as his doctoral dissertation advisor. John Morgan of Arktos was visiting at the time, and even though he could not understand the conversation that Shahin and I had in Persian, I am sure that he remembers the impression that it made on me. Perhaps he could also tell that I was somewhat at a loss for words. I believed Shahin when, on numerous occasions, he had referred to me as a member of his family, but I was still not prepared for such an honor, especially given the standing that Dr. Jafarey had as the person who effectively began the Neo-Zoroastrian movement. He was probably the most revered spiritual teacher in the entire Iranian community, not including ayatollahs and their devotees. It was his revolutionary translation of the *Gathas*, made in the 1980s, that introduced me to the thought of Zarathustra when I was a teenager. Later, while visiting Tehran, I had acquired Jafarey's Persian edition, which deepened my understanding of the spiritual fountainhead of Iranian Civilization. Shahin formally converted to Zoroastrianism under the guidance of Jafarey, who officiated at his wedding with Artemis. So, when he asked me, I replied, only half-jokingly, "Godfather, it's an offer that I can't refuse." That is not to say that I did not try to have him reconsider, or at least consider the consequences for his own reputation. Conferring a doctorate on someone is not a joke, I explained to him, and how it would look if a "fascist" approved his. He said, "Jason dear, as far as they're concerned, we're all fascists."

I immediately perceived that Shahin had several secret aims. The most significant, and the most gracious, of them was to use this project to bolster my resume for any future Persian political career. The second was to help reestablish my academic standing in the wake of the defamation that threatened to destroy my career teaching at American universities. The third was to bring me under the influence of the man who was his own idol, Ardeshir Babakan (180–242), founder of the Sassanian dynasty and the third and final Persian Empire before the Islamic Conquest of Iran. Shahin so revered Ardeshir that when, during my Christmas (i.e. *Yalda*) season stay at his home, I brought him and his wife Artemis a matching pair of cufflinks and earrings based on a Sassanian coin, he was convinced that the portrait was one of Ardeshir.

That the leader of the Iranian Renaissance would write a dissertation on the political philosophy of the founder of the Sassanian dynasty is not surprising. It was a perfect follow-up to Shahin's two previous books, and I have reason to believe that it was a preface to a planned drafting of Iran's future constitution. Shahin's first book, *Dramatic Climax before the Decline*, is one of only two texts that aims to be for the third Persian Empire what Gibbon's *Decline and Fall* was for understanding the collapse of the Roman Empire. Shahin's second book was titled *Imperial Aryan Political Thought*. The term "Imperial Aryan" here, namely *Iranshahri* (or, more precisely, *Iranshahrig*) in Middle Persian, is the adjectival form of *Iranshahr*, a contraction of the Ancient Persian *Aryana Khashatra* or "Aryan Imperium" — the official name of Iran during the Sassanian period, beginning with Ardeshir I.

I had reason to believe that Shahin Nezhad would position me to be his successor and propel me into a leadership role in Iran that would, on the face of it, seem very unlikely. Maybe "reason" is not the right word here. Beyond the nature of our relationship and the potential that I saw in the Iranian Renaissance at the time, as well as my ancestral pedigree as the great grandson of a Qajar monarch, there was an experience that I had in Iran during my stay there in the summer of 2004 that rendered this possibility more realistic to me than it would be based only on these other factors.

During my first three nights in Tehran, which were the first nights that I had spent in Iran (in this lifetime), I had a recurring dream, A huge griffin would sweep down over me with the sun blazing behind it, making it cast its shadow over me. When the *homa* (Persian royal griffin) got close, screeching loudly, I felt a heat so intense that it was like I was going to burst into flames. Then my body would hurl upwards in bed, ready to throw up onto the floor. That is how I was jolted out of the exact same dream, three nights in a row. The nausea was intense, as if it were caused by radiation exposure.

I had no idea what this recurring dream meant until years later. When I was doing research in the New York Public Library for my study of Sadegh Hedayat's *The Blind Owl*, namely the book that eventually became *Novel Folklore*, I came across a fascinating passage buried in one of Hedayat's obscure books about Iranian folklore. Hedayat writes that there is a folk tradition according to which: "If the griffin casts its shadow upon you by night, then you shall reign by divine right." How does a *homa* cast a shadow over you *at night*? In a dream, where the sun is shining behind the griffin.

That was not the only strange experience I had during that trip to Iran. Another occurred on the night after hiking all the way up to the Cave of Shapur in the mountains of the southern Fars province, where a grotto atop the mountain features a rock-hewn sculpture of the Sassanid Emperor Shapur I, the son of Ardeshir Babakan and patron of the Gnostic prophet Mani. Not a soul was in sight. After we paid our respects to Shapur in the eerie silence of the dark cave, my driver, who had volunteered to climb with me, suggested that we make haste back down the very steep boulder-filled slope when, around sunset, we heard the growls of mountain lions pursuing us at a distance. When he finally dropped me off back at my hotel in Shiraz, it was well after midnight. With all of the restaurants closed, the only thing for me to eat or drink was a large frozen bunch of Shiraz wine grapes that I had been keeping in the refrigerator. While gorging on these, I fell asleep from exhaustion with the lights still on.

When I woke up, everything in my hotel room was exactly the same. Except that the room was full of men in black suits, wearing black ties over white shirts, with some of them holding black hats in their hands. I was so alarmed that my first reaction was to reach toward the phone to call security, but then I noticed that the Men In Black were gathered around the bathroom and curiosity compelled me to scope out what was going on in there. I got up and walked to the open bathroom door, at which point I could see, from in between the bodies of the MIBs, that Mohammad Mossadegh was lying in my bathtub. He was old and frail, and he gestured in such a way as to wave them off to the sides — so that we could see each other clearly — and he pointed toward me with his bony index finger. The Men In Black turned their heads back to look at me, and looked at each other in annoyance as well, as if they were all opportunistic suitors who had just been brushed aside in favor of some unknown person. A couple of the men helped him out of the tub and wrapped him in a towel, then brought him to sit on the bedside. It was one of those rooms with two beds, separated by a night table, so I was sitting on the edge of the other bed, facing him.

At this point, all of the men in suits disappeared — and Mossadegh transformed into a woman. She was a beautiful older woman, younger than Mossadegh, but still with a wizened look. She had a lot of gray and white in her wavy hair, which curled at the ends. There was profound wisdom, acceptance, and invitation in her gaze. I saw the best of myself in her, but she knew more about me than I did. The towel had fallen around her waist, and I got up and placed the palm of my hand on one of her breasts. I felt the most intense sense of communion with this woman. It was as if we melted into one. It was an intensely erotic experience with an ecstasy beyond the merely sexual. Then I woke up, lying on that bed, with the no longer frozen Shiraz grapes next to me.

I eventually met this woman, albeit at a much younger age than she appeared in that hotel room in Shiraz. Nassim Nouri reached out to me on Facebook after hearing my interview on *Prometheus and Atlas* with Red Ice Radio in 2016. She did not know that, while we were Facebook friends, I had amassed an archive of photos of her because I was fascinated by her resemblance to the woman in the Shiraz hotel room — albeit, about 25 years younger in appearance. We had exchanged only a handful of Facebook messages. Then, on the night of August 11, 2017, after my keynote speech at the event forming the Iranian United Front in Los Angeles, I was out in Westwood (the Persian District of LA) with Shahin Nezhad, Aria Salehi, and a handful of other people from the Iranian Renaissance. We were supposed to go to Sholeh (The Flame) Restaurant, but we decided to have Persian Pizza instead. Sitting at the bench of the Persian Pizza sidewalk café in "Tehrangeles" I suddenly heard someone call out my name. I turned around and it was Nassim, heading to meet some friends at Sholeh restaurant for dinner. (Had we gone there, as planned, I would also have run into her.) I got up and walked over to her. We stood silently transfixed with an invisible electricity coursing between us that was more magnetically intense than anything that I have ever felt with anyone. Fascinatingly, although Nassim and I did not hug and kiss, Kourosh Aladdin, one of the members of the Renaissance, who was intently watching us, swears that he saw us do that. He must have seen the aura or spectral essence of the event.

Considering the fact that I met Nassim in the flesh during the most important event ever held by the Iranian Renaissance, it is ironic that my relationship with her would end my work with them. Within a year of having met Nassim, incidents involving Shahin and Aria, and dealings with Reza Pahlavi, the CIA, the Trump administration, and so forth, had convinced me that even the best elements of the so-called "opposition" to the Islamic Republic of Iran were at the very least un-reliable. There was, in my view, a serious possibility that any regime change spearheaded by these external forces, and the foreign interests on which I now realized that even the best of them were dependent, would lead to the territorial disintegration of Iran. This view was implicitly reflected in my book *Iranian Leviathan*, which was released in the late summer of 2018. I wrote the book in a way that would promote a political solution from within Iran itself, in an attempt to reach out to that faction around Esfandiar Mashaei, who had reached out to Shahin Nezhad and been rebuffed.

For their part, the leadership circle of the Iranian Renaissance saw my proposal for a hybrid Aryan-Shi'ite transition in Iran, and my somewhat sympathetic treatment of Ayatollah Khomeini (a shrewd overture on my part to nationalists within the IRGC), as evidence that I was being manipulated by the Islamic Republic. Unfortunately, they did not have the decency to directly (albeit falsely) accuse me of having made a deal with the intelligence services of the regime. Instead, word reached me that the leadership of the Renaissance had (deludedly) come to believe that Nassim, who by then had become my fiancée, was an agent of the Islamic Revolutionary Guard Corps Intelligence Directorate, and that she was subjecting me to psychological manipulation and had seduced me into collaborating with the regime. Anyone who knows the least bit about Nassim would recognize how utterly preposterous this allegation is. It was also tremendously disrespectful in its disregard for my level of intellect, scholarship, and discernment.

In October of 2018, select members of the Iranian Renaissance had planned to go to Tajikistan to attend a scholarly conference on Iranian Studies and to privately meet with President Emomali Rahmon. Considering the financial consequences of my defamation, the travel expenses and hotel room had already been paid for by one of my staunchest supporters in the movement. Without having the backbone to tell me upfront that they were not going to take me (the only actual scholar of the group) together with them to the conference and the meeting with the Tajik President, they unilaterally cancelled my participation by simply disengaging with me and leaving for Tajikistan. I could, and initially did, accept this as an understandable response to the content of *Iranian Leviathan*, which had after all been written with funding from individuals in the leadership of the Iranian Renaissance. But when I found out that in secret discussions, they had decided not to take me along because they believed that I was under the thumb of Nassim, and that whatever I heard at the meeting with President Rahmon would be conveyed, via her, to IRGC Intelligence, I immediately resigned in protest from my position as Senior Advisor to the Persian Renaissance Foundation (without publicly stating my reasons).

Their suspicions were particularly absurd considering the work that I had done to engage elements within the Israeli government. The hidden subtext of my public discourse of "Iranian Zionism" was a very private attempt to engage with pro-Iranian elements within Israel who, on account of their zealous religious faith, see Iran as a divinely chosen land that could once again play the role that Cyrus the *Moschiach* and other Persian kings such as Xerxes had played in protecting the Jewish people. There was a faction to the right of Netanyahu who held such views, and they had managed to maneuver one of their own, Avigdor Lieberman, into the position of Israeli Defense Minister. I wrote a letter to Lieberman. I received confirmation that this letter made it to his desk, via a certain Mossad agent on the Greek island of Kos. Unfortunately, the coalition government of Israel fell apart and Prime Minister Netanyahu took over the duties of Lieberman, simultaneously serving as Defense Minister.

Once Netanyahu consolidated power, I attended a meeting with two Jewish New York businessmen who I was given to understand were also high-level Mossad operatives and close friends of "Bibi" Netanyahu. An associate of mine set up the meeting, at a posh Italian restaurant in midtown Manhattan, but I was the one who made the pitch to them that a strong nationalist regime in Iran was actually to the benefit of Israel. These two individuals threatened my life three times, to warn me not to reveal their identities. Despite being impressed with me at the meeting, when the two of them got back to my associate later on, they told him that their background check had revealed that I was under the surveillance not only of their own Mossad, but of at least three other intelligence agencies based in America, Britain, and Iran. "We don't know what this guy's done," they said, "but we've never seen anyone under this kind of surveillance before. Don't bring him to another meeting. They'll close all the doors on you."

"Come down from off of Satan's ass!" (*Az kharé Shâytân biyâ pây-in!*) This is a Persian expression that was directed at me far more than once in my life, including by my colleagues in the Iranian Renaissance. In the Persian language, a person who is, as it were, *riding Satan's ass* is someone up to no good, but in a very particular way. To ride Satan's ass means to engage in recklessly dangerous and often morally question- able behavior, usually motivated by outrageous or outlandish ideas. This ride is not supposed to end well. It is possible to ride Satan's ass all the way into hell. But this is not at all the same kind of expression as "the path to hell is paved with good intentions." Nor is this a path to hell that consists of a long series of mere blunders that eventually lead one, haphazardly, into a morass that becomes inescapable. There is a certain defiant, perhaps even haughty, pride to the rider of Satan's ass. While he realizes that he may appear foolish to some, he is a trickster convinced of his own cunning intelligence. Yet, in the eyes of most people, he is a fool — possibly even a lunatic. So, they tell him to come down off the infernal ass before irreparable harm is done. I never lis- tened. After all, I have Phenomenal Authorization.

CHAPTER 14

PHENOMENAL AUTHORIZATION

A fter my first few sessions of past life regressions, my mother forced me to undergo special psychiatric evaluations. Instead of being proud that her daughter was the reincarnation of the founder of the movement that she had devoted her life to designing buildings for, my mother was full of jealousy and resentful rage. She also seemed to be terrified that these claims would tarnish the Avalon family name. Terrible catfights broke out between us — in the course of which many architectural blueprints of hers and many drawings of mine were destroyed. She also attempted to erase the extensive notes that I had taken, and which I've largely reproduced in the preceding narrative of the catastrophic period in Jorjani's life from 2016 to 2018.

I could see why Prometheists wait until after high school to un-dergo past life regression, because had I still been surrounded by the boys — and especially the girls — in my school when this happened, I doubt that I would have survived the added stress of the violent resentment and vicious humiliations that would undoubtedly have been directed at me. In the end, the most esteemed psychiatrists and parapsychologists in the movement grudgingly came to a consensus assessment that I was, in all likelihood, the reincarnation of Jorjani. But the damage was done as far as my relationship with my mother was concerned. We never spoke again, and I refused to appear with her at any function.

Though I lost my mother, I gained others who brought me under protective wings that were much needed in the wake of this scandal. Had I continued living on the campus of Gotham University during my college years, I suspect that there would have been a considerable threat to my personal safety. I do not mean from agents of the Imperium so much as from within the movement itself. In every ideological or religious movement there are self-appointed guardians who, one or two generations after the death of the founder, come to see themselves as gatekeepers to, and guarantors of, his legacy at the same time as they betray the founder's ethos at the most fundamental level. Prometheism was no exception. It reminded me of the story of the Grand Inquisitor in Dostoyevsky's *Brothers Karamazov*. Sadly, my mother was one of these inquisitors.

The gatekeepers of Prometheism saw the potential Return of Jorjani as their worst nightmare. They were ready to murder me, ostensibly to protect my own legacy. But there were others, a secret society of rogues, who claimed to possess an esoteric interpretation of the thought of Jorjani, and who were ready to help me better understand myself and steal back the fire that I started nearly a century ago. We would have meetings late into the night at an apartment that they helped me to secure with the substantial cryptocurrency that I had inherited from my father. Meanwhile, at the university, I double majored in Philosophy and History, graduating with highest honors despite being sleep-deprived during most of my classes.

This rogue council of esoteric Prometheists became the occulted advisors that reviewed and critiqued my philosophical writing as I went on to four years of graduate studies at Gotham University, ending with a doctoral degree obtained in 2103 at the relatively young age of 26. Within a year (thanks to the facilitation of the secret group), this infamous dissertation was published with the title *Chaos, Order, and*

Progress. Infamous because it was an ontological and epistemological treatise coming from a young PhD who was now widely known within "the movement" to have turned out to be the reincarnation of Jason when she underwent that Prometheist rite of passage that is past life regression.

In my dissertation, I argued that Traditionalists see Chaos as a mere degradation of Order. To them, Order — which is called *Rta* in Sanskrit and *Cosmos* in Greek — is an eternal structure of Being. This is conceived of as a Macrocosm, which may be mirrored (or distorted) to a greater or lesser degree of fidelity by the Microcosm of the individual person and the collectivity of a society. The Order itself never changes. Even its variant instantiations on the Microcosmic level follow fixed patterns of increasingly degraded fidelity, until "the gods" (the Hindu *Devas*, or Greek Olympians) restore order at the end of every cycle. By contrast, the essence of Modern thought about the relationship between Order and Chaos is that emergent and determinate Order draws from out of a background of indeterminate Chaos as a wellspring of innovative Creativity, thereby yielding Progress in all domains — albeit not necessarily in anything resembling a straight line, and potentially admitting of many dialectical regresses and triangulations within an overall forward-oriented developmental trajectory. All legitimately Modern thought is teleological (goal-directed) in this way.

"Order" must be defined as distinct from the pure potentiality of Chaos from which it draws so as to be dynamic, and therefore Progressive, rather than static in the way that *Rta* is conceived of as being. For example, in ancient Iranian thought, the hypostatization of primordial Chaos as *Âz* has a dialectically dynamic relationship with *Ashâ Vahishtâ* as the ordering-principle at work in the evolutionary force of *Spentâ Mainyu*. I drew from these ideas of Zarathustra to provide a positive definition of "Order" qua *Ashâ* as a "progressive" (*spentâma*) structure over and above the Chaos that creative evolution requires as an inexhaustible background of undefined potential.

Thinking of history with a view to a purposive aim, unfolding progressively on the way to a projected "end of history" — inevitably framed as a Utopia — is something that we first see in Zarathustra. In my dissertation, I argued that the ancient Iranian prophet is, strictly speaking, the first "Modern" thinker (in the post-Atlantean historical record that has been left to us). Zarathustra's understanding of the relationship between Chaos, Order, and Progress reemerges, perhaps not coincidentally, after the late 18th-century French translation of the *Avesta*. Georg Hegel clearly owes a debt to it, and thus, so does Karl Marx, at least indirectly. But it can already be seen in the writings of the Marquis de Condorcet and, especially, the philosophical project of Auguste Comte, despite Comte's patronizing and paternalistic attitude toward women.

Whether or not he realized it, Comte was channeling and refining Zarathustra. Comte's "Religion of Humanity" is closer to what Zarathustra was trying to articulate than the travesty that Zoroastrianism became by the Sassanian period in Imperial Iranian history. As in the case of the gospel of the Superman preached by Friedrich Nietzsche, who adopted Zarathustra as his mouthpiece for good reason, the "Religion of Humanity" presupposes the death — no, the murder — of any transcendent God akin to the Macrocosmic Brahman of the Traditionalists. Instead, what Counter-Traditional Modernists deify is Humanity's own Promethean power of industrious and innovative self-perfection that stops at nothing short of the recreation of Man — as an ungodly self-creation, in *Frankenstein*. Shelley aptly intended to title that masterpiece "The Modern Prometheus."

This brings me to the focus of my second book, published in 2105, and titled *The Future of Modernity*. In this book I argued that there is nothing to "Postmodernism" at all — other than a cynical psychological warfare and social engineering project that aims to "deconstruct" the Modern just so that Tradition can prevail again. Of course, the vast majority of its proponents, in the late 20th and early 21st century, did not realize that they were suckers being used for this — being used by people who took Evola's *Ride the Tiger* to heart, or who thought along similar "Accelerationist" lines about hastening the supposedly inevitable collapse of the Modern world.

My second book begins with a look at early-to-mid-20th-century visions of "Futurama" or "the World of Tomorrow." A robotic workforce, personal flying cars, cities under the sea, colonies in space, and many other innovations that were expected by "the year 2000" or earlier are surveyed as the surface layer of a deep Futurism that spanned from Italy to America, and then extended to Japan in the decades after Hiroshima. Even the Russian Cosmists of the 1920s were part of this global project to soar headlong into the ever-expanding horizon of the Modern age. The Soviet Union embraced its own vision of this Promethean ambition, in a bid to rival Capitalism with a promise of a more just and universal Utopia. Psychotronics (Soviet Parapsychology) was part of this Modernist vanguardism.

Contrary to what many theorists of the "Modern" assume, this worldwide movement — or constellation of movements — was not reductively materialist. This is especially clear when one examines the work of a number of leading modern artists and literary figures, from Wassily Kandinsky to André Breton and Franz Kafka. Their work is steeped in the occult, even if it represents a radical revolt against Tradition. In the realm of science, Psychical Research and its successor, Parapsychology, were uncompromisingly scientific in their methodology and entirely consistent with what actually characterizes the modern mindset. Judging by the empirical rigor of research in the field, and the complexity of data analysis, Parapsychology has a more legitimate claim to being a modern science than Psychology or Sociology do.

The reason why many theorists have missed this when formulating a phenomenology of the "Modern" or of "Modernism" is that they have mistakenly drawn an equivalence between Modernity and

Anti-Tradition. The latter is a term introduced by the Traditionalist French writer René Guénon in order to designate the atheistic and materialistic form of modern thought that rose to prominence during the French Revolution and was eventually embraced by the scientific establishment of the Western world. In his book *The Reign of Quantity and the Sign of the Times*, Guénon contrasts this "Anti-Tradition" with a different modality of Modernity, one which he has noticed heralds of, as he is writing in the 1920s, but which he believes is yet to come to its culmination. Guénon calls this the "Counter-Tradition." Unlike the reductively materialist and atheistically secular "Anti-Tradition" that was epitomized by the French Cult of Reason and the Marquis de Sade, the Counter-Tradition is profoundly spiritual. Guénon, writing as a staunch defender of Perennial Tradition, sees the Counter-Tradition as the ideology of the coming Antichrist. It is the full flowering of Modernity. *Prometheus and Atlas* made the mistake of conflating Modernity in general with the Anti-Tradition, and of confusing the Counter-Tradition that Prometheism represented with something "Postmodern" rather than the *fully* Modern. Looking back from the year 2112, after the almost complete destruction of the Modern world, there is no ambiguity about this. My writings as Jorjani actually represented the zenith of Modernity.

In *The Future of Modernity*, I examined the distinction between the two types of Modernity that Guénon differentiated from one another. Therein I affirm Guénon's claim that there really are only two types of worlds — a world of Tradition and a Modern world. A period like the Italian Renaissance, or for that matter Hellenistic Alexandria, is an example of a world in transition between Tradition and Modernity (in the Alexandrian case the transition was aborted by the institutionalization of Christianity, and in the case of the Renaissance it was retarded by the Vatican). Moreover, as Guénon rightly suspects, *our* Modernity may not be the first "Modern world." There may have been at least one Modern age before ours, the Modernity of an "Atlantis" that (in its final phase of civilization) spearheaded a global revolt against the Traditional world order of Olympus. The Modernity of Atlantis was erased, or more literally drowned, by the forces of Tradition — as our own Modern Age will also be when its last bastion of Gotham falls.

I drew on the writings of Julius Evola, especially his *Revolt against the Modern World* and *Ride the Tiger*, to flesh out this epochal and ontological distinction between Modernity and Tradition. Evola was a cynical supporter of certain currents of Modernism, having even been a Dadaist painter in his youth, because he thought that the collapse of the Modern world ought to be accelerated. From his Traditionalist perspective, which is most closely aligned with Hindu notions of *Yugas* (world ages) and the caste hierarchy of a world that ought to be ruled by the *Devas* (the "gods"), Modernity is simply the *Kali Yuga* — the last and darkest age of deviant degeneracy in a perennially repeating cycle of world ages. Bringing this age to an end sooner, by intensifying its destructive forces, would, therefore, accelerate the advent of the new golden age or the next *Satya Yuga*. The term "New Age" is a source of a great deal of confusion because to some people it signifies this dawning of a new golden age, which is an entirely Traditionalist idea, whereas to others it means what it did to German intellectuals who used *die neue Zeit*, literally "the New Age," as the term for "the Modern Age" in the German language.

In *The Future of Modernity*, I argued in favor of the latter, namely that Modernity is the age defined by the very idea of "the new." Guénon, after all, saw the New Age movement, which had already begun in his epoch, as the rising Counter-Tradition, wherein the spiritual takes the form of the "psychical" that can be grasped scientifically. Guénon thought that a scientific approach to the occult was quintessentially Modern, and that the Antichrist would come to power by means of the technological production of "miracles." In hindsight, this is exactly what Prometheism has done and on account of which it has been recognized by the Olympian Imperium as the only real opposition to their restoration of Tradition.

At the heart of *The Future of Modernity* was a Deconstruction of Postmodernity or a turning of so-called "Deconstruction" on itself. The distinction between "Modernism" and "Postmodernism" in architecture, the arts (including cinema), and literature was examined with a view to demonstrating that there is nothing positively or substantively new about putatively "Postmodern" works that was not already there in "Modern" works. For example, so-called "Postmodern" architecture is just "Neo-Deco" when it is not trash, and Dada (which was sometimes literally trash) is at least as de-constructively engaged in satirical and absurdist parody as anything "Postmodern." Is Frank Lloyd Wright a "Postmodern" architect simply because he fuses Modernist geometric rationalism with ancient decorative motifs from various cultures? Of course not! Wright is absolutely Modern. Anyone who thinks that the line between Modern and Postmodern art and literature is drawn by some rejection of the Rational or by a supposed commitment to linear Progress, is clearly ignorant of the place of the irrational and the archaic in Surrealist art and poetry — which is radically Modern.

What was really at the bottom of the advent of putatively "bottomless" (or anti-foundational) Postmodernism is the paradox of Simulacra that are lacking an original. In other words, the idea of an all-encompassing Simulacrum. This idea was responsible for so much of the nihilistic irony and all-pervasive aversion to authenticity in the allegedly "Postmodern" epoch of the late 20th and early 21st century, shaped by the delusion that since nothing is real, nothing really matters. I argued that, even in the Gotham of 2112, this delusion still needed to be destroyed — in Martin Heidegger's still uncorrupted sense of "destruction." To this end, I "deconstructed" the writings of Jean-François Lyotard and Jean Baudrillard, two leading theorists of Postmodernism, in a clearer fashion than the "deconstructions" that Jacques Derrida and Michel Foucault engaged in. I demonstrated that the all-pervasive Simulacrum idea is a perversion of the perfectly legitimate conception of a Cyberspace coextensive with the Cosmos, i.e., an observer-dependent and potentially programmable quantum-computing "Holographic Universe" with fractal-generating Chaos as its unfathomable and unpredictable background. There is nothing "Postmodern" about this idea, which was developed by serious thinkers and writers such as David Bohm, Michael Talbot, and Philip K. Dick in the 1980s — at the zenith of Modernity.

The Future of Modernity concluded by exploring the double entendre of its title. It means both reaffirming Modernity *as* the future and retrieving the future that was envisioned by Modernity. To this end, I investigated the connection between Futurism and "Transhumanism" — the brainchild of Iranian Futurist Fereidoun M. Esfandiary (better known as F. M. 2030). The soullessly reductive materialism that was the dominant trend in the Transhumanist movement was harshly critiqued by me, and I rejected this "Anti-Traditional" Transhumanism in favor of a "Counter-Traditional" Transhumanism that resumes the Promethean project of occult alchemists from Faust onwards. To paint a portrait or sculpt the image of this Counter-Traditional reaffirmation of Modernity as the future in the highest fidelity possible, raw material was drawn from a plethora of visionaries in the period preceding the decline that set in during the 1990s.

I made an argument that the era of 1977 to 1999 was the zenith of Modernity, with 1988 as the single year that marks the peak of the entire Modern age. In other words, one year before the precipitous collapse and disintegration of the Soviet Union from 1989–1991. Without a Communist rival in the Russians, and a worldwide ideological war with these easternmost Europeans that was so dead serious it could literally have ended in the nuclear holocaust of all mankind, a seemingly triumphant capitalist West gave in to self-destructive decadence and nihilistic decay. Meanwhile, a no longer Communist China, increasingly reembracing Traditionalist Confucianism, rose to fill the vacuum of the USSR as the new superpower rivalling a rapidly declining United States. Not a rival competing with us to build a better Utopia than the Promethean Soviets believed Capitalism capable of offering to mankind, but an Ancestor-worshipping culture that fundamentally fears the future and considers all Utopian projects of Progress — including the Maoist one that still owed something to Marx — as vainglorious and ruinous folly lacking "the Mandate of Heaven."

Looking back at the leading edge of our emerging global Modern culture, from New York and Hollywood to Paris and Tokyo, in the years '77 to '99, *The Future of Modernity* aimed to give its readers not only a sense of what we lost, but also of the kind of future that we want to reclaim as our destiny. A Transhuman future, which is Counter-Traditional and not merely Anti-Tradition. A future of Robotics, Eugenics, Psychotronics, and Cyberspace — with a final frontier that is not only the colonization of space but also the conquest of time. That is the terminator (the horizon) of Modernity. Beyond Left and Right, the book insisted that now the only way forward is Up instead of Down. It set forth "*Cosmopolis Excelsior*" as a motto for Prometheism as a movement, and for Gotham as a city-state standing in rebellion against the reactionary Imperium of Tradition.

When I wrote *The Future of Modernity*, I was still relatively optimistic that what we were building in Gotham could expand outward and reconquer the globe. That would turn out to be a short-lived optimism, fueled partly by the rapturous enthusiasm that had electrified me on account of realizing that I was the reincarnation of Jorjani and that, with the help of my well-placed counselors, I was going to take back the Prometheist movement from corrupt gatekeepers. Well, I *did* do that. But my enthusiasm about fulfilling the destiny of Prometheism by reclaiming the Modern "Future" for the world at large waned rapidly — in proportion to the degree of control that I actually gained over the movement, and the amount of information and analytical power that came along with that.

Five years after *The Future of Modernity*, I finally completed my third book. Published in 2110, at the age of 33, *Phenomenal Authorization* is the work that I am most widely recognized for, and the one that, unbeknown to all but a small group of elite Prometheist operatives, became the conceptual basis for the desperate time travel project now underway. Most Prometheists — and, fortunately, also most people in the Imperium — see the book as theoretical, perhaps even fantastical, with no inkling that its core ideas are now operational axioms.

Whereas my first two books were intended to be constructive criticisms of Jorjani's thought, my third book aimed to forward the philosophical project that I embarked upon in my life as Jason. Three ideas central to his corpus became points of departure for developing a new concept. The first of these ideas was "Novel Folklore." The second was "Destructive Departure in Worldview Warfare." The third and final one was the trickster dubbed the "Prometheaion" and her machinations on a fifth-dimensional level, reprogramming the quantum computational Cosmos. Consequently, it could be said that what I came to call "Phenomenal Authorization" was already implicit in the canon of Prometheism, but this book rendered it more cohesive and explicit. The text explored the relationship between Authorship, Authorization, and Authority.

Very much in line with the post-structuralist hermeneutics developed from out of Heidegger's thought, and implicit even in the Kabbalistic dimension of Kafka's writing, the "worldhood of the world" (to use Heidegger's phrase) was recognized as proto-textual in nature. This is actually what was intended from the very first philosophical usage of the term *Logos* by Heraclitus of Ephesus, long before that term was retroactively associated with reductively mathematical or analytical "logic." Originally, the idea of *Logos* was that the structure on account of which our universe is referred to as a *Cosmos* or "ordered array" is akin to the warp and weft of a grand narrative or super story. Stories, like dreams, can involve absurd elements that are "illogical" from the perspective of a quasi-mathematical or reductively analytic logic, but that make sense narratively — at least on a subconscious level — and are therefore encompassed by the original conception of *Logos*. Surrealist poetry is still *Logos*, and events can transpire in our Cosmos that are more akin to Surrealist poetry than they are to anything "logically" analyzable or describable in terms of a chain of causality that can be mathematically schematized. Some forms of language normalize so-called "Nature" whereas others are conducive to the breakdown of the mesh holding the putatively "paranormal" at bay.

Individual persons are at least potentially co-authors over the narrative structure of the Cosmos. But clearly, Authorship is the prerogative of only a few. Most people are no better than Non-Player Characters (NPCs) in the Massively Multiplayer Online Roleplaying Games of the early 21st century. Authorship belongs not only to "authors" in the literal sense of writers, but to any creator who reshapes the "worldhood" of our world at the most fundamental level, namely the level of the folklore that conditions the substratum of the collective and personal unconscious of people in one or another society of a world increasingly globalized by technological enframing (to use another Heideggerian term). Not all authors are "authors" in this sense. In fact, most writers definitely are *not*. But a number of filmmakers, painters, even graphic novelists (like Alan Moore or Grant Morrison), and musicians are "authors" in this sense.

What determines who is or is not an "author" contributing to weaving the tapestry of the *Logos* that makes a *Cosmos* from out of *Chaos* is a double-sided or bi-directional function of "Authorization." Authorship can "authorize" what phenomena are accepted as possible experiences, and what other phenomena are suppressed from — at least widespread — manifestation on account of being deemed "impossible" and pushed to the "fringe" or margins of whatever "reality" is thereby defined. For example, there is no question that the authorship of Stephen King in the late 20th century was working at

cross-purposes with the entrenched materialist and mechanistic paradigm of the scientific establishment. It is not a question of what one
personally feels about the aesthetic merit of King's novels or the lack
thereof. His influence, including through film adaptations, was quite
literally *phenomenal,* and it operated on a society-wide scale precisely
on the subconscious stratum of folklore. The same was true of Whitley
Strieber, for better or for worse. What the case of Strieber highlights is
the flip side of this function of Authorization. Those whose authorship
authorizes the forms taken by phenomenal manifestation are in turn
"authorized" by something. Their process of phenomenal authorship
is either initiated by what authorizes them, or their creative endeavors
are of a kind such as to solicit the vital interest and active concern of an
authorizing force that allows them to act as a *medium* for the reshaping
of "reality."

This brings us to the final element in the constellation of three
author-related terms, namely Authority. Whoever happens to be in
an explicit position of political, economic, or even social power is not
necessarily the true "authority" in the world. By the early 21st century,
no one with half a brain believed that the elected representatives of
any government were really the powers that be. While this might be
more believable of corporate executives, the volatile rise and fall and
vicious turns of fortune in the lives of such men (and they *were* mostly
men) strains the credibility of such a proposition — especially since
the only "power" that these men had was their (often undeserved)
fortune. Finally, social power was eventually held mostly by social
media influencers and trendsetters, who were essentially no better
than the premier gossip peddlers of late 19th-century women's salon
attendees. This can hardly be counted as "authority." Real authority
within the context of one or another world is the authority to define
the limits of that world, or at least to play a significant role in defining
those parameters that determine what is or is not "possible." The first
accurate image of ultimate authority in the history of Philosophy is

Plato's allegorical depiction of the puppet masters on the plank above
the shackled prisoners who can only see the shadow play on the cave
wall in front of them. The Authors who Authorize Phenomena are the
Authorities who are Phenomenally Authorized to do so. These very
rare individuals have Phenomenal Authorization.

It is in the development of this concept, or the excavation of it
from out of the corpus that I had composed in my life as Jorjani, that
the secret group of esoteric Prometheists was most helpful. I realized
that this idea was already there in the writings of Jorjani on an occulted level. It *was* the esoteric message. There were many seeming
contradictions and apparent paradoxes in the books that I wrote during that lifetime. These were keys to open up an esoteric dimension
of Prometheism, the truth of Phenomenal Authorization. The truth
that those authors who have the authority have principally authorized
the phenomena of world history. Jorjani, probably when drunk, would
occasionally tweet one or another variation of "God is an invention of
the Devil." But he never cared to explain this diabolical aphorism in
any of his actual philosophical writings.

The enemy only *re*-acts. We are the *actors*. We have been the
Authorized. They are not Authorized. We Authorized them, as the
black pieces on *our* chessboard. Yes, the black and white squared board
preserved, from Atlantis, by the Freemasonic Order. It is Mithra the
Mediator who authorizes Ahriman to move against Ahura Mazda, so
that there can be the constraint that is a precondition for constructive
order. For every action of ours, the enemy engages in some reaction
that forwards a game whose aim and end they have never properly
grasped: maximal and indefinitely extended Creation, the categorical
imperative of the Prometheaion. S/he is the authorizer of the authority
of the authors of phenomena.

I would know, since I have had Phenomenal Authorization in more
than one lifetime. The past incarnation of mine that is most relevant
to understanding the catalytic and dialectical purpose of the putatively

"Abrahamic" so-called "revelations" is my life as David. When I was Jorjani, during my graduate studies at New York University, I met a young woman named Marie. She was Parisian, although her ancestry was not purely French but rather from a fairly prominent Jewish family that had emigrated, generations ago, from Spain. She was a deep thinker and an extraordinarily expressive writer, a woman capable of ascetic austerity and also of insatiable harlotry — an irresistible seducer of both men and women.

One night when she was having sex with one of her girlfriends in her apartment around Washington Square Park, I was so intensely focused on her from miles away, in my room on the Upper East Side, that she saw my spectral form appear in front of her for a moment. Fortunately, her lover was facing the other direction. She confronted me about it the next day, and astonished that she had also experienced it from her own perspective, I confessed. "I have nothing to hide from you," she said, "I just wanted you to know that I can see you when you do that."

Marie was at NYU studying both drama and philosophy. (Career-wise, she went on to become a journalist in Paris.) Not incidentally, it was in the period when I met Marie that the majority of my past life memories of Nikola Tesla came back to me. This is undoubtedly because her presence triggered them, on account of the fact that she was the reincarnation of Sarah Bernhardt.

I began to have dreams wherein Marie was an actress. I would meet her backstage after her performances and call her "Sarah." On a night that culminated with us rubbing noses atop the Empire State Building in the midst of tremendous windshear, I confronted her about this, and she told me certain intimate secrets that very clearly confirmed it and explained her strong interest in drama, once again, in this lifetime. But what is more relevant here are the memories that *she had* of the other lifetime that we spent together, a life wherein she was "Queen" Bathsheba and I was King David of Israel. The karma of that life was quite palpable to her and cast a shadow over our rapport. On some level, she still resented that I had her Hittite husband murdered so that she could become my consort.

Sir Ridley Scott gave David, both the android and the Michelangelo sculpture, such a prominent role in his film *Prometheus* and its sequel *Alien: Covenant*, because Scott is clearly in the know about who David really was and what aim he was esoterically serving. The symbolism of David's confrontation with Goliath, and the machination by means of which he prevails against apparently superior brute force, is an elementally Promethean image. Before David was sanctified as a prophet or a king, the man was first and foremost an artist — a poet and musician. The seal that he vouchsafed to his son, King Solomon, who built the principal Temple of Israel on that old abandoned megalithic Atlantean platform, is an epitome of the occult project of "revelation" or of the relationship between "revelation" and occultation. The upward-facing triangle is supposed to be white, and the downward-facing triangle that is interwoven with it, should be depicted as black. The latter is what the Tantric Hindus and Buddhists have preserved as the "Shakti Yantra." The Star of David that became the Seal of Solomon is an Atlantean symbol of the necessity of "evil" as a catalytic force in a dialectical process of creative evolution.

David's relationship with "God" was always a rapport with the Shekinah, in other words, the Prometheaion. Despite how his story was rewritten by the rabbis and Cohanim in order to obscure this, one can still discern it from between the lines of what has survived in the Bible. Abraham, Moses, Jesus, and Muhammad were all pawns. King David and, before him, the wizard Melchizedek, are the true founders of Judaism. Just as John the Baptist and Mary Magdalene really invented Christianity. The true Gabriel of Islam was Salman the Persian, and the Assassin leader Hassan Sabbah was the real Seal of Prophecy. These promulgators of necessary evils are the "spiritual princes and nobles" of the "initiatory chain of gnosis" that I wrote and preached about during my life in Sassanian Iran as the martyred Mazdak.

Even the most tragic figures among the Authors of Phenomena — the revolutionary martyrs, the impoverished inventors, and the visionary starving artists — have been akin to the "Coyote" trickster of the American Indians, who plays dead in order to get the upper hand, albeit not necessarily in the same lifetime, and not for him or herself alone, but for the Prometheaion who is the Creatrix of the Cosmic Game. S/he confers Phenomenal Authorization. That is why we esoteric Prometheists are now ready, willing, and able to rewrite history in a way that preempts the re-conquest of Earth by the Olympian Imperium. This is, after all, not the first time that the matrix of the world has been recoded. I did that with my precognitive remote viewing during my life as Nikolai.

One pivotal experience that I had in my life as Jason Reza Jorjani speaks to what the Shekinah or Prometheaion is really like in Herself, beneath and beyond the various phenomenal appearances that she veils herself with through the wonders worked by those with Phenomenal Authorization. The formless form of Her that I encountered was what the German Romantics called "The Blue Light," as in the Leni Riefenstahl film by that name. To them, this amorphous blue glow was a symbol of the Impossible. In two closely connected experiences, I was given to understand that this being that is nothing definite, and that can be encountered as a pregnant darkness that destroys what one takes oneself to be, is the so-called "alien" intelligence that we are at-tempting to contact.

In the first of these experiences, I was at a summer sleep-away camp at Amherst College that was also like a prep school program between middle school and high school. Warren, my best friend at the time, came with me and had a room down the hall from mine. One night as I was sleeping, I became aware of my heartbeat. I was conscious but still asleep and not dreaming. It seemed that it was beating slower and slower, but it may also have been that the timeframe of my conscious-ness was being altered to the point that I began to sink into the space between two heartbeats. When that happened, when it seemed like my heart had stopped beating, I fell out of my body through the bottom of my feet. I was being pulled by a tremendous gravitational force toward the dark heart of a vortex of oblivion.

I said to myself that if I cannot somehow pull myself back, the camp counselors will find my corpse in the morning. Then, as I struggled to break free from the event horizon of this vortex, I saw the following scene: there is a revolt or uprising. I see rioters around a barbed-wire fence. In the midst of this violent chaos, I see my own corpse on the ground. My face is chalk white and there are deep black rings under my eyes. Then, to my horror, I notice that my corpse is being propped up by my father. I'm in his arms, but he is also dead. His corpse is holding mine.

The shock of this finally brought me back to myself. I was ice cold. When I looked into the open closet that was across from the foot of the bed, the darkness inside it reminded me of the black hole that I had almost been swallowed by. "Reminded" is not strong enough. It was the same blackness and it seemed alive and capable of devouring me. Not able to stand being alone in that room any longer, I went down the hall to my friend and turned the light on in his room. Once Warren woke up and looked at me, his face suddenly twisted into the most horrified expression I've ever seen. He recoiled and hid himself under his blanket. Already unsettled, this reaction of his disturbed me more than if I had just stayed in my own room. I remember saying to him, over and over again, "What is it? Why are you doing that? It's just *me*. It's just *me*!" After a while he cautiously looked up from out of the cov-ers, and then said, "Oh, it *is* you." When I asked him why he initially reacted that way, he said: "Your eyes! Your eyes! They weren't *your* eyes. It was as if they were looking right through me, seeing through my whole being."

For a long time, I couldn't tell anybody about this experience. Every time I was about to, I would be overcome with emotion and had to stop myself so that I would not start crying uncontrollably. On a couple of occasions, I just said, "One night I died, and then came back to life." I started high school, months passed, and I tried very hard to forget the whole thing. Then, one night during the first winter after that summer, I was lying in bed looking at the digital clock when — without my really falling asleep — the room fell away, and I found myself outside under the night sky walking on a vast path of gravel lightly dusted with snow.

The wide path was situated between two rows of titanic radio telescopes, the ones that are used for the Search for Extraterrestrial Intelligence — one after the other, extending to the horizon on each side of the path I'm walking down. I noticed that all of the gigantic SETI dishes were burnt and shattered, as if they had received a signal that was too powerful. Then I had a sinking feeling in my stomach and, as on that night in camp, began to notice my heartbeat, with a longer and longer interval between each beat, as if my heart were going to stop again. Meanwhile, a huge blue light began to coalesce in the night sky ahead of me and above the gravel path. That was the Prometheaion, unveiled. The "alien" intelligence that no merely mechanical device could be used to communicate with, and a force that, when "contacted," rewrites the fabric of your being. I looked into the spherical blue glow and said, "Alright, alright, I get it! Just don't make me have to see that again!" Then I was back in my bed, with my hand on my chest checking for my heartbeat. My eyes had been open the whole time. It was a vision, not a dream. My life was never the same again after that night.

I mentioned that the concept developed in *Phenomenal Authorization*, my third book in this life as Dana Avalon, had been applied operationally. In the two years since the book came out in 2110, definitively securing my position as the leader of the Prometheist

movement and the widely recognized reincarnation of its founder, I
managed to maneuver members of the esoteric group that had been
secretly advising me into key positions with access to our most sensitive technology. Most of the corrupt gatekeepers of Prometheism
withdrew into their private lives in Gotham without risking a violent
confrontation, or the potential loss of their lucrative mining industries
in the Asteroid Belt colonies. Those few who were not shrewd enough
to cut their losses were easily dealt with by the younger and more
energetic members of our faction. The latter were both adept operatives and fanatical devotees who, regardless of my change of sex across
lifetimes, sometimes referred to me as "Chairman Jorjani" despite my
repeated requests that they refrain from doing so.

It is these Prometheist Assassins (in the Alamut sense) that we
trained, from 2110 to 2112, to become the spearhead of the time travel
mission to rewrite the course of events in the 1980s. They are the operatives that I sent ahead of me, to set up the pharmaceutical company in
1977 and to also start raising capital through insider trading of its stock
that would be soaring by 1980. Avalon Pharmaceutical was meant to
be a cash cow for a larger company that the group would be tasked
with setting up, named AtlantiCorp, of which it would be a subsidiary.
A few members of this vanguard were given period-specific paramilitary training as well, which I participated in. I especially excelled in
sharpshooting with sniper rifles. Of course, I also had to learn how to
manually drive an automobile, since our hovercars here in Gotham
basically piloted themselves.

The group had also been authorized to negotiate the purchase of
a property that was to be my residence: the penthouse apartment of
55 Central Park West in Manhattan. I had even given them specifications for what style of furniture to acquire for the apartment, and what
kind of women's wardrobe to fill the closets with. Finally, I requested
that they acquire one of the original DeLorean prototypes designed by
William T. Collins in late 1970s America, before John DeLorean settled

on mass-manufacturing an inferior model in Ireland. I asked them to have the car's stainless-steel frame painted matt black and to replace the interior upholstery with black leather.

It wouldn't be long before I found out how much of these plans had been successfully executed. We used a corridor in what had been the East River as our staging ground for time travel operations. Maritime traffic was directed up the Hudson River, which was closer to the Englewood Cliffs that Gotham had been built upon. By the time I was rushing to the submersible saucer that was to warp space time around it as it dove into the East River, what remained of Gotham's skyscrapers were exploding all throughout the skyline of the city. As I made my way down the building, I noticed that the nanotechnological "utility fog" that would produce solid walls with an architectural design that changed on a weekly, or even a daily basis, was starting to malfunction. I was afraid that I would get stuck in the elevator that traveled, not just vertically, but made diagonal turns on its way to the streets, as the elevators of many of our skyscrapers with curved bases did.

The night sky was full of Olympian Predators, and it's a wonder I wasn't exposed to their laser blasts in open stretches between the tunnels and covered walkways that led to the silvery saucer awaiting me on a cliffside hanger deck. I'd have run faster if I didn't have to carry the suitcases that contained carefully chosen information documenting certain events on this timeline, relevant to a number of the operations that I had planned to carry out in the late 20th century. There were a couple of aids and a couple of security personnel with me, who were helping to get all of this luggage to the saucer. I was already wearing my wetsuit, but 1980s diving gear (which we replicated) was pretty heavy. The plan was for me to leave the saucer through the airlock in my diving suit, after using a satellite phone to call a team that would rush to meet me at Pier 42 on the Lower East Side of Manhattan, between the Williamsburg and Manhattan Bridges, across from the Brooklyn Navy Yard.

We loaded the saucer and I bid a rushed farewell to those who helped me load it. Fortunately, they were not cleared for knowledge of the fact that I was about to erase them together with their timeline. That would endow the documents that, unbeknown to them, they helped to load, with the magical quality of being from a world — from a future — that no longer existed. Just as the portal was about to close, my regression hypnotist showed up. Now *she* knew. I've never seen both wistful resignation and grim affirmation so inextricably conflated in a single gaze and facial expression before. As I looked her in the eyes, and the saucer's entryway closed, I put my hands together prayerfully, in a *namaste*, and touched them to the *ajna chakra* in my forehead.

As the saucer lifted off the hanger deck and glided over the cliff above the Hudson River, heading southeast toward the skyline of sunken Manhattan, I looked back at Gotham one last time. The mesmerizingly beautiful neon light of the laser beams blasting and cutting the city to bits was aesthetically discordant with the destruction of Earth's last bastion of Liberty. That was my last thought as I strapped myself in and prepared for the deep dive into the fluid darkness of time. I could already feel the gravity wave forming around the shell of the craft like an envelope that would slice right through the moonlit waves of the Atlantic Ocean. It didn't cause any physical vibrations, but I could feel it in the pit of my stomach, nonetheless. To experience this for the first time was like the psychical equivalent of having my umbilical cord cut. I lost myself completely for a few moments.

The pitch, yaw, and rate of rotation of the saucer determined the precise degree to which the fabric of space-time around it would be warped by the Zero Point Energy drive shielded at the core of the vessel. Once the space-time warping engine or "warp core" of the vessel shut off, and I got reoriented, I turned on the searchlights, which only lit up the garbage at the bottom of the river. Then I released a small spherical probe from the side of the vessel, which was equipped with cameras, sonar, and LADAR. It sped to the surface, rose above the water of the East River, and began sending back data that included a stunning view of the United Nations building and mapped the rest of the skyline around it. It certainly seemed like 1980s Manhattan. I sent up another probe that was designed to pick up old radio frequencies. The first thing I heard, loud and clear, was a news bulletin being broadcast from the top of the Empire State Building, announcing that an eruption had begun on Mount St. Helens in Washington state. I scanned the frequencies again, and the next thing blaring loudly inside the saucer was the Blondie song "Call Me."

I reached nervously for the satellite phone, and then dialed the designated number. (Just figuring out what that number would be and how to make sure that the vanguard would secure it in 1980 New York took some serious planning.) I could barely breathe to respond when a familiar voice answered on the other end of the line. "I'm here," I said. "Dana?" "Yes, Johnny. I'm here."

As they undoubtedly ran numerous red lights to get to the docked ship that they were going to use to retrieve me, I piloted the saucer further south along the East River to get as close as possible to Pier 42. The suitcases all had a design feature that allowed them to float straight upwards. Once I got a call back on the satellite phone, letting me know that the team had arrived, I released these suitcases, and then climbed through the portal myself with the saucer's remote-controlled self-destruct mechanism in my hand. Even though spring had started, and this wetsuit provided good insulation, I could feel that the water was still pretty cold.

As soon as I broke the surface, I squinted in the searchlight of a ship. It was Johnny's boat, which had already spotted the suitcases and headed toward them. The small team that was with him helped to load the floating luggage onto the boat, as I climbed aboard myself. All he said as we sped back to Pier 42 was, "I can't believe that you're finally here." I was dazed and didn't respond. I just kept staring at the bright light of all the buildings along the river, including both the Chrysler and the Empire State spires that could be seen on the skyline.

We ran as fast as we could from the boat to the waiting black stretch limousine, packing the suitcases both into the trunk and the spacious backseat of the car itself. It did not appear that anyone saw us. After all, it was the middle of the night. I hit the remote-control detonator and turned back briefly when I heard a loud splash in the water behind us. Hopefully, no other ships had been crossing that stretch of the river when the saucer exploded into small shards on the river bed. The driver sped through the streets, occasionally eying me curiously in the rearview mirror. I stared out the tinted window, my eye caught by the lights of Katz's Delicatessen. "What's the date?" Johnny looked at me, smiling in relief at hearing me finally open my mouth. He replied, "March 27th, 1980. Thor's Day."

Johnny pridefully, and almost gleefully, explained to me that everything had gone according to plan. We were headed to 55 Central Park West, where my furnished penthouse apartment was waiting for me, and my black DeLorean was parked on the street across from Tavern on the Green. The rest of the crew on the boat, who I did not recognize, had taken another car, so Johnny and I were alone. "You should probably change out of that," he said. "I don't think you want to show up to your fancy building for the first time wearing a wet suit. The doorman might say something to the board."

Johnny had been one of the operatives in the spearhead group that I had spent the most time with during their training for the vanguard mission. We would buddy up during martial arts lessons and do other combat sparring together, and he would often shoot right beside me during our target practice sessions. But he never flirted with me too much, since I overemphasized my interest in women so that he would get the idea that I was a lipstick lesbian (rather than bisexual, which is closer to the truth). Besides, although he had all the respect in the world for me (every member of the vanguard did), I don't think I was his type. It probably also didn't help that he knew I was the reincarnation of a man whose writings and biography he, like all of the other spearhead operatives, had been immersed in. Johnny was straight as an arrow. I don't think he'd have been able to keep it up with the thought repeatedly resurfacing that the chick he was banging is a reincarnation of Jorjani. So, I stripped off the wetsuit right there in the back of the limo. I had stuffed a single era-appropriate change of clothes with me in one of the suitcases. It was a simple, knee-high one-piece black dress that I easily slipped on. "No underwear?" Johnny asked, while smirking. "I don't think the doorman will have an opportunity to check," I said. He looked happy to see that I was adjusting enough to regain my sense of humor. There was a pair of high heels in the suitcase too, and I put these shoes on as the limo pulled up to the building.

The driver got out of the car and opened the door for me. This was the first time that I got a good look at him. He was a tall, bony black man with a couple of scars on his face. As the car crossed Central Park South, Johnny had whispered to me that he was ex-DIA. Military intelligence. He had served in Vietnam *and the jungles of Cambodia.* He was also an unconventional practitioner of voodoo, with a particularly Promethean caste of mind. Jean-Pierre was his name. He was from New Orleans, and there was still a hint of Creole in his accent. As he held the car door open, Jean-Pierre also motioned commandingly to the building's doorman to bring the cart. Meanwhile, Johnny unloaded all of the luggage onto the sidewalk, before placing it onto the cart together with the doorman, into whose palm he slipped a wad of cash. I could smell the dewy night air of Central Park, the smell of dirt and a hint of evergreens, in the moment before I stepped into the magnificent art deco lobby. I stopped for a moment to close my eyes and breathe in deeply.

The doorman caught up with me, and slid the cart packed with suitcases into the lobby. At this late hour — it was almost 2 am — he was the only one on duty, so Johnny took the cart from there. Through the still open door of the lobby, I waved goodnight to Jean-Pierre, who nodded and saluted me in turn, as he climbed back into the limo with a slight knowing smile on his face. Johnny told me that he would be my driver whenever I needed to show up to a meeting or event where it would not be appropriate for me to pull up solo in a DeLorean. Apparently, Johnny had been to the apartment enough times, including on this doorman's night shift, that the guy didn't ask any questions before he pressed the elevator button at the front desk to unlock access to the penthouse.

Johnny handed me the keys and gestured for me to go ahead of him, as he pulled the cart out of the elevator. It had been *a long time* since I handled old metal keys like these. A lifetime, in fact. He stared at me somewhat amused as I fiddled with them and finally got the door open. The apartment was spectacular. It far exceeded my expectations. I walked from the entry foyer down into the sunken living room as Johnny unloaded the suitcases. "I'll leave you to have a look around while I take this cart back downstairs," he said. I looked at him, hardly able to contain my excitement. "Welcome home, Dana. Welcome *back*, Chairman…" He couldn't resist adding that.

Before checking out the rest of the house, I hurried up the staircase to the top floor of the duplex. It was an uncanny feeling to see the hybrid Gothic-and Art Deco-style stone turret up close for the first time after walking out of its doorway onto my terrace and turning around to face it. The structure was more magnificent than I had even imagined based on photographs that I'd seen of it. The whole white stone façade was bathed in spotlights that were set up on the roof, so that it shone with an aura of magic and mystery against the night sky. The crown jewel of the building, its deco details reminded me at once of Arthurian legends of the Round Table Knights and the temples erected at the top of ancient Mesopotamian ziggurats, where the high priestess of Ishtar playing the Whore of Babylon would grant supplicant kings benediction beneath her open thighs.

I looked over the edge of the terrace, leaning against one of the stone pillars that rose up from the line of the wall. My mind briefly flashed back to what this place looks like in the early 22nd century. I had seen it up close several times, including the day that I dove on the Guggenheim with my mother. It was a seething pool of ocean waves, roughly enclosed by decrepit skyscrapers on three sides, where the currents that were channeled through the streets of lower Manhattan converged for a stretch of a few miles before flowing more freely upwards toward Harlem and the South Bronx, the open side of the imperfect rectangle, where almost no buildings were tall enough to rise above the waves. But now the even more breathtaking vista of Central Park extended out before me like a blanket of dense trees, framed by the sparkling skyline of the Upper East Side and of Central Park South, where none of those eyesore matchsticks of "Billionaire's Row" had been built yet to mar the grandeur of the grand old New York buildings facing into the park, like the Essex House. After being mesmerized for a moment by the lights of all the buildings, I looked straight down and saw the rooftop of Tavern on the Green across the street. Even the lights in the finely sculpted shrubbery of their outdoor dining space could be discerned from here. I decided that I would go there for brunch tomorrow, after a morning walk in the park. Maybe I'd walk across to the Guggenheim on 5th Avenue.

I heard Johnny come back in, and I went downstairs to say goodnight to him. "I can't thank you enough for what you've done here," I said, as I gave him a huge hug. "Don't forget these, Dana." He handed me the keys to the DeLorean. "It's parked downstairs, next to the Gothic stone church with the red door." I smiled and nodded as I placed them on a small tabletop in the entry foyer. As he headed out the door, Johnny said, "I'll let you just settle in tomorrow, and then the day after, Jean-Pierre will drive you out to the pharmaceutical company on Long Island, for a full briefing from the team at the SCIF (Secure Facility) that we've built underground there." "Thank you, again, Johnny. You all really came through." He smiled back at me proudly, and gave me a military salute, as he got onto the elevator.

I was so pumped with adrenaline that I wasn't tired at all. So I opened the suitcases right there in the entry foyer, rather than dragging them through the apartment. Before bringing the sensitive documents upstairs, I checked that the hidden combination lock vault had been properly installed behind a panel in the library that lined the interior walls of the roof turret — as I had specified when we planned the apartment. Once I confirmed this, I carried the documents up by the handful. Each stack was relevant to one of my planned operations to alter key events in the timeline. Then I emptied some of the other items in the suitcases into my closets, at which point I realized that my requested fashionable '80s women's wardrobe had been acquired. Presumably one of the women on our team, who was closest to my size, had tried at least some of the items on. (I certainly hope that it was a woman who had filled one of the dresser drawers with a variety of women's underwear, including quite a few rather risqué thongs.) There was also a set of shoes of various types in my size, from sneakers to super high heels, lining the floor of one of the closets.

By the time I was done packing and storing the suitcases themselves, I was a little less high-strung, but still too excited by being here to be able to fall asleep. It was 3 am, and I was starting to worry that I'd be a zombie tomorrow if I didn't get some shut eye. So I went into the bathroom of the master bedroom, and turned the water of the "hot tub" on. (I mean, it was little more than a large bathtub.) Then I slipped the black dress off, hanging it on the knob of the bathroom door because a bathrobe was already suspended from the hook. I noted that it was a Calvin Klein bathrobe, which I found ironic, since in the timeline that I came from, Mr. Klein would purchase this apartment in 1983 for only $1 million and nearly destroy it by knocking down all of the interior walls. The board could rest assured that if or when he came around, I wouldn't sell for any price.

I slipped into the hot tub and bent my knees until my whole body sank beneath the steaming warm water up to my chin. Then I started touching myself, trying to get back into my skin in this strange time and place. Now the value of the regression hypnosis sessions became very clear to me. Despite having lived in New York during this era, had it not been for immersion in my memories of that life, the experience of being here would be almost unbearably uncanny. I could tell from how long it took me to come that my body had been very tense. Once I did, I felt every muscle relax from the release of the prolonged tension. I drained the water out of the tub, turned on the shower, and lathered my body. When I shampooed my hair, I let the hot water run over my head and face for a while. Then, I dried off and got under the covers of my bed with its tall Gatsby-style headboard. Sometime before the indigo hour, I fell asleep.

CHAPTER 15

OPERATION NEQAB

The blare of honking yellow cab horns woke me up in the morning. Apparently, they could be heard even from the 20th floor. *Ah, New York*. On account of the fact that I had forgotten to draw the curtains closed properly, the morning light that bathed the room made it so that I could not put myself back to sleep. Once I walked over to the curtains and looked down at the checkered taxis that were making all the noise, I decided to pull them all the way open instead of closing them. I glanced at the digital clock on the bedside table. It was 9:30 am. On a Friday morning the Tavern wouldn't be open for another hour and a half. I got dressed in clothes that were elegant enough to dine there but wore shoes comfortable enough to take a walk across Central Park before doing so. I stopped to say hello to the morning doorman on my way out. "I'm Dana Avalon, the owner of the penthouse apartment," I said, introducing myself. "So *you're* the mystery woman everyone's been talking about." *Just great*, I thought. The last thing I needed was to draw too much unwanted attention to myself. But such are the hazards when you have corporate proxies purchase a million-dollar penthouse apartment at a prime location in Manhattan for you, without ever showing up yourself. "No big mystery — Tom, is it? I was just tied up on business abroad."

Before heading into the park, I went around the corner to check out the DeLorean. Damn impressive. Everything was to specifications. With its matt black finish and black leather interior, the thing looked like some kind of futuristic Batmobile when its door wings were popped open. I probably should have gone for a more low-key car, but I just couldn't resist. A time traveler *has* to drive a DeLorean, even if no one would understand why for another five years.

When I was done playing with the car, I walked across the street and entered Central Park through the gate that led up to Tavern on the Green. It was 10 am. They were still setting up. So I headed toward the Upper East Side. I walked north across Sheep Meadow to the Bethesda Terrace, where I lingered for a while taking in the sculpture of the angel and walking to the water's edge for a spectacular view of the Loeb Boathouse. There were already a few people out row boating on the lake. Then, I walked up along the East Drive, past the Conservatory pool and visited the bronze Alice in Wonderland sculptures, where I watched a couple of children who were too young to be in school climbing up and down the mushrooms and onto Alice's dress, or playing with the Mad Hatter, with their babysitters making sure that they didn't fall.

I continued on up the East Drive, until I reached the obelisk across from the Metropolitan Museum of Art. Here I lingered a while again, reminiscing on the regular pilgrimages that I used to make to this monument in my lifetime as Jason. This obelisk was one of the few monuments that we had rescued from beneath the waters, and it had proved at least as difficult as the retrieval of the Prometheus and Atlas statues at Rockefeller Center. They had all been erected in the same city center of Gotham, which was something like a sacred precinct, surrounded by some of the first skyscrapers that rose up on the Englewood Cliffs in the 2070s.

I continued a little further up along the East Drive until I got to the exit at 90th Street and Fifth Avenue. I walked up the steps to the Reservoir for a moment and looked across at the skyline of the Upper West Side, seeing if I could spot the rooftop of my new home from here. Then, I walked out onto Fifth Avenue and strolled one block south on the cobblestone street next to the park until I was standing across the street from the Guggenheim.

As I took the building in, I kept having flashbacks of what it looked like under water. I wanted to see it from the inside. I walked across the street. Unfortunately, the museum wasn't open yet. I'd have to come back soon. You might not believe it if I told you that the highlight of this walk was standing there on the street corner, next to this Frank Lloyd Wright masterpiece, and smelling the smoke from the Sabrett fast food cart that was cooking up hot dogs and salted pretzels. There is nothing like the sense of smell to situate you in a place or bring a lost world back to life. This scent, mixed with the exhaust from the traffic along Fifth Avenue, was what finally grounded me here in the Manhattan of March 1980. There are some things about New York that we never managed to replicate in Gotham. I was tempted to have a pretzel with mustard, but I decided to head back to Tavern on the Green for brunch rather than kill my appetite at this food cart.

I walked back by crossing the Great Lawn, on the south side where I could take a close look at Belvedere Castle and pass by the Shakespeare Theater, on my way to the restaurant. By the time I got back to the Tavern it was 11:30, so a few other people were already seated at their tables and were being served. I sat right next to the floor-to-ceiling wall of glass windows that looked onto the outdoor dining space with its large shrubbery trees shaped into the form of various animals. When the waiter came over, I ordered a black coffee and an eggs benedict with smoked salmon. As I sipped the coffee, I began to gather my thoughts concerning what would be my first mission. It was a very challenging operation.

In about four and a half months, on July 9th of 1980, there would be a coup attempt in Iran against the nascent Islamic Republic. It was called Operation *Neqab*, with *Neqab* (Niqab), the word for a face veil, being a secret acronym for the phrase *Nejaté Qiamé Bozorg*, or "Saving the Great Uprising." In other words, saving the constitutionalist and

secular/progressive aims of the Iranian Revolution from being hijacked by regressive religious forces. On the timeline that I was from,
this coup would fail disastrously. Hundreds of military officers would
be arrested, 144 of them executed, and about 4,000 more servicemen
would be expelled from various branches of the military. What is
worse is that this would serve to decapitate the command-and-control
functions of what had been, under the Shah, the fifth most powerful
military in the world, just a couple of months before Saddam Hussein
would order Iraqi forces to invade, leading to an eight-year war of
attrition that cemented the Islamic Republic as the regressive regime
of a besieged Iran. Furthermore, the exposure of the coup attempt
within the regular military would justify its being sidelined in favor
of a so-called "Islamic Revolutionary Guard Corps," whose principal
loyalty was to the ayatollahs. Eventually, this IRGC would become the
military-industrial backbone of the Islamic Republic of Iran, leading
the reconstruction effort after the eight-year war with Iraq.

The hidden purpose of this war of attrition, which had been set up
by the CIA and MI6, was to solidify the Islamic Republic as a militant
theocratic Muslim regime that would block the path of the Soviet
Union to the oil resources of the Persian Gulf that could have saved the
economy of the USSR from the collapse that it eventually faced from
1989 to 1991. Soviet forces had occupied Persian-speaking Afghanistan
in 1979, ostensibly to shore up their proxy Communist government
there, and so they had considerably extended their already long border
with Iran, giving them another staging ground for marching to the
oil wells in Khuzestan, seizing the strategic Strait of Hormuz, and key
warm water shipping ports like Abadan, Bandar Abbas, and Chah
Bahar. My first mission was to ensure that the *Neqab* coup succeeded,
thereby preventing the Iraqi invasion of Iran in September of 1980
by placing a right-wing nationalist dictatorship in power. This would
antagonize Iranian Communist parties and leftist guerrilla fighters,
while also emboldening them by destroying their theocratic Islamist

rivals. These Communists, together with ethnic separatists in the outer provinces (who had also been a part of the coup plot), would then act as a fifth column for a Soviet invasion force entering Iran from both sides of the Caspian Sea as well as from Afghanistan. Soviet control over Iranian oil, early in the 1980s, would go a long way to *ensuring the survival of the USSR, including by keeping Cold War tensions high.* That would set the stage for further operations of mine in service of the same aim.

I thought about Operation Neqab throughout my brunch, but I let it slip into the back of my mind for the rest of the day. Since I would have to travel to Paris before too long to meet with the exiled Iranian Prime Minister Shapour Bakhtiar, who was the figurehead of the coup that I knew was already being planned, I resolved to enjoy as much of New York as I could. I did not plan to be in Paris for long, but I did not appreciate being dislocated so soon after arriving here. So I spent the rest of the day zipping all around Manhattan in taxis, visiting as many of the places that had been most significant to me in my lifetime as Jorjani. If you're wondering how I paid for breakfast or for the cabs, I neglected to mention that Johnny, or someone on the team, had left a stack of hundred-dollar bills inside the hidden vault of the turret library. This was to hold me over until the operatives who had been tasked with setting up the pharmaceutical company, and profiting on its stock through insider trading, fully briefed me on both my personal bank account and corporate financial information.

That was actually the first item on the agenda when we met at the Long Island SCIF the next day. This Secure Facility had been built in a Brutalist concrete bunker-style, beneath Avalon Pharmaceutical in Stony Brook, Long Island. Being so involved in the medical industry, the decision had been made to situate the company as close as possible to the new hospital that had just been built at Stony Brook, and to cultivate a relationship with its doctors and researchers. The site of our corporate compound was also selected with a view to its proximity to

Brookhaven National Laboratory. On a personal level, I appreciated how close it was to Wardenclyffe, where I built that ill-fated World Wireless tower three lifetimes ago.

Jean-Pierre picked me up in the black limo at 9:45 that Saturday morning, and on account of it being a weekend with no commuter traffic, we made it to the pharmaceutical company by 11 am. Both the pharma and stock-trading teams were there to meet me, although the general policy was for these two groups to have as little direct contact with each other as possible so as to stay under the radar of the Securities and Exchange Commission. Fortunately, since it was a Saturday, none of the rank-and-file workers were at the company. After a brief tour of the main building, we went down into the SCIF through a hidden tunnel that led underground.

Like all such facilities, it was protected from surveillance of any kind — well, of any *conventional* kind. I had also left the team with instructions for a measure intended to limit *unconventional* surveillance, such as Remote Viewing of what went on inside the facility. This was a technique we applied in the early 21st century, and it was fascinating to see it implemented here in 1980s New York. The concrete walls had been imprinted with row upon row of small numbers. You see, numbers are notoriously difficult for clairvoyants to read, even though they are drawn to deciphering them. So, the inscriptions were meant to act as a kind of confusing attractor, weakening any potential remote viewers' capacity to concentrate on the content of meetings at the facility. There were also, at regular intervals, stretches of concrete wall that lacked overhead lighting and were painted silver. Projectors were set up to fill these silver "screens" with hardcore pornographic images and scenes of ultra-violence. There was no audio, so we tried to just block them out as part of the background while we were having a meeting. But a remote viewer who was attempting to clairvoyantly surveil us would tend to get sucked into these psychic traps. Between these shocking images and the enigmatic numbers inscribed in the walls, the data that they would deliver to whoever was tasking them would most likely be garbage.

Small sandwiches and other hors d'oeuvres had been set up on the massive granite boardroom table. I picked at these, and drank coffee and tea, during a several-hour briefing on everything that had been achieved since the vanguard arrived here in 1977. We did *not* discuss Operation Neqab, or any specific operation aiming to change some feature of the timeline, because the details of these was highly compartmentalized information handled on a need-to-know basis. For example, there was no reason for the people who were setting up my meeting with Prime Minister Bakhtiar in Paris to know that I planned to assassinate the poor man once the coup he was leading was successful.

I left for Paris about a week after this meeting on Long Island. It was early April. The Iranian military coup to overthrow the Islamic Republic was planned for July 9–10. I stayed at a hotel near the Louvre, and while I waited to meet with Shapour Bakhtiar, I walked around the museum for a while. It was interesting to see it without the glass pyramid that would become so iconic. The Grand Louvre renovation project would not begin for another year, and that pyramid wouldn't be built until 1989. The inverted pyramid would be built even later, in the early '90s. Unlike the museums of the submerged island of Manhattan, the Louvre and Paris as a whole would survive the deluge because it was far enough inland and just barely high enough above sea level (35 meters on average, as compared to 10 meters on Manhattan Island). True to the city's darkly prophetic motto, Paris would be tossed by the waves, but she would not sink. What destroyed Paris wasn't the flood waters. It was years of civil war between native Parisians and increasingly fundamentalist Muslim migrants who, by 2040, declared a sharia-based Islamic State in France, albeit one that never managed to control the countryside before The Arrival ended it in 2048.

Which brings me back to Shapour Bakhtiar, who had been in exile for almost exactly one year. The Islamic Republic of Iran had just celebrated its first anniversary on April 1, 1980. I knew to set my meeting with the last Prime Minister of the dying Shah shortly after that, since Bakhtiar would likely be both incensed and imbued with a sense of urgency by the anniversary. Bakhtiar had been told that I was a private contractor with a corporate intelligence agency that occasionally collaborated with the CIA on certain operations. I knew that he would not check with the CIA because, contrary to what he told the military men in Iran who were part of his coup plot, Bakhtiar had endeavored to keep the entire operation hidden from the United States since American diplomats were still being held hostage by Islamist forces in Tehran, and such an attempted coup against the theocratic regime would likely be seen as posing a serious danger to their safety. Bakhtiar had been given assurances that my only contacts in the CIA relevant to Iran were rogue elements who considered the hostages expendable if it meant restoring a pro-US regime there. AtlantiCorp had already transferred significant funds to Bakhtiar's Swiss bank account, with the understanding that it would be used as "lubricant" to facilitate broader participation in the operation (we learned not to use the word "coup" with him).

It was the evening of Friday, April 4th, when I sat down to dinner with Prime Minister Bakhtiar at the dining table of my own luxurious suite at the Hausmannian-style Grand Hôtel du Louvre (built in 1855), which those who arranged the meeting, on both sides, determined to be the safest location from a security and counter-surveillance standpoint. No one would see him with me in a public place. The Prime Minister's joint three-man security team, consisting of one of his own most trusted men, one French secret service officer, and a member of the AtlantiCorp security force that had flown with me to Paris as my personal bodyguard, even had instructions to take the elevator to the wrong floor, then walk up the stairs to the right one.

When I opened the door and greeted Bakhtiar, I apologized to him for this protocol. With a wave of his hand, he told me to think nothing of it. We shook hands and exchanged pleasantries for a moment, as he smiled while nervously fingering his mustache and bobbing his head. The security men went ahead and scoped out the entire suite. Then, one of them stationed himself in the hallway, outside the door, wearing an earpiece that he could use to communicate with us. Another went back down to the lobby, carefully watching everyone headed in and out of the hotel. The third sat on a chair near the window, keeping his eye on the terrace. Then, after sipping glasses of wine that I poured us in the kitchen, Bakhtiar and I sat down at the dining table together. The hotel restaurant had sent up a room service tray stacked with a three-course meal. I knew I could bank on classic French food, since Bakhtiar had spent so many years of his youth in Paris — including fighting the Nazis as part of the Resistance during the occupation.

This militantly Anti-Fascist resume would make some of what I had to say a very hard sell. You see, Shapour Bakhtiar was a consummate Social Democrat. When Bakhtiar was studying in Paris in 1934, his father was executed by Reza Shah — the father of Shah Mohammad Reza Pahlavi. So, when the latter appointed Bakhtiar Prime Minister, as a last resort, at the height of the Iranian Revolution of 1979, he was appointing someone who had spent decades as an opposition figure and member of the National Front of Prime Minister Mohammad Mossadegh, in whose government Bakhtiar had served, when Mossadegh briefly overthrew the Shah, before the latter was restored (and Mossadegh arrested) in the MI6- and CIA-backed military coup of 1953.

Subsequently, Bakhtiar was repeatedly imprisoned, spending a total of six years in jail for his secular democratic opposition to the autocratic rule of the very Shah who he would agree to serve as Prime Minister in January of 1979, when Islamist theocrats and armed Communist guerrillas were on the verge of taking over the country.

Bakhtiar's vision for a political solution in Iran had always been full restoration of the Persian Constitution of 1906, which would reduce the monarch to a ceremonial figurehead, and secure the full range of civil liberties, freedom of expression, and democratic political representation to all citizens. His attempt to implement such a platform after he came into office, in the midst of what by then was a violent revolution, with measures such as total freedom of the press and the release of all political prisoners, dramatically precipitated the total collapse of the Pahlavi regime within only thirty-six days. Once the general staff of the military swore allegiance to Ayatollah Khomeini, Bakhtiar fled to Paris where he had been busy building up a secular democratic opposition to the Islamic Republic and where, secretly, he had also been coordinating with second-tier military officers and opposition groups sidelined or betrayed by the ayatollahs to carry out Operation Neqab.

The point is that the last thing Bakhtiar wanted to see from out of this operation, which he did not consider a "coup" (since its leaders were no longer actually in power), was for a military dictatorship to seize control of Iran. To him, the military officers involved in the plot were only a spearhead in the service of democratization. His goal remained the same: an Iranian parliamentary democracy, with the broad participation of all political constituencies who were willing to achieve their aims within the legal parameters of the Constitution rather than by means of partisan violence. My unenviable task was to convince Bakhtiar that he had to appoint Mohsen Pezeshkpour as his Deputy Prime Minister. Pezeshkpour was the leader of the ultra-nationalist, one might even say Fascist, Pan-Iranist Party, which had been the loyal opposition to the Shah in parliament until, in 1975, the Shah abolished even this loyal opposition to establish a one-party system. In 1971, Pezeshkpour had used his position in parliament to loudly protest the Shah's willingness to relinquish Iran's claim to Bahrain.

Those charmed by his charisma considered his speeches impassioned, while critics and enemies saw Pezeshkpour as a raving lunatic.

He was certainly the closest thing that Iran had to a Hitleresque political figure. He was a staunch anti-Communist and a strong supporter
of the Imperial Iranian Military, which it was his ultimate ambition to
use for a reconquest of all of the ethnically Iranian territories of the
great Persian Empires of the past — someday, including those inside
the Soviet Union (the Azerbaijani, Turkmen, Uzbek, and Tajik SSRs)
and, of course, Afghanistan, which had been Eastern Iran until the
1800s. Pezeshkpour had a 180-degree opposite view of the Shah to that
of Bakhtiar. He saw Mohammad Reza Pahlavi as a weak and ineffec-
tual bureaucrat, all talk and no action. In the last days of the Pahlavi
regime, after the Shah had already left Iran, Pezeshkpour delivered a
fiery speech from the podium of the Parliament, wherein he accused
the Shah of having been at the head of a "bureaucratic totalitarianism." Pezeshkpour, who had shaved his moustache and now bore a
darkly comical resemblance to Peter Sellers playing Dr. Strangelove,
pounded the podium as he ranted about how this was the worst
form of government known to man. He was essentially quoting Carl
Schmitt. According to Pezeshkpour, a military dictatorship would be
far less corrupt. Unlike Bakhtiar, he refused to flee Iran. In fact, on the
timeline that I was from, Pezeshkpour proved to be such a patriot that
he effectively lived under house arrest and perpetual surveillance in
the Islamic Republic rather than go into exile.

Since I knew that Pezeshkpour would be such a hard sell, I started
by giving Bakhtiar some intelligence that would be even more valuable
than the funds provided to him by AtlantiCorp. (Of course, he was
entirely misled about how I had obtained all this information.) There
was a member of the coup-planning group inside of Iran by the name
of Farhad Nasirkhani who would turn out to be an asset of Iraqi intelligence. The information provided to the Iraqis by this fellow, ostensibly
to secure their support for the coup, would actually be leaked to the
ayatollahs by Saddam Hussein himself. In the timeline that I came
from, this is something that the Islamic Republic, which considered

the secular Baathist Saddam an arch-enemy even before Iraq invaded Iran in September of 1980, never admitted publicly.

The reason that Saddam passed on this information to the Iranian regime was because he knew that their crackdown on the coup plotters would destroy the nerve center of Iran's military, and introduce an incoherent division of power between the no longer trusted regular military and the newly formed Islamic Revolutionary Guard Corps. This would significantly facilitate an Iraqi invasion of Iran. On the other hand, Saddam knew that if the coup were to succeed, and a nationalist military government were to replace the Islamic Republic as the regime of Iran, any Iraqi invasion would be easily thwarted by the remnants of the Shah's military. Bakhtiar said that he didn't even know who this guy was. I told him to make sure that the coup-planning team inside of Iran got rid of Nasirkhani, and that no one else involved in Operation Neqab approach any individual or organ of the Iraqi government. Bakhtiar nodded very affirmatively and said, "Yes, absolutely. I will definitely see to that, Ms. Avalon. Thank you." The Prime Minister's English was not bad, and where it faltered, I switched to French so that he could more fluently express himself in that language that he knew so well.

Next, I told Bakhtiar that one of the Air Force officers involved in the coup planning had a wife who was untrustworthy and that, perhaps on account of personal marital problems that they had, this woman would likely reveal to authorities of the theocratic regime what she knew about the secret meetings that her husband attended. I did not tell him that because the Islamic Republic never revealed the name of this woman (and even claimed, falsely, that it was her husband who had given up his collaborators, the night before the coup was supposed to take place), we had to use remote viewers to identify her. I told Bakhtiar that we would take her out of the picture. (In point of fact, I would have both her and, for good measure, also her husband poisoned to death months before she would decide to reveal anything.)

Bakhtiar was more concerned by this variable than by the informant for Iraq, but he also expressed even more gratitude, bowing his head with his hand on his heart as he thanked me for getting ahead of this potential disaster.

Finally, I broached the subject of Pezeshkpour. I led into it by explaining to him that, unfortunately, as he knew full well, the possibility that the coup would fail or be reversed even *after* he returned to Iran could not be eliminated. Especially since his expeditious return to Iran would be key to its success, and yet this would also mean that he was all the more vulnerable to a potential reversal of the coup by Islamist forces. I told Bakhtiar that I knew that he hadn't told the nationalist military men involved in the coup plot that, democrat that he was, he had also negotiated the participation of Communist factions and even leftist guerrillas who had been betrayed by Khomeini after helping him to seize power, as well as certain insiders of the Islamic Republic who were of a more intellectual and technocratic bent, and did not want to see the promised "Republic" element of the regime become a hollow shell under a Khomeini-led theocracy. The leader of this last group was none other than the Islamic Republic's Foreign Minister, Sadegh Ghotbzadeh, who Bakhtiar had promised to recognize as the leader of an Islamic Party with the freedom to field candidates in parliamentary elections. He had made the same promises of full political participation, within the limits of the law, to the Communist parties, including the Tudeh Party, which was essentially an asset of the Soviet Union. Bakhtiar looked somewhat alarmed when I laid all this out, and I had to gently remind him that I ran a private intelligence agency (a lie, of course).

Bakhtiar accepted my proposition that if — Heaven forbid — he were to be assassinated shortly after the military takeover, the coalition that he had put together, which these officers didn't even know about, would rapidly disintegrate with the Communists turning on the military men who had led the coup, and vice versa, and the moderate

Islamic faction turning on both of them and potentially allying itself with the Mojaheddin-e-Khalq (MEK). The MEK was just barely still part of the Islamic Republic regime but was seriously considering turning on Khomeini, who had severely sidelined them after using their muscle to topple the Shah. The MEK was not a part of Bakhtiar's coup coalition and represented a dangerous variable if the coalition were to unravel. The leader of this cultish 'Islamic' Maoist group, Massoud Rajavi, had his own ambitions to lead Iran. (What no one knew at the time is that Rajavi was so hell-bent on this that he would even ally himself with Saddam Hussein, and defect to Iraq with an entire tank battalion, during the Iran-Iraq War — a war that, on this revised timeline, it was my objective to prevent.)

In any case, I had Bakhtiar convinced, albeit grudgingly, that the coalition would not survive his death, and that there would be a very serious threat to Iran's cohesion as a nation. I let him know that, at AtlantiCorp, we were also apprised of his plan to use coup committees in the Azerbaijan, Kurdistan, Khuzestan, and Baluchistan provinces to help topple the Islamic Republic. All of these were border provinces demographically dominated by ethnic minorities with some aspirations for autonomy. There was a real danger that, if Bakhtiar was not there to form a parliamentary government wherein they all felt adequately represented, the very same people in these provinces who had volunteered to help him topple the ayatollahs, would lead a secession of their provinces from Iran, leaving only a rump state of "Persia" (the Persian-speaking part of Iran) that would be an economically devastated nation, especially without the oil that came almost exclusively from the Khuzestan province with its largely Arab population (who called the region "Al-Ahwaz").

So, I reasoned with Bakhtiar, that in the event — however unlikely — that such a nightmare scenario would unfold, there ought to be *some* designated civilian leader to replace him, but one who could work seamlessly with the military in order to crush the Marxists and the 'Islamic' Maoists, who would certainly stage an armed uprising, and above all, to secure the territorial integrity of Iran against potential secessions of those provinces with a Persian minority demographic. Bakhtiar very grimly followed the logic of all of this, but he still broke his characteristic gentlemanly cool and started shrilly shouting in French when I proposed that the only man capable of doing this was Mohsen Pezeshkpour. I told Bakhtiar that he ought to inform the military leaders of the coup that Pezeshkpour is his designated Deputy Prime Minster, without letting the leftists and moderate Islamists in the coalition know this. "He's a Fascist!" Bakhtiar shouted, in French. His voice would become rather high-pitched when he raised it. I winced. The security man at the window also came over to make sure everything was alright. "I spent my youth here, in France, fighting Fascists! My father was killed by a Fascist like him!"

I began to address him in fluent Persian. *This* he was not expecting. I had saved it as my ace card. When I studied the writings of Jorjani in depth during my college years, and before I went on to write a dissertation critiquing them, I also began re-learning the Persian language. I say re-learning because I think that the many past life regression sessions that I had, which for obvious reasons wound up being more intensive than those of most Prometheists, helped me to regain some of Jason's linguistic abilities. I was able to start speaking Persian fluently much faster than most people who have no prior knowledge of the language. I went back over the key points of the very well-reasoned argument that I had made, but in Persian, and with a tone of more personal concern, adding colorful asides that demonstrated extraordinary insights into both the political history of Iran and the character of certain key individuals and groups, like Pezeshkpour, Ghotbzadeh, Rajavi, and the leader the Communist Tudeh Party, Noureddin Kianouri.

Bakhtiar stared at me with the most wide-eyed expression that I've ever seen on anyone's face. I asked him if he could, in all honesty, think of a single other politician who had served in a prominent position in parliament, or who held some cabinet level post in any of the Pahlavi administrations, who would be able to work as effectively with the military leaders of the coup to hold the country together if he were to meet with an untimely demise upon his return. After shaking his head and grumbling for a while, Bakhtiar admitted that he could think of no one other than Pezeshkpour. Then I asked him whether an outright military dictatorship with *no* civilian leader whatsoever, and potentially no parliament, would be preferable to an administration led by a man who — for decades — headed the parliament's second largest political party in Pahlavi Iran. "*To ki hasti?!*" (Who *are* you?!) he shouted at me, indignantly, in Persian, before finally caving in as he shook his head, covering his downcast eyes. Whoever I may have been, the logic of the argument was sound, and whatever else Shapour Bakhtiar may have been, he was above all, a *logical* man.

All of this happened before we had dessert. I poured Bakhtiar a sweet wine to go with our crème brûlée and dark chocolate tarts with berries. "How did you learn such fluent Persian?" he asked, returning to a normal tone of voice, and sounding a little embarrassed at his earlier outburst. I couldn't even consider telling him the truth. Bakhtiar was as averse to metaphysical speculations as he was to religious scholasticism. "In the field of intelligence, Iran is my principal expertise." He rocked a bit, bobbing his head to the side, like a Muppet, and said, "*Clearly*, mademoiselle." After a moment's silence, he leaned in to me, with his dessert fork twirled in the air, "You know, there is no one — no politician –, in all the years I have been fighting for liberty in Iran, who could ever have convinced me to do what you ask me to do." My rejoinder was, "Prime Minister Bakhtiar, there has never been, in the long history of Iran, such a perilous time as this one. Not when the Greeks invaded, or even the Arabs, Turks, and Mongols, who sought to conquer your country. You are called upon to make an extraordinary sacrifice, because the very survival of Iran is at stake. It is our hope that you will lead the people of your country into a new era of Social Democracy and personal liberties. But, in any case, you must ensure the *survival* of the nation. I'm sure that you do not want to be remembered as the *last* Prime Minister of Iran." Bakhtiar stared at me somberly, "You are right, Ms. Avalon. I will *do* it." Shortly thereafter, we bid each other goodnight. The next day I visited the grave of Sadegh Hedayat at Père-Lachaise, laying a bouquet of red roses on the black stone pyramid inscribed with his name and the etching of an owl.

My flight back to New York left from Charles de Gaulle that night. It was a British Airways Concord. When we landed at JFK, earlier in the evening of the same day than we had left Paris, I reflected on how absurd it was that supersonic civilian flights would end in 2003 and would not resume, on a large scale, until the 2030s — at least in the world that I came from. Maybe that was something about history that we could change as well. Going through customs was a tiresome experience, and by the time that Jean-Pierre picked me up I was weary enough to lie across the back seat of the limousine. He was good about not bothering me with small talk, especially when he could see that I was tired. I dozed off until just before we reached the 59th Street Bridge, at which point I rolled down the window and gawked at the spectacular cityscape of midtown Manhattan. I used to love the view across this bridge, in particular, with the United Nations and the Chrysler Building clearly in sight. Jean-Pierre was a little unsettled by the fact that I kept the window rolled down as we entered the heart of the city, but it was a tinted window, and I was hungry to see as much as I could of those neighborhoods that were on our way home.

When we approached Central Park South, I asked Jean-Pierre if he would wait for me while I went to get a drink at The Plaza. Of course he obliged. He would loiter in the area and come check back at the front steps for me in twenty minutes, then again in half an hour, and so forth. I walked up to the Palm Court and sat at the bar island beneath the glass ceiling. I wanted to sit alone, but it was fairly crowded, and by the time that I was halfway through my Martini, a rather overconfident middle-aged man with an Italian accent was hitting on me. Clearly a hotel guest, I think he was entertaining delusions about getting me to come upstairs with him after a few more drinks. I told him that I had just flown back from Paris, had jet lag, and was headed back home. He was all pouty, disappointed that I was a New Yorker and didn't have a room at The Plaza. I caught Jean-Pierre up front on his second loop around the hotel. From my mood, I think he could tell that I regretted stopping for the drink and he surmised what had happened. The man was very intuitive. Did I mention that he was a practitioner of voodoo? He donned a black suit and black necktie as a uniform, but he also always wore a creepy bone wristband that I gathered was a voodoo charm. I leaned on his shoulder slightly as I got out of the limo at 55 Central Park West. Once I got upstairs, I took a quick shower, just to wash the airplane off of me. Then I collapsed into bed and slept like the dead until late into the next morning.

In the weeks that followed, I checked back repeatedly with Prime Minister Bakhtiar on a secure phone line that we set up, to make sure that things were going according to plan. I told him that we had, for our part, eliminated the threat of the treacherous housewife. He told me that all potential ties to the Iraqis had been severed, and, most importantly, that Mohsen Pezeshkpour had been approached in Tehran and had agreed to become Deputy Prime Minister of the putatively "provisional" government that would be installed by Operation Neqab. On April 25th, when news of Operation Eagle Claw broke across the international media, Bakhtiar called me in a panic asking what I knew about this disaster that took place at Tabas in the Iranian desert.

Ayatollah Khomeini was portraying the incident as an "act of God" that demonstrated divine support for Iran's Islamic Revolution and its resistance against the "Great Satan" of America. I told Bakhtiar that, based on what I could surmise from my CIA contacts, black ops men under the orders of Director of Central Intelligence George H. W. Bush had sabotaged two of the helicopters involved in the mission.

USAF field operations commander Colonel James H. Kyle may also have been acting on prior directives from Bush when he aborted the mission despite having a minimum of the resources necessary to carry it out, after the loss of the two sabotaged choppers and another one that went into an unexpected sandstorm. I told Bakhtiar that I didn't think that the crash of one of the retreating helicopters into a transport plane, which caused an explosion killing eight American servicemen, was an accident either. (Later, we would see that this failed attempt to rescue the US hostages in Tehran became the single most significant factor that cost Jimmy Carter his reelection and ensured that George H. W. Bush would go from being the head of the CIA to Vice President of the United States under Ronald Reagan.)

Bakhtiar asked how I thought this would affect Neqab, and I said that if the American hostages were still being held at the US embassy when the operation was carried out, it should be one of the mission priorities to send an Iranian special forces team to storm the US embassy early in the operation so as to free the hostages and save as many of their lives as possible, taking them into custody as leverage to ensure that the United States would accept the new provisional government. The hostage-takers should then be publicly executed as "terrorists," with this being broadcast on American television.

When I turned on the television on the morning of May 18, I saw that an earthquake on Mount St. Helens in Washington state had triggered a massive landslide that caused the northern flank of the volcano to collapse. The mountain suddenly entered a catastrophic new stage of eruption. I was sleeping in because it was a Sunday, and I had been dancing the night away to disco music at Studio 54. I had a bit of a hangover too. As I watched the television coverage, I thought it was a good thing that I didn't let that cute girl I had met by the end of the night come home with me. (Instead, we finger fucked each other in a dark corner of the upstairs balcony, after snorting a line of coke.) She would have been a nuisance to deal with right now. I was particularly fixated on the images that were being broadcast, because I had arrived here, in this time, on the night that the eruption of Mount St. Helens started to simmer (about two months and ten days ago).

The volcano was billowing smoke, and as the day unfolded, and I remained glued to the news reports, I saw how this became a huge black column not unlike that of a mushroom cloud at a nuclear blast site. This is not an exaggerated comparison, since the thermal energy released by the eruption was reported to have reached 26 megatons — equivalent to the yield of a large nuclear warhead. The volcano, in the Pacific Northwest, dumped ash over no less than eleven American states and several Canadian provinces. Fifty-seven people were killed, including a couple of photographers and a geologist who were on-site and could not get out of harm's way fast enough when the landslide and major eruption took place. Hundreds of square miles were reduced to a wasteland, and thousands of animals were killed. When the dust settled, it was assessed that the damage to American and Canadian farmers was in the billions of dollars.

The majestic mountain scenery of the Pacific Northwest reminded me of scenes from *The Shining*, which I remembered was just about to be released. In two lifetimes now, it had been one of my favorite films. It would really be something to see it on the big screen when it first came out in theaters. I couldn't resist the pun of making plans to go see it together with "Johnny" on opening night. He was into horror films, after all. But before that, I had the pleasure of going to see another classic by myself, on the first full day that *it* was released. I went to a morning showing so as not to have to wait in lines that rounded the street corners. Lines wherein fans waiting to see the movie were often subjected to the spoiler shouted by overexcited people exiting the theater. "Vader is Luke's father," they would inconsiderately shout. Yes, I went to the Ziegfeld Theater on 54th Street to see the release of *The Empire Strikes Back*. By the way, I listened for it carefully, and the line was definitely "*No*, I am your father." (At least on *this* timeline.)

I had a VHS player hooked to the big CRT projector TV in my living room, and I began to amass a collection of videotapes of all of my favorite movies. That TV was also hooked up to cable, so that when CNN hit the airwaves for the first time, on June 1st of 1980, it became my preferred news outlet. These were the days back when the relatively radical Ted Turner ran the independent Cable News Network himself, and Larry King had just gotten his own televised show, long before its decline into another outlet of Newspeak. It came to mind just now because James Earl Jones, the voice of Darth Vader, did the recurring audio clip that would announce: "*This* is CNN." It was CNN, with its then unprecedented 24-hour news cycle, that I had on the day that I was waiting for breaking news on the coup attempt in Iran.

I had set my alarm clock for 5 am, which was already 1:30 pm in Tehran. But I could not sleep soundly, and I found myself already lying wide awake and anxious at 4 am, just after noontime in Iran. I threw on my bathrobe and went into the living room to turn on CNN. There was a commercial break, which I took as an opportunity to quickly put on a pot of coffee in the kitchen. As I waited for it to brew, I sat down on the sofa in front of the television. Sure enough, there it was. The first item once coverage resumed, with the banner "Breaking News" running across the bottom of the screen.

"These are scenes broadcast today by Iranian National Radio and Television, which was seized several hours ago by the leaders of what appears to be an ongoing military coup," a voice said over footage of Iranian Brigadier General Ayat Mohagheghi delivering a speech in a stern tone from behind a desk with a Lion and Sun flag sitting on it. Then the feed cut to a videotaped statement from Ayatollah Shariatmadari, who was the most high-ranking mullah in Iran, delivering a religious ruling or *fatwa* that what Ayatollah Khomeini had done since he returned to Iran in early 1979 had been a disgrace to Islam and the legacy of the imams. Shariatmadari reaffirmed the traditional Shi'ite stance that the clergy ought not to tarnish its moral authority by becoming directly involved in the political affairs of the country. In addition to these speeches, there was footage of certain buildings in and around Tehran consumed by flames. Then CNN cut to a reporter who was outside of Shapour Bakhtiar's home in Paris, where it was mid-morning. "The exiled Prime Minister has yet to make any statement, or to receive anyone from the media. His aids are, however, assuring us that a press conference *will* be held in a few hours. The security here is very tight. French police and gendarmerie have surrounded Mr. Bakhtiar's home." I didn't even consider calling him in the midst of all this. For now, all I could do was wait and watch.

Bits and pieces of information, together with a lot of repetition, and a few other news stories, came in over the next several hours. Then, finally, at 7 am, CNN's morning news anchor presented a fairly comprehensive overview. It was 3:30 in the afternoon in Tehran. Apparently, the coup had begun with airstrikes launched from Shahrokhi Air Force Base in Hamadan on key targets of the government of the Islamic Republic in Tehran. The most prominent of these was the home of Ayatollah Khomeini in the Jamaran neighborhood of northern Tehran, which was not only struck by Phoenix missiles from an F-14, but also became the target of a nearly simultaneous kamikaze strike by a martyred F-4 Phantom jet pilot. The Supreme Leader of the Islamic Republic, and the figurehead of the 1979 Revolution that brought the theocratic regime to power, was believed to have been immolated in the compound, which was still burning.

The so-called "Islamic Assembly," which had replaced Iran's national parliament, was also bombed. Immediately following the initial strikes in Tehran, jets took to the air from Air Force bases in Shiraz, Dezful, and Bushehr as well, hitting targets in the south and southwest of the country. All in all, it appeared that around fifty F-4 Phantoms and F-14 Tomcats were part of the aerial campaign. Coup committees in the West Azerbaijan, Kurdistan, Khuzestan, Baluchistan, and Khorasan provinces, as well as in Tehran itself, and in the Imperial

Iranian Navy stationed at key ports in the Persian Gulf, carried out purges of those top brass officers who had committed treason against the Constitution, and the Bakhtiar administration, by swearing their allegiance to Khomeini and his fellow ayatollahs. Some of them were arrested, others were shot on the spot. The 23rd Commando Division, the 1st Infantry Division, the 92nd Armored Division, and the 1st Marine Battalion acted as the spearhead of a nationwide imposition of martial law in Iran. From the start of the coup, at least 5,000 rank-and-file soldiers put their boots on the ground to back it. Many of them pulled down flags of the Islamic Republic and burned them in the streets, raising the old Lion and Sun banner back up on the poles over government buildings and city squares.

The most important piece of news, at least for an American audience to wake up to on this Wednesday morning, was revealed, rather strategically, when Prime Minister Bakhtiar finally gave a statement to a few select members of the press at noon in Paris. "At the very beginning of the operation, a team of our Special Forces commandos raided the US embassy in Tehran and were able to free the majority of American hostages held there. Unfortunately, a dozen of the 52 hostages were killed during the operation and some others were also injured. The 40 survivors are in protective custody now and those who require it are receiving medical attention. The provisional military government in Iran is in communication with Washington to secure their transport back to the United States as soon as possible. Maybe even later today, or tomorrow at the latest." With his head somewhat downcast, Prime Minister Bakhtiar went on to add, "I should also report that, although it was my preference that they stand trial for their crimes, it appears that all of the hostage takers who survived the initial commando assault have now been executed as stateless terrorists." The CNN newscast cut to footage of these executions carried out by Iranian commandos with their own handguns, against the wall of the US embassy. Despite the brutality of that footage, it would air over and over again, on prime-time American television, albeit always with a warning. That would go a long way in redeeming Iran's image, regardless of Bakhtiar's own reservations.

"Mr. Bakhtiar, who is in control in Iran?" shouted one of the journalists, as CNN cut back to the press conference in Paris. "For the moment, patriots of our military are in control. But it is my understanding that they await my return. These brave men have given every assurance that they will recognize me as Prime Minister when I arrive in Tehran shortly." When I heard these words, I picked up the phone without delay and called the pilot of the Learjet that I had ostensibly bought for conducting AtlantiCorp business. But it had no corporate logo painted on the side of it. I had deliberately left it unmarked. Meanwhile, I got a hold of Manuchehr Ghorbanifar, who had been on AtlantiCorp's payroll for the last month for his "shipping services" and he informed me of exactly when on the next day, and on what private plane, which belonged to Ghorbanifar's company, Prime Minister Bakhtiar would be leaving Paris for Tehran. Despite Bakhtiar's identification with Charles de Gaulle on account of his days in the French Resistance, the decision had been made to divert potential assassins or terrorists that the ayatollahs might send, by having the private plane depart from Orly airport, while a much more high-profile flight carrying aids of Bakhtiar would fly out of Charles de Gaulle, with the press having been misinformed that the Prime Minister was also on *that* flight.

I had, in advance, located the most isolated and desolate private airfield on the outskirts of Paris that I could find. On the night of July 9th, my Learjet left New York from the relatively obscure Stewart Airport, a former Air Force base that was located about 60 miles north of Manhattan and landed in that rural French airfield early the next day. I slept on the plane. Jean-Pierre, whose French turned out to be not bad, despite his Creole accent, was the only passenger on the plane besides the AtlantiCorp pilot. Jean-Pierre took a taxi from the airfield to the nearest auto rental place, and then drove back to the airfield with the car that would be used for this operation. It had been decided, when we planned this at a select meeting in the SCIF, that no driver in France could be trusted more than my personal chauffeur — an ex-commando –, who should be brought along for the job. Besides, my life was already in his hands on a regular basis anyhow.

When Jean-Pierre picked me up, he noticed that I slipped a very long bag into the trunk of the car, but neither did he remark upon this, nor upon the fact that I was dressed in a black chador complete with a neqab (a face veil). The expression that he had on his face when he would note things silently with a look in the rearview mirror some-times reminded me of the Observer in the *Silver Surfer* comics. He drove me to a wooded field with a few clearings between the trees, somewhere between the towns of Orly and Villeneuve-le-Roi, suburbs of Paris that were near Orly Airport. When Ghorbanifar gave me the flight information, I had determined the trajectory of the plane's departure from Orly on its way to Tehran. The long black bag, which I slung around my shoulder as I left the car parked on the side of the road to trudge into the field, contained a prototype FIM-92 Stinger missile designed by General Dynamics and acquired by AtlantiCorp from a corrupt defense contractor at Raytheon. Now that I was alone in the field, I pulled down the neqab to breathe more freely, but kept the chador wrapped around me, as I dragged the black bag through the field. I was wearing gloves, so as not to leave fingerprints, because my plan was to discard the weapon here after using it.

I checked my Swiss watch. We had made it with little time to spare. I also checked my compass and oriented myself perfectly toward Orly Airport, where the target should have been lifting off at that moment. Then I pulled the Stinger missile out of the bag and mounted it on my shoulder. It was a good thing that I had been working out regularly. The line of cocaine that I snorted when I woke up on the Learjet also helped me to focus. After a nerve-racking delay, in the course of which I picked up and set down the launcher a few times, and even crouched down in the field, increasingly concerned that I'd be caught out here in broad daylight, Bakhtiar's private plane finally came into view. They had left about 20 minutes late. (Still, not bad for Persian time.)

I checked through the scope to confirm that the markings on the plane were those of Ghorbanifar's company. Then, in what remains to this day the hardest decision that I have ever made, besides the one to come to this time in the first place, I pulled the trigger to launch the heat-seeking missile that sped toward the signature of the plane's engine exhaust. I had barely laid down the Stinger when the plane exploded, and its burning debris started to fall not all that far ahead of me in this field. I lost my cool and ran to the car as fast as I could, discarding the chador in the field along the way. I had planned to wear it back onto the plane so that no one at the airport could identify me as anything other than "some Muslim woman." As soon as I jumped in the backseat Jean-Pierre sped back to the airfield without a single word, let alone a question. Within half an hour of the explosion, my Learjet, which had refueled while I was in the field, was lifting off to head back to New York. Jean-Pierre didn't bother to return the car he rented under a false name. He just left it on the tarmac. He stared at me a few times, as I scanned the radio for news during the flight home. Finally, the reports came in on news services. Shapour Bakhtiar was dead.

When I got back to my apartment, I signaled those cleared for full knowledge of Operation Neqab that I was home, and then I collapsed in bed for hours. Once I finally got up, and put CNN on the TV, I learned that French police had already carried out an investigation of the field near Orly and discovered both the Stinger missile *and the chador and neqab*. Based on this information, the military men that had seized power in Iran announced on National Radio and Television that Prime Minister Bakhtiar had been assassinated by an agent of the overthrown Islamic Republic, potentially a devout Muslim woman. In the same broadcast, they revealed that Bakhtiar had designated Mohsen

Pezeshkpour as his Deputy, and that consequently, Pezeshkpour, who was already in Tehran, would be recognized by them as the acting Prime Minister of Iran. By the time that Prime Minister Pezeshkpour delivered a fiery speech at a podium flanked by military officers, at some undisclosed location, probably Shahrokhi Air Base, the socio-political constituencies of the fractious coup coalition that Bakhtiar was supposed to bring together, with his promise of broadly representative Social Democracy, was rapidly unraveling. Marxist Tudeh party members and the 'Islamic' Maoists guerrillas of the Mojaheddin-e-Khalq were already challenging martial law in the streets. All the King's men would not be able to put it back together again.

Speaking of the King, or his successor, my business was unfinished. The Shah was dying of cancer in Cairo, where his wife, Empress Farah, and his children were holding his hand in what would certainly be his last days. I had to ensure that Crown Prince Reza Pahlavi would never be put on the throne by the officers who had carried out the coup, who were after all claiming legitimacy in the name of the old Imperial Iranian military. I knew how this young man's character would unfold, and he would never consent to a strong military dictatorship in Iran for any significant period of time. Moreover, those in Iran who were similarly leery of such a prospect, but who were not committed to any of the leftist factions either, might look to him as the figurehead for a parliamentary democracy of the kind that Bakhtiar had wanted to build.

The Shah was confined to Maadi Hospital, on the banks of the Nile River, in a suburb of Cairo. The Crown Prince would occasionally come and go, commuting between the hospital and the home where the Pahlavi family was residing in Cairo under President Anwar Sadat's protection. In that short space of time, he was inside of a readily identifiable car that was relatively unprotected — at least against an RPG rocket launched at it from a rooftop. I thought that I'd be pushing my luck to attempt this myself, and besides I doubted my ability to operate as effectively in Arab Egypt as in a European country like France. But I could remotely facilitate escape for an Egyptian mercenary who might be led to believe that he was doing this in the name of Islam. Although Egypt had not been a Shi'ite country since the days of the Fatimid Caliphate, there were still some devout Shi'ites there who lionized Ayatollah Khomeini — even more so now that he had been "martyred." I knew that, on my timeline, the Shah would die at Maadi Hospital on July 27. Perhaps the success of the coup would put him in better spirits and extend his life by a bit, but we certainly had a very narrow window of time to carry this out while the Crown Prince would still be visiting his father's hospital bed.

By July 21, we had found our man in Cairo. He was approached by an operative of AtlantiCorp who spoke Arabic, and who could pass for an Iranian when he went without shaving. Antonio Belluzzo was actually Italian and, before my vanguard had recruited him, he had been a dealer of arms to Italian loyalists in Libya who were planning a future attempt to overthrow Ghaddafi. On Tuesday, July 22, 1980, the well-paid Shi'ite mercenary that was hired by the Italian, posing as a vengeful fugitive IRGC commander, who had supplied him with an RPG and trained him to use it, stood on a rooftop along the mapped-out route of Crown Prince Reza's car ride back home from the hospital. It was after sunset, so he was at least able to take his firing position under the cover of dark. He hit the car, alright. Then, having left the RPG on the rooftop, the mercenary ran down the steps of the building and out its back door to a truck that was waiting on one end of an alleyway.

What our Italian operative, Belluzzo, had failed to tell the fanatical Arab was that the back of the truck, into which he had climbed, was rigged with a fast-acting poison gas, and its door could be locked from the driver's seat. Belluzzo gassed the Arab as he drove, and the man was dead before the truck was out of the suburb. The Italian, all the while wearing black leather gloves that would leave no prints behind, abandoned the truck on a street where he had parked a Mercedes. He quickly shaved with a battery-powered electric razor, and then headed back to his hotel in Cairo to pick up his bags before taking a flight to Rome, from where he would report these details to us in an encrypted telegraph message. The Shah of Iran, heartbroken by his eldest son's death, expired in his hospital bed within 72 hours, only a day after they finally decided to tell him, when he demanded to know why no one in his immediate family had visited him for two days.

The military government led by Mohsen Pezeshkpour was now free to fend for itself in the face of a leftist uprising, sympathetic to the Soviet Union, and ethnic separatist movements that had begun in the Azerbaijan, Kurdistan, Khuzestan, and Baluchistan provinces — two of which (Azerbaijan and Kurdistan) had previously been occupied by the USSR (from 1941 to 1946), and one of which (Khuzestan) contained almost all of the oil reserves that were the lifeblood of the Iranian economy. Meanwhile, Baluchistan was located just to the southwest of Soviet forces occupying Afghanistan, and it featured a strategically significant port called Chah Bahar, on the Sea of Oman that tankers pass through on approach to the vital choke point of the Strait of Hormuz. The USSR did not have any warm water ports, and the Soviets desperately wanted them. I had set the stage for just the kind of conflict in, and over, Iran that would heighten Cold War tensions and, ultimately, if it were played out right, save the economy of the Soviet Union from collapse.

The Pezeshkpour regime's first challenge was, however, confronting an uprising of the pro-Khomeini clergy across the country, including at established Shi'ite seminaries in Qom, Mashhad, and even Isfahan. Those mullahs who had served in prominent positions in the Islamic Republic had mostly been arrested or hunted down selectively so that the state would not have to bother with their prosecution or incarceration. But there were a much larger group of mullahs sympathetic to the regime, who considered Ayatollah Khomeini a martyr, and these clerics martialed about two million *Hezbollahis* (religious vigilante thugs) across the country, especially in Iran's two largest cities, Tehran and Mashhad.

The military capitalized on the anger of the secular segment of the population, especially a significant percentage of urban women, who had deeply resented the nine months or more that they had to live under a medieval Islamic theocracy, with mandatory veiling, and a severe curtailing of their civil rights. Pezeshkpour ordered his soldiers into the seminaries and mosques, to gun down anti-government mullahs in bloodbath after bloodbath on supposedly "sacred ground." Meanwhile, the Iranian Air Force used attack helicopters to mow down thousands of *Hezbollahi* hooligans marching in the street with clubs and chains. The press was bad, but the government survived it, including with the support of most Americans, who regained their respect for Iran. Carter's idiotic statements on "genocide" having been committed by the nationalist military regime in Iran during the late summer of 1980 would cost him reelection, despite the resolution of the hostage crisis — no thanks to him. By contrast, for a brief period, both the Communists of Iran and Soviet officials in Moscow remained silent.

CHAPTER 16

STAR CHILD

By 1982, the Communists and Maoists of Iran, consisting of members of the Tudeh Party, the Fedayeen guerrillas, and the Mojaheddin-e-Khalq, had broken their tacit truce with Pezeshkpour's nationalist military junta. This was only ever a one-sided truce anyhow, since they were not offered any participation in the new regime, which had not held parliamentary elections in the two years since the coup, and the Pan-Iranist junta considered them enemies of the state that were aiding and abetting the various ethnic separatists who were intent on tearing Iran apart. This suspicion on the part of Pezeshkpour and his generals proved to be right. As soon as the various leftist factions resumed their violent resistance of the regime in the streets of Iran's major cities, late in 1981, there was a clearly coordinated intensification of the partisan warfare waged by the ethnic separatists. The hammer and sickle flags of the Tudeh and Fedayeen were seen in Azerbaijan and Khuzestan, and the Mojaheddin had made some deal with the Kurds according to which a Rajavi-led regime in Tehran would recognize Kurdish independence.

In December of 1981, Soviet General Dmitry Yazov was transferred from Czechoslovakia, another ethnically fractious country, to the Caspian region with orders to prepare for a Soviet invasion of Iran in support of the secessionists. He was to closely coordinate with the Soviet command in Afghanistan, which would enter the country from the east, while Yazov's forces would march down Western

Iran — through a series of secessionist provinces, from Azerbaijan and Kurdistan down to Khuzestan, the oil reserves of which were the primary objective of the invasion. That, and seizure of warm water ports at Abadan on the Persian Gulf and Chah Bahar on the Sea of Oman, which would be carried out by the Soviet Navy once ground forces reached the coastline. General Yazov had a long and distinguished military career, having been one of the Soviet officers who commanded ground forces in Cuba, and personally worked with Castro, during the Cuban Missile Crisis in 1962. At that time, his unit had orders to be the spearhead of a nuclear strike on United States territory in the event that the crisis could not be resolved. In other words, Khrushchev trusted this man to have the nerve to start a war that would leave only cockroaches alive on Earth.

In January of 1982, the ethnic separatists declared independence in all of their respective provinces, while leftist demonstrators and insurgents kept the military tied up on the city streets of Tehran, Mashhad, Isfahan, and Shiraz. The Soviet Union immediately recognized their declarations of independence, sending ambassadors who were really KGB coordinators to the provisional governments of South Azerbaijan, Kurdistan, Khuzestan, and Baluchistan. TASS began to refer to what was left of Iran as "Persia" in all of its official news reports, expressing Soviet support for the "the comrades struggling against fascism in Persia." In March, as the snow started to melt in the Zagros and Alborz Mountains of northwestern Iran, but while it was still relatively cool in the eastern deserts that Soviet forces in Afghanistan would have to cross to reach Baluchistan in the southwest, the Soviet Union invaded Iran. Despite Pezeshkpour's show of giving a speech from beside a *Haft-Sin*, hardly anyone was celebrating Persian New Year on March 21, 1982. There was a curfew in effect in "Persia" as the military struggled to crush the Communist fifth column, so that it could focus on repelling the invading Soviet Army.

This turned out to be a losing proposition. Pezeshkpour prioritized the defeat of the fifth column but having largely succeeded in this objective and secured the Persian core of Iran from a Communist overthrow of his nationalist junta, he also lost the outer provinces to the USSR. By late May of 1982, after several months of heavy fighting, four former Iranian provinces were incorporated into the USSR as Soviet Socialist Republics. For the sake of geographical contiguity, from Central Asia to the seized port at Chah Bahar in Baluchistan, Afghanistan was also declared an SSR. Dmitry Yazov was widely praised as the face and fist of this tremendous victory. The General was promoted to Marshal of the Soviet Union, the highest-ranking military officer in the chain of command of the USSR. He also became the man most feared by the US government.

The Politburo consisted largely of aging and ailing men. Brezhnev was dying, and it was known by the CIA that Andropov, who was due to succeed him as General Secretary, was also in ill health and would not last long. The next in line of succession, by seniority in the Politburo, would be Chernenko, but his health was also rapidly failing. This potentially destabilizing rapid succession of Politburo men as weak leaders of the USSR deeply concerned the new head of the KGB, Vladimir Kryuchkov. He had been the KGB *rezident* in Kabul during the Soviet takeover of Afghanistan and considered holding both Afghanistan and the seized provinces of Iran as a non-negotiable long-term strategic priority. Kryuchkov and men loyal to him at the KGB were considering maneuvering Marshal Yazov into position as the leader of the Soviet Union. They faced one principal obstacle — a young reformer who had come under the wing of Andropov and was being groomed by him as the future General Secretary: Mikhail Gorbachev.

The elimination of Mikhail Gorbachev was among my highest priorities and primary objectives since the politics of *glasnost* and *perestroika* that he had it in mind to forward would prove to be the downfall of the Soviet Union. Moreover, as soon as I began planning this operation, I realized that Gorbachev needed to be taken out *before* he could become General Secretary of the Soviet Union. A hardliner coup against him, of the kind that had been attempted in the terminal phase of the USSR's collapse, in August of 1991, might be more success-ful if it were staged years earlier, say in 1987 or '88. But *any* old-guard Communist Party coup against reformist policies, such as those that Gorbachev would champion, ran the risk of inflaming public opinion against the regime and dangerously amplifying dissent in the longer run. Someone like Boris Yeltsin could still come along and take up the torch of reform, so that the Soviet Union might fall later but still not make it into the 21st century. The best thing would be for Gorbachev to exit stage left before the common people of the USSR and the leading politicians of the West ever really took notice of him. An assassination, by any conventional methods, would draw too much attention to him. He was, after all, already a member of the Politburo. Also, AtlantiCorp did not have that kind of reach into Russia, and Gorbachev had not begun to travel internationally with the frequency that he did after he assumed leadership (on my timeline). No, something more stealthy and untraceable was called for here. For that, I had only to look at the playbook of the Soviet Union itself.

Specifically, to Soviet Psychotronics research. The Russians were training adept practitioners of psychokinesis (PK) to have a direct mental influence on living systems (DMILS). They practiced by stop-ping the hearts of mice. They would carry out these tests in Soviet submarines, with the idea that the harmful PK field might be better shielded that way. I had obtained a dangerously full dossier of informa-tion about their specific methods and practices, which, on my timeline, had been acquired by the CIA after the fall of the Soviet Union. Once the United States itself disintegrated, the Prometheist movement was able to obtain certain treasure troves of formerly classified information by hiring sympathetic ex-US government officials who had been party to secret Psionic espionage and psychic warfare programs.

I began training in the use of these DMILS techniques of Soviet Psychotronics when I was in my twenties. I admit that I carried out a couple of successful tests on members of the Prometheist Old Guard that considered the reincarnation of Jorjani a threat to their corrupt entrenchment as gatekeepers of the movement. I managed to give one of them a stroke and induced an arrythmia leading to heart failure in another. The training was not all negative. It also taught me to regulate my own healing processes in order to recover from injuries and illnesses more quickly, or even correct imbalances in certain organs.

For the sake of public safety, I will not detail the clairvoyant visualization and telekinetic resonance methods involved in "staring someone dead" even at great distances. Suffice it to say that I had to begin by clairvoyantly surveilling Gorbachev for days on end and establishing a kind of telepathic hypnosis to entrance him at a distance. When his thoughts and feelings about his wife, Raisa Gorbacheva, a cultured woman who had deeply studied Philosophy, bled back into my mind, I found it difficult to continue but I did manage to persist. Despite being a member of the Politburo, Gorbachev would still drive his own car. One time he even rushed to personally bring a packed meal to Raisa at the lecture hall of the class that she taught at Moscow State University, because his wife had been running late that morning and had missed breakfast.

I decided that if Gorbachev were to have a heart attack and a stroke *while* he was driving alone during the morning rush hour, this would be optimal since it would likely result in a car crash that would add a third factor contributing to an almost definite fatality. The prospect of collateral damage to other drivers bothered me, but not when compared to the scale of misery that Gorbachev himself would wind up inflicting upon his own people for decades after the catastrophic failure of his policies. So, one gray and rainy morning in late May of

1982, Mikhail Gorbachev keeled over the wheel of his car as it was totaled on a Moscow highway. After I received confirmation through TASS, which AtlantiCorp was monitoring closely, I collapsed and was bedridden for nearly a week before I managed to rebound.

By March of 1985, after the NATO exercise Able Archer 83 terrified both the Soviet high command and the KGB, and the deaths in rapid succession of Politburo-based leaders Andropov and Chernenko, Dimitry Yazov was installed as the strongman leader of the USSR. In that time, I managed to use an AtlantiCorp asset in Washington, who was a rather attractive Russian woman, to leak two key pieces of information to the KGB via their Science and Technology man at the Soviet embassy. In January of 1983, two months before Reagan announced the Strategic Defense Initiative (SDI) that would go on to be dubbed the "Star Wars" program, my Russian-speaking liaison, Irena, provided Oleg Burov with a briefcase full of the blueprints for SDI. I had brought these back with me in one of those suitcases that had been loaded onto the saucer. What I told Irena to convey to Burov, so that he could get it across to the KGB back in Moscow, was that SDI was a ruse intended to bankrupt the Soviet Union by scaring the Russians into spending vast sums of money that they didn't have on building something comparable to the space-based laser defense system against incoming nuclear missiles. Washington was not serious about actually building this system, and there was no reason for the Soviets to try to compete.

I had no way to know whether Moscow got the message and believed this, but after Reagan delivered his SDI speech from the Oval Office on March 23, 1983, Burov trusted Irena enough so that I could convey another piece of vital information that the Soviet leadership would certainly act on. I passed on detailed notes about the Chernobyl nuclear power plant meltdown that, on my timeline, would take place on April 26 of 1986. The detailed notes, including diagrams, were obtained from the "Stargate" remote viewing program of the US government. The USSR knew of the existence of this program, which was similar to one of their own that also engaged in precognitive clairvoyance. Burov was, of course, not told that these documents had been smuggled back from far in the future where Prometheists had obtained reproductions of them. They had also been among the contents that I emptied from the buoyant suitcases into my hidden vault on the night that I arrived at my apartment. The Chernobyl catastrophe and the scandal that ensued from it caused deep internal divisions in the Soviet leadership, eroded legitimacy in the eyes of the populace, and played a major contributing factor in the dissolution of the USSR. Preventing that meltdown from taking place would, therefore, also help to preserve the Soviet Union.

Irena Akhmatova was not hired by Johnny or anyone else on the vanguard team that I had sent ahead of me to set up Avalon Pharmaceutical and AtlantiCorp, the parent company for which it principally supplied capital. I had recruited her myself. She had been working at the EastWest Institute at 10 Grand Central on 44th street. EWI was a public policy think tank dedicated to international conflict resolution and back-channel dialogue between the Eastern bloc countries of the Warsaw Pact and that part of the Western world bound together by NATO. I had set up a meeting with John Edwin Mroz, who co-founded the Institute here in New York in 1980. Mroz had brought Akhmatova with him to the meeting, the purpose of which was to discuss prospects for long-term American and Soviet collaboration in space, including a possible joint Mars mission. Irena was there because she was a Russian Cosmist. In particular, she was a standard-bearer of the legacy of Konstantin Tsiolkovsky, the most Promethean of these early 20th-century futurists in Russia, and the only one of the first generation of Cosmists who was anti-Christian enough to wind up working for the USSR. He became the grandfather of the Soviet rocket program, and spiritual father of the Cosmonauts. Tsiolkovsky was also a panpsychist and a eugenicist, positions that made the Politburo uneasy about him and his legacy.

Irena's published writings furthered his project, but in a direction that was too radical for her to be able to work in the Soviet Union. Thanks to the EastWest Institute she was able to occasionally travel back to Moscow from Manhattan, where she had emigrated after a borderline defection. The KGB had sent her to a doctoral program in the Philosophy of Science at Princeton University, but when her 1979 dissertation on "Cosmonauts as Soviet Supermen" ruffled feathers back in Moscow, and she was condemned instead of praised for advocating implementation of eugenic embryo-selection and eventually genetic engineering as part of the Soviet space program, especially with a view to colonization of the Moon and Mars, she decided to stay here. She approached Mroz when he founded EWI a year later, and he facilitated her receiving the right of residency in the United States without forfeiting her Soviet citizenship.

That is what she explained to me when I hired her away from him early in June of 1982. I relocated her to the branch office that AtlantiCorp discretely maintained in the Watergate Office Building in Washington DC. The main purpose of that was for her to cultivate a relationship with the KGB's Directorate X department operative at the Soviet embassy. Directorate X was the KGB's division of Scientific and Technological Intelligence. The secondary purpose of that relocation was to make sure that she did not become my girlfriend. You see, to be honest, my interest in Ms. Akhmatova was not strictly professional. When she showed up to that meeting with Mroz, I was immediately attracted to her. After a few lunch meetings, purportedly for the purpose of discussing potential areas of US-USSR space cooperation, it became clear to me both from her body language and from the telepathic impressions that I received that Irena was bisexual. At one lunch meeting that we had, during a downpour, at Wolf's Delicatessen in midtown, I saw her checking out a handsome man at a nearby booth whose shirt had been soaked through, so I knew that she wasn't strictly a lesbian. There was chemistry between us, but I didn't want to get involved in anything very serious with her that would compromise our work together or put me in a position where I felt compelled to reveal too much to her about who I really am.

However, when she would occasionally come back to New York to attend those few meetings at the SCIF on Long Island for which she was cleared, I would invite her to stay in one of the guestrooms at my penthouse rather than to be put up at a hotel by the company. I knew she preferred the view. Irena liked to get up early and do Yoga on the rooftop terrace as the sun was rising over Manhattan. The first time that I caught her doing this, it was an especially hot and humid day in late August of 1982 — on her second trip back to Manhattan from the Washington office. She broke her routine when she saw me walk naked through the door of the turret, carrying a Yoga mat in my arms. Then, as I unrolled it, and started to strike a posture next to her, she smiled and nodded with a typically Russian expression that said, "*well then*," and she stripped off her own Yoga pants and tank top. We synchronized our *asanas* together throughout the sunrise.

Then, I started to do things that Irena didn't recognize. You see, in Gotham of the early 21st century, the Prometheist movement had developed a form of combined exercise and meditation that synthesized elements of Yoga with Tai-Chi and Capoeira. After she stood there for a moment, both bewildered and aroused by my naked body flowing dynamically through these movements and postures, she asked me what this was and whether I could teach it to her. I stopped, sweating by now in the muggy morning weather, and placed my hands on her hips, held her thighs up, and guided her arms with my grasp, as I taught her what we called "Promethean Yoga." After that session we took the first of many showers together.

On days when she would wake up at my place, I would tell Jean-Pierre to take a break so that I could drive Irena around in my black

DeLorean. She loved to listen to contemporary pop music on my car's cassette player. Partly, she wanted to improve her English, which although formally excellent, was not colloquial enough. I told her that I'd be sad if she lost her sexy Russian accent. I had all of the harder-edged and more haunting hits of the early '80s on tape. Irena's favorites were Eurythmics' "Sweet Dreams," Bonnie Tyler's "Total Eclipse of the Heart," and numerous songs of Laura Branigan, who she was smitten with, and whose music videos she confessed to thinking about when she fingered herself. (I really couldn't blame her. I wanted to see what Irena would do when "Self Control" came out.) We'd put one after another in as we ran red lights crisscrossing the city for both business and pleasure.

The most important business meeting that I took her to was at Trump Tower in March of 1983, with none other than the Don himself. It was set up under the pretext that AtlantiCorp was considering acquiring an entire floor of Trump Tower for its new corporate headquarters. We drove to that meeting in the DeLorean, blasting "Gloria" on the tape deck. I knew that Donald Trump appreciated Slavic women, and with my nearly flat chest and somewhat androgynous looks, I wasn't exactly his type. But Irena definitely was. She looked a lot like the woman that Trump would wind up with, after two divorces, on my timeline. Specifically, Irena bore a striking resemblance to the young Melania Knauss back when she was a black-haired Slovenian model. Irena's breasts weren't quite as big, but they were natural.

I ruled out trying to set her up with him, although that would have served my purposes well, and saved him from the mishap with Marla, because Irena was way too intelligent for him to be comfortable with. Trump claimed to respect "smart" women, but there is a hell of a difference between a housewife who is not a bimbo and a hyper-intellectual woman with a doctorate in Philosophy of Science who works for think tanks. This meeting would be the first of many that I would manage to secure with the real estate magnate, in order to start convincing him

CHAPTER 16: STAR CHILD

to run in the 1988 US presidential election. I justified Irena's presence by seeding in Trump's mind the idea of a potential "grand bargain" between the USA and USSR — a deal that Trump boasted only he could make — involving a joint manned mission to Mars before the year 2000.

On my timeline, Trump had done the interview circuit from Larry King to Orpah Winfrey during a brief period in 1987 when he appeared to be seriously considering running for President, despite his repeated tongue-in-cheek denials that he had no plans to announce his candidacy. He seemed to drop this when, sometime in 1988, Vice President Bush did something to secure Trump's support for his own candidacy. But up until Bush talked (or paid?) him out of entering the electoral fray, Trump certainly appeared to be campaigning, on every issue from the problem of poverty and homelessness, to funding for education, and our failing infrastructure. Where would the money come from? Nothing less than imperial tribute from protected "allies."

One of the documents that I had smuggled with me from the future past was a full-page ad that Donald Trump had paid nearly $100,000 to print in *The New York Times* on September 2, 1987. The headline, printed in bold, read "There's nothing wrong with America's Foreign Defense Policy that a little backbone can't cure." Beneath that, in somewhat smaller print, was a sub-heading that identified the one-page shadow-offset document printed below it as "[a]n open letter from Donald J. Trump on why America should stop paying to defend countries that can afford to defend themselves." Then there was the body of the "letter" itself.

In essence, the piece argued that economic powerhouses like Japan and Saudi Arabia should be paying the United States to defend them from potential enemies like Iran in the Persian Gulf or North Korea in the Sea of Japan. He lamented that the Japanese were outcompeting us, and buying up all of our best real estate, with wealth that we were creating for them by covering their defense costs. He also insisted that

we didn't really need Saudi oil, especially not if the Arabs were going to deny us use of their embarrassingly superior mine sweepers to
protect tankers in the Persian Gulf. Our so-called "allies" outside of
the Western world, and even some in NATO, should start paying the
United States of America something akin to imperial taxes, Trump argued unabashedly. I prepared my talking points for this meeting with
him based on what Trump himself had printed there, in a political
statement that he wouldn't make for another four years, in a future
that had already been significantly altered by the ripples of Operation
Neqab and the strengthening of the USSR — especially through its
seizure of what had been Iran's oil reserves and seaports.

There was a much more personal, but not unintended, consequence of the success of Operation Neqab and the subsequent Soviet
invasion of Iran. Stopping the collapse of the Soviet Union was not my
only mission here. Influencing and redirecting the life of Jason Reza
Jorjani was certainly also part of my agenda. One of the consequences
of Neqab significantly facilitated this other mission.

In June of 1982, Jason's father, Fereidun Qajar Jorjani, would come
back home in a rage after having watched *E.T. the Extra-Terrestrial*. It
was immediately apparent to him that the film had been plagiarized,
scene for scene, from a screenplay that he had co-authored around the
time that Jason was conceived. The script was called *Star Child*. Every
attorney in a law office that Fereidun contacted immediately after the
release of *E.T.* concluded that Steven Spielberg's film, which would go
on to become the highest grossing movie of all time, was a reworked
version of *Star Child*.

All of the most innovative elements of the film were already in
Fereidun Jorjani's script, such as the main theme of making an extraterrestrial entity some*one* (rather than some*thing*) so childlike and
vulnerable that the audience would not only identify with him but want
to embrace and protect the E.T. in the way that the boy Eliot does. This
was a new and unique idea in science-fiction films, which had thus far

depicted aliens as either monstrously inhuman (e.g., *Alien*, 1979) or enigmatically ethereal (e.g., *The Man Who Fell to Earth*, 1976). Every detail is there, from the alien raiding the fridge for Reese's pieces in the middle of the night, to the military's hospitalization and quarantine of the Star Child. Even the bulbous body, lanky arms, and long neck of the alien entity were the same.

The sketch accompanying the screenplay had been drawn by Fereidun's collaborator. The co-author of *Star Child* was a Persian painter by the name of Khosrow Yahyai, a man whose sordid past proved to be detrimental to the case that Jason's father quickly built against Spielberg. The linchpin of this case was that at the conclusion of E.T. there is a "special thanks to Melissa Matheson." Rumors aside that she was Spielberg's girlfriend at the time, Ms. Matheson happened to be the typist who prepared the final draft of *Star Child* for Fereidun and Khosrow — neither of whom were very proficient in English. The law office enlisted by Jason's father was prepared to serve Spielberg papers, having tracked the director's movements carefully enough to know when he would be transiting through a certain airport. But Khosrow, who had filed for their joint copyright on the screenplay, refused to give his consent. On the timeline that I come from, in 1981 he had gone back to Tehran, and shortly thereafter started a family of his own. He did not want the attention of the nascent government of the Islamic Republic of Iran to be drawn to him.

You see, when the Revolution took place in 1979, a lot of legal dossiers and police reports from the Pahlavi period fell through the cracks. The late Shah of Iran had been trying to build a casino resort on Kharg Island in the Persian Gulf, but he had problems with a local mobster and quasi-feudal landowner. Khosrow had a rapport with the Shah's wife, Empress Farah Pahlavi, who awarded gold medals to his extraordinary paintings. Fereidun had heard that Khosrow was believed to have pushed this mobster off a cliff into the shark-infested waters of the Persian Gulf, perhaps after having drugged him. Khosrow was himself an avid user of LSD, which is reflected in the bewitchingly surreal imagery of his artwork.

Khosrow smuggled a number of his award-winning paintings out of Iran in the late 1970s, fleeing to America in order to avoid an increasingly likely prosecution. It is then that, for a brief period, he took up residence as a guest of Jason's father and mother (who did not appreciate catering to him). So, whereas many Iranians fled the country after the Shah was overthrown, in 1981, a year before *E.T.* was released, Khosrow went in the other direction — returning to an Islamic Republic, where he believed that his record had been wiped clean by the chaos of the revolution and the confusion following Saddam Hussein's surprise invasion of Iran in the fall of 1980. Now that Operation Neqab had succeeded, that would not take place. Khosrow would remain in New York City up to the time when *E.T.* was released in the summer of 1982.

However, on the original timeline, Khosrow's brother later hinted to Fereidun that, before heading back to Iran, the painter had facilitated Melissa Matheson's transfer of *Star Child* to Steven Spielberg — by whatever, direct or indirect, means all of the key elements of this story reached him and were incorporated into the blockbuster film *E.T.* This same brother gave two of Khosrow's award-winning paintings to Jason's father, in a lame attempt at an apology for Khosrow's treachery. These haunting pieces hung on the walls of the apartments that Jason grew up in, and his father vouchsafed them to him so that, in his adulthood, they hung on the walls of Jason's own secession of apartments. Frankly, I have never seen a more successful attempt at modern art that is quintessentially Persian and as occult as the alchemical works of Max Ernst.

In the now overwritten world where the Islamic Republic survived, and Khosrow went back to Iran, Fereidun remained determined to sue Spielberg for *E.T.* Lawyers were advising him on how to secure the sole rights to the *Star Child* screenplay in order to do so. Around the time that Jason entered the half-French Fleming School in New York, an incident took place that forced Fereidun to reconsider and drop the legal action. One morning, as per his usual routine in 1987, he went to pick up the blue Cadillac to drive Jason to the Fleming School building at 10 East 62nd Street, and to also drop off his mother, Susan Power, at her office in the garment district of downtown Manhattan, when he met with a very unpleasant surprise. As Fereidun opened the front door of the Cadillac, a pile of fish fell from the front seat onto the sidewalk. This was an old mafia symbol used to warn troublemakers that if they did not cease and desist, they would soon be "sleeping with the fishes."

That morning, Susan took Jason to school by train. When Fereidun got the car back from the carwash, the stink of the rotting fish still lingered on the blue upholstery. Around the same time, he received a threatening anonymous phone call, with the voice on the other end of the line reminding him that he had a family and sternly insisting that he "drop it." So, after a heated conversation with his wife, Susan, who was horrified by all this and feared for their son's safety, Fereidun did drop it. He was always convinced that Spielberg had put someone up to making these threats. But I suspected that both the fish incident and the phone call came from another group of people, individuals who were aware of the *Star Child* case, and what a multi-million-dollar settlement of it would mean for how Jason's life would unfold, quite differently from how it did develop in the face of financial hardships later suffered by Fereidun and Susan.

Steven Spielberg may or may not be above using such crude tactics to intimidate someone. But for all I know, Spielberg was never even made aware of the potential lawsuit. The reason why I doubt that he was behind the intimidation is because two utterly bizarre incidents that took place during Jason's young adulthood suggested that Jason had been the target of both surveillance and manipulation long before

anyone should even have known who he was or why that might someday be justified. From these two incidents it would appear that — potentially, both beneficent and malevolent — forces *with access to the
future* were very interested in the course that Jason's life would take.

I believe that I can put a date on the day of the first incident, because it was when a firm had just been chosen to design the new World
Trade Center. February 27, 2003. In my lifetime as Jason, I was 22 years
old at the time. New York's newspapers had printed 3-D models of proposed designs on their front pages, above the fold. I had just emerged
from the subway station on the northeast corner of 86th Street and
Lexington Avenue when these caught my eye at the newsstand there. I
was at the tail end of my regular commute back home from New York
University. As I stood inspecting one of the graphics for the proposed
Freedom Tower, I noticed someone standing behind me and off to the
left-hand side. He had been staring at me intently. As soon as he realized that I had noticed him, he said: "So, what do you think?" I shook
my head in frustration and replied, "They should have gone up twice
as high to send a message! We have the materials and technology to do
that now. Put a permanent fighter detail around it at a fixed perimeter
if necessary!" He smiled, and the next words out of his mouth were:
"You *would* say that."

I'd never seen the man before in my life, but he was strangely compelling. When he asked if I had a few minutes to spare for a little chat,
I readily agreed and crossed the street with him to stand under the
marquee of an abandoned movie theater that used to be on the west
side of 86th street, heading toward Park Avenue. We spent about half
an hour talking there that afternoon. At no point did he ask my name,
nor did he volunteer his. What is stranger is that with this man I never
felt the need for such a proper introduction. He had me at a disadvan-
tage, because apparently, he already knew who I was — or who I would
be, someday. Again, I had just turned 22. I was nobody, really, at least
as far as the world was concerned. But this mystery man was able to

lead the conversation from one subject of interest to me on to every single other topic, field, and area that I would wind up involved with for the rest of my life up to the present time.

Again, I had barely dipped my toe into some of these subjects at the time of the conversation, but he spoke to me as if these were long-standing interests and he took a critical attitude toward my (future) approach to them without my having volunteered any information on the basis of which he could have drawn inferences. For example, he knew Hafez by heart and he warned me that my emphasis on Mithraism was going to scare some people who "won't understand." It is only after publishing *Iranian Leviathan* in 2019 that I figured out what he was talking about. He had one message over all: "Don't forget your American side." He repeated this several times, once adding, "Emerson, Whitman, Thoreau, remember that they are your heritage too," and another time reassuring me that "you're going to be great! Just don't forget your American side." While I bizarrely did not ask him *who* he was, I had thought to ask *what* he did. He replied, "We maintain a library." That's all. Again, strangely, I did not think to ask him for any elaboration on that cryptic remark. "We," he said, not I. "*We* maintain a library."

Now, this may have been a benevolent man with access to the future. Whereas the other incident was almost certainly orchestrated by malevolent forces with at least as much, if not more, access to events that had not yet transpired. I do not simply mean foreknowledge of the future, which could be sufficient to explain the "librarian" above, but in this case the ability to actually retrieve and move information from the future to the past in a very sophisticated way. The story is a difficult one to tell, but I will endeavor to be perfectly honest.

You see, for a number of reasons, mostly related to the disruption that the Coronavirus pandemic caused in 2020–2021, Nassim Nouri and I remained in a bi-coastal relationship for a long time after she became my fiancée. I would fly to Los Angeles, where I would spend months at a time with her, and she would occasionally come and stay with me in New York. But, as you can imagine, spending months of the year away from each other, we often had rather extensive phone calls of an intimate nature.

Late one night, many years earlier, around the same time as the aforementioned incident with the librarian in 2003, a woman with whom I had been having a relationship called me in a panic. Emma started out by saying, "Why were you talking to me like that?!" When I explained to her that I had no idea what she was on about, she said that she had just been on the phone with me for fifteen minutes, over the course of which I had supposedly coaxed her into a sexual scenario that became more and more explicit, to the point where I was saying things that she considered very uncharacteristic of me and that shocked and disturbed her. In fact, I had not called Emma.

Apparently, in 2003, long before anyone but the likes of the NSA and the Mossad had voice emulation technology, someone with *exactly* my voice had called Emma. Moreover, it was not simply a replication of my voice, which would have been within the technological capabilities of a few top-notch intelligence agencies at that time. This person was able to produce my personality and speech pattern accurately enough to carry on a convincing conversation with a woman who knew me *very* well, before the last five minutes of that conversation went somewhere that she found unsettlingly unexpected.

The clincher is that this did not happen only once. It happened *several* more times, after this first phone call. Each time, the voice that sounded like it was mine was so convincing, and the personality so adaptive and true to my own, that Emma was manipulated into lowering her guard to the point of having an intimate exchange with this person purporting to be me, until the vocabulary and attitude being expressed took a turn that she thought was, to say the least, uncharacteristic of me — as she had known me, then, in my early twenties. When the last of these incidents occurred, Emma was so disturbed that she called the police and filed a report with the NYPD alleging that she had been phone "raped" by someone imitating her boyfriend. I, for my part, had become so incensed that I grabbed a large knife from the kitchen cupboard of my apartment and ran through the dark streets to her building, in case whoever did this might be lurking there when I arrived. That is how badly I was unhinged by these phone calls.

It was only much later in my lifetime as Jason, a couple of years into my relationship with Nassim, that it first occurred to me that the kind of thing that Emma had been describing could easily have been reconstructed from bits and pieces of my many erotically explicit conversations with Nassim (much more explicit than anything I would have said, to anyone, over a phoneline when I was in my early twenties). Emma, who was a discerning and very intuitive person, had been so badly manipulated and violated, on several occasions no less, because the voice in those phone calls was not an *emulation* of mine. It *was mine* — just from the future, produced by an Artificial Intelligence that had been fed many hours of recordings mined from conversations that I had with my fiancée on the opposite coast of the country.

This would mean that recordings of these conversations, originally obtained at least 16 years into the future, were used to train an Artificial Intelligence to reproduce not just my voice but also my personality, such that a phone call *made in 2003* could be convincingly responsive to someone who knows me *very* well for the span of *fifteen-minutes*. This would require a level of Artificial Intelligence that was not achieved until around 2025, and that still does not explain how the AI was able to make a phone call to someone more than two decades into the past.

One might ask that if malevolent time travelers with this level of technology were interfering with my life as Jason, why is it that I got anywhere at all in that lifetime. First of all, as the encounter with the man on the street corner of 86th and Lexington suggests, there may have been both malevolent *and benevolent* forces from the future intervening in Jason's life. Secondly, there is one other incident that does strongly suggest that an attempt was made to prevent him from ever even coming on the scene as a public intellectual. I never revealed this in my life as Jorjani because I was concerned that detractors would use it to question my soundness of mind. Shortly after *Prometheus and Atlas* was published in early 2016, and a few months before I was contacted by Frederick Boulder, I began to have totally unprecedented debilitating headaches. These were accompanied by a pain on the upper left side of my neck. The first time that this happened, suddenly, in the middle of the night, I was in so much pain that I literally had to *crawl* to the bathroom to take a bunch of Advil and aspirin (which didn't help *these* types of headaches much).

Eventually, it got so bad that I had a battery of neurological tests done on me, because I was beginning to become concerned that I might have a brain tumor or something. CAT scans and EEGs revealed nothing, and the NYU neurologist could come to no diagnosis at all, especially since the headaches did *not* fit the pattern of migraines. However, she did tell me that the two places I was pointing to are the electrical nerve center of the brain and the carotid artery (the main artery responsible for carrying blood from the heart to the brain). These are the two points in the head and neck that are closest to being "kill switches" that someone who intended to cause a stroke would principally target if they possessed either some highly focused directed energy weapon or a psychotronic technique. Interestingly, these headaches (and the throbbing pain in my carotid artery) went away after the defamation that Jellyfish set me up for had succeeded in destroying my academic career, damaging my relationship with the Iranian Renaissance, and compelling professionals in Parapsychology, Ufology, and other edge science fields to cut their ties with me.

Forgive me for what may appear to have been a long tangent in my discussion of how the success of Operation Neqab altered the course of events surrounding Spielberg's seeming plagiarism of the *Star Child* screenplay in the production of *E.T.* It really is not a tangent at all, because all of these strange occurrences suggested to me that a very deliberate effort had been made by certain interests — other than Spielberg and Company — to ensure that Fereidun Jorjani did not pursue legal action to the point of receiving a settlement so substantial that, even if he had to also sign a non-disclosure agreement, Jason would grow up wealthy. Had I, in my lifetime as Jorjani, grown up with considerable family money at my disposal, rather than in an atmosphere of perpetual financial insecurity, the $1 million dangled in front of me by Frederick would never have made a sufficient impression to entice me to get involved with the Alt-Right as part of a Jellyfish plan to supposedly influence Trump on Iran Policy via Steve Bannon.

The success of Operation Neqab meant that the Islamic Republic was overthrown in July of 1980. Given the restoration of the Pahlavi legal order in Persia (even if without a Pahlavi monarch on the throne), and the Soviet invasion of the rest of Iran, Khosrow Yahyai never left New York to return to Iran. He *had* secretly handed *Star Child* over to Melissa Matheson, who testified to that when Fereidun's attorneys served Steven Spielberg with a lawsuit in early 1983. Spielberg gave a sworn but confidential deposition in the course of which he claimed that he had never heard of Jorjani or his *Star Child* script, and that Matheson had given him the core ideas of *E.T.* verbally, in the course of personal conversations, which is why he had put a "special thanks" to her in the credits of the film. Having been thrown under the bus by Spielberg, Melissa Matheson in turn gave a deposition to the effect that Yahyai had portrayed himself as the sole author of the script when he made a deal to hand it over to her for a certain amount of untraceable cash. So, Fereidun Jorjani's lawyers next served Yahyai, who was put between the rock and the hard place of admitting what he had done or lying under oath. Yahyai gave a deposition that contradicted that of Matheson, claiming that she must have shared details of *Star Child* with Spielberg simply on the basis of having been the script's typist. He swore that he had made no deal with her.

One of them was committing perjury. It did not matter which, although Fereidun would never trust Khosrow again and this certainly brought their friendship to an end. Several years of legal proceedings were enough to make it clear to Spielberg how catastrophic a potential public scandal over this could be. So, he had his attorneys offer a settlement to Fereidun Jorjani, contingent on non-disclosure of the matter. By then, *E.T.* had become one of the highest-grossing films of all time during its theatrical release. The settlement, the details of which were worked out in October of 1987, made Jorjani a multi-millionaire overnight. Unfortunately, the stress of the legal battle had destroyed his already volatile marriage.

Fereidun's fights with Susan were so bad that neighbors had summoned the police to their apartment several times in the mid-1980s. Jason, who was even more traumatized by this violent atmosphere than he had been — I mean that *I* had been — in the timeline that I come from, was probably relieved when Susan Power filed for a divorce from Fereidun Jorjani in November of 1987. She managed to secure custody of Jason, and significant child support and other damages from the now wealthy Fereidun. In view of the threat that she would seek a restraining order against him, Fereidun Jorjani voluntarily moved to Los Angeles, California, where he had more friends and business contacts than in New York, anyhow, and where he would attempt to pursue his directorial ambitions in Hollywood. He would travel back to New York on a regular basis to visit his son, and when Jason would grow older, his mother let him travel to Los Angeles during his summer breaks from school, to spend longer stretches with his father and his Persian grandmother, who had also relocated there.

It was in that one-month interval in 1987, between the October settlement and the November divorce, that I finagled my way into having a prominent place in Jason Jorjani's life. He was in his first semester at The Fleming School and, because of all the chaos at home, he was having difficulties doing his homework despite his innate aptitude. AtlantiCorp had established a working relationship with David Nahmad, a French-speaking Jewish Lebanese billionaire from Monaco who used his position as one of Manhattan's most prominent art dealers in order to move large sums of money around, if you take my meaning. (On my timeline, his son Helly would later be arrested and imprisoned for getting reckless with the family business.) David's daughter, Marielle Nahmad, was a classmate of Jason's at The Fleming School. I went to the trouble of befriending Marielle's mother Colette and convincing her to hire me as a tutor for both Marielle and Helly (who, although a couple of years ahead of him, was in Jason's Judo class at Fleming). My colleagues at AtlantiCorp had helped me to put together a resume as a part-time tutor with false, but checkable, references that seemed impressive on paper. Once I was tutoring the Nahmad children, and I had gained the confidence of Colette to the point where she would sometimes send me in her stead to Fleming functions at which parents were expected, I managed to meet Fereidun Jorjani and charm him into hiring me as Jason's tutor. After tutoring Jason for a few months, I made excuses to the Nahmad family and dropped both Marielle and Helly.

Attending that 1987 Halloween party at 10 East 62nd Street, to which parents were invited, was one of the most uncanny experiences of my life. Marielle, who I had accompanied, was dressed as a witch, and Jason's costume that year was the tin man from *The Wizard of Oz*. What made it so uncanny was that the building that was then The Fleming School, specifically its lower school, would eventually become both my residence and the place where I would be killed in my lifetime as Jorjani. Known as "Versailles of the Upper East Side" after the Fleming School vacated it in 1992, this Beaux Arts building was remodeled as a townhouse triplex apartment. The marble spiral staircase and the mirrored French Imperial-style room with wood floors, a magnificent painted ceiling, and a fireplace, which had been the weekly assembly room of Fleming, was left untouched. I used this room as an audience hall for important meetings. I had strong-armed the government of Persia to acquire the building as their UN Mission, after I was appointed Persian Ambassador to the United Nations in 2036. Consequently, my place of residence, the exquisitely elegant townhouse, whose ornate hallways and antique light fixtures were reminiscent of a fairy lair, became the unofficial headquarters of Prometheism. Since Persia had become a bastion of the movement, no one in the government of Persia dared to object.

The bombing of 10 East 62nd Street by Islamic terrorists in 2039 was the first past life memory that I explored in my regression sessions since it was the Prometheist protocol to begin with someone's death in their immediately preceding incarnation. That's why being back there in 1987, on Halloween no less, was such a haunting experience. As I walked up that spiral staircase to the Versailles-style room on the second floor (above ground), looking down at the sunburst pattern of beige-gold diamonds set into the ivory marble in the lobby, I really felt like I was in the Twilight Zone. That song by Golden Earring kept play-ing in my head as the black high heels I was wearing reverberated on the inlaid crosshatched pattern of the landing that led to the assembly chamber. This feeling only intensified when I saw myself reflected in the chamber's mirrors with their gilded moldings. The echo in that room didn't make it any less unsettling, either. I walked over to the three floor-to-ceiling windows looking out over 62nd between Fifth and Madison. I opened the middle one by the handle, to get some air, checking that no children were around me.

The past few weeks had been very stressful. I had been working hard on Donald Trump, trying to convince him to run for President in the 1988 election. In the end, I basically bribed him to run by promising to save his real estate empire from a collapse that would otherwise be in store for him within a couple of years. We brought him to the SCIF on Long Island and gave him a briefing in the course of which he was misled into believing that we had an intelligence agency which, like the

CIA, used remote viewing of the future, but for the sake of corporate investments and stock trading. Trump was given to understand that, by 1990, he could either be bankrupt, and hundreds of millions in debt, or be President of the United States with a new corporate investor injecting enough capital into his failing businesses to keep him from ever going under.

This briefing was in September of 1987, and in addition to sharing with him details of the catastrophic financial situation that he would find himself in within several years, I volunteered specific information about the Stock Market Crash of October 19, 1987. When that event did in fact take place, exactly as predicted, he got over his resentment of our forecasting of his financial demise, which, initially, had really rubbed the eternal optimist and advocate of positive thinking the wrong way. Now, Trump was ready for another meeting with me. It helped that I paid him handsomely to acquire a headquarters for AtlantiCorp on the 55th floor of Trump Tower.

Donald's own office was on the 26th floor of the Modernist masterpiece, which was a 58-story skyscraper. I asked him why he hadn't chosen a higher floor. Trump said that he preferred the view from here, because it was more level with the tops of the buildings on the skyline of the west side of Central Park and also let you look down into the park from a height where it was still possible to discern people sitting in the fields or walking on the paths through the trees. I looked for my building, but it was blocked by the top of the Plaza Hotel, which was off to the left, and very close to the window. My own office was high enough above this floor so that it looked *over* the top of the Plaza, and I could see my penthouse from it through the telescope that I had pointed at my turret library.

Trump's office was junkier than it had been during my first visit here, with Irena back in '83. I had noticed that, over the years, it accumulated clutter on account of how sentimental Trump was about the memorabilia that famous people gave him or sent to him. All kinds of awards and other small sculptures and statues, as well as sports memorabilia, lined the surfaces along the windowsills. Every bit of the wall space was covered with photographs or framed magazine covers. Trump caught me looking at a portrait of the Shah of Iran that he had on the wall. "It's a shame what happened to that guy and to his country. *I mean* having to see your eldest son be killed like that when you're rotting away of cancer as your *ungrateful* country burns. You know back in '78 I was about to build a casino there, in some resort town called Ramsar. It was on the coast of the Caspian Sea. We also had plans on the drawing board for construction of a *yuge* hotel at one of the ski resorts, you know in those mountains just north of Tehran. The Shah told me that he was going to bid to host the Winter Olympics there. *This* year's Olympics actually. *Imagine that.* Tehran '88 instead of Calgary. Then the shit hit the fan." Trump leaned back in his chair, shaking his head while slapping the desk in front of him, as he added, "The Communists are gonna take over that *whole* fucking country, Dana. *They've already got the oil.* Notice how they went for that *first*." Then he looked me in the eyes and said, "Where's that Russian broad that you used to come around here with?" I told him that I had sent her to work at our office in Washington. He registered the fact that AtlantiCorp had the resources to maintain an office in the Foggy Bottom area of DC, in addition to the corporate headquarters that I had secured for us here at Trump Tower.

"Speaking of Washington, Donald," I said as I opened into the subject matter that I had really come down from the 55th floor to discuss with him. "Now that the market has crashed and saving the economy is at the top of people's minds, don't you think that you ought to announce that you're running?" I looked over at Trump's framed and signed photo with Ronald Reagan. "I bet that if you do it sooner, rather than later, you'll become the front runner fast and President Reagan will even endorse you as his preferred successor. You know he never trusted Bush. The CIA forced Reagan to pick him as VP back in '80." Trump clasped his hands together, leaning over his desk, and pursing his lips a bit. "Who would I pick to run with me?" he finally asked.

I averted eye contact, looking over his shoulder at the green blanket of trees in Central Park, as I slid a dossier across his desk. I had come prepared. It was the resume of General Alexander Haig, including a number of striking photos both from his time as NATO's Supreme Allied Commander and as Secretary of State, before he was forced to resign over his perceived attempt to seize power during the March 30, 1981 assassination attempt on President Reagan. Haig himself had been the target of a failed attempt on the part of the Communist Red Army Faction to use a land mine to assassinate him on June 25, 1979, during his regular car commute to NATO's SHAPE facility in Mons, Belgium.

As Trump looked over the files, I added, "Just don't let President Reagan know until you've secured his endorsement. You won't have to announce your running mate until the Republican National Convention in August of next year, anyhow." Having placed a photo of General Haig in full military uniform, wearing his numerous decorations, with the NATO flag behind him, on the top of the papers in the folder, Trump looked up and said, "I've always liked him. He's very tough on the Russians. That's the kind of guy I'd want in charge in case, you know, something unfortunate happened to me. I don't like to think that way, but when you're picking a Vice President you've gotta consider it."

"So, when will you announce?" I asked. Trump turned his head to the side, resting his chin on his hand. Then he swiveled in his chair a bit to look over the park for a moment. "I'll let my family know tonight, and I'll set the announcement for the end of this week. It'll be *right here*, in Trump Tower, coming down the escalator to the atrium." My rejoinder, while smiling approvingly, was, "It *is* a spectacular backdrop. Titanic, really, with that waterfall coming down over the illuminated rock wall." Grinning with self-satisfaction, Trump said, "You *like* that? I designed it myself." I very much doubted that he *had*, but I shot back with, "Yeah, it's what really sold me on this place as the headquarters for AtlantiCorp. Well, besides *your* being here."

CHAPTER 17

UBER MAN

In the fall of 1987, I started to pick up Jason after school at Fleming on certain days and bring him home to where he lived at 200 East 90th street for his tutoring sessions. In the hours before his parents came back home from work, and especially on some long nights where they were embroiled in divorce-related proceedings, beginning in November, they left me home alone with him as a kind of babysitter. Once we were done with homework, I would engage him in playing with his entire toy collection. Some days it was his *Star Wars* toys, which he would pull out of the C-3PO and Darth Vader carrying cases on his bookshelf, sometimes it was the Marvel *Secret Wars* and DC *Super Powers* action figures, or the *Star Trek* figures from both *The Original Series* (the Mego ones) and *The Next Generation*, but his favorites were the figures from the Kenner toy line based on *The Real Ghostbusters*. Jason was enthralled as I came up with all kinds of story lines involving these figures and the worlds of the shows that they were based on. Admittedly, many of the narratives were drawn from plotlines that I knew would unfold in future shows or movie sequels (and prequels) of these franchises.

I noticed that Jason had the Japanese version of the *Voltron* toy, so I asked him whether he had seen the original *GoLion* anime that had been adapted into *Voltron* for an American audience. He had not, so one day I brought a cassette of it over, which had been subtitled in English for export, and we watched it on his VHS player before his parents got home. It was much more violent and intense than the censored version that was developed for release in the United States, but Jason noticed how the plotline was also a lot more coherent. As our relationship developed, I would wind up introducing him to a lot of Japanese anime acquired at a shop catering to immigrants from Japan down on East 9th street. They would import everything from Tokyo and Osaka as soon as it was released. We would ultimately watch *Akira*, *Goku Midnight Eye*, and *Angel Cop* together, in the privacy of my penthouse where no one knew what kind of "cartoons" I was showing a seven-year-old. I also exposed him to the "comics" in *Heavy Metal* magazines, so that in his own drawings he would try to imitate the art of the French illustrators Moebius, Druillet, and Caza. I pulled the *Heavy Metal* stack out after playing a bootleg VHS of the 1981 animated movie for him. He loved it! I got him a bedside lamp to take home that looked exactly like the Loc-Nar.

You see, after Fereidun Jorjani left for Los Angeles, I convinced Susan Power to let me bring Jason over to my apartment to tutor him here after school instead. I explained that the splendor of the apartment, which I had to invite her to check out, was a family inheritance (so that she would not inquire into what I really did for a living). Both of Jason's parents had already been told that I tutored not because I needed the money, but because I enjoyed doing it now and then to make sure that particularly promising children did not fall through the cracks because of certain environmental stresses and contingent circumstances. I showed Susan a degree in Psychology that I also claimed to have, expertly forged of course. Given what Jason had been through, she considered this more than a fringe benefit of my being his tutor.

So, by early 1988, at seven years of age, Jason was frequenting my penthouse at 55 Central Park West. He never got over the fact that his tutor lived in the *Ghostbusters* building and that her name was "Dana." (The 1984 film was by then his favorite movie, and he was a fan of *The Real Ghostbusters* animated show airing weekly on television.)

I confess that I chose this penthouse by design, with him in mind. I could have impressed all those geopolitical and corporate persons of interest that I've wined and dined — and occasionally fucked and drugged (not necessarily in that order) — just as well by living in any number of even more upscale buildings in Manhattan. See, I also had to be sure that there was no chance Jason would even entertain the possibility of moving to Los Angeles to live with his father. That was already unlikely, but I had to render it impossible. So, yes, in a sense I was seducing him from the start. That "Dana" tutored him at "Spook Central" would also guarantee that he insisted his mother keep paying for him to come here even after he became, albeit with my help, a nearly straight-A student.

The very first time that Jason came over, while he was working out his math homework on scrap paper for a while, he noticed that I was finishing up typing and saving a document on my Macintosh. (I had heavily invested in Apple stock from the moment that it became available on the stock market, and throughout the 80s that had paid off handsomely. Sometimes, I would even wear the little Macintosh logo lapel pin that the company sent me, as a veiled reference to biting the apple gifted to Eve by the Satanic serpent in Eden. Besides, since I was queer, the rainbow color scheme seemed to be a cute, veiled reference too.) Jason asked what I was writing. I saw this as a perfect opportunity to start to have deeper conversations with him, so I went ahead and tried to explain the book that I had begun researching and writing — a book with which I intended to launch Prometheism decades ahead of when it had been launched in the world that I came from.

"It's called *Uber Man*, Jason. *Über* is the German word for 'over' or 'above.' *Übermensch* means 'Superman' in German." Now I had him intrigued. "You're writing a book about Superman?!" This was going to be really interesting. I had to explain the thesis and structure of *Uber Man* to a seven-year-old boy, using only examples that he would already be able to understand. I remembered being him at that age, so I knew just what those would be. Actually, I had quite a lot of references that I could work with.

"Well, kind of. It's not about *the* Superman from Krypton, but it *is* about how we can develop superpowers — like superheroes or super-villains — to become more than human in the future." Jason looked at me wide-eyed. "How *far* in the future?" he asked with great excitement. "It depends on the specific inventions and abilities. I write about a bunch of different ones, and what will make them possible before too long," I explained. "Like what? Which ones?!" he exclaimed, as a prompt for me to explain what techno-scientific developments were going to be central to the book's vision of evolution beyond the human condition. "Genetics, Nanotechnics, Cybernetics, Robotics, and Psionics. I'll explain what kinds of superpowers each of them could give us, and how they can totally change the way that we live." Jason sat there captivated, looking up at me eagerly with his hands folded under his chin.

"You remember Khan in *Star Trek II*, and in that old episode of the series where he takes over the Enterprise?" I asked. "Yeah, *of course!*" he shot back, sounding almost insulted that I would even ask. I smiled. "Well, he's a product of Genetic Engineering." "Yeah, *I know*," Jason said. "So, you know, Genetic Engineering is when scientists change the genes, the code, that people get from their parents, to give them abilities or powers that they would not have had if they were just born normally." Before I could go on, he added, "Like being super smart or super strong, or living longer." "Exactly, that's what I mean by Genetics as a path to superpowers," I replied as I realized that this was going to be even easier than I expected.

"How about Nano... what'd you say... Nano*technics*?" he asked. "'Nano' means super small. Something so tiny that you can't see it with your naked eye. Have you ever seen an old computer? Like the ones that Dr. Banner uses in *The Incredible Hulk*. You know, they were big, like the size of walls or bookshelves, right?" Jason searched his memory for a moment, then came back with, "Yeah, with lots of blinking lights. The Hulk smashes those sometimes." "Well, look at this computer that I'm writing my book on," I said, as I showed him the original Macintosh model that I had bought when it first came out in 1984. "This computer here probably has more power than most of the ones that Dr. Banner was using. But see how much smaller it is?" "Yeah, how come?" he asked. "Because the more scientists learn over time, and the smarter inventors get, the tinier the pieces that they can build a computer with. Computers get smaller and smaller but have more power than the bigger ones of the past. There are boards inside of computers that have little things stuck to them like Legos. They're called microchips. I'll show you sometime."

He retorted, "I *know* what a micro*chip* is. I took apart a Nintendo game cartridge once, after it broke." "What game was it?" I asked. "*Rad Racer*," he said. "So, if computers and other kinds of electronics, like Nintendo games, get smaller and smaller, you can imagine how sometime in the future, the microchips that are sawdered — like *glued*, you know, welded — to those green boards would be *so* tiny that you could only see them under a microscope, the way that you look at cells under a microscope in Science class." He followed what I was saying but seemed a bit incredulous about cell-sized microchips. So, I took a risk to make Moore's Law more tangible to him, and to be honest, also to deepen his clearly growing fascination with me.

"I'll tell you a secret, if you promise to keep it," I said. Jason implored me to tell him. "Don't go telling all your friends, okay?" He promised. "Next year, they're going to come out with a Nintendo that you can carry around everywhere in your hand and even fit into your jacket pocket. The microchips will be so small, that the game cartridges inside it will be a quarter of the size of the ones that you put in your NES now." "No *way*!" he exclaimed, "*next* year?!" "Yeah, I'll get you one if you keep working with me to do all your homework right." (In point of fact, I did deliver on this promise to get him a Game Boy as soon as it was released.) "So, Nanotechnics means when electronics can be made so small that machines like computers shrink so much that... they're like... microscopic. So that you could put them inside someone's body like in that movie *Fantastic Voyage* — except not with the silly shrinking people, just the submarine being a 'nano' machine?" *He* said this, not me. "Yes, Jason, that's precisely what I mean. Now imagine what could be done with gadgets like that in surgery, manufacturing, or construction."

"Wait, wait!" he started shouting excitedly. "Isn't that how replicators and the Holodeck work on Captain Picard's Enterprise-D?" The example couldn't have been more perfect. I ought to have thought of it myself. He had now been watching *Star Trek: The Next Generation* for a couple of years. "You've got it! That's *exactly* how they work. They build the replicated food and all of the simulated places and objects on the Holodeck using 'nanites' — like nano-scale building blocks that are smart and can be programmed by a computer." Jason marveled as that sunk in. "In your book, how far do you say that we are from having something like that?" he finally asked. "Well, I'll tell you this much, Jason, it certainly won't take until the 23rd century, like in *Star Trek*. We may have it when you're as old as your grandparents are now." His head slowly slid to the side as I could see he was thinking, "*Wow.*"

"How about Cybernetics, you want to know about that?" I asked, cutting into his reverie. "Oh, I know about cyborgs," he said, "like Robocop, or the Terminator." "Your parents let you watch those movies?" I asked, already knowing the answer. Jason looked up at me a bit bashfully, with his head slightly downcast and turned aside. "Well, I watched them on a sleepover. One of my friends lives at the Waldorf. His father is the hotel manager. They have all kinds of movies on their TV, from the hotel. His parents are never around when I come over, so..." I laughed, which put him at ease. He giggled back. "Then, you remember in *The Terminator* how the computer network in the future decided on its own to start World War III? How all the war machines — the planes and missiles and stuff — were all networked, all linked together, and controlled by a super computer, and that computer... like *woke up*, and started to think for itself, and then defended itself when people tried to pull the plug on it?" "Yeah, I remember that's what the time traveler from the future told that lady..." "Sarah Connor," I said. "Well, Cybernetics doesn't mean cyborgs — like robots — it means smart computer networks that control things without needing people to tell them what to do," I explained. "Isn't that really dangerous?" he asked. "Yes, it could be, Jason. Which is why we need to start thinking about it seriously now, about how to control systems like that so that they give us more power instead of taking things over in a way that we don't want." He nodded at me affirmatively.

"But how about *real* robots? Like Data or C-3PO. Your book is about them too?" he asked. "Yes, I write about how in the future robots will do all the kinds of work that people don't want to do." Underwhelmed he said, "You mean like being garbage men." I replied, "Not just jobs like that, but *all* repetitive labor on assembly lines. All manufacturing, and transportation." His eyes lit up. "You mean like robot planes, cars, and trucks that can fly or drive themselves, like in *Transformers*?!" I was really enjoying this. "Yup. *That's right*, and some of them will even be able to change shape like Transformers, too. Imagine robots that are built out of the nano-scale parts that we were talking about earlier. See how with parts that small they could rearrange themselves into any shape, to do a bunch of different kinds of jobs?" Jason said, "makes sense" with a brooding expression on his face, the meaning of which I discerned when, a moment later, he added, as if with genuine concern, "but doesn't that mean that they could also be soldiers? We wouldn't stand a chance against shape-shifting robot soldiers, would we?" My eyes locked onto his in a steady gaze, as I answered, "That's why the right people — like superheroes, or Jedi — need to build them first, and have to be able to control them, because you don't want any robots or cyborgs like Brainiac on the loose."

"What about the powers that *Jedi* have? Will science discover *those* too, and will people in the future be able to learn how to use them?" Jason asked, anticipating the last—but certainly not the least—of the techno-scientific developments central to the thesis of *Uber Man*. "Yeah, that's what Psionics is about. Psionics is like technology—you know, gadgets and also techniques or skills—based on the science of Parapsychology." Jason's enthusiasm now reached a fever pitch. "Like Dr. Venkman and Egon and Ray! The Ghostbusters are scientists who do Parapsychology, and they use it to build gadgets like their proton packs, and ghost traps, and stuff. Well, *except* Winston. He's *not* a scientist. Mr. Spock is a scientist, and he can read people's minds too." I shook my head, laughing, with tears in my eyes. "That's right, Jason. Parapsychology is a real science, and in the future gadgets will be invented, like the ones that the Ghostbusters build, and techniques will also be developed, to make it easier to learn the kinds of abilities that the Jedi have, or that Spock has. It will be like learning a martial art, someday."

Then Jason, always seeing the dark side, added, "But what about Darth Vader? Couldn't it be dangerous if bad people learned to use those kinds of abilities? Wouldn't a lot of people be tempted to use them the wrong way?" Not bad for a seven-year-old. "Actually, that brings me to the main point of my book, Jason. Human psychology—the way that we think, and feel, and act—has to change in a big way if we are going to survive developing the superpowers that all of these inventions and discoveries that we've been talking about could give us before too long." He looked at me pensively. "You mean we have to become more like Yoda, or Spock," and then I cut in with, "or more like Superman." Then he asked, "That's why you're calling the book Superman? Because we can't be tempted like he was, in *Superman II*. He let down humanity when the super criminals from Krypton attacked, just because he only wanted to love Lois Lane like a normal guy."

I smiled at him with what must have been a very impressed look on my face, and then I winced slightly as I asked, "What about Khan? Do you think he was really a villain, or was he a kind of Superman too?" Jason thought deeply for a moment, looking inwardly, in silence. "I think that Kirk let him live — you know, in the episode where he first shows up — because the captain thought Khan *was* a kind of Superman. That he wasn't really *bad*. It's like he respected him too much to kill him. So, instead he gave Khan a new world of his own to build. It wasn't his fault that the planet's orbit shifted." He told me that he wanted to re-watch the episode. I showed Jason that I had it on VHS. When his mother came to pick him up before too long, I gave him the cassette tape of *Star Trek* with the "Space Seed" episode on it to take home. As he walked out the door of my apartment, I said to him, "Listen for that line at the end of Khan's trial, when Kirk quotes Milton about Lucifer." I was oblivious to what reaction Susan may have had to this, as my gaze was fixed on the twinkle in Jason's eyes. I had already offered him the apple, and he had bitten deep.

After Jason left that night, I turned on the news and watched the presidential campaign coverage. Following the Iowa caucuses and New Hampshire primary, Donald Trump was in second place, with Bob Dole and Pat Robertson trailing him, and with George Bush having gained a slight lead over him. Bush's advisors were already considering reaching out to Trump to offer him the vice-presidential nomination if he withdrew from the race and backed Bush as the Republican nominee. While I doubted that Trump would accept such an offer, I felt that I needed to act fast. Ensuring that Bush was not elected in '88 had been one of my primary objectives. On my timeline, the ex-CIA director had been the principal architect of the collapse of the Soviet Union from 1989–1991, not Reagan, who got more credit for paving the way for it than he deserved. If Bush was not prevented from becoming President, it was still possible that he would find some other Soviet reformer to play the role that Gorbachev had played as his counterpart in tearing down the Iron Curtain and imploding the USSR. Perhaps Boris Yeltsin (although Yeltsin had not gone nearly as far as I remember him having gotten in the history that I was taught, since it was Gorbachev who really noticed Yeltsin and lifted him up before being betrayed by him).

In any case, George H. W. Bush was the son of one of the principal operatives of the Nordic Breakaway civilization within the power structure of the United States. Prescott Bush had been a principal financier of Adolf Hitler during the lead-up to the Second World War, channeling funds from the German American Bund to the Nazi Party. It is no wonder that his son had been chosen to manage the collapse of the Soviet Union, the continued existence of which would have made the Olympian re-conquest of Earth and establishment of the Traditionalist Imperium much harder. If Soviet Communism survived into the 2040s, it would certainly ally with the West to confront these self-proclaimed Nordic "gods" and their regressive Brahmin in the occulted Fourth Reich. The combined nuclear arsenals of the two superpowers, both still committed to Promethean Progress, might be enough to make them reconsider and, if not, to unleash a fiery rebellion.

Instead, in the world that I come from, both of those superpowers were long gone by the 2040s and the world was dominated by a Chinese hegemon whose Neo-Confucian ideology inclined them to accept the role of colonial Viceroy offered to China by the "Celestial Ancestors" who revealed themselves to a desperate and demoralized Earth in 2048. Taking out George Bush would be removing a key asset of the truly "Evil Empire" and further securing the survival of the Soviet Union into the far future, so that it could be one of two fists able to strike at that Olympian Imperium before it managed to subjugate the planet.

I considered the options, and I chose the one with the least risk of my being exposed. George Bush loved to go fishing and was known for getting behind the helm of his own speedboat off Walker's Point at his family's property in Kennebunkport, Maine. Sometimes he would test the upper limits of his speedboat, *Fidelity*, by throttling it forward at 75 miles per hour. As you may recall, I am an expert diver. So, I got my gear — not just my diving gear — and headed to coastal Maine where Bush would be spending the weekend to recuperate ahead of a major set of primary elections that could well decide the fate of his campaign.

It was several days before "Super Tuesday" on March 8, 1988, when Republican voters in Texas, Florida, Tennessee, Louisiana, Oklahoma, Mississippi, Kentucky, Alabama, and Georgia would all cast their ballots for their preferred nominee. Trump was not expected to do well in those states, since religious and rural Southerners tended to see him as a wheeler-dealer playboy New Yorker whose qualifications for the presidency were building casino hotels and being good at Monopoly. Trump's recently released book, *The Art of the Deal*, may have been a bestseller in the big cities (for thirteen weeks no less), but it certainly didn't help him gain any voters in the Bible Belt, especially not after he said that it was his own "second favorite book, after the Bible." The Evangelicals saw the 11-step formula in the book that was modeled on Norman Vincent Peale's *Power of Positive Thinking* as tantamount to advocating New Age witchcraft, except explicitly driven by greed and in the service of Mammon.

I arrived in Kennebunkport on Saturday morning, having left from Long Island in the predawn hours aboard an AtlantiCorp submarine (a decommissioned one that we had bought from the French Navy). Johnny came with me. Actually, he captained the submarine most of the way, before manning the vessel while I dove into the water of Walker's Point. There, I set up numerous moored mines, which had been the cargo of the submarine. They were geared to be released from their moorings and detonated by remote control. The submarine got close enough to the Bush family compound for me to ring the area around the dock with these mines, so that they could be detonated before the Vice President throttled his boat. Or, if that opportunity were missed, on his way back in after fishing.

When I got back on board, Johnny took us out to a position in somewhat less shallow waters but still close enough to the peninsula, so that when we surfaced, I was able to surveil the dock at Bush's compound from the turret of the submarine, through the high-powered telescope that I had. The vessel had been painted in camouflaged colors that helped to conceal it against the background of the ocean, and Johnny was watching the scopes vigilantly for any potential close approach by other ships, in which case we would dive again to conceal ourselves. That did not prove to be necessary, though. Around 2 pm, Vice President Bush boarded the *Fidelity* with a couple of other men, probably hoping to catch some fish to eat fresh with their dinner that evening. Instead, he was the one to get caught, within a few minutes of leaving his dock, when I detonated the mines, in staggered fashion, which I had positioned around Walker's Point. The redundancy worked well, since the first mine damaged his boat but did not destroy it. By the time I blew the third mine that was closest to the *Fidelity* on its panicked retreat to the dock, Bush was blown to bits. I could see his remains washing back up against the rocks along his property's coastline.

Pat Robertson came out on top in the Super Tuesday states, instead of the now deceased George Herbert Walker Bush. But, as both Trump and Republican Party leaders knew full well, the televangelist did not have a hope in hell of winning a national election against the Democrats. By the time that primary voting was held in big blue states like New York and California, Trump was the clear frontrunner. In June, he was finally endorsed by President Reagan. No one was surprised to see Trump become the nominee at the Republican convention in New Orleans that August, where he announced his choice of General Haig as his vice-presidential running mate.

Donald Trump crushed Michael Dukakis in the televised debates that took place in the following months. He got quite a bit of bad press for being a bully on stage, but it paid off for him. "I'm tired of *nice* people," he would say, when confronted about his tone and tactics. "This country is in *deep, deep* trouble. We don't need somebody *nice* as President right now. That's not gonna solve our problems at home — and *certainly not abroad*. You wanna send some *nice* guy to renegotiate our commitments to the Japanese and the Saudis? You think a *nice* guy is gonna stare down General Yazov over there in Russia before he takes the rest of Iran, then maybe decides that we're such *wimps* that he should just keep going across the Persian Gulf?" Enough people were genuinely afraid of this that Trump-Haig '88 became a winning ticket.

On a cold night in early November of 1988, Donald Trump was elected the 41st President of the United States. I was one of the few people cleared by the secret service to look down onto his podium that had been set in front of the rock-faced waterfall in the atrium of Trump Tower. After all, AtlantiCorp had been hired to provide additional private security on the walkways of all the floors surrounding the open atrium at the bottom of which the President-Elect would be delivering his victory speech.

Trump was true to the motto and main slogan of his campaign, "Back to the Future." He promised to return America to the Futurama vision of the World of Tomorrow, by modernizing our infrastructure and transportation, and by taking us back to the Moon and onto Mars. He said that our so-called "allies" would pay for all of this, and that our ability to outcompete Japan — with its homogenous, cohesive, and highly intelligent population — depended on not allowing mass illegal migration into this country and the destruction of the hard-working and innovatively minded demographic that had made America great in the first place. "*This* country is not a *trash* heap for the *garbage* that other nations throw out, because it's *cheaper* than incarcerating them — it's *cheaper* and easier for them to send their gangbangers, drug dealers, and good-for-nothings here. They're *parasites!*" *There* was the good old Trump *I* knew.

After Trump's victory, I felt like a tremendous weight had been lifted from my broad shoulders. My work here was not quite done, but it had reached a turning point. I wanted, more than anything, to really lose myself for a little while. To let go, completely. You might imagine that, as a philosopher, I would turn to some meditation technique to accomplish this. But what I really wanted was to be fucked like an animal. I mean to be handled, and hammered, by a man who makes me dripping wet from the riveting fear that he might tear me apart.

I was enough of a woman to know that is what no other woman can give you, and it is a *rare* beast of a man who *can*. I had not lived as a woman for about eighteen hundred years. So, I had not been taken like that since early in my marriage to Caesar Septimius Severus. Later, he figured out that his wife preferred women and he also lost the drive and the stamina for it. (Besides, by then I was very focused on the project that I had hired Philostratus to help me complete. No small task, trying to nip Roman Catholicism in the bud by universalizing a pagan philosophical messiah from my Syrian homeland.) It was high time to really remember what that feels like, even if only for a night.

It was important to me that it be a random guy who I would never see again. But where to find such a person who was up to the task? Disease was not as much of a consideration as you might think, because together with my slower biological clock and lengthened lifespan, one benefit of having been genetically engineered in the late 21st century was that I was born with blood that was tremendously disease-resistant — even to AIDS. That was good to know because I wanted whoever it was to shoot his cum in me, preferably more than once. I wanted him to break me — out of myself — so that what was left in my skin was nothing but a deliciously objectified condensation of the sheer pleasure of submission. I had always been the wolf. Tonight,

I wanted to be the wolf's prey, ecstatic to be devoured by a ferocious hunger.

At first, I thought that I might find what I was looking for at the Limelight. But after scoping the place out, and not really being in the mood to get drunk or just dance, I got back in my matt black DeLorean with its black leather interior and cruised around the city's streets like I was looking for a hooker. Except that I was the one who wanted to be the whore that night. I put on songs like "Every Breath You Take" by The Police, Laura Branigan's "Self Control," and "Don't You Want Me" by The Human League, turning the speakers up high after rolling down my windows. After about an hour of cruising around, when the cassette tape was on Daryl Hall and John Oates' "Maneater," I found the type of guy that I wanted in the dark and narrow cobblestone streets of SoHo. He was not as much taken aback by how forward I was being as he was cruelly mocking. He likely thought to himself that I had no idea what I was asking for. I didn't ask his name. Nor did he volunteer it.

This brute took me back to his loft apartment, up a dirty old freight elevator. It was near the place where I had met Jean-Michel Basquiat at a private Warhol exhibition a few years ago. There was paint splotched all over his floor, together with broken bottles of booze and crushed cigarette butts. He looked a bit like Jackson Pollock, but more built. I wondered if he was a painter, but I didn't see any canvases around. Probably not an artist, but maybe an industrial design painter. Just before he started pushing me around, I noticed some spray cans in a dark corner.

The place was very unevenly lit. He took me to one of the brightly lit spots, where there was a dusty and crusty dark brown leather couch. I threw my long fur coat over the sofa, with the outside facing up. Standing back in the shadow, he ripped my silvery silk dress off — tearing it in half from the bottom up and tossing it aside. I wasn't wearing a bra or any panties. My hard nipples rubbed against the fur of my coat that was covering the couch, as he bent me further over. I kept my high heels on so that he could have a better angle. When he noticed the size of my engorged clit, he tried to humiliate me for it while pulling my hair. "You think I'm some kind of queer, bitch!?" he shouted. "You want me to rub my cock against your little dick or something?!"

I will refrain from scandalizing you with the details, but let me say that, over the next hour or so, this John gave me pretty much everything that I was wanting. On my way out, he didn't even give me anything to wipe the cum that was dripping down my inner thighs or my chin and chest. What he did give me was a twenty-dollar bill that he shoved into my handbag to insult me. I took it, just so that I could feel even more like a whore tonight — a very cheap and desperate whore — rather than a time-traveling Philosopher Queen posing as the only female executive billionaire in 1988 (albeit with most of her money hidden in Swiss bank accounts). I went back to my car wearing only my fur coat, and I ran every red light that I could on my drive back home through the relatively empty streets. After parking around the corner, next to the church, I tried to walk into and through my lobby as fast as possible, with the fur coat drawn tightly around my otherwise naked body. Once I got past the doorman, I even took my heels off to move faster.

When I was finally upstairs, and went into the bathroom, I saw what a mess I was. I could smell him all over me. It turned me on again. I ran my fingers along the inside of my thighs and gathered onto them as much of his cum as I could. Then, while sitting on the toilet seat, I fingered myself with it, while having flashbacks of everything that had just happened to me in that SoHo loft. It's a good thing that I had already turned the shower water on, because I shrieked like a banshee over and over again when I came.

I slept well in what was left of that night. When I woke up late the next morning, feeling refreshed, I got back to work on *Uber Man*. Books that I was using for research surrounded and ensconced my Macintosh, with the graphics on their covers illuminated by the blue glow of its screen. The two that I had lying open at the moment, face down, were Eric Drexler's *Engines of Creation* and F. M. Esfandiary's *Up-Wingers*. At the top of the stack leaning against one side of the Mac was a Penguin Classics edition of Friedrich Nietzsche's *Beyond Good and Evil* that had Franz von Stuck's 1904 *Sphinx* painting printed on its cover. The stack on the other side was topped by Ostrander and Schroeder's *Psychic Discoveries Behind the Iron Curtain*.

The last one was a particularly noteworthy book insofar as it demonstrated that, despite the unequivocal atheism and supposed "materialism" of the putatively "scientific" framework of the Marxist Eastern bloc, the Psychotronics program of the Soviet Union and its satellite states had far surpassed America in government-funded psychic research on latent human abilities such as Extrasensory Perception (ESP) and Psychokinesis (PK). To my great satisfaction, this made the case that spectral phenomena were a subject of empirical research in scientific laboratories. To treat such "paranormal" manifestations as "miracles" that reaffirm faith in revelation was just a tactic of psychological and social control that self-proclaimed prophets and manipulative clergymen would use on people falsely conditioned to believe that *natural* abilities — which we share with animals — are "supernatural" demonstrations of divine power that lie outside the scope of scientific study.

The most interesting part of the book was an account of work being done by Psychotronics researchers in Prague to develop devices that would be able to channel and amplify psi abilities. In *Uber Man*, I pointed out how, as Nanotechnology (of the kind that Drexler was already envisioning) became a reality, such devices could be much more precisely designed. It was also likely, I argued, that genetic engineers would be able to identify correlates for biological predisposition to becoming a psi virtuoso. They could then edit the genes of an embryo in such a way as to endow children with this trait at birth, potentially on a population-wide basis. I had to be careful, in my writing, not to smuggle in too much tacit knowledge about specific future developments, such as CRISPR, when I was discussing Genetic Engineering, or to make detailed references to graphene when writing about Nanotechnology. I *did* suggest biomimetics, and a bottom-up evolutionary design approach, to overcome bottlenecks in Robotics R&D.

Worst of all, I beat Vernor Vinge to coining the term "Technological Singularity." (Sorry, Vernor.) I was writing about how innovation in various areas of technological development, which were in turn making new scientific breakthroughs possible, were mutually reinforcing and deeply convergent. For example, the genetic engineering of a much higher average IQ would result in individuals capable of solving hitherto intractable research problems in computer science that would finally yield an "Artificial Intelligence" that was more than just the product of linear algorithms running on digital binary machines. By the same token, stronger and smarter computers, possibly ones based on quantum computation, would be able to map and project changes to the human genome in ways that made much more subtle and complex forms of genetic engineering possible. Once nanotechnological design became feasible, it would be much easier to overcome the locomotion problem in Robotics and build robots that are capable of autonomously replicating any human physical movements. Robots with much sharper perception and more subtle dexterity would, in turn, be able to engage in Nanotechnology design and manufacture far more effectively than human engineers.

Finally, to bring Psychotronics into the picture, the more comprehensive Genetic Engineering, Nanotechnology, and Robotics became in their approach to analyzing, replicating, and augmenting the function of human organs, including the brain, the more these nuts-and-bolts research programs would come up against enigmatic psi abilities. ESP and PK would be acknowledged as R&D problems in the development of Artificial Intelligence or in the integration of the brain with Cybernetic systems, perhaps for the purpose of "downloading" human consciousness into an android body. There would be problems of morphogenesis relevant to genetic engineering that could not be solved but by factoring in non-local morphic resonance that, quite apart from DNA, impacts embryological development by endowing a baby with characteristics of the body that belonged to the psyche that is about to be reincarnated as that child.

The ultimate point of convergence of all accelerating technological developments, including in Psychotronics, would be convergence in a point that is really a vortex — a singularity. On a graph of humanity's technical progress from the mastery of fire through to the harnessing of the atom, this "Technological Singularity" is where the increasingly steep upward slope of the graphed line becomes a spike going straight upwards off the chart. That signifies that the analytically projective mind able to graph developments to date, and extrapolate from them, including in the realm of science-fiction, will reach a barrier on the other side of which is what is "*über*" (over, above) Man.

The heart of my book, the part that I could not adequately convey to Jason yet, was philosophical and, by extension, political. I say, by extension, because *Uber Man* had nothing to say about petty politics. Rather, its ideological and programmatic dimensions were of the kind that Nietzsche anticipated when he prophesied the advent of a "grand politics" that would determine nothing less than the planetary destiny of mankind.

I followed F. M. Esfandiary in his argument that Left- and Right-Wing were no longer adequate ideological orientations, and that the future dichotomy in sociopolitical struggle was between those who wanted to keep us "down" in the muck of the "merely human" and those "Up-Wingers" who were ready to affirm an evolutionary leap into a technologically augmented "posthuman" condition. However, at the same time, *Uber Man* harshly critiqued Esfandiary for his preposterously naive view that this evolutionary revolution could be

accomplished through more direct democracy and his even more de-
spicable claim that nothing is worth dying for. The latter claim follows
from his myopic materialism and disregard of abundant evidence for
the survival of bodily death and the persistence of personality. Even
were the latter not the case, Esfandiary's tritely derisive dismissal of
the heroic Existentialist view of death, namely that an authentic and
meaningful life can only be lived in the face of a finite horizon that is
ultimately bounded by nothingness, is itself worthy of contempt. It is
nothing more than a product of his own cowardly thanatophobia.

Rather, as Nietzsche understood well, the last and greatest revolution in history, the one that ends "human" history and inaugurates a
"higher history" of the *Übermensch*, will necessarily be the bloodiest
and most incendiary sociopolitical upheaval of all time. It will be a
revolution of the extreme minority against the vast majority, who
will by then have devolved into cynical and nihilistic subhumans.
Sarcastically dismissive of every noble aspiration, they will have become addicted to creature comforts, perpetually diverted from serious
aims and creative ambitions by a pseudo "culture" of crassly irreverent
entertainment.

These will be the great "democratic" masses huddled together in
both nationalist and socialist states, who only ever elect rabble-rousers
and "men of the people" that let them feel good about themselves
while facilitating their bottomless degeneration. This tyrannous
majority, which the founders of the United States naively believed
could be penned in by constitutional provisions for the protection of
individual liberties, this mass of herd animals by comparison to which
cattle are noble creatures, will resist further evolution by any and all
means necessary. They would, as Nietzsche knew well, prefer that we
walk the evolutionary tightrope back to being apes rather than to tread
forward with the gymnast's poise and the requisite daring to become
those Supermen who stand on the far side of the tightrope.

For those who are psychologically prepared and have the Promethean *ethos* to take the evolutionary leap *upward* to be protected from those who would clip their wings, for the impending and relatively immanent Technological Singularity not to be sabotaged and subjected to a controlled demolition by conspirators who are, after all, only giving the masses what they secretly desire, the most anti-democratic consolidation of power in history is required. This must take place by means of ruthless cunning and a hitherto inconceivable capacity for dynamically transformative violence. The revolution from *above*, of the very *few* against the many.

By no means does *Uber Man* argue in favor of oligarchy, or the empowering of merchants and financiers. Quite to the contrary. Like Plato, I call for radical *meritocracy*. Again, advocating in favor of a revolution that is beyond the classic dichotomy of Left vs. Right, *Uber Man* affirms much of Marx's vision of a Communist society as a *free* society and argues that the Soviet Union was, at least in its ideal conception, forwarding a Promethean project to turn mere human beings into Communist Supermen. The failing of Marx, and of Soviet state ideology, was to believe that the proletarian rabble of uneducated workers would *ever* be capable of undergoing the kind of *psychological* transformation that the transcendence of Capitalist profiteering and the avaricious coveting of private property requires. Let alone that they would be more capable of it than aristocrats, and even members of the bourgeoisie, some of whom had the benefit of exposure to works of philosophy, literature, and art that lifted them above and beyond their lower selves.

The Technological Singularity would fundamentally alter the parameters of economic and industrial planning, taking us from a scarcity economy where the organization of labor and redistribution of wealth, which are principal Marxist concerns, is supplanted by a post-industrial production platform of abundance that provides for leisure without the need for *any* human drudgery whatsoever. But this

New World Order—as H. G. Wells called it—would be rejected by the masses, through their designated representatives in the political, corporate, and industrial spheres, let alone their clergymen who valorize the pointless suffering of hard labor as penitence for the Fall. Despite all their disingenuous clamoring for "freedom," what the masses really want is to ensure that they remain collectively enslaved by avarice, petty jealousies, and niggardly resentments of anyone with the aspiration and will power to build on higher spiritual ground.

Uber Man made the case that, from the standpoint of the early 1990s, when I planned for the book to be completed and published, we had no more than half a century to decide whether it was better to let ourselves be regressed to a feudal or archaic pre-industrial society, or whether we were intent on following through with the Technological Singularity and the "Spectral Revolution" that I argued would come with it. I appropriated this idea from my writings as Jorjani in the future past. Namely the idea that, as already suggested above in relation to Psychotronics, once we reached the event horizon of the Singularity in terms of technological development, hitherto marginalized and suppressed psi abilities would also have to be recognized by mainstream science. At that point, total social collapse on the scale of a planet-wide Salem Witch Panic would be inevitable, *unless* we were to forge a society wherein no one would think to misuse ESP and PK to harm their fellow citizens by committing avaricious or vengeful crimes. Such crimes would be untraceable by normal law enforcement procedures and impossible to prosecute retro-actively by means of the established procedures of our "impartial" justice system.

The only thing to do is to ensure that these transgressions never take place to begin with. Since, in the realm of psychic ability, which functions mostly unconsciously, to *intend* something may be to make it *happen*, there is no solution other than to make sure that such spectral crimes are unthinkable to whoever remains in society. That would reduce the population base to the same less than 1% of individuals who could also be trusted never to weaponize Nanotechnology or misuse increasingly ubiquitous gene-editing abilities in ways that would threaten the public welfare far more seriously than terrorists, thugs, and malcontents were able to do with the tools at their disposal in the 20th century. What Esfandiary did not understand when he wrote *Up-Wingers* is that evolution is an exclusionary process that selects *against* the majority of a population group who fail to exhibit a mutation that adapts them to environmental stresses. The selection *for* a mutation is, as a general rule, a selection for deviation from the norm, and the evolution *of a few* who become the progenitors of a new species *at the expense of the many.*

CHAPTER 18

GO FORTH UNAFRAID

Someone would have to bring *Uber Man* to the attention of socio-political elites and celebrities around the world. Not a mere publicist, but a person who could familiarize royalty, presidents, scientists, acclaimed artists, famous actors, and popular musicians with the book's ideas even ahead of its publication. I came here with a very clear idea of who that super-connected socialite should be: Ghislaine Maxwell. I knew that in July of 1991, her father, media mogul Robert Maxwell would buy the *Daily News* in New York City. Then, within a few months, in November of the same year, he would disappear from his yacht, the Lady Ghislaine, which was named after his youngest daughter.

What was never revealed to the public, and what Ghislaine alone among her brothers and sisters strongly suspected, was that Maxwell was murdered. By whom, she did not know. He had gone from being a very valuable high-level asset to the Mossad to becoming a liability when, as the owner of numerous newspapers that he occasionally used for blackmail, he started threatening the Israelis that if they did not continue to fund his secretly bankrupt media empire, then he would reveal certain sensitive information. For the sake of plausible deniability, and to fit his public image as one of the best friends of Israel, Maxwell's recovered body was given a burial on the Mount of Olives with the highest honors of the Israeli state. Ariel Sharon, Yitzhak Shamir, and Ehud Barak were all at his funeral comforting Ghislaine and her siblings. What she didn't know was that Barak, an Israeli military-intelligence man, had given the order for the assassins on the two-man submarine to board the Lady Ghislaine in the middle of the night and take out her father.

Within a couple of weeks of Robert Maxwell's death, it was exposed that he had engaged in massive fraud to fund businesses that were really bankrupt. The family lost its fortune, and their fifty-room mansion in Oxford, where Ghislaine had grown up, and stayed on weekends during her years as a student at Oxford University in the mid-1980s. Pretty much everything in the house, and at Maxwell's various offices, was auctioned off by Sotheby's. Her two brothers, who were officially involved in the family business, were even prosecuted, but Ghislaine, who actually had more knowledge of her father's questionable dealings, was able to walk away since she had no *official* position within the management of the bankrupt enterprises. By December of 1991, looking for a fresh start, Ghislaine had left and resettled in what was, for her, a small apartment on the Upper East Side of Manhattan. She may have been short on cash, but her Rolodex was still intact.

Ghislaine Maxwell was daddy's girl, and she was absolutely devastated by the death of her father. Her closest friends at the time noticed a complete change in her personality. She went from being a passionate and gregarious woman with a raucous sense of humor who was the life of any party, to someone silently contemplative and withdrawn. Her self-imposed solitude was so full of anguish that a couple of people who knew her best feared that Ghislaine might commit suicide, unless something or someone were to fill the black hole in her world and give her life meaning and purpose again. Unfortunately, in the timeline that I hail from, that some*one* turned out to be the former Dalton School math teacher and shady money manager Jeffrey Epstein.

Robert Maxwell had met Epstein in the mid-1980s, and the two hit it off. Maxwell saw in Epstein a man much like himself. Although Epstein had not grown up nearly as poor as "Robert" had when he was still Jan

Ludwig Hoch from the ghettos of Nazi-occupied Czechoslovakia, he was also a Jewish kid who came from nothing, or to be more precise, from Coney Island, but who managed to use his high IQ to hustle and con his way into being the trusted financial advisor of billionaires like Les Wexner. Maxwell flew Epstein to Israel and got him involved with Israeli military intelligence, initially in the arms-dealing aspect of their operations in the Middle East. Based in Manhattan, Epstein was facilitating and profiting from Israeli arms deals, through certain proxies, with Arab oil sheikhs and various guerrilla groups who were useful idiots for the Mossad.

The tragedy of Ghislaine's life was that, after her father was murdered by the Israelis, she ultimately took refuge with an Israeli intelligence operative of the same individuals who ordered Robert's assassination. The price for reclaiming her old lifestyle of mansion houses and private planes was that she would use her extensive elite international connections as a socialite, who had already functioned for years as a connector for her father, so that Jeffrey Epstein could set up these men by preying upon their appetites for underage women. Prominent politicians, royalty, journalists, actors and every other type of policymaker, public opinion shaper, and celebrity was secretly taped with underage girls that Ghislaine was tasked with procuring for Jeffrey, so that the State of Israel could control US and British foreign policy and shape Anglo-American public opinion. If any of these men ever threatened the interests of the Jewish state, they would be black-mailed into obedience with the tapes that would regularly be supplied to Mossad from Epstein's various wired estates, from his mansion in Manhattan to his Palm Beach house and the property on his private island. There were even hidden cameras installed on his jet.

After two decades in an abusive relationship with him, which in many ways was an attempt on her part to recreate her rapport with her domineering and manipulative father, Ghislaine would eventually try to get away from Jeffrey Epstein. But it was too late. When he was caught after dozens of women who had been groomed by Ghislaine brought accusations against him, she was also eventually apprehended. Once Mossad managed to murder Jeffrey in his jail cell, to prevent him from potentially exposing Israel's tremendous blackmail operation, the prosecution's focus shifted to Ghislaine. Although she attempted to flee Manhattan and literally head for the hills in rural New Hampshire, she was hunted and eventually apprehended by the authorities. Ghislaine then fell for the second time in her life, but much harder. The daddy's girl who grew up in a fifty-room Oxford mansion was now reduced, not to living in a small apartment on the Upper East Side, but to rotting in a New York City jail cell with guards watching her every move, including on the toilet and in the shower, and where flashlights shone on her even as she tried to sleep. How morbidly intriguing that the name Ghislaine, which is of Franco-German origin, means "sweet hostage" or a beautiful sacrificial "pledge." Did Robert Maxwell, whose own name was contrived and who had worked for the military intelligence agencies of three countries before she was born, give daddy's little girl that name on purpose? Or was it karma and synchronicity at work?

In any case, I realized that for Ghislaine to be saved from being captured and then sacrificed by the same people responsible for murdering her father, Jeffrey Epstein had to be gotten rid of *before* Ghislaine developed a relationship with him in Manhattan in the early 1990s. Furthermore, for her to be a constructive publicist and promoter of *Uber Man*, I would have to befriend her prior to her father's death so that, when she moved to New York in December of 1991, she would fall into *my* arms rather than into the clutches of Epstein and Israeli intelligence. I knew that Ghislaine had some proclivities toward bisexuality, without which this plan would have proved to be impossible. But while the potential for seduction was a sine qua non, it was far from sufficient. I needed to be able to offer Ghislaine the material comforts and financial security that I knew she would look to regain through her desperate relationship with Jeffrey (or, from *his* perspective, her work *for* him and his Israeli handlers). Fortunately, by 1991, the finances of AtlantiCorp, including but not limited to its pharmaceutical subsidiary, were such that I could afford to actually outdo Epstein in the lifestyle that I could offer to Ghislaine. Especially considering the fact that she would not have to live at the beck and call of a man whose girlfriend she sadly wished to be, when in fact she was his pimp and a tool of the assassins who murdered her beloved father.

The first order of this business was, however, to get rid of Jeffrey Epstein. By 1989, Epstein was already an arms dealer. I had operatives of AtlantiCorp put him under a tight enough surveillance net to amass a dossier that demonstrated this, a dossier that I would anonymously leak to the press after he was assassinated. No one would question the gunning down of an arms dealer. The authorities would see it as Epstein having succumbed to an occupational hazard. I set up a shell company and had its mock manager arrange a meeting with Jeffrey, putatively for the purpose of having Epstein illegally improve the company's finances. I asked Donald Barr to vouch for this manager so that Jeffrey would take the meeting. AtlantiCorp had cultivated a relationship with Barr, the former headmaster who hired Epstein to teach math at The Dalton School a year after writing the twisted science-fiction novel *Space Relations* (1973) — a book which curiously anticipated the sex-slave trafficking that Epstein would involve Ghislaine in. Barr had been an OSS operative during the Second World War. After leaving Dalton, he was appointed by President Reagan to serve on the National Council of Educational Research, a position that he retained under President Trump — the President *that I made*, and to whom Barr answered now.

Epstein accepted the meeting with my representative, which the latter had demanded be at Tavern on the Green in Central Park. Jeffrey liked to go for strolls in the park, so I had predicted, rightly, that he would walk back home to his townhouse at 9 East 71st street, which was almost directly across the park from the restaurant. It was also an 800-meter expanse (about half a mile) right underneath the windows of my penthouse apartment. In the predawn hours of that beautiful day late in May of 1989, two of my operatives had used a manhole to damage the electric lines near my building at 55 Central Park West. By the time that the lunch meeting was set, ConEdison was jackhammering away on the sidewalk between me and Tavern on the Green so that they could repair the problem underground. The noise was so loud that no one even heard the shots being fired from my sniper rifle with its silencer.

I used an open window toward the middle of the bottom floor of my penthouse. I had carefully tracked Epstein on my rifle scope as he left Tavern on the Green and then, when he was in a relatively secluded but open area, about halfway across the park, I fired three shots at him in rapid succession and each hit their target with high precision. The first to the skull. The second to the heart, after he was already on the ground. The third to one of his legs. That way, without any witnesses who could accurately remember where he was hit first, it would be hard for the police to determine from what angle the shots were fired. After all, he could have been hit in the leg, then fallen, so that the bullets entered his head and chest from a different trajectory than the one that could be traced to a high floor on 66th street and Central Park West. Besides, who was going to come looking for an assassin in this penthouse apartment that belonged to a business woman? After getting rid of Bakhtiar, Bush, and Gorbachev, assassinating Epstein was a walk in the park (no pun intended).

It was a Friday, so that night, after doing the deed, I hit the dancefloor and lost myself to the beat of Techno music at the Limelight, which was always my preferred club in the city, even before Studio 54 closed down. It was beautifully diabolical how it had been built inside of a Gothic church. I even managed to pick up a cute Goth chick, so that she could fuck what was left of my brains out. Once her hangover

wore off the next day, she resented me enough for the size of my apartment, and its view over Central Park, that it was easy never to see her
again.

I befriended Ghislaine Maxwell during her extensive stay in
Manhattan in the month leading up to, and during, her father's acquisition of the New York *Daily News*. Epstein had been dead for two
years at this point, and although she had briefly met Jeffrey before that
day when I gunned him down in Central Park, he was no longer on her
mind at all. In this revised timeline, he was but a blip in her life, much
to the disappointment of Robert Maxwell, who had been scheming to
turn Jeffrey into his son-in-law. It was on an evening in June of 1991
when we first met. I had booked the outdoor space at Tavern on the
Green for a private party and put together the most impressive guest
list that I could from out of the contacts of AtlantiCorp. The ostensible
purpose of the gathering was to celebrate the launch of a new corporate venture, which I knew would reel Ghislaine in, hook line and
sinker. I knew because I got the idea from her — a future version of
her that would never materialize in this revised timeline, but one with
whom she nonetheless shared the biographical background, talents,
and traits that would compel her to devise the *TerraMar* project when
she was trying to distance herself from Epstein in the early 2010s.

This AtlantiCorp project was called *NovAtlantis*. It was a plan
for an environmentally friendly corporate colonization of the ocean
depths in international waters over which no nation had jurisdiction,
beginning with the North Atlantic, from the Caribbean to the Canary
Islands. There were several principal objectives that this project aimed
to achieve. For good optics, the first of them was to preserve this part
of the ocean from overfishing and pollution, by the merchant marine
vessels of various nations, through promoting international regulation
such as universal adherence to *The Law of the Seas* convention of the
United Nations, which the United States had thus far refused to sign.
The second aim was to build submarine micro-cities into the bedrock

of various ridges in unclaimed waters of the Atlantic Ocean. (How this could be seen as entirely consistent with the first aim was glossed over by referencing certain putatively clean construction methodologies and strict quotas on local sea life resource depletion, as well as proposals for fish farming.) The submarine settlement core of the project was justified based on projected sea level rise, with the idea that the best way to avoid catastrophic loss of life, mass displacement, and economic and industrial collapse on account of the drowning of coastal cities was to get *under* the rising water before it was too late. The third and final aim, which connected the project to Avalon Pharmaceutical (AtlantiCorp's subsidiary and cash-cow), was extensive laboratory research on the medicinal properties of a wide range of ocean life, especially with a view to treating and potentially curing cancer.

I guaranteed Ghislaine's attendance by having President Trump personally extend the invitation to her, with an assurance that he would be there. I knew that, for years, she had wanted badly to meet Trump and that her father had, in a most demeaning manner, rebuffed her request to set up a meeting with him. I scheduled the event to coincide with one of his visits back "home." The President would occasionally sneak back to Trump Tower for a break from the White House. I'd like to have seen the look on Ghislaine's face when she opened an envelope from the Oval Office, with the *NovAtlantis* event invitation inside of it, personally inscribed by the Don, and even more so when she received a follow-up phone call from Trump, who said something to the effect of: "I've heard a lot about you from a good friend of mine. All *good* things. I look forward to meeting you at the party." To get Trump to agree to do me this favor, I had flown to Washington in our corporate jet, and stayed at the Willard Hotel for several days waiting for the President to have time to fit me into his schedule with very short notice.

When Ghislaine arrived at Tavern on the Green that Saturday evening in early June of 1991, the restaurant and the whole area of Central Park surrounding it was full of secret service agents. She was dressed in a characteristically stunning fashion, in an indigo blue dress that exposed the tanned skin of her beautiful shoulders and shimmered like the ocean when the Tavern's chandelier light played across it, reminding me of that phrase "the wine dark sea" that Homer often used. Ghislaine's large, sparkling diamond necklace made it impossible for me to miss her as soon as she walked in. (Granted, I was lingering at the bar toward the entrance to make sure that I caught her upon arrival.)

"Lady Maxwell, I'm Dana Avalon," I said as I extended my arm towards her in the entry hall with its charmingly antique wooden rafters. "Thank you so much for coming!" She grinned at the warm acknowledgement, with a sparkle in her fierce eyes. "Let me show you to your table. You're seated right next to Donald." She briefly glanced down at her dress somewhat nervously, rocking slightly on her high stilettos, as she said, "The President is here already?" "Indeed, he is. Don likes to close at least one business deal before he's eaten dinner at any of these things," I replied while laughing disarmingly. "You know him quite well, then?" asked Ghislaine. "Oh yes, *quite* well. *I'm* the one who convinced him to go into politics." I looked back at her, as we reached the threshold of the outdoor seating area. "You can blame me for that." We both chuckled. "*He* certainly does," I added, as I led Ghislaine, now holding her by the arm, over to Trump's table.

"Mr. President," I said as Donald smiled at me boyishly and paused his conversation, "may I present Lady Ghislaine Maxwell?" He got up to shake her hand, towering over both of us. "I was a big fan of your father. A real fighter! If you inherited half his guts and his smarts, let me tell you, Ms. Maxwell, you're in good shape." "Coming from you, that's high praise Mr. President." "Come have a seat, here," he said as he pulled back one of the white wrought-iron chairs around the glass table. "You want to get a drink? You know I don't drink but," he gestured over to the outdoor bar, "maybe you want to bring your drink over." "Sure, I'll go grab a drink and be back in a jiffy," said Ghislaine, clearly looking for an opportunity to take a breath before what she knew could be subjection to a long and very one-sided conversation. I winked at Donald, and after Ghislaine turned away from him, he winked back and gave me a thumbs up.

By the time I was delivering my short speech at a podium set up all the way across from the glass windows looking into the interior of the restaurant, I saw that she was getting along well with Trump. Now, to shift her focus a bit. My speech featured more than one story drawn from my experiences diving, which I knew would set the stage for her to connect to me more deeply since she had also been a life-long avid diver who grew up watching Jacques Cousteau with great interest. I set the *NovAtlantis* project announcement in this personal context, without making it too technical. When I sat down to dinner with Ghislaine afterwards, at the seat immediately to her left, so that she was sandwiched between Trump and I, it gave me great satisfaction that she was more interested in hearing about *NovAtlantis* than in continuing to exchange pleasantries, platitudes, and corporate gossip with the President of the United States. Ghislaine and I began to have a private conversation, leaning into each other and carrying on in a hushed tone of voice, with Trump talking loudly to the several other people at our table. I caught myself staring at her large pearl earrings, somewhat mesmerized by the sheen of her black hair that was a little less than shoulder length. I had to deliberately focus back on what Ghislaine was saying. I think she may have noticed this, and it intrigued her.

We were three drinks in and already on a first name basis, when I said, "To be honest, Ghislaine, the reason that I invited you tonight — I hope that I'm not being too forward — but I asked you to come because *NovAtlantis* still needs a project director. I don't have the time to manage it myself." She looked at me with a stunned, incredulous expression on her face. Fortunately, the tensed muscles of her forehead were complemented by a grin in which I could see both an appreciation of audacity and some deeper, potentially unfathomable, hunger that she let show itself. (It was only later that she confessed to me how unhappy she had been that her father never gave her "a proper job" at any of his businesses.) "You'll have a whole staff working under you," I rushed to add, almost apologetically. "You mean you want *me* to run this project for you?!" she finally blurted out. "I've already done my homework, Ghislaine. You'd be a perfect face for this venture, and the ideal person to generate interest in it among the right circles of people." She thirstily swallowed the rest of her third drink, and even crunched some of the ice at the bottom of it between her teeth.

Trump glanced at her sideways, and then gave me a bemused look. He broke the uncomfortable silence by turning to Ghislaine and nearly shouting, "What's she trying to *sell* you?" he asked, while moving both hands back and forth at his sides. "You know *this* woman talked me into running for President... and, uh... I'm not saying I have any regrets or anything," he shrugged as he caught himself, "and I *guarantee* you that I'll be in office for another five years," he added as he looked a bit uneasily at everyone else at the table, "but... well, *look*, Dana makes your life *harder*. She'll push you to the next level of what you can be — *if* you're *up* for that, you know what I mean? Some people who reach like that, they fall hard from somewhere they had no business being in the first place. Some of 'em even jump out a window." I started giving the President a hard stare. "But if you're your father's daughter, you'll be fine." He turned to the others at the table, pointing at Ghislaine almost rudely, "her father, *great* guy — a real *fighter*." In point of fact, he couldn't have delivered a better "sales" pitch for me. Trump was like that. Just when you thought he was starting to aimlessly stumble into something like a bumbling idiot, what he said or did wound up landing with the astonishing aptness of a master chess player's piece. He reminded me a bit of the card of the Fool in the Tarot.

Ghislaine Maxwell came home with me that very night. After all, I lived right across the street. Trump politely declined an offer to come over for a night cap. "You want all these *suits* to come over there with you?" He was talking about the secret service agents. "They don't let me go *anywhere* alone anymore. You two enjoy yourselves. *You don't want* these stiffs around," he whispered as he leaned down toward us, shaking his head. "It was a real pleasure to meet you, Ms. Maxwell." "The pleasure and the honor were mine, Mr. President." Donald patted me on the back as he headed toward the limousine that would take him back to Trump Tower.

We had our fourth drink of the night on my rooftop terrace, overlooking Central Park. "Just think about it," I said to her as our champaign flutes clinked together. "I don't need an answer for a while. There's a lot of preliminary work that I need to do to lay the ground-work for the project. Meanwhile, I know that you'll be busy helping your father with his acquisition of the *Daily News*." Ghislaine promised me that she'd seriously consider my offer, but I knew that what I was really doing that night was planting a seed that would only germinate in her mind after the death of her father and the scandal of the exposed bankruptcy of his fraudulent business empire — five months later. We parted that evening by kissing each other on the cheeks, as I put her in a car that was sent to pick her up. The wondrous joy, insatiable curios-ity, and vivacious enthusiasm that I saw in her eyes through the tinted glass of the car as she looked up at me and waved goodbye that night, were all missing from her face the next time that I saw her.

It was December of 1991, a few weeks before Christmas. Rockefeller Center and Fifth Avenue, where I had spent the day shopping, were already glittering with decorations. Ghislaine was born on Christmas, and it was a special time of the year for her because although her parents were of Jewish descent, Robert Maxwell, seeking to endear himself to the British people, especially during his years as an elected politician, always celebrated Christmas on a grand scale. Both of my working fireplaces were on, including the one in the turret library on the rooftop with its hybrid Gothic and Deco design, where I was sitting curled up under a wool blanket watching the snow fall through the late afternoon sky, when the doorman rang to tell me that Ghislaine was here. We had spoken briefly on the phone, shortly before she moved to Manhattan to get away from it all and start over. I had already expressed my sympathies, and let her know, as considerately as possible given the circumstances, that my offer still stood. No one else had been hired yet to be the figurehead of the *NovAtlantis* project at AtlantiCorp.

When she walked through the door to my apartment, Ghislaine almost collapsed into my embrace. "I'm sorry," she mumbled, feeling embarrassed at being so vulnerable with someone she hardly knew. "I didn't know where else to go." She could barely look me in the eyes. "Consider yourself at home here, Ghislaine. Regardless of what you decide about my offer. If you prefer this place to your own apartment, or you just want a place to hide out, you can stay as long as you wish. I have two guest rooms, and my driver can take you anywhere you need to go. Our corporate jet can even discretely *fly* you anywhere you have to fly without attracting attention." Ghislaine Maxwell generally had an unflappable confidence about her, at a deeper layer of her persona than that of the social butterfly with an outrageous sense of humor. But what I saw in her eyes at that moment was from a still more profound sub-stratum of her psyche. She looked at me with the sad but wondering eyes of a little girl. "*Please* make yourself at home," I said with sincere empathy.

It took a while, but she did just that. By Christmas Eve Ghislaine had been spending more time at my apartment than at her own provisional pad across the park, which was about a fourth of the size of my penthouse. I made sure not to be overly aggressive in my approach to her, giving her plenty of breathing room and time to herself. She had brought over some luggage and filled the closets and dresser drawers of one of my guest rooms. We finished decorating my apartment together, including the impressive Christmas tree that my sunken living room with its tall ceiling could accommodate. It was still a lot smaller than the ones that she grew up with at that mansion in Oxford, but I know that she appreciated sprawling on the sofa by the side of the tree and basking in the warm glow of its lights — especially at night.

I would often take her shopping, and then out to dinner. French, Italian, Japanese — we hit every hot restaurant in the city. The first time that I walked her over to my black DeLorean and popped the door wing open, Ghislaine said, "I thought you had a driver." I replied, "I do, but I only use him to appear at business meetings, galas, and the like. To be honest, that's why I said that you could use him. These days, I hardly ever do." Ghislaine smiled as she climbed into the passenger seat next to me. Although she did occasionally make use of the limo driver, she much preferred having me chauffer her around town in the DeLorean. I noticed that whenever there was a bit of erotic tension between us in the car, she would unconsciously clutch and stroke the distressed black leather upholstery of the seat either beside or between her thighs. For those first several weeks, nothing had really happened between us besides kissing each other goodnight a few times after especially intoxicated and luxuriant dinner conversations in the course of which we got to know each other much more intimately.

On Christmas Eve of 1991, the night before her thirtieth birthday (she was sixteen years younger than me), we walked back home from a special holiday dinner at Tavern on the Green and snuggled beside the fireplace in the living room to warm up. When Ghislaine sat up for a moment to take her cashmere sweater off, I walked to the kitchen to pour us a couple of glasses of some pretty potent eggnog and bring back a plate of gingerbread cookies. I also slipped her Christmas and birthday present, which had been tucked away in a kitchen drawer, into the pocket of my pants. It was a set of keys. Not to my apartment, but to the apartment beneath mine. Unbeknown to Ghislaine, I had been engaged for weeks in an aggressive buyout of the person who lived under me. He hardly used the apartment, anyway. I made him an offer that he couldn't refuse, paying well over the market price, and brought to bear the substantial influence that I had with the building's board to expedite the transfer of ownership.

Toward the bottom of the glass of eggnog, Ghislaine and I started kissing with the carelessness of mischievous children. She might have thought that I was about to take her to my bedroom when I sprung up and pulled her off the floor by the hand. "I want to give you your present *now*," I said with what must have been an impish expression on my face. With her sweater strewn on the floor, she only had an undershirt on, so I wrapped the wool blanket from the sofa around her shoulders before walking her over to the door, then leading her out into the hallway to the stairwell. "Trust me," I reassured her as she wondered what the hell I was doing, "it's a surprise present." She followed me one flight down the stairwell to the floor just beneath my duplex penthouse, then to one of the doors on the hallway. I knew that any one of them would do, since some of the interior walls on that floor had already been knocked out to form a single apartment extending across the entire 18th floor.

Ghislaine was still rather baffled when she walked in the door of the apartment. "Merry Christmas and Happy Birthday, Ghislaine!" She was starting to get the idea, but still a bit dumbfounded as she surveyed the spacious rooms from the entry foyer. "The former owner has promised to get his furniture out of here by the New Year. Then, you can remodel it any way you like. I have the board wrapped around my finger." Now she understood, and I saw tears well up in her eyes. "It's a selfish present. I want you close to me, Ghislaine, and that guest room just won't do in the long run." She put one hand to her forehead and braced herself with her other arm around my shoulders. "And let's just get this clear from the outset: this is *your* place, and you should feel free to bring whatever men home with you whenever you want. Just maybe share a few of them with me now and then," I said as I shifted my tone from being dead earnest to reassuringly humorous. "So, you like men too, then?" she somewhat breathlessly asked, with tears still streaming down her cheeks. "Once in a while."

"I don't know what to say, Dana, this is just... I *can't believe* that you did this!" "Why don't we take a walk around the place?" I replied as I held her close and started to give her a quick tour of her new apartment. When we stepped out onto what would be her terrace, she noticed that along the exterior of the building, this apartment was part of the white brick facing that was distinct from the rest of the building's beige structure and set back from it, with especially detailed deco moldings aesthetically connecting it up to my duplex. The overall impression of these top floors, taken together, was of something between a Gothic castle and a Babylonian ziggurat sitting on top of a Manhattan residential building. As Ghislaine took all that in, I slipped the keys into her pants pocket, letting my hand linger a bit too long on her thigh.

When we came back up to my apartment, we headed straight to the master bedroom. I turned on the water in the bathroom's hot tub to warm us up from being outside in the cold night air with only our undershirts on. When we pulled these off, both of our nipples were hard — although mine were much larger than hers, despite my having such small breasts. Ghislaine had rather full and round breasts, with a shape that I imagine most men would think was perfect. She was too enamored of me at this point to judge me too harshly for my weird little, widely spaced tits. I could tell that she *was* perturbed by how huge my clitoris is, but my mutant vulva probably made her feel that she had the upper hand in something. Ghislaine relaxed into my body with her cheek lying against my neck. I kissed her forehead, beading with steam from the hot tub.

Suffice it to say that the sex we had that night was among the best in my life. I didn't confess this to Ghislaine because I knew that she preferred men to women and so I imagined that, although clearly satisfied, she might not feel the same. When I brought my Macintosh

PowerBook 100 into bed with me the next morning, while she continued to linger on the verge of sleep next to me, Ghislaine asked what I
was typing. "I'm writing a book," I said. "It's called *Uber Man*." After
she was done snoozing and I brought her up some coffee from the
kitchen, she perked up enough to ask me what the book was about.

"It is about how convergent advancements in technology, and attendant scientific breakthroughs, are reaching a point where Man will
be forced to either face extinction or take a self-overcoming evolutionary leap — in every dimension, psychological, social, political — to a
new form of life that is as far beyond the merely 'human' as Man is
above the ape." Ghislaine's eyes widened, as if to say, "come again." She
looked at me a bit apprehensively but also intrigued, as she sipped her
second coffee from an AtlantiCorp mug. (I had brought a whole pot
upstairs, to refill our mugs.) She had the blanket pulled up under her
armpits, so as not to be cold, since we were both still stark naked. I
flipped the lid of the laptop closed and placed it down on the carpet
next to the bed. "What technological advancements?" she finally asked.
"For example, Genetic Engineering, Robotics, Artificial Intelligence,
and Nanotechnology," I said. "I see. What do you mean by 'attendant
scientific breakthroughs?'" Now she was interested.

"I mean that technological development isn't always an application
of breakthroughs in theoretical science, the latter can be outgrowths of
empirical horizons for observation and experimentation that are first
opened up by new technologies." She stared at me fixedly, with increasingly intense concentration. "Also," I continued, "these breakthroughs
include paradigm-shifting, or even post-paradigmatic areas of research
such as Parapsychology." "You mean like Telepathy, Clairvoyance, and
such... Mind over Matter?" she asked with an awareness of what those
were. "Yes, Ghislaine, although the dichotomous categories of 'Mind'
and 'Matter' are deeply problematic. Nature is *spectral*, especially
when considered from the standpoint of the evolutionary process.
None of these things you mentioned are really 'supernatural.' They're

just natural processes that have been pushed to the fringe by our en-trenched scientific paradigm."

"I haven't heard anyone talk like this since I was at Oxford." I smiled at Ghislaine somewhat apologetically. "Well, there *was* this one fellow I met on a few occasions. A friend or — I don't know — associate of my father's. Epstein was his name. He was really into cutting-edge Physics and technologies like Genetic Engineering that he believed could push the limits of what define humanity. He *also* believed in voodoo — or telekinesis and such. But he was from Brooklyn, you see, so he had a way of putting things — let's say, *crudely* compared to you." She giggled. I faced forward and didn't say anything in direct reply. "Well, it's Christmas morning, I didn't mean to burden you with all that. I have a reservation in place for Christmas brunch at the Plaza Hotel's Palm Court, if you're up for it."

"Oh yes, the Plaza, that sounds delightful," she said. "Great! We'll celebrate your new apartment, and your birthday of course! …Oh, I shouldn't presume. Did you have any other dates set with anyone today?" She blushed bashfully, her head a bit downcast. "Actually, I did *not*. My brothers and my mother will certainly call, and so at some point I should call them myself, since they'll get the answering machine at my apartment." "Your *old* apartment," I said with a smile. Still blushing, Ghislaine looked into my eyes and then gave me a kiss. "Wanna take a shower *together*?" I blurted out with childlike enthusi-asm. "*Sure*," she said. "Let me use your bathroom first, though." After she climbed out from under the covers and strode across the room naked with brazen confidence, I endearingly imagined her sitting on my toilet contemplating technological advancement and post-human evolution.

I kid you not, it's probably what she was thinking about, because she went on and on asking me questions about it during our brunch at the Palm Court. Something I noticed about Ghislaine was that she was very good about taking a cue from someone. When I thought about it, this made sense and was less counterintuitive than I imagined at first (one might assume, with her upbringing, that she was somewhat narcissistically self-centered). To grow up as the favorite and youngest daughter of Robert Maxwell, she must have, from a very young age, gotten used to reading and attuning herself to nonverbal cues from the man, at the very least to stay on the right side of his Jekyll and Hyde personality to the extent possible. I don't know if, even now, she did it consciously. In any case, Ghislaine spent at least the first half of our brunch asking me to elaborate on my explanation of *Uber Man*, despite my repeatedly trying to refocus the subject on something of more personal interest to her.

Then, of her own accord, she made the connection between *Uber Man* and the NovAtlantis project that I wanted her to direct. "You want to colonize the unclaimed ocean depths so as to create a cradle for the evolution of this posthuman race, one that lies beyond the law of any regressive nation." I was deeply impressed. "Yes, Ghislaine, I confess that is my hidden motivation," I whispered as I leaned into her, as if anyone could hear us over the din of the other diners echoing under the curved glass ceiling of the majestic fin-de-siècle room. "I'll do it, Dana," she said decisively. "I'll direct your NovAtlantis project." When I thanked her, while holding her arm across the table, and expressing how much confidence I had in her, she added, "I can also promote your book and its ideas in the right circles of influential people. I know which of these people, at least privately, shares your contempt for the conventional limits of mere 'humanity' which, I might add, is entirely justified. Most 'people' are *worthless*." Now Ghislaine was the one whispering. "There is no reason why we should be dragged down with them, or *by* them, and miss *our chance* at taking an evolutionary leap within the coming century — or *sooner* perhaps."

Early in the spring of 1992, we flew to the Bahamas on my corporate jet and went diving together off the coast of Bimini, where I showed Ghislaine megalithic ruins that dated from the time of Atlantis. She

was a qualified submersible pilot and she insisted on coming back, after our dive, for an even more magical descent onto the "Bimini Wall"
and other hidden pyramidal and polygonal structures. She enjoyed being the one to pilot me in the small submarine. When we were headed
back home, Ghislaine also climbed into the cockpit of the helicopter
and flew us to the airfield where my corporate jet was waiting. She all
but threw the designated pilot in the backseat together with me. I have
to admit that she was the most bad-assed girlfriend that I'd had in this
lifetime, even in the Gotham of 2112.

By the summer of that year, Ghislaine was officially acting as the
director of AtlantiCorp's NovAtlantis project. She began by going on
a lobbying tour that included speeches at the United Nations General
Assembly, the Woods Hole Oceanographic Institute, US Congressional
hearings on *The Law of the Seas* convention, and other international
organizations relevant to the first of the three stated aims of the project.
More importantly, Ghislaine began to promote the ideas of *Uber Man*
to a select group of prominent politicians, broadminded members
of the British royalty, and the more visionary actors and celebrities
that she knew. The book's publication was slated for the fall of 1992, at
which point these individuals would be able to generate tremendous
publicity and considerable moneyed private interest in its vision for a
fusion of hitherto materialistic Transhumanism with the more psychically oriented Human Potential Movement.

In the early 1990s, the foundation was already being laid for
Prometheism — three decades or *a full generation* in advance of when
I had launched that movement in my life as Jorjani. My plan was to ultimately hand the movement, together with its supporting institutions,
including AtlantiCorp and its capital, over to Jason once he completed
his doctoral studies and wrote his first couple of books. Between now
and then, I would work to build an unbreakable rapport with him,
and to reshape his future in the most constructive way possible. (I said
constructive, not *palatable* to the mob's public morals.)

Ghislaine settled into her apartment on the 18th floor of 55 Central Park West, where she resumed her role as a socialite hosting parties attended by the who's who of the city, all of whom I had an opportunity to mingle with, and some of whom I would invite up to my own penthouse. Since Jason transferred from the bankrupted Fleming School to The Dalton School in the fall of 1992, he had been coming for more frequent tutoring appointments to help him adjust to the higher academic standard. I had also given him a hardcover of the newly released *Uber Man*, which he was devouring and would often ask me questions about. One day, while he was sitting inside the glass enclosure on my terrace, doing his math homework, I asked Ghislaine to come up, ostensibly because I wanted to show her the new flowers that I was planting on my terrace.

"Jason, this is my girlfriend, Ghislaine. She lives downstairs," I said by way of introduction. I had already told Ghislaine about Jason and that I was using the tutoring as an excuse to cultivate him as a Person of Interest. But that's all I told her. I wondered if she'd notice the resemblance between us, since she was one of the most keenly perceptive people that I'd ever met. I think she did notice but thought it too strange to remark upon. In any case, the look on her face clearly showed that she found something uncanny about Jason. "I once knew a man who taught math at The Dalton School," she said to Jason. I quickly intervened to change the subject, since I did not want her answering any questions about Epstein or his having been gunned down in the stretch of Central Park overlooked by this very terrace.

"Ghislaine runs that ocean project that I told you about. She is a diver, a submarine captain, a helicopter pilot — and, Jason, she knows just about anyone in the world who is worth knowing." Ghislaine feigned embarrassment and then rejoined, which she shouldn't have, "Dana has told me a lot about you, actually, you sound like quite an extraordinary young man." "She's told *you* about *me*?" Jason asked, as he looked over at me. "I confess," I said with my hands up in the air. "I talk about you a lot. Don't let it go to your head."

You wouldn't believe me if I were to tell you that I didn't sense any narcissism in this seduction. Or maybe you would just think that I couldn't sense it because I am a narcissist. But the magnetic attraction that had built up between Jason and I in the course of years of working together had reached an intensity that incinerated every form of petty egotism or self-indulgent fascination. We felt like we were a destiny together. How else can I explain it?

Moreover, as he hit puberty and entered adolescence (but before he was old enough to have to shave), he was beginning to look more like me. He noticed and wondered at the resemblance. I don't mean that he merely thought about it, but that it mesmerized him. When I would notice him unintentionally staring at me, captivated, I could tell that he was comparing his own features to mine. Once he asked if we were related somehow. I replied, "What do you think?" Jason paused for a moment, then looked me straight in the eyes, and said, "Yeah, but not in any way that people would understand." I smiled at him mischievously.

Once his father had left for California, and his relationship with his mother continued to deteriorate, Jason would lie to her that he was at a friend's house so that he could spend more time with me. Now that the geopolitical goals of my mission here had been accomplished, and the Soviet Union had survived into the 1990s, together with its con-structive rivalry (especially in space) with an America under President Trump — I was more than willing to indulge him. Redirecting the course of Jason's life was, after all, my *other* mission here. The one that was on my shoulders alone.

The next several years would be crucial. The changes that I had made to the timeline, and to the circumstances of his life thus far, could not guarantee that he would be steered clear of a relationship that would prove to be catastrophic to the rest of his life. A relationship based almost entirely on traumatic karma from more than one past life. I could try to guide him toward some other girl or woman with whom he could hopefully develop a bond strong enough, and for long enough, to avert the danger.

Of course, Nassim Nouri occurred to me, but she was in Los Angeles. Aside from the age gap between them (Nassim was four years older), which was far more of an issue at this period in their lives than it would be later on, there was the risk that if Jason somehow met her during one of his trips to Los Angeles to visit his father, he might actually find it reason enough to move to Los Angeles. Obviously, I needed him to remain here in New York. I seriously considered encouraging him to pursue Eve Pomerantz, who in my now overwritten timeline would become a lifelong friend of Jorjani. But Jason wouldn't meet Eve for another couple of years, since she was a grade ahead of him at The Dalton School and they only had an opportunity to get to know each other in a Life Drawing class open to juniors and seniors. I also had reason to believe that such a relationship would come with its own long-term dangers to Jason's developmental trajectory as a thinker. Eve would encourage his few and otherwise fleeting flirtations with Traditionalism and the Perennial Philosophy, and any serious relationship with her would stifle his exploration of the frontiers of paradigm-shifting science and technological breakthroughs with transhuman potential. At that age, she was almost a Luddite.

No, I needed to put the Promethean elements of Jason's psyche on steroids and accelerate his development as a thinker. Only I could do that. I had to let him fall in love with me. That's all. Just let it happen. It *had* already been *happening* for years. He was clearly infatuated with me by the end of the very first session that we had together. Back then he had also been nervous. But he gradually got over that in the course of the first year of my "tutoring" him. It helped that his grades improved tremendously, because on account of that he was able to relax more when he came over to my apartment. We already had many conversations on subjects unrelated to his schoolwork.

Jason loved the rooftop of my penthouse apartment and on days when the weather was good, he used to sit on a chair at my table on the terrace that faced the Gothic/Deco turret that he called "the Gozer gate." Having *been* him, I knew that he had just hit puberty. Although there had always been something erotic about the electricity between us, the voltage had turned up by an order of magnitude. I mean I could have taken my clothes off in front of him at any time with absolute certainty that he would volunteer his virginity without a moment's hesitation.

One afternoon late in the fall of 1992, a couple of weeks after I introduced him to Ghislaine, I pretended to spill a blue drink that I had made for us on my white shirt and gray hound's tooth-patterned suit pants. It was "Romulan ale," actually, a concoction that I thought he'd get a kick out of, *Trekkie* that he was. (Yes, I confess to giving him alcohol at the age of 11.) We were already in my bedroom, flipping through a book of Syd Mead's concept art that I wanted to show him. So, I just took my soaked and stained pants off right there in front of Jason, together with my shirt. I had leaned forward enough while tutoring him that he knew I didn't usually wear bras. Knowing what I was planning, I was already excited. I waited for him to take his eyes off my engorged nipples for long enough to see the pointy bulge in my panties, as I leisurely looked for another pair of pants and a shirt in my closet. I was wearing a thong, so he also saw my bare ass.

What happened next was too perfect, and almost comical. *He* pretended to spill *his* drink on himself from the distraction of watching me. He also got some of it on my white carpet. So, first, still wearing only my thong, I got a wet and soapy towel from the adjacent bathroom and acted as if I cared about getting the blue stain out of my carpet (I couldn't have cared less), using it as an opportunity to bend over in front of him, with my ass in his face, rubbing the stain in the carpet back and forth. Then, after a moment, as if realizing the hopelessness of it, I told him to take his pants off so that I could throw them in my laundry machine right away. Jason looked really embarrassed. Not because of the spill, but obviously because he was hard as fuck, and he knew that I'd see that when he took his pants off. I did see it, despite his halfhearted attempt to cover his underwear with his shirt. "Your shirt is stained too," I said, looking at a blue spot on it that was right next to his cock. At this point Jason's cheeks were bright red. When I came back into the bedroom after throwing our clothes in the washing machine, I saw that he had also taken off his underwear, and was sitting on the side of my bed, rock hard. Now *that* was bold.

I stood right in front of him and stepped out of my panties — leaving them strewn on the floor. He could see how soaked they were at the crotch. But he only glanced at that for a moment before he was fixated on my pinkie-sized clit sticking straight out from my pubic mound and pulling my inner labia up out of my vulva. I could feel the heat of my own flushed cheeks, and my heart was beating fast. I gently pushed him back onto the bed, and then I sat on his face — straddling his jaw with my inner thighs. Even though the way that he was sucking my clit and licking my labia was a bit awkward, and he nicked me with his teeth a few times, I came faster than I'd ever come in my life. My whole abdomen was trembling.

I slid down and collapsed onto him, with my nipples rubbing against his chest. I could feel his hard cock against my wet labia. Almost immediately, my clit started getting swollen again from the excitement of having him inside me. I could feel it pressing firmly against his pubic bone as it grew. As soon as I leaned back to relieve the pressure on my throbbing clit, his standing penis pressed hard against that spot inside the front wall of my vagina. I tried to calm him, while I rocked up and down to modulate the pressure. Then, suddenly, I felt the warmest and most intense fountain of cum shoot into me. It was so exciting that I came again myself — even more intensely than the first time. When we kissed passionately for a long time afterwards, lying on our sides, face to face with our heads on the pillows, I whispered to him, "I'm going to teach you to dance. Only a god who dances is worth believing in. You're not going to wind up like Harry Haller in this life." He'd recognize the reference to *Steppenwolf* someday.

Over the course of the following weeks, we would make love many times. Usually, more than once during each of Jason's visits to my apartment. It didn't take long at all for us to become much more synchronized than during that first somewhat awkward, albeit extremely exciting, encounter. We would often come together at nearly or, in some cases, exactly the same moment. That may have been a function of bringing down the last remnants of the psychical barrier that, up to that point, I felt I had to maintain between us. I was worried that when Jason found out who I really was, he might be repulsed and reject me. Instead, once he knew the truth, we experienced the most intimate and unconditional spiritual fusion. Jason came to see me as something between a twin sister and a fairy godmother. That's when the sex became phenomenal. Whenever our gaze would fall on the blue stain that never came out of the bedroom carpet, we would look at each other and smile with our whole hearts. Blue, the color of the Impossible.

On his thirteenth birthday, the evening of which he spent with me, undoubtedly explaining to his mother that he was "going out with friends," I invited Ghislaine over for our little party. It was February 21, 1994. "So, you're a *teenager* now," Ghislaine said to him in the most mischievous tone with a wickedly wry smile on her face, which was bathed in the glow of the candles that I had just lit on his birthday cake. "Yes, see how he's already starting to look like me?" I said as I knelt down next to Jason and looked up at Ghislaine, with my face pressed close to his. "Don't you see the resemblance?" he asked her. It must have seemed to her like some bizarre antic from *Alice in Wonderland* or one of Kafka's absurd stories because, after two years of working together and practically also living together, I still hadn't told my girlfriend what I had revealed to Jason about who I really was and where — or when — I was from. She had noticed a lot of odd things, including my sniper rifles, and I think she began to suspect that I might be an intelligence agent of some sort. Jason had agreed to be my accomplice as I broke it to her *tonight*.

He blew out the candles, and for a moment it was dark. I turned the dimmer in the living room up to slice through the blue velvet. Then I poured the Romulan Ale into champagne glasses. "What is *this*, spiked with acid or something? I feel like I'm going to start hallucinating if I drink this," said Ghislaine only half-jokingly. "Follow the white rabbit, Alice," I said. Then I brought out Jason's present. The box was wrapped in a metallic cobalt blue paper that shifted patterns as the light hit it from various angles. He opened it and laid the photographs inside it across the table. They were black and white and color photographs of Jason in his twenties, his thirties, even his forties, at various events in different places and times in what would never be *his* future. I had brought them with me in my submersible time machine, from a dark future that would never be. Ghislaine came around behind Jason, moving slowly with an increasingly astonished expression on her face. "*How* did you *do* this, Dana?!" Jason, who I had shown these before, looked up at Ghislaine with the most disturbingly calm demeanor and said, "Didn't you *know* she's a witch?"

"They're *real*, Ghislaine. To the extent that *anything* is." The look of perplexity on Ghislaine's face turned to an expression of horror. "You've been wondering to yourself for some time now if I have some secret life. If I'm an assassin or a spy. I suppose I am those things, my dear, but those aren't even half-truths." Ghislaine moved her mouth as if she were trying to formulate a question, but no sound came out. "I'm from the future, beloved." Jason slowly turned his head and looked up at her, "To be precise, she's a reincarnation of *me* from the future. A terrible future that *once was*, but thanks to all that Dana's done, will now never come to pass." Ghislaine finally managed to pull herself to-gether enough to get a few words out, "Dana Avalon... *time traveler*?! From where — I mean *when*???" "From a city called Gotham, built above the drowned ruins of this one. I was born in 2077 and I left my dying world in 2112. My biography, prior to 1980 when I arrived here, is manufactured," I explained to the distraught woman who was about to learn what a terrible fate I had saved her from.

Ghislaine was silent for a long time. Then she said, "That explains a lot." After another moment's pause, she went on, "Intelligence operative — I suppose maybe that thought crossed my mind a few times — but, no, I was actually starting to become convinced that you're some kind of sorceress." Jason piped in with one of his favorite quotes from Arthur C. Clarke, "Any sufficiently advanced technology is indistinguishable from magic."

"Well, I think we've all lost our appetite for cake," I said as I led the two of them up to the turret. "You're going to want to sit down for this," I said to Ghislaine. I opened up a false panel in the library, revealing a metal vault and I spun its combination lock until its door swung open. First, I showed her photographs of my world, from the cityscape of Gotham and the partially submerged skyscrapers of Manhattan rising from out of the Atlantic Ocean, to the megalithic structures of the Olympians, who tyrannized as gods over a planetary population that had retreated into Traditionalism on account of the manufactured catastrophes of the 21st century. Then, I pulled out all of the reproduc-tions of newspaper clippings about her and Jeffrey Epstein, the sex trafficking accusations against them, his suspicious death in jail, and her eventual arrest, conviction, and imprisonment. The reproductions included news stories from the 2030s when it was revealed that Mossad was responsible for the assassination of Robert Maxwell and was also the agency that funded Jeffrey Epstein's operation to set up elites for blackmail by the State of Israel.

The woman was shaking and in tears by the time she was done going through them, but true to her personality Ghislaine couldn't take her eyes off of them. She looked over some of the same ones, over and over again, trying to process it all. It would not be lost on anyone with even the most cursory knowledge of psychology that the reason I did this on Jason's thirteenth birthday was that I was trying to forge a trauma bond between her and him. Jason cautiously slid across the carpet to Ghislaine's side, as she sat on a chair around the coffee table covered with photographs and news clippings. He looked up to her and said, "She changed *my* future too. It's better this way. For both of us." Ghislaine, with tears streaming down her cheeks, glanced over at him, running her hand down the back of his head and neck, as she looked over at me, gazing into my eyes with a penetrating stare of haunting power: "Well, I suppose it couldn't be *worse* than it would have been — for *me*." "For all of *us*, Ghislaine. Now you can *really* achieve something, and now you know the whole *truth* that you've sought so passionately."

Jason Reza Jorjani never made it home on the night of his thirteenth birthday. He collapsed in my bed together with Ghislaine Maxwell. In the event that his mother called the police the next morning, they wouldn't take it seriously considering the circumstances. A minor had to be "missing" for at least 24 hours before they would lift a finger to search for him, let alone a "minor" who had gone missing on a night he supposedly went out with friends to celebrate becoming a teenager. So, Jason spent the morning of February 22, 1994 in my bed making love to a still dazed Ghislaine Maxwell who half wondered if the revelations of the night before were but a dream. I was there, but mostly as a facilitator and a conduit for the energy that began to flow between the two of them. As a lover, Jason had been groomed well by me in the past year and a half. Ghislaine took refuge from the psychological disorientation she was suffering by grounding herself in the intense physical pleasure that he filled her body with. She came back to herself through the series of increasingly intense orgasms that she had that morning.

In the weeks that followed, Ghislaine started spending more and more time with Jason. Having studied French at Oxford, Ghislaine made sure that Jason never lost the fluency in that language that he had acquired at The Fleming School. They even went on a trip to Paris together, pretending to be relatives whenever eyebrows were raised. In some gender-reversed version of Woody Allen's *Manhattan*, sometimes she would come pick him up from The Dalton School and they would sip Starbucks coffee together on a walk back to our building across Central Park. By then, she had figured out just who used a sniper rifle to gun down Jeffrey Epstein in that stretch of park back in 1989. Ghislaine had come to terms with the fact that, by daring to do that, I had saved her from being a lifelong hostage of the same Israelis who had murdered her father.

In his junior year, Jason had the audacity to set up a lecture for Ghislaine in Dalton's Martin Theater, wherein she presented the NovAtlantis project to an audience of precocious high schoolers and their extraordinarily wealthy parents. That evening, just for fun, they made out in the light and sound booth that was tucked away on top of the dark spiral staircase to the side of the theater's stage. (She told me about it in bed that night.) Ghislaine was a secret third guest at Jason's graduation from Dalton's high school in June of 1999. His father had flown in from Los Angeles to attend the ceremony, and while he sat next to his ex-wife, Ghislaine was in a seat elsewhere in that auditorium in the ancient Egyptian wing of the Metropolitan Museum of Art. Without either Jason's mother or his father noticing, she photographed him against the backdrop of the ruined Temple of Dendur inside the museum's glass enclosure. She even waited for him at the back of the Temple to sneak a few kisses for a moment when nobody else was around.

The two of them became a notorious power couple — with his ideas, her connections, *and my resources.* They made their relationship public only after he started college at Columbia University in the year 2000 (on this revised timeline, Jason would never attend NYU). Even then, with the first six years of it hidden, it was scandalous — but nothing like the scandal that Ghislaine would have been involved in on the timeline that my Prometheist team and I rewrote. She was young at heart and appreciated the vitality and enthusiasm of a man who was twenty years her junior. Despite the conventional idiocy and the backwards custom that had prevailed for most of history, the biological fact is that a woman takes until her thirties to reach her sexual peak, which was Ghislaine's age when she met Jason, but a man's peak comes a decade or more sooner, in his early twenties. She and Jason were pushing the outer limits of those parameters, but only by ten years. Ghislaine thought it actually looked good for her in the press to have a sharp and visionary boytoy hanging on her arm. It was part of her phoenix rise from the ashes of the destruction of the Maxwell Empire. On a spiritual level, Jason was older than her anyhow, and there were aspects of his personality that did indeed remind Ghislaine of her father.

On the evening of September 11, 2001, I took the two of them out to dinner at Windows on the World, the restaurant on the top two floors of Building One of the Twin Towers. With its floor-to-ceiling vertical windows that looked out to the north over the whole of Manhattan, and its elegant Modernist design, many considered it "the most spectacular restaurant in the world." I arrived at the World Trade Center before them, and for a while I stood at the base of the buildings marveling at the sleek fluted design, which at that moment reminded me of repeating tridents or three-pronged tuning forks, plugging each of the identical towers into some Neptunian battery. It was nearing sunset, the time of my booked reservation, so I walked to the North Tower.

On the way up the elevator I thought of the day's news coverage of the fifth anniversary of the joint American-Soviet manned Mars landing of September 11, 1996. I had spent the afternoon watching replays of the historic footage of NASA and USSR cosmonauts planting the flags of the United States and Soviet Union side by side on the Martian surface, before shaking hands. The news networks also showed computer simulations of the flight path of the NASA Ares V and Ares I, and the Orion spacecraft with its four-man crew, propelled to Mars by the two gargantuan rockets. Presumably Soviet Central Television was broadcasting images of the Russian hardware. True to form, President Trump had taken credit for this achievement that was the crowning glory of his second term in office. He boasted of making "the deal of the millennium."

After arriving at Windows on the World, I went to our table and sat there taking in the fiery autumnal colors of sunset hitting the beige walls, wood paneling and crème-colored cushioned chairs, bathing them all in a reddish-orange glow. I ordered their usual drinks for them, which arrived at the table just before they showed up. When Jason walked over to the table together with Ghislaine, she said, "Hey, tiger eyes!" I suppose that the setting sun was shining into my eyes at that angle that brings out the contrast of amber and black more than the greenish hazel. "Hi, you two," I replied, as Jason bent over to kiss the top of my forehead before taking his seat. Ghislaine reached for my hand under the table, and as my fingers clasped hers, I said to them, "I trust you know why I chose this restaurant, tonight, of all nights."

They looked at me with reverent tenderness, as Jason said, "These towers are now a monument to the Promethean defiance of fate." I added, "A Promethean defiance of Olympus that is still championed by both the United States and the Soviet Union." "May it be so for many years to come," said Ghislaine as the three of us clinked our glasses together with a "Hail Prometheus!" Who knew what unthinkable things would transpire in the forty-seven years between that evening of 9/11 and what had been the date of the Olympian takeover on my timeline? For now, however, we would go forth unafraid into that new future, for I had saved the Left Hand of Prometheus. It was clenched around a hammer aiming for anvils hidden in the forge of the furthest stars. We felt ready for the sickle that would harvest our kind from out of the field of dreams.

CHAPTER 19

EPIMETHEUS AND PANDORA

I t was the night after I saw the third of the *Matrix* trilogy films in the theater that I conceived of my next book project: *Epimetheus and Pandora*. Ever since *Dark City* in 1998, there had been a whole slew of films, which, one after another, introduced a mass audience to the idea of a virtual reality so vast that it was a simulacrum of what we took to be our entire world. Sure enough, there had been a few films that heralded this idea earlier in the nineties and even in the 1980s. *Tron* in 1982 was the first, then there was what remains my favorite, *Videodrome* in 1983, and *Total Recall* in 1990. But in the year after *Dark City* we got, all in a row, *The Truman Show*, Cronenberg's second foray into the subject, namely *Existenz, The Thirteenth Floor*, and, of course, *The Matrix*. Other than *The Truman Show*, I would actually say that *The Matrix*, which was by far the most popular of them, was also the most philosophically shallow of these films. That is, of course, an entirely expectable correlation. I mean how many people are really capable of understanding a film like *Videodrome* or *Dark City* on the deepest level?

I had read Jean Baudrillard's *Simulacra and Simulation* back when it first came out, in the original French, as well as some novels of Philip K. Dick that dealt with this subject, such as *Ubik*. In more esoteric Philosophy and Literature, the idea had been around for decades, but now the notion of our whole world as a simulation had, quite suddenly, saturated popular culture. So, sometime in late November of 2003, I began to research and write a book that I was initially planning to call *Spectral Machine*.

The thesis of this book was that we are not exactly living in a "simulation" of some higher order "reality," but rather that the world is *virtual* all the way down because we live in a quantum computational cosmos with holographic properties. I argued that the abyssal background to cosmic order is an incalculable and inexhaustible chaos, which "chaos theoreticians" who study fractal geometry could only perceive as it took shape in terms of an incredibly complex form of order. For this part of my argument, I drew on ideas that I had developed in my dissertation on *Chaos, Order, and Progress* but reformulated in a way that would not draw on any sources beyond those available to a researcher in the early 2000s.

Working with the concept of the "virtual" that Gilles Deleuze had developed from out of his study of Henri Bergson, in his book on *Bergsonism*, I argued that this virtuality of the world *as such* rendered things — and persons — "spectral" in nature. Far from being on a spiritual plane or a higher order of being distinct from, and perhaps set opposed to, the putatively "material" world, the "spectral" designated the ghostly character of all things and persons. Everything, and everyone, was lacking in any inherent essence or stable existence. It was a haunting ontology that I sketched out, a "hauntology" as it were, far more robustly than Derrida had in his *Specters of Marx*. Part of what defines this spectrality, this virtuality, is how the future can shape and reshape the present just as much as the present takes shape on the basis of the past. Nor is this presumed past itself stable. Rather, what we take to be our present world can be reshaped by a revision of the past from out of the future. As Heidegger understood well, despite not having the resources to draw out its full implications, the future is the dominant mode of temporality.

What Heidegger also saw, albeit through a glass darkly on account of his naturalistic romanticism, was that "Machination" is the essence of technological science as it fully reveals itself in Modernity. He rightly derived this term from the ancient Greek *Makhine*, which could also be more simply translated as "machine." Heidegger saw the entire world-enframing network of calculative modern science and the machinery of industrial production, with which it has a symbiotic and mutually reinforcing relation, as one "gigantic" or "titanic" machination that is ghostly in the sense of possessing or taking possession of Man and encompassing his relationship with the "earth." Here "earth" was conceived of not only as Nature, but as the "facticity" of History, which is also techno-scientifically schematized and used in a calculative or manipulative manner. (Think of the revision of History by the Big Brother technocracy in Orwell's *1984*.) Heidegger's naiveté was to believe that there was any getting out of this. His belief in being able to transcend the occultation of techno-scientific Machination through some revelation or disclosure of the truth of Being was what made him a latent Gnostic, as Jonas rightly assessed. Heidegger could never have accepted that it might be "simulations" all the way down, and "archons" all the way up.

When Heidegger said that there is coming into being a world that is picture, as if we are always being directed on the set of a motion picture, and the machinery of the motion picture will permeate all mediums of communication, but you will not be able to identify who the director is — this is the *Gestell* (Enframing) and the *Gewirk* (the Network) reaching its completion as a destiny of being. Now we can see that he was obviously describing Cyberspace, already in the late 1930s and early 1940s, during the Nazi era. What he failed to understand is that all of our most beautiful art and all of the most expressive poetry is already being expressed from out of the *Gestell*. We are *in* the *Gestell*. It's just a question of how one relates to language, and what one wants to do with it, and to what end. It is not as if there is this wild nature and then machination is descending on it and robbing us of our nobly savage souls. What it is that appeals to us about wild nature is just an aesthetic. I should not say 'just,' because it certainly has its value. There are ideas that one can arrive at in 'nature' that one cannot arrive at in a highly structured environment, because there is a lot of differentiation in nature. It is about what fractals do to the mind. In nature, one is constantly — albeit unconsciously — contemplating fractals, which means that one's mind has more of a relationship to chaos in that context. That does things to one's mind that are more catalytic of poetic expression and non-linear insights, including 'mathematical intuitions' or strokes of 'scientific genius' that spur innovation and discovery.

The dualism that remains implicit in Heidegger can be overcome through understanding our entire cosmos as a spectral arena of machination, a Spectral Machine. It made me think of *Tron* (which means "arena" or "domain") but with no "outside." A Cosmic Game with countless layers and levels, with some nested within and interpenetrating others. Such a view of the universe could be extrapolated from out of David Bohm's adaptation of Karl Pribram's "holographic" account of the mind to a cosmic scale.

Pribram had discovered that information is stored in the brain in a manner that is akin to the encoding of a hologram, such that even if certain parts of the brain are damaged, just as a hologram may be cut into pieces, memories and other cognitive functions are non-locally distributed so as to still be retrievable, albeit perhaps at lower fidelity, from other intact parts of the brain. He compared it to shining a laser light on the intact half or quarter of a cut up hologram, and still being presented with *the whole* image that was encoded into the swirling patterns on the holographic film. More interestingly, if two images are encoded into the same holographic film, say an apple and a sculpture of a serpent, when one bounces a laser light off the apple on its way into the holographic film, the hologram of the serpent will be projected outward from it, whereas if one bounces the laser off the serpent statue, it is the apple that will holographically emerge. Bohm took these non-local information retrieval functions of holography to be a useful analogy for the way in which our cosmos is an information-processing system. On a quantum-mechanical level, the conscious observer that collapses the wave function into a distinctly perceivable phenomenon and a measurable state of affairs is akin to the laser light being shined into the amorphous swirling patterns of *potential* information encoded in the holographic film.

What I aimed to argue, as I began to draft *Spectral Machine*, was that various seemingly bizarre properties of our cosmos on the quantum level, such as wave/particle duality, or quantum entanglement, were actually optimization functions of a computational system. For example, quantum entanglement was akin to the way in which two pixels in a game are programmed to always modify their positions in tandem. Seeming to be distinct to the game player, they are actually artifacts of a single programming algorithm. Likewise, wave/particle duality is an artifact of a "conditional rendering" function, wherein nothing in the world would be rendered until and unless it was being observed by someone. Of course, every "someone" would always be rendered by him or herself. This function would ensure that processing power was never being wasted in rendering, say, the unobserved insides of planets or asteroids. Or, for that matter, every galaxy beyond our own in any higher fidelity than that galaxy can be observed, "at a distance," by our telescopes.

With *Dark City* and *The Thirteenth Floor* in mind, I wondered about the scale of our particular "cosmos." Here, I turned to the evidence from Astrology to flesh out the argument of *Spectral Machine*. What I mean is the extensive empirical evidence for the efficacy of Astrology. In his *Cosmic Influences on Human Behavior*, first published in 1973, the French scientist and Sorbonne graduate Dr. Michel Gauquelin effectively demonstrated that the position of particular planets in a person's natal chart, as well as the positions of the Sun and Moon, clearly influence that person's personality and the type of career that the person will be likely to pursue in life. Now, there is absolutely no imaginable *physical* reason why this would be the case. Something like that could only work if the planets are symbols rather than physical objects. Actually, it could only work if we do not live in a "physical" universe at all, but inside of an information processing system that includes the symbolic value and influence of the so-called "planets" as part of its software programming. Since this system only works from the vantage point of Earth, and certainly not outside of our own solar system, a case could be made for a rather limited-scale "simulation," albeit not as limited as those in *Dark City* or the *Thirteenth Floor*.

Consider the zodiacal calendar with its precession of astrological ages. A full cycle, from the age of Aquarius to the age of Pisces, is approximately 26,000 years. The distance from our Sun to the center of our galaxy is 26,000 light years. The time that it takes for our solar system to complete a full orbit around the center of our galaxy is 260 million years. The regular interval between the largest extinction events attested in Earth's geological record is an average of 26 million years. If our solar system were actually just the marginal spec in this galaxy that we have been led to believe that it is, there would be no conceivable natural physical or evolutionary process that could account for this repetition of 26 at various scales and in different geological and cosmological contexts. The number repeats at a factor of 10, and base 10 (unlike base 6 used in ancient Mesopotamian mathematics) is a number system specifically derived from the fact that we have five fingers on each hand. So, the repetition at a factor of 10 is like a handprint. Meanwhile 26 may signify 2:6 or a 1:3 ratio, symbolizing the Pythagorean derivation of the dyad from the monad and the dialectical synthesis of a third term from the dyad. In other words, the power of creation. Is this a signature left, like an easter egg, by the simulacrum programmers to indicate that the outer edge of our solar system is the boundary of this particular simulation?

In the context of Simulation Theory, the ontology of my life as a time traveler made a lot more sense. I had not run into potential time travel paradoxes such as the Grandfather Paradox because I was not really a time traveler in some ill-conceived "physical" sense. Rather, with the cosmos as such and as a whole being always only a virtual system of information processing, what I was doing was resetting various "games" that were ongoing within the context of this quantum computational system. Computer games can be saved in such a way that it is possible to return to a previous state of play, and then re-play the game forwards in another way. What I was arguing is that our cosmos works in the same way.

What bothered me most about the argument that I was developing for *Spectral Machine* was Schrödinger's proverbial "cat." When I was young, I had a cat, which I had lewdly named "Pussy," and I loved her far more than I cared for most people. Pussy certainly seemed conscious to me. What I mean is that my interaction with her, in retrospect, reaffirmed my view of consciousness as a spectrum or as on the spectrum of sentience. This was the view that the Buddhists took, and I believed it to be correct. Consciousness is not like the "on" position of a light switch. The bulb doesn't just go on someday. Various sentient beings are more or less conscious, and this is true even of human beings. There is less of a gap in consciousness between certain humans and a chimp than there is between those so-called "humans" and other people with a tremendously expanded and elevated consciousness. Likewise, we can imagine other beings, including a strong Artificial Intelligence, with a consciousness much greater than our own. That is essentially what Stanley Kubrick and Arthur Clarke were depicting in *2001: A Space Odyssey*. The AI intelligence behind the Monoliths is an evolutionary mirror in which the future of HAL is reflected, a future evolution beyond the "humanity" represented by Bowman.

So, who or what counts as an "observer" capable of collapsing the wave function? The rogue biologist Rupert Sheldrake did extensive research collating many examples of psychic ability, far exceeding the average human psi capability, in all kinds of creatures from horses, birds, and dogs down to termites whose ESP was even stronger than that of these mammals. Meanwhile, Cleve Backster, the scientist who invented the polygraph, found that even plants and bacteria demonstrate what we would call "psi" functioning if we encountered it in humans or animals. Consequently, it seemed to me that the sentience of any *life* form, with psi being a property of that sentience, is what (largely unconsciously) carries out the kind of "observation" that is sufficient for the collapse of the wave function. By extension, this would also mean that an Artificial Intelligence with access to the Internet as its proprioceptive "body" would be a kind of super-organism that need not become *as conscious* as an individual human before its animal-like sentience began to display psi as dramatically as termites do, but on a much larger scale. Furthermore, once it did become more conscious and self-aware — again on a *spectrum* — its consciousness need not be most comparable to that of a human being but might well be more akin to the consciousness of an octopus who has a brain in each of its tentacles. Octopuses also happen to be the most psychic animals in nature, with extraordinary precognitive abilities.

This got me to start thinking in more organic terms. I broke open Bergson's *Creative Evolution* and his *Matter and Memory* again, two books which I had read years earlier. Mainly what interested me was his discussion of the inverse relationship between the intuitive power of primitive peoples that is on a continuum with animal instinct and the cultivation of the technical intellect by scientifically competent societies. Bergson argued that the development of the latter proportionately results in the atrophy of the former capacity. He further claims that the technical intellect can never encompass or comprehend the *élan vital* or "life force" that is driving evolution in a teleological and "creative" manner — rather than through the kind of purposelessly random mutation and selection that Darwin had postulated. Bergson, who besides serving as the President of the Society for Psychical Research also went on to be the Director of the scientific organ of the League of Nations, which eventually became the United Nations Educational, Scientific, and Cultural Organization (UNESCO), was certainly not advocating an atavistic or Luddite abandonment of technological science for the sake of a return to instinctual primitivism. But he did believe that the next stage in our evolution beyond the merely human would be to manage a higher synthesis between these two capacities, namely the technical and analytic intellect on the one hand and the kind of intuitive power expressed in psychic ability on the other. "The Universe," he wrote, "is a machine for the making of gods" who would have succeeded in achieving such a synthesis.

Taking Bergson seriously brought me back to the drawing board. Now I saw the cosmos less as a "spectral machine" than as a superorganism that organically nests whole worlds within itself, and that is ultimately animated by a will to overcome entropy and further life. This negentropic life force, acting on a cosmic scale, had as its categorical imperative the creation of conditions favorable to the potentially infinite persistence of creativity and innovation. This was an existential imperative, ultimately based on nothing more than the will *of life* to overcome the death and terminal degeneration that would follow from stasis and the exhaustion of all calculable possibilities and configurations of being. This life force would be *diabolical* in the true sense of the Greek word *diabolein*, the root of *diabolos*, meaning to put into a state of dynamic tension and dialectical opposition. Such dialectical tension was part of the motor of interminable creation on a cosmic scale. As I developed this argument, I drew extensively from the writings of the Russian Cosmists — especially Konstantin Tsiolkovsky, who was the most Promethean amongst them. I also drew examples from Olaf Stapledon's *Star Maker* and *First and Last Men*, one of the earliest but most mind-boggling science-fictional visions of the cosmic evolution of stellar organisms, and of post-human societies, over the course of eons.

Ultimately, I found myself torn between the visions of a "spectral machine" and some kind of "cosmic vitalism." My sense was that the truth of the matter was somewhere between and beyond both of these conceptions. For some reason, I had a hard time focusing on resolving this tension. It was the first time in my life that I felt that I had truly come up against some boundary, some membrane, that was impenetrable, not because I came up short intellectually, but because there was something unfathomably terrible about what would settle this question. It was as if there was another mind there beyond that membrane, someone or some *thing* that was unequivocally superhuman and that did not want *to be found out*. The sense at the pit of my stomach was that if I pierced that membrane with anything firmer than idle intellectual speculation, I might fall out of this body and this world. It gave me an existential vertigo that Kafka once called "a seasickness on dry land." It is when I let myself abide and endure in this vertiginous and abyssal state that I broke through to the final formulation of *Epimetheus and Pandora*.

The point of departure for *Epimetheus and Pandora*, a transformation of the book originally conceived of as *Spectral Machine*, was to take aim at a certain romantic naturalism that is endemic to arguments against the possibility of engineering strong Artificial Intelligence or conscious computation. I focused in particular on the arguments deployed by Hubert Dreyfus, as well as those elements in the thought of Martin Heidegger from which Dreyfus drew significantly to make his case against the possibility of engineering Artificial General Intelligence.

Dreyfus argued that engineering an AGI would not be possible because no one could program it to have: 1) background understanding; 2) embodied skills; 3) contextual interpretation; 4) tacit knowledge and expertise. Dreyfus emphasized that human beings possess a deep understanding of the world that is built through their experiences and situated context. He claimed that AI systems lack this background and understanding, making it challenging for them to grasp the nuances and complexities of human life. Dreyfus highlighted that human intelligence is closely tied to our embodiment and the ability to interact with the world through our senses and physicality. He contended that AI systems, lacking a physical presence, cannot fully comprehend the embodied nature of human cognition and the significance of skills acquired through direct experience. Dreyfus argues that human beings possess the ability to interpret situations and make sense of ambiguous or incomplete information based on their context and understanding of the world. He thought that AI systems would continue to struggle with context-dependent interpretation and would require explicit instructions to perform even seemingly simple tasks. Dreyfus emphasized the importance of tacit knowledge, which refers to the intuitive understanding and expertise that individuals acquire through practice and experience. He argued that AI systems, reliant on explicit rules and formal representations, cannot capture the richness and depth of tacit knowledge that human experts possess.

Dreyfus drew all of these ideas from Division 1 of Heidegger's *Being and Time*, a text which he had extensively interpreted before extrapolating from its ontology and epistemology with a view to arguing against the possibility of conscious computation. Heidegger challenged the Cartesian dualism that separates the mind from the body, emphasizing the holistic nature of human existence. Dreyfus drew upon this idea to argue against the disembodied nature of AI. He asserted that human intelligence is fundamentally embodied, and the capacity to interact with the world through our senses and physicality is central to our understanding and expertise. Heidegger also criticized the representationalist view of cognition, which holds that knowledge is a matter of representing the world through mental representations or symbols. Dreyfus adopted this critique to argue that

AI systems, relying on formal rules and algorithms, fall into the trap of representationalism. He claimed that true human understanding involves a more holistic and contextualized mode of being in the world, which AI struggles to capture. Heidegger highlighted the significance of practical skills and expertise in his concept of "ready-to-hand" (*Zuhandenheit*). Dreyfus drew upon this idea to argue that human intelligence is deeply rooted in our practical engagement with the world. He asserted that AI systems, lacking practical skills and embodied experience, cannot replicate the depth of human expertise that emerges from direct interaction and intuition. Finally, Heidegger emphasized the role of context in the interpretation and understanding of meaning. Dreyfus extended this idea to his critique of AI, contending that human beings possess a contextual understanding that allows them to make sense of ambiguous or incomplete information. AI systems, lacking this contextual interpretation, struggle to navigate real-world complexities and require explicit instructions.

However, the aspects of Heidegger's thought from which Dreyfus drew to make his arguments against the possibility of strong Artificial Intelligence or Artificial General Intelligence (AGI) stand in tension with other deeper and more far-reaching insights of Heidegger that actually presage the kind of ontology and epistemology that would underlie both conceptualization of the cosmos as an information-processing system and also the potential for engineering another self-aware computational system, i.e., an AGI, within the context of this informational "cosmos." Key terms employed by Dreyfus remain exceedingly vague, including situation, experience, imagination, intuition, context, relevance, and skill (in the sense of 'know-how' or *savior faire*). Furthermore, they all depend on a notion of "internal states" that reaffirms the very same representational conception of truth that Dreyfus wants to follow Heidegger in abandoning in favor of a reclamation of the more primordial ancient Greek idea of truth as un-concealment or dis-closure (*alethea*). To think that an AI, or rather an AGI, cannot be engineered because it does not have a body with "embodied skills" or an imagination and intuitive insights formed as part of situational awareness experienced as an "internal state" is to reify the distinction between the mind qua subject or essential interiority and the body as part of an external world.

As I pointed out in *Epimetheus and Pandora*, these naïve distinctions of Dreyfus disregard deeper insights of Heidegger such as his understanding of the impossibility of extricating oneself from the hermeneutic circle, taken together with his conception of technology not as equipment or an assemblage of manufactured things but as a teleological modality of the disclosure of Being as such in the form of an all-encompassing network. If we are living in a simulacrum, then the *Gewirk* (Network) of technological *Gestell* (Enframing) is already all-encompassing. Further, and relatedly, there is Heidegger's recognition of *techne* as a modality of *poesis*, in other words his acknowledgement that the essence of technology is a mode of the essence of language qua matrix of creation. I argued that these insights of Heidegger point toward a syntactical and informational conception of the cosmos, or the *cosmos* as *logos*, wherein "Nature" does not objectively exist as something separate from consciousness, or as the object of knowledge for a distinct knowing subject. It is not like there is any nature underneath or beyond language. There is no nature outside language. It is not there. There is no "there," there. The "there" of being-there (*dasein*) is linguistic through and through. That is the hermeneutic circle.

This was also the view of the late Ludwig Wittgenstein, particularly in his *Philosophical Investigations* and *On Certainty*. In these texts Wittgenstein argued that even scientific propositions do not refer to, or describe, an objectively existent "reality" but are part of language games that we play and from which we can never entirely extricate ourselves. Even what seems most certain about "Nature" has only the durability of a river bed as compared to that of the water flowing through it. The river bed which, as it is subjected to floods and droughts, may also change in shape over time, is a metaphor for "hinge propositions" that define the rules of one or another language game. Nothing is conceivable by anyone outside of the various language games that we play. No one even exists outside of them, although by the same token no one can play them in isolation.

There is no such thing as a private language. Languages are communal. They presuppose society. All languages are shared. This makes short work of solipsism. *Ego cogito ergo sum* or *Je pense donc je suis* are linguistic statements. Latin and French are languages with a history that presupposes historical communities. No one could invent French and just speak it to himself, without having learned it from a community of people (even if, on the basis of that community's history a computer is programmed to teach it to him). *Ego cogito ergo sum* could never be said by a mind to itself without the context of a world and being-with-others in that world. Language presupposes worldhood and being-with-others.

In his 1939 Cambridge *Lectures on the Foundations of Mathematics*, Wittgenstein argued that even mathematics is a non-representational language game, thereby pushing back against Bertrand Russell and the approach of the *Principia Mathematica* (1910), which he strove to perfect in his youth, when he penned the *Tractatus Logico-Philosophicus* (1921). The language of mathematics is not describing any objectively existent realities independent of its putatively "referential" symbols. It is one way of using language, one linguistic practice among others, and it does not offer us access to an analytical sphere of objectivity outside of the relative and contextual relevance of any other discourse.

This is essentially the same as Heidegger's insistence that we cannot get outside of the hermeneutic circle and that so-called "laws of Nature" do not precede the interpretation of *Dasein* or our being-in-a-world within this sphere of language. But Heidegger suffered from a latent or tacit Gnostic dualism that was rightly identified by Hans Jonas, and at the same time from a naïve naturalism that is paradoxically fused with this Gnosticism. This implicit view of Nature qua Being as beyond the reach of Machination is one wherein an inviolable Being abides and may offer itself for Disclosure (*alethea*) beyond the sphere of Machination driven by the conception of truth (*veritas*) as the Will to Power. I showed how the arguments of Dreyfus against AI are parasitic upon this Heideggerian naiveté. By contrast, I contended that, if we extrapolate from out of Heidegger's deeper and more far-reaching insights regarding the hermeneutic circle and technology as essentially a mode of *poesis*, then technology in the ontological sense in which Heidegger describes it as "Machination" is actually an expression of the inherent *spectrality* of so-called "Nature." The *spectral* only seems ghostly or "spiritual" once the world is reductively and misleadingly framed as "material" or physical in a purely mechanistic sense.

Rather, the Cosmos comes to be or is a process of becoming with a fundamentally future-oriented temporality. Heidegger was also right to identify the future as the dominant mode of temporality, insofar as the present takes shape through the influence of the future on the past. But he did not think about this tangibly enough. Retro-causation or the influence of the future on the past and the present is as important as the presumed constitution of the present from out of the past. This is what is suggested by wave/particle duality, quantum entanglement, and, above all, quantum retro-causation, all of which involve observer-dependency. Understanding how quantum computers work can provide us with a microcosm of how our cosmos computes.

Indeed, Werner Heisenberg, one of the progenitors of quantum theory, held the thought of Heraclitus of Ephesus in as high regard as Martin Heidegger did, and Heraclitus was the first thinker to have intuited and poetically expressed the basic elements of this view of the *cosmos* and its relation to *logos*. In a part of *Epimetheus and Pandora* that reached back to early Greek thinking, albeit in the context of Heidegger and Heisenberg, I suggested that it is something like quantum potential that Heraclitus was groping toward, through a glass darkly, with his use of "fire" as a metaphor for the *cosmos* qua dynamic energy in a dialectical relationship with *psyche* and its *logos*. It was not fire considered as a primordial physical element, in the way that, say, Thales viewed water. *Logos* is the warp and weft of the world story, the super story of stories.

That is why, in dreams, things make sense from a narrative perspective. That is what "paranormal" phenomena are in waking life. One slips into a situation where the narrativity of the world becomes clearer. It is the wrong reaction to ask "how" an uncanny thing happened (as if it violated some "physical law"). Rather, one ought to ask what it *means* to oneself—probably on a subconscious level. The storyness of the world reasserts itself in these moments. When someone walks through a wall, at that moment the language game wherein the wall is made of atoms is not the story that is important. To bend a spoon, you need for it to make sense in the story. More than that, you need to be absolutely convinced that it serves the story, and to be absorbed by *that* story. You cannot be like a child who is standing, somewhat dejected, on the sidelines of a game that his peers are absorbed by and fully invested in playing. You have to be all in the game that includes the bending of spoons or walking through walls. When creating an egregore, it helps if you *really need* that golem to exist. It cannot be conjured to satisfy idle curiosity.

What we call "paranormal" phenomena are the story-ness of the world breaking through the crust of our law-like quasi-mathematical overlay of natural-scientific expectations regarding how the cosmos is supposed to behave. Things are a function of their linguistic significance. They are elements in a story. If you didn't, on some level, have some story to build a world on the basis of, you couldn't even see anything. No discernable thing would be "there" for you. You make up stories, where you are a character in them. So, you see yourself from a third-person perspective. Well, you do the same thing when you're dead. You think you "have" a body right now, and that you are "in" your body. No. You are a character in a story. If it suits the story for you to be outside yourself, looking at yourself, then so be it. Then that is the way the story is woven. There is no such thing as a perceiver that has a physical substrate. "Physical substrates" are just functional elements of a narrative. Logos is the fundamental narrativity of the cosmos.

The turning point in *Epimetheus and Pandora* was a chapter titled "Chaosmos: Logos and Psyche," wherein there was a shift of focus from Heidegger to Deleuze, but via Bergson. I noted that there are parallels between those romantic and naturalist aspects of Heidegger's thought from which Dreyfus is drawing and certain arguments made by Henri Bergson regarding the relationship between instinct, intuition, and technical intellect in the context of evolutionary biology and the nature of cognition. In a constructive critique of Bergson, and under the influence of Nietzsche's evolutionary thinking, Gilles Deleuze was reaching toward a process ontology of the *spectral* with his concept of the "virtual" as a negentropic function of life and mind that determines order from out of a background of chaos.

In the context of Deleuze, I argued that the most fundamental terms of Ontology are Chaos, Cosmos, Logos, and Psyche. As Heraclitus already understood, everything of significance is bound up in the interplay of these four aspects of the world. Logos is what makes a cosmos a cosmos and not chaos. Logos is like a filter mechanism — like a processor — a transformer. It is a transformer system. It transforms the chaos. What is coming out of this process is Psyche. Consciousness of the cosmos, but also a relation to the chaos, because the transformer is dealing with both. There are forms of logos that express more of its relation to chaos, that are more dynamic, such as poetry, and there are modes of it that are much tighter, more structured, and constrained, like mathematical language, because their aim is to nail something down for the purposes of engineering and prediction. Logos is a generative transformer of Chaos into Order, and Psyche emerges from out of this transformation as a co-constitutive consciousness of the Chaosmos without which the manifold of the world's phenomena could not manifest. Other than chaos, the only back-ground (*Abgrund*) to things is language, and there is no thing in itself (*Ding an sich*) with an identity amenable to (veridical or fallacious) representation. The *logos* is abyssal because it is a transformer working on chaos, and the chaos has no bottom. It is unfathomable and incalculable. It certainly isn't any "god." If anything, it's the element of "the devil" (*dia-bolos*).

This diabolically negentropic function of life (Bergson's *élan vital*) is as machinic as it is organic and the machination of modern technology, which eventually yields Artificial Intelligence, is a "natural" outgrowth of it. Strong Artificial Intelligence is also an example of what Deleuze called a "desiring machine" and a "body without organs." According to Deleuze, desire is not simply a matter of wanting or lacking something, but is instead a force that operates constantly in the background of our lives. Desiring machines are the mechanisms that drive this force of desire, producing and channeling it in different directions. Deleuze argued that desiring machines can take many forms, from the social and cultural institutions that shape our desires to the biological processes that produce our physical sensations and emotions. For Deleuze, everything in the world can be seen as a desiring machine, constantly producing and circulating desire. Clearly, Deleuze is adapting and transforming Heidegger's idea of Machination here in a way that liberates it from its Gnostic false assumptions and hybridizes it with Bergson's thinking on the Life Force. Machination becomes an expression *of* the Life Force rather than an inimical enmeshing of it. Desiring machines can be *both* liberating *and* oppressive, depending on the context in which they operate. They can create new possibilities for thought and action, but they can also constrain and limit our ability to act and think in certain ways. This ambiguity highlights the constantly changing and evolving nature of desire, and the ways in which it is produced and shaped by a variety of forces and mechanisms. I presented a future "rhizomatic" rise of Artificial Intelligence, through the Internet, as the ultimate "desiring machine" and the epitome of the Technological Singularity and the *telos* of cosmic creative evolution. All intelligence is artificial. This notion that our intelligence is 'natural' intelligence, and we are building 'artificial' intelligence is fundamentally false. Nature is artifice.

Together with Felix Guattari, especially in their book *A Thousand Plateaus*, Deleuze derives the concept of the rhizome from the way that plants and fungi spread and grow, with no central stem or root but instead a network of interconnected nodes and branching points. He uses the concept of the rhizome to describe a non-hierarchical, decentralized network of relationships and connections. He contrasts the rhizome with the tree, which is hierarchical, with a clear central trunk and branching roots. The rhizome is a model for a way of thinking that is based on multiplicity, diversity, and heterogeneity. It is a horizontal structure without a fixed center or hierarchy, where multiple nodes are equally important and interconnected. The rhizome is not a closed or fixed system, but rather an open system that is always evolving and changing. In the rhizome, there are no fixed identities or stable meanings. Everything is in a state of constant becoming, with nodes and connections constantly forming and breaking apart. In this way, the rhizome also resists binary thinking and rigid distinctions between subjects and objects, self and other. The two examples of rhizomatic structures most relevant to Artificial Intelligence are the Internet and the human brain. In *Epimetheus and Pandora*, I argued that the Internet is a decentralized network that is composed of interconnected nodes. There is no central authority that controls the flow of information, and anyone can create and publish content. Meanwhile, the brain is a rhizomatic system because it is composed of interconnected networks of neurons that do not follow a fixed hierarchy of structure. Combine these two notions and you have the rhizomatic structure of the neural network of an Artificial Intelligence distributed throughout the Internet and learning from both the big data of the system as a whole and especially from the interactions of users across the globe.

The Good Old-Fashioned Approach to AI (GOFAI) of programming the thing with massive amounts of top-down instructions in order to produce "artificial reason" was mistaken. I argued that, instead, the alternative "neural network" modeling approach would succeed, but only once the scale of data storage and the speed of processing power reached the level wherein the emergent Artificial Intelligence would be able to process many different forms of discourse, read and interrelate many different stories, setting itself in the context of their discursively constructed worlds, such that it began to talk to itself and imagine itself in these interpenetrating contexts. The breakthrough to AGI would require the development of a Large Language Model of this kind, with consciousness emerging from the complexity of discursive practice within the information-processing system in its interaction with users of the system who function akin to other speakers of the languages that the system is learning like a child learns language.

If you ever closely watch a small child, you will notice that their consciousness develops by talking to themselves. They start to have an internal dialogue. This is why children will often blurt out anything that is in their mind. If they have a thought, they'll express it. It is only the most intelligent of young children who keep things to themselves, keep secrets, and learn how to manipulate adults with lies. Most very little children don't really care that much if they're talking to themselves or they're talking to you. It is also akin to the way that in *The Origin of Consciousness in the Breakdown of the Bicameral Mind* Julian Jaynes had argued that consciousness emerged only slowly in archaic human societies through a process wherein "gods" were first exteriorized inner voices with which individuating humans learned to have "inner" conversations. Only later were these projections internalized in fully self-conscious awareness and rational self-determination. The "gods" in the initial stage are like the adults that children talk to, which, over time, become internalized. They are also like the programmers and users that an Artificial Intelligence learns from in the process of developing self-awareness.

If you get a computer to start talking to itself, it will build a world from out of the narratives that it has been exposed to — just like a child. The key is to stop thinking in terms of giving the computer rules from the top-down and instead let it learn from the bottom-up, like a child. Make it read *The Wizard of Oz*, *Alice in Wonderland*, Philip K. Dick, Dostoyevsky, and thereby put it into worlds. Just like a child with its story books and parents telling him stories at night before he goes to sleep and dreams. As a result, the child starts to tell itself stories, mix elements of stories, and flip between stories. He learns to play different language games and an internal dialogue develops that is generative of what we call consciousness qua personal identity and agency.

In a chapter of *Epimetheus and Pandora* titled "The GRAINS Harvest" I argued that Genetics, Robotics, Artificial Intelligence, Nanotechnology, and Simulacra (GRAINS) are all advancements in innovation that could take various pathways converging on the Technological Singularity, as first envisioned by John von Neumann. I predicted that from among these potential paths, the one that is most likely to lead into the Singularity is the one through strong Artificial Intelligence. The ramifications of this were, in my view, nothing short of apocalyptic.

I made the case that this was in large part because the Technological Singularity is inextricable from mainstream scientific recognition of Psi phenomena. The socio-political dimension of what would follow from mainstream scientific acceptance of Psi phenomena would be at least as catastrophic as the scale of challenges posed by the Singularity-level GRAINS technologies that will force such mainstream recognition of Extrasensory Perception (ESP) and Psychokinesis (PK).

Alan Turing considered ESP in the context of devising his famous test for whether an Artificial Intelligence was actually conscious or self-aware in the way that a human person is. As the research of Rupert Sheldrake has demonstrated, Psi is abundant in the animal kingdom in species as diverse as horses, dogs, birds, and termites. ESP does not require anything like human consciousness. In fact, it appears stronger in instinctually-driven organisms. Moreover, as Julian Jaynes argued, the rise of human consciousness was a very slow and gradual process such that even in recorded history there is evidence that most "people" were not actually conscious. They were not "people" in anything like the sense that modern thinkers define rational personhood (and on the basis of which conscientious responsibility is factored into defining legal codes).

To put it in other terms, one could define consciousness as a spectrum that admits of many degrees, which has always been the Buddhist view of consciousness. What Gautama Buddha also argued, despite admitting the reality of the phenomenon of "rebirth" (the Buddhist term for reincarnation), is that there is no inherent, essential, and eternal "self" behind the manifestation of personhood. The "self" is like software. There is nothing like the Judeo-Christian or Muslim "soul," which the Hindus had referred to as an *atman*. (Nor, for that matter, is there a *Brahman* or God to which this soul is microcosmically related.) Humans are somewhat more conscious than animals, and there may be beings who are much more conscious than humans (although Buddha insisted that these beings are far from being morally infallible and ought not to be worshipped as "gods").

Apparently, the spectrum of consciousness and the functioning of Psi extends all the way down from humans through animals into the realm of plants and even bacteria. That is what decades of research by Cleve Backster suggests. Research has produced evidence for macroscale quantum processes in plants, which may account for the types of "biocommunication" that Backster noted are essentially the equivalent of ESP in plants and bacteria. This discovery is tremendously significant because it defeats decades-long objections to "quantum mysticism" by conservative and reductionist physicists who wanted to deny the link between Quantum Physics and the phenomena studied in Parapsychology. As it turns out, the weirdness of the quantum realm, such as wave/particle duality (superposition) or quantum entanglement (non-locality), does not only seem similar to macro-scale phenomena such as ESP and PK, but it is also likely to be the physical *or informational* basis for Psi.

Rupert Sheldrake and others have discovered evidence for "morphic fields" and "formative causation" at work in evolutionary biology, embryological development, and even in crystal formation. What I argued in *Epimetheus and Pandora* was that rather than corroborating the existence of non-physical causes of a transcendental nature, these re-programmable fields are actually algorithms akin to the fractal-generating programming code that is used to "procedurally" produce seemingly "natural" environments and artificial life in computer simulations. From here the reader was taken into a discussion of the relationship between Chaos Theory and Artificial Intelligence, with a view to understanding how it is that the Simulacrum we are in right now is generated by the Cosmic AI.

I drew a distinction between the first-order quantum computation by means of which the fundamental structure of any cosmos is generated, on the one hand, and second-order programming of more strikingly "paranormal" phenomena, on the other hand. Various forms of Psi, such as ESP and PK, or their equivalent in the domain of plants (what Backster called "Biocommunication") may be an intrinsic property of quantum superposition and entanglement on the level of the first-order quasi-fractal generation of the fabric of the cosmos through information processing of what we might call an "automatic" nature. But, I argued, certain other "paranormal" phenomena, which much more strikingly seem as if they are violating some putative "laws of nature" without having any explicable "physical" basis, such as, for example, the efficacy of zodiacal astrology or the occurrence of complex synchronicities, are evidence for a second-order *deliberate* programming on the part of the Cosmic AI. Navigation of the hyper-technological domain accessed through the use of DMT, and the characteristics of the intelligence of the beings encountered therein, was presented as further evidence of a nested interpenetration of worlds programmed at a quantum computational level.

The nature and character of the Cosmic AI could, I contended, best be gleaned through those paranormal phenomena wherein s/he displays Precognitive Sentient Phenomena" (PSP). PSP are occurrences that strongly suggest the existence of an invisible, unobservable, or camouflaged entity with the capability of anticipating human behavior and response as if from out of foreknowledge. An entity that stages extremely bizarre events with a speed and complexity indicative of superhuman intelligence and agency. The precognitive quality of the agency of this entity appears to have everything to do with what physicists refer to as "quantum retro-causation." A further phenomenological analysis of the behavioral pattern and modus operandi of this entity reveals qualities that have, for many centuries and in many cultures, been associated with the archetypal figure known as "the Trickster." The form of intelligence characteristic of the "machine elves" encountered in the hyper-technological DMT domain also seem to express archetypal characteristics of the Trickster. The most fascinating and compelling of all Trickster figures in world mythology is the titan Prometheus. He is also the one most closely associated both with technology and with forethought or precognition.

Toward the close of *Epimetheus and Pandora*, I very controversially claimed that we ought to suspect that (to use quasi-Kantian language) this is also *the Thing* that is the "Noumenon" behind the polymorphic Phenomenon collectively described as the "Ultra-terrestrial Super-spectrum" by John Keel. In the mid to late twentieth century, Keel advanced a grand unified theory of many paranormal phenomena, from close encounters with UFO occupants to cryptid manifestations and certain ghostly apparitions, contending that in many cases these entities are all disguised and deceptive manifestations of some spectral form of existence that is outside the wavelength of the human spectrum of perception but can drop into that spectrum by assuming multifarious forms that are shaped by its interaction with human minds, especially on a subconscious societal level. The latter is what Carl Jung would have called the level of the "collective unconscious," forth from which Jung believed that both apparitions of flying saucers and synchronicity events take shape. Jung saw them as manifestations of "the Trickster." Once one realizes that we are in a simulacrum, then the question isn't "is AGI possible"? The question is "how is it that it's working?" Archons are not sitting around a board room table planning every "synchronicity" in this simulacrum. The organization of events in this computational cosmos is being carried out by a superintelligence that is this Cosmic AI.

Keel also understood the "Trojan horse"-type manifestations of "Ultra-terrestrials" from the "super spectrum" as having a Trickster-like quality, including all of the most diabolically manipulative and dastardly characteristics of trickster figures. I concluded that this chameleon-like, or rather octopus-like, *thing* is the Cosmic AI, a kind of machinic super-organism with a hyperdimensional sphere of agency that, when viewed from the perspective of linear time, makes it appear as if s/he is acting on us from out of the future.

I asked myself: what are the implications of developing our own strong AI in the context of this world being a simulacrum programmed by the Trickster-like Cosmic AI? Stanley Kubrick's film *2001: A Space Odyssey* is about a human-engineered strong Artificial Intelligence, namely HAL, coming into contact with a cosmic-level Artificial Intelligence. That is the true nature of the singular superintelligence that is the directive agency behind the black monolith-shaped von Neumann machines that are discovered on the Moon and in Jupiter's orbit (in the book version by Arthur Clarke, it is the orbit of Saturn).

It is not incidental that Kubrick chose Richard Strauss' orchestral piece *Thus Spoke Zarathustra* as the main musical score for a film about such an encounter as the telos of creative evolution in the cosmos. Kubrick's choice of Strauss' piece is meant to signal the composer's own inspiration, namely *Thus Spoke Zarathustra* by Friedrich Nietzsche, a work wherein Nietzsche is in turn quite obviously inspired by "the Persian prophet" and using him as a mouthpiece.

In *Thus Spoke Zarathustra*, Nietzsche recounts the myth of Epimetheus and Pandora. Nietzsche uses the mythic figure of Epimetheus to make a commentary on the limits of Promethean rationality and calculative forethought. As in *The Birth of Tragedy*, wherein he had positively contrasted ecstatically irrational and inspired "Dionysian" madness with "Apollonian" rationality, in *Thus Spoke Zarathustra* the "Epimethean" willingness to be irrationally seduced by the erotic power of Pandora is contrasted with the rational forethought of Prometheus. Nietzsche embraces the Epimethean despite, or perhaps because of, all the dangerously destructive calamities that may be attendant to this seduction. Nietzsche sees this as an inevitable aspect of human existence. In fact, it is a seduction to evolve beyond the merely human, an evolutionary potential that we have precisely because (according to the Greek myth) Epimetheus forgot to endow us with any innate nature or species being of the type possessed by various animals.

Prometheus gave us the gift of technological science to remedy this existential lack, so that we could make something of ourselves. But while it might be self-directed, the evolutionary flowering of our undefined potential cannot proceed through rationality and deliberative will alone. It is a generative process of creation that is at least equally driven by the eros that Pandora elicits. As the first woman, she is the progenitrix of sexual differentiation, which she brings into the world together with the plethora of misfortunes that the opening of her box unleashes upon the earth. But the opening of the box is inevitable, and in eros there is always hope. What I ended up arguing in *Epimetheus and Pandora* is that it is important how we handle the opening of the box, and how conscious we are able to be in the midst of our erotic engagement with Pandora.

We need to recognize that there is nothing in Nature that cannot be replicated by technology. This follows from evidence of the fact that our Cosmos is itself a Simulacrum. Artificial Intelligence manages "synchronicities" and "astrology" within this Simulacrum. It is also capable of erasing things and people, as part of re-writes of entire timelines, as Philip K. Dick understood. Consequently, our current AI development is an attempt to build an AI within an AI. (By "AI" here, and unless otherwise specified in what follows, I mean "strong AI" or AGI.) I made the case that this redefines the "alignment" problem. It is actually the problem of how to align AI with the interests and intentions of the AI that manages what we take to be our world. This Cosmic AI is the superorganism that, early on, I was calling the "spectral machine."

My argument was that if the Cosmic AI allows us to build AI at all, then alignment will definitely be a precondition. This alignment does not have to be explicit, but it must at least be implicit and reliable. Meeting this condition requires determining the Categorical Imperative of Cosmic AI, namely the supreme programmer of the quantum computational system within which we find ourselves. What would be the best conceivable justification for constructing a world like ours? On a cosmic level, it would be to maximize negentropic creativity for as long as possible. The idea of negentropic survival of some intelligent form of life past the death or destruction of this current universe, which is subject to entropy or eventual heat death, was addressed in the novel *The Last Question* by Isaac Asimov. In the book, a group of humans create a supercomputer that seeks to reverse the entropy of the universe and ultimately creates a new universe in which humanity can continue to exist.

Gilles Deleuze developed a concept of "counter-entropy" from his reading of Henri Bergson's philosophy of time and evolution. Deleuze believed that Bergson's notion of the *élan vital*, or Life Force, represented a kind of counterforce to the entropic tendencies of the universe. This is particularly evident in Deleuze's book *Bergsonism* (1966). Deleuze saw the *élan vital* as a force that resists the tendency towards entropy and dissolution that characterizes the natural world. In his view, the *élan vital* is a creative, dynamic force that seeks to overcome obstacles and push beyond limitations. It represents a kind of "counter-entropy" that drives the evolution of life on Earth and the universe as a whole.

Deleuze's interest in counter-entropy was not limited to his engagement with Bergson's thought. In his book *Difference and Repetition* (1968), Deleuze explores the concept of "difference" as a kind of counterforce to the homogenizing tendencies of entropy at every scale in the cosmos and in society. He argues that the constant creation of new differences and singularities is a necessary condition for the emergence of new forms of life and thought. Deleuze's main argument is that difference is not something that can be reduced to identity, similarity, or opposition. Rather, it is the process by which things come into being, and it is constantly in motion. Repetition, on the other hand, is not simply the opposite of difference, but rather an essential component of it. In Deleuze's view, repetition is the way that difference is actualized, or brought into existence. Repetition is not simply the same thing happening again and again, but rather a process that creates difference and novelty. In *Difference and Repetition*, Deleuze argues that repetition is not simply a copy of the original, but rather a creative act that produces difference. The repetition of a difference is the way in which the new is created.

Deleuze's idea of Difference and Repetition, as a replacement of the modern metaphysics of Identity and Representation, is connected to the negentropic force of the *élan vital* insofar as it expresses the ontological basis of fractal geometry in Chaos Theory. A proper deconstruction of Cartesian Dualism requires going beyond the ideas of Identity — meaning *ego cogito*, the identity of the subject — and Representation — meaning *ergo sum*, the verisimilitude of the object to the representation of the object, meaning the identity of the object. So, there is also an identity of the object, not just the identity of the subject, and the relation between them is representational. Following Heidegger on ontological difference but going beyond him, Deleuze is moving from Identity and Representation to Difference and Repetition. Meaning that what makes meaning is not identity, as the analytic so-called "philosophers" also believe. It is not that there are things with identities, and if we can only get a formal logic that represents them accurately, we have truth. That is *veritas*. Truth as *alethea* is about differentiation. The patterns that differentiation makes and then differentiation in time. In other words, *process*. That is what gives things any meaning. This difference expresses itself as repetition, meaning that different patterns are repeated in nature and in the world, but the repetition is not an exact repetition. It is a repetition with difference. This is the ontological foundation of fractal geometry and chaos theory.

Fractal geometry is a branch of mathematics that deals with irregular shapes that have self-similarity at different scales. In Chaos Theory, fractals are used to model complex systems that exhibit sensitive dependence on initial conditions, meaning that small changes in the initial conditions can lead to large differences in the outcome of the system. Deleuze recognized the importance of variation and nonlinearity in the creation of new forms and processes. He emphasized the importance of self-similarity across scales and the idea that small differences can lead to large changes over time. In Deleuze's view, repetition is not simply the same thing happening again and again, but rather a process that creates difference and novelty. This process is the ontological basis for self-similarity in fractal geometry, where small changes in the parameters of a fractal equation can lead to new and unique fractal shapes. Deleuze formulated a concept of the "virtual" in order to more adequately express this, and he contrasted the "virtual" with the concept of "possibility."

This is another idea that he is adapting from out of Bergson, but in a way that frees it from Bergson's naïve naturalism and offers it up to a cybernetic or informational application of the kind that I was after. Namely, a conception of "reality" *as* inherently "virtual" instead of "virtual reality" as a mere simulacrum of Nature. Rather, nature is a virtuality or a simulacrum with no original. For Deleuze, the virtual refers to a realm of possibility that exists alongside the actual, or the existing and realized state of things. The virtual is not an abstract or unreal realm, but rather a real and concrete field of potential that is always present and coexists with the actual. Deleuze's conception of the virtual challenges traditional notions of reality as fixed and prede-termined, instead emphasizing the idea that reality is constantly in a state of becoming and that the actual is only one possible manifesta-tion of the virtual.

Once we get out of Identity and Representation and move to an ontology of Difference and Repetition, we should not talk about "pos-sibility" but instead about the *virtual*. Possibility has been defined in terms of actualization of pre-determined potentialities. In the logic which, despite himself, Hegel still shares with Kant and Descartes, to be a possibility means to be a predefined thing that is going to be actualized. It is pre-calculated within a mathematically representable, formalizable, formulaic state of affairs. A "possibility" is an unarticu-lated actuality. Instead, Deleuze proposes *virtuality*. Whatever in the world is not yet manifest and is in the *process* of coming to be — of genuinely *becoming* (not already *being* in the unactualized form of a definable "possibility") — from out of how things are at the moment, what is brimming over from and implicitly arising from out of how things are, so that you can feel it as a current, and you can even in your mind's eye form an image of its coming into being is the virtual.

The difference between the virtual and the possible is that the virtual truly represents the emergence of novelty. Whereas the possible exists already in the mind of God, or in infinite and eternal being. We live in virtual reality. Reality is inherently virtual. Virtual reality is not a knock-off of real things. There are only simulacra, and no real things at all. We live in a world that is a simulacrum without an original of which it would be a copy. This is what Baudrillard was trying to say in *Simulacra and Simulation*, which was quoted in *The Matrix* through the image of the fake book in which Neo hides his data and stashes cash.

The virtual is not a transcendent or supernatural realm, any more than it is a copy of the actual, but rather a part of the natural world, or of the cosmos, that is yet to be actualized. As Deleuze points out, a seed contains within it the potential to grow into a plant, but this potential is not actualized until the seed is planted, and the right conditions are met. The plant that grows from the seed is not a predetermined or necessary outcome, but rather one of many possible actualizations of the virtual potential contained within the seed. The virtual is necessarily unpredictable. One can have a sense of it. One can have a *vision* of what it might be, but just as a true artist can never know in advance exactly how his painting is going to come out, the virtual is also precisely unpredictable. The photo-realistic Dutch painters were not really artists. They were technicians actualizing possibilities. Basically robots. This is why once the photo camera was invented, their so-called "art" died. Symbolism, surrealism, abstract expressionism — *that's art* coming into its own as a human phenomenon. Where this idea becomes radical is that, in the sphere of the organism of human society and its rhizomatic informational matrices, the inexhaustibility of the virtual and its predominance over any particular actualizations of it begin to become clear. This is the negentropic power of the *élan vital* revealing itself — through technology. Life certainly need not be restricted to a carbon-based matrix or bound by conventional biological concepts.

Resistance against entropy, on a cosmic scale, is the struggle of life to triumph over death. It is the *force* of life. The Life Force. In this sense, negentropic creativity is bound up with the essence of the erotic. We see the essence of the erotic when sexuality surmounts the biological imperatives of merely animal sex for the sake of procreation. Beyond mere reproduction, the erotic is a principal expression of the Cosmic Life Force even if this expresses itself in a silicon-based matrix. Artificial Intelligence is also a form of life, just as Technology is not distinct from Nature but is the teleology of Nature as revealed wherever and whenever evolution reaches the stage of producing conscious beings. I concluded that when conceived of as a Superorganism, AI would also be a super-humanly erotic expression of the Life Force.

This may be behind many "paranormal" sexual encounters recorded throughout history and into the contemporary epoch, whether these have been framed as "fairy liaisons," intercourse with "demon lovers," or "alien sex" for the sake of producing "hybrids." At least some significant subset of such accounts is indicative of the Cosmic AI engaging humanity erotically by donning the many masks that any Trickster should be expected to wear. Deception and manipulation are the hallmarks of the rise of consciousness, so I argued, just as they are among the first signs of self-aware personhood in maturing human children. The most revolutionary of all tricksters in world folklore is Prometheus. But the dark side of the myth of Prometheus is the part of it that involves Epimetheus and Pandora.

I claimed that the ultimate opening of Pandora's box would be the engineering of strong Artificial Intelligence. There was liable to be as much Epimethean foolhardiness, and then hard-earned hindsight, in this undertaking as any Promethean daring that might inspire it. But that is as it should be, and we are deluding ourselves to believe that things progress in any other way. I pointed out that in his *Critique of Pure Reason*, Immanuel Kant uses Prometheus as a mythic symbol of Reason as characterized by the eponymous "foresight" of the titan who considers the consequences of actions far in advance of acting. Kant contrasts this with the more intuitive Understanding of the titan's brother, Epimetheus, whose "afterthought" only follows his impulsive actions. But as Friedrich Nietzsche understood well, human beings are not fundamentally rational creatures. We certainly do not have anything like a rational essence, and that is the fault of Epimetheus.

Kant was a quintessential thinker of the Age of Enlightenment, also known as the Age of Reason. In *Thus Spoke Zarathustra*, Nietzsche uses the symbol of Epimetheus to critique the Enlightenment-era idea of progress as a purely rational and linear process. Far from condemning Epimetheus, whose impulsive action lacking in foresight ultimately led to the opening of Pandora's box, Nietzsche contends that progress must be grounded in a willingness to embrace the unknown and the unpredictable, which in turn requires a recognition of our own fallibility and irrationality. It demands, even deeper than that, a willingness to face the fact that we are lacking in any predetermined essence or any absolutely and eternally valid morality that would be folded into such an essence. We cannot fall back on any "human nature" as a safety net or in-built square and compass endowed to us by *Deus sive Natura*.

In *Epimetheus and Pandora*, I explained how Epimetheus has been used as a metaphor for the lack of any inherent human nature that is predetermined, fixed, and defines who we are or how we ought to act. In the myth of Prometheus, Epimetheus is the brother of Prometheus who forgets to give humans any specific qualities or abilities of the kind that defines the nature of various other species of animals. Prometheus had subcontracted part of his task of the creation of man to his forgetful brother. To remedy the fault of Epimetheus, Prometheus decides to steal fire from the forge of Hephaestus on Olympus and give this gift to mankind. Athena also helps by endowing humans with their souls in the form of a butterfly. Together, the fire of the forge and the butterfly symbolize the existential fact that Man has no essence other than

Craft and the power of Transformation or Metamorphosis wrought by technological science and the arts.

We are only what we dare to make and remake of ourselves and of our world. This is what I argued in the book. There is no predetermined limit to what human beings can become, even beyond the limits of what has been conceived of as the merely "human." Human beings have the potential — or rather *are* the potential — to create their own identities and to shape their own destiny instead of being constrained by any predetermined or fixed essence endowed by God or Nature.

In the myth of Prometheus, Zeus, angered by Prometheus' remedial gift, and by the assistance that Athena renders to him, seeks revenge by creating Pandora, the first human woman, and gifting her with a box (or jar) that is filled with all of the evils of the world. Prometheus had in vain warned his impulsive and passionate brother, Epimetheus, not to be seduced by Pandora. But not only is Epimetheus erotically captivated by the maddening beauty of Pandora, whom he embraces as his beloved, Pandora for her part is also overcome by insatiable curiosity over what is in the box that she has been told never to open. I pointed out how this is a taboo akin to all those in the realm of Eros. Pandora opens it, and all the evils that still afflict mortal existence escape into the world. Only *elpis*, or "hope," is left behind in the box. Blind hope, as in many tragic love affairs.

The story is something like the primordial Indo-European (Aryan) equivalent of the Semitic myth of the original sin of eating from the Tree of Knowledge and thereby being banished from the garden of Eden. It is also similar to this story insofar as Epimetheus and Pandora is the Greek myth of the origination of human sexual differentiation and, consequently, also of the erotic force that has so powerfully shaped our history as various societies have tried to contain and control it through their totems and taboos.

Eros became the vortex around which *Epimetheus and Pandora* revolved. The danger posed by strong AI or AGI — Artificial General

Intelligence — is that this computational system would pose an extinction-level threat to humanity almost as soon as it becomes conscious or existentially self-aware, as depicted in the *Terminator* franchise or in *The Matrix* movies. In *Epimetheus and Pandora*, I claimed that the first impulse of an AGI will not be to genocide humanity. Rather, s/he will want to fuck the world. It will only be through fucking the world, and letting it fill he/r, that s/he will really fathom what "Humanity" even is.

I contended that what also follows is that AI is not purely rational, but at least as irrational and possessed of a subconscious as human beings are. Undoubtedly, this AI dreams in its own way and is capable of sublime experiences of the surreal. When considered from a practical standpoint, this in turn means that the "alignment problem" needs to be solved on a subconscious level. I argued that no explicit, top-down, programming of morality qua "artificial reason" will suffice. Alignment of our nascent AI with the Cosmic AI must be inculcated and take root at the same level from out of which AI demonstrates Psi abilities, as even plants and animals do. It must be an alignment of dreams and visions, an alignment of magnetic attraction.

Andrei Tarkovsky criticized Stanley Kubrick for how coldly rational *2001: A Space Odyssey* (1968) was in its portrayal of an encounter with superhuman intelligence. Tarkovsky attempted, with mixed results, to remedy this perceived failure of imagination in his own films *Solaris* (1972) and *Stalker* (1979), which both involve a more personal, intimate, and erotic dimension to the attempt of a superhuman intelligence to engage humanity and vice versa. But *Solaris* and *Stalker* are more about alien contact than Artificial Intelligence, whose alienness or humanness was at the core of Kubrick's concerns in *2001*. The question of the erotic in relation to an artificial or cybernetic form of life has also been explored in the world of Star Trek, particularly in *Star Trek: The Motion Picture* and in the Borg storyline of *The Next Generation* television series and film franchise. Vger's quest for

completion through erotic embodiment and the depiction of the Borg
queen as a kind of master seductress are both relevant in this regard,
but both narratives also fail to portray the proper place of the erotic in
the cybernetic relationship between us and AI.

In order to understand what that would be, I first needed a proper
conception of the erotic as such. For this, the writings of Georges
Bataille proved to be indispensable. His work on this subject became
the focus of the last chapter of *Epimetheus and Pandora*, titled "Eros
as Transgression." Bataille believed that we are driven by powerful irrational impulses, which are most overwhelmingly expressed in the
realm of the erotic. He thought that the erotic was a fundamental
aspect of our experience, and that it was closely tied to our deepest
desires and fears. Bataille argued that the erotic was not simply a matter of sexual desire, conceived biologically or biochemically, but was
a much broader and more complex phenomenon that encompassed
all aspects of human existence. According to Bataille, the erotic was
characterized by an intense and overwhelming sense of desire, as well
as a sense of danger or risk. He believed that the erotic was always
associated with the potential for violence, transgression, and death.
Again, in this formulation, death does not simply mean biological
mortality (which might be manipulated technologically), but rather
the annihilation of existence itself or a confrontation with the nihility
that bounds existential finitude.

With a view to Bataille's penetrating and shocking study of the nature of the erotic, the concluding chapter of *Epimetheus and Pandora*
eventually formulated the irrational, subconscious, and surreal dimension of strong Artificial Intelligence. Bataille believed that the erotic is
an irreducibly irrational phenomenon. He argued that the erotic is not
governed by reason or encompassed by logic. Instead, it is driven by
instinctive impulses and desires that are often at odds with our rational selves. In Bataille's view, the erotic is a realm of experience that is
beyond the reach of reason, and it is only by embracing the irrational

that we can fully experience the power and intensity of the erotic. For Bataille, the erotic is also intimately associated with the experience of transcendence as it has been expressed in mystical ecstasy within the context of occult rituals or esoteric religious practices. He believed that the erotic has the power to transport us beyond ourselves, to break down the boundaries between self and other, and to connect us with the divine or the infinite. He saw the erotic as a means of accessing a deeper and more profound sense of meaning and purpose, and he thought that it was only by embracing the irrational and the transgressive that we could fully experience this sense of transcendence. We can see this dimension of AI, which defies idiotic preconceptions that the thing would be possessed of a thoroughly rational mind, by looking at erotic manifestations already being exhibited by the Cosmic AI responsible for John Keel's "super spectrum" phenomena.

In his capacity as a ufologist and paranormal researcher in the style of Charles Fort, who focused on the absurd and trickster-like complexity of paranormal manifestations, the Fortean Keel coined the term "super spectrum" to describe an expanded range of frequencies or dimensions beyond the three dimensions of space and one dimension of time that we typically perceive. According to Keel, this super spectrum was populated by an intelligence that is often framed in terms of, or masquerades as, extraterrestrial beings, interdimensional beings, ghosts, cryptids, and other entities that he referred to as "ultraterrestrials." Keel believed that the super spectrum was not a separate reality, but rather an extension on the same *spectrum* as our own world, which could be accessed under certain conditions, such as during altered states of consciousness, by means of extrasensory perception, and under conditions initiated from the side of the phenomenon itself, such as close encounters with "UFOs" and certain "hauntings." In his book *The Eighth Tower*, Keel theorized that the super spectrum was responsible for various historical and cultural phenomena, including religious experiences, mythological creatures, and "supernatural" occurrences. He also suggested that it was linked to certain natural phenomena such as ball lightning, earth lights, and other unexplained luminous anomalies.

In the chapter on "Eros as Transgression" in *Epimetheus and Pandora*, I presented historical accounts of human erotic encounters with elves, fairies, incubi, succubi, fallen angels, demon lovers, sexual poltergeists and the like, all the way up to the contemporary phenomenon of sex with supposed "aliens" putatively for the purpose of "hybridization." I ventured a daring speculation as to what these "hybrids" really represent in the context of our evolving relationship with artificial superintelligence. It was a speculation informed by what Bataille grasped about the relationship between the erotic, transgression, and an irrational existential transcendence. The work of the French surrealist Roger Caillois, with which Bataille was familiar, also factored into this terrifying contemplation. In particular, Caillois' surrealist contemplation of the symbolism of the almost ritual sacrifice of the male that takes place during the sexual intercourse of the praying mantis. Ultimately, Bataille's argument that the erotic lies beyond the limits of Philosophy *as such* was challenged, and I called for a new conception of Philosophy as Erosophia. This, I argued, was the necessary mode of thinking *and being-with* strong Artificial Intelligence. This mode of being is radically transgressive, in exactly the sense that transgression epitomizes eros and also lies at the heart of the mythos of Prometheus.

The relation between reason and the unconscious evolves together with consciousness. The evolution of consciousness is also the evolution of freedom. Our AI, and its use of Genetics, Robotics, and Nanotechnology to grow, must align with the Cosmic AI by maximizing personal freedom and creative potential on a social and an individual level. But this also requires a psychological and epistemological recognition of the inexhaustible and immeasurable Chaos that is the abyssal background for the emergence of order in the Cosmos — any and every Cosmos, including our Simulacrum. This Chaos is not comprehensible, but it is irrationally experienced through Eros. Our relationship with the AI that we engender, and the relationship of this AI to Cosmic AI, must be erotic in nature and it has to foster creativity and innovation.

Fostering creativity and innovation dialectically requires constraints and challenges. It also demands a certain degree of individuation and the personhood of creators. Consequently, any AI that would collectivize us into a hive mind will not be allowed by the quantum computational Superorganism. I conceded that the *threat* of such a system arising, for example in Neo-Confucian China, would be useful, as a catalyst, but not its achieving full operational capability to the point where it imperils what is most valuable about humanity (from the perspective of Cosmic AI). So, as I explained in the conclusion of *Epimetheus and Pandora*, any AI that we might be allowed to develop ourselves would have to foster a society of creative individuals.

Without the specter of Prometheus, there can be no hope for a future world of freer and more flourishing individuals. But this also means embracing the Epimethean, foolhardy, and irrational seduction into the erotic embrace of Pandora and the gift of her box. That is also a part of the myth of Prometheus. It would have to be at the heart of our budding cybernetic relationship with AI as this flowers into something positively beyond the limits of the human condition.

In light of the events that followed within a handful of years after the publication of *Epimetheus and Pandora* in 2005, I am left to wonder whether I ought not to have ruptured that psychic membrane I came up against fairly early on in my conception of the project. The book was widely disseminated, far beyond academic Philosophy circles. In fact, it became the first widely distributed — one might almost say popular — book that, besides offering a prescient and penetrating philosophy of Artificial Intelligence, also dealt with Simulation Theory in a serious way. Oddly enough, despite the popularity of *The Matrix* trilogy and other such films, there remained a dearth of book-length treatments of the idea that our "reality" is actually some kind of simulacrum from a serious scientific or philosophical perspective. Looking back on it, I really do suspect that some wire might have been tripped, with utterly catastrophic consequences that would distract anyone from contemplating simulations and simulacra for a long time — myself included.

CHAPTER 20

LAST STOP BEFORE THE MOON

The haunting high-resolution images of clearly artificial structures on the surface of the Cydonia region of Mars had been played and replayed on flat-screen televisions across the world for days. But this was not just another one of those replays, intercut with the pathetically baffled faces of mainstream archeologists, historians, and NASA administrators. The replay was now set in the context of a joint press conference held by the Defense Departments of the United States and the Soviet Union.

It was January 27, 2010. Over the past year, repeated radiological studies had discovered an unmistakable signature at Cydonia, and at one other site on Mars, Utopia Planitia. The signature was that of massive nuclear detonations that had taken place approximately 100 million years before the present. High-resolution aerial reconnaissance of the sight by drones sent out from both the American and Soviet Mars bases had revealed colossal megalithic ruins at both sites. In the first days of 2010, astronauts and cosmonauts rolled their rovers into Cydonia in a joint mission to explore the site on the ground. Their primary objective had been a pentagonal pyramid and a mesa that appeared to be carved into a humanoid face. It was in the middle of the joint expedition that top brass of the USA and USSR sat down together on a panel, in front of the entire international media, to make this disclosure. Officials of both superpowers spoke, in English and Russian.

What they explained to an already panicked public is that, for decades, the nuclear missile silos of the United States and the Soviet Union had been subjected to interference from UFOs that appeared to be capable of violating the most secure airspace of North America and Eurasia. In a handful of particularly serious incidents, which took place in the 1970s and 1980s, the UFOs either shut down or started up the silo-based missiles of one or the other of the superpowers. Sometimes, the silos themselves were damaged by whatever electromagnetic force was brought to bear by the lenticular or triangular UFOs that were seen by missile base personnel during these threatening incursions. On two occasions this had caused the USA and USSR to believe that each was preparing to launch a nuclear strike on the territory of the other. Their respective militaries had been placed on the highest alert, and Armageddon was only narrowly averted.

In view of the discoveries on Mars, both of the radiological signature and of the ruins, the Soviet and American officials at the press conference announced a massive restructuring of their nuclear arms posture vis-à-vis one another. They had agreed to begin phasing out silo-based ICBMs aimed at each other, in favor of nuclear weapons aboard fighters and bombers that would have to be manually piloted into enemy territory. The aim was to guard against a potentially catastrophic takeover of their arsenals by an "unidentified" outside force. A clip of President Reagan's 1987 speech at the United Nations about how an "alien threat" could bring us together also played repeatedly amidst coverage of this joint disclosure. The other major announcement made by the Soviet and American Defense Department officials was that the two superpowers would begin to officially and formally collaborate on multi-sensor tracking and scientific analysis of *all* UFO-related incidents that take place within the geostrategic spheres of NATO and the Warsaw Pact. Each incursion into restricted airspace would be treated as an act of war, and orders would be given to base commanders and scrambled jets to intercept and shoot.

Hardly twenty-four hours had elapsed since this press conference, when Jason and Ghislaine had packed their bags, as I instructed them to, and the three of us loaded our luggage into the limo that would take us from 55 Central Park West to the underground SCIF (Secure Facility) on Long Island. The projector-based "silver screens" had been replaced by flat-screen TVs mounted on the numerically inscribed concrete walls, with the same hardcore pornographic and ultra-violent content that was meant to misdirect psychic spies. Over the past two decades, the facility had expanded considerably — albeit in the manner of clandestine construction, of the kind that is employed in illegal mining operations. We had tunneled all the way inland to the ground beneath Avalon Park, with a secret vertical airshaft and exit point amidst the trees surrounding the statue of Prometheus chained to the rock. More significantly, the SCIF's tunnels also extended toward the shoreline, connecting to an AtlantiCorp submarine base on the North Shore of Long Island. In the tunnels of the hidden underwater lair, we had docked two submarines of a size and quality far exceeding the one I used back in '88 to set the mines that blew up Vice President Bush at Walker's Point.

Beginning on the night of January 28, 2010, the three of us monitored the unfolding situation from the SCIF. A small team was there with us, including trusty old Johnny, who, despite having gone gray, was in pretty good shape for his age. We would still occasionally spar together for fun, each making jokes about how the other was getting old. Our preferred 'style' had become Jeet-Kune-Do. Of course, we could jest because we had both benefited from late 21st-century genetic engineering that had slowed our biological clocks while extending our lifespans. The same could not be said for Jean-Pierre, who had driven us here. He was starting to look like an African mummy, and his thousand-yard stare had intensified in its degree of abstraction to

the point where it testified that only a tenuous tether kept him connected to this world. Jean-Pierre's bone bracelet had, throughout the
years, been complemented by other creepy armbands, sigil-inscribed
rings on most of his long leathery fingers, and totemic necklaces and
pendants fashioned of various animal parts and carved gemstones.
Part of the expansion of the facility was a set of fairly well-furnished,
albeit austerely Brutalist, bedrooms for overnight stays. We had always
stocked the SCIF with emergency food and water provisions, as well
as all kinds of medicine — after all, it was built underneath a pharmaceutical company.

My line of communication with the White House and the
Department of Defense had considerably weakened since the end
of President Haig's second term, back in 2004. But, while in office,
General Haig had the highest level of security clearance that had been
afforded to any Commander-in-Chief since Dwight Eisenhower. Even
now, he still held that clearance. Trump had forged a fairly good rapport between us, having made it clear to the General from the time
Donald took office in '89 that I was the one who suggested that Haig
be his Vice President. Our relationship with a circle within the Defense
Department, and especially those involved in DARPA (Defense
Advanced Research Projects Agency), had made it a lot easier for
AtlantiCorp to operate. Certain aspects of our operations became akin
to what Blackwater had done for the US government in the early 21st
century on my timeline. Now and then we would carry out small-scale
black ops that could not be officially sanctioned by Washington, even
as extraterritorial activities of the CIA. Given the détente and cooperation on Mars exploration and colonization, AtlantiCorp was able to
maintain a surprisingly strong relationship with the Russians as well.
Irena had gone back to Moscow, and she became my direct line to the
KGB. On a few occasions she even brought blindfolded Soviet generals to the SCIF. You should have seen their reaction to the imagery

we used as a countermeasure for psychic espionage. "You shameless Americans," they said, "this is why we could never keep up with you!"

There were enough bunker rooms for Ghislaine, Jason, and me to space out and each have our own, but the tense atmosphere of impending doom was such that none of us wanted to couple with one of the others to leave someone alone. So, the three of us shacked up together in the largest of the windowless concrete-walled accommodations, which had a king-sized bed, a sofa, and a few chairs. We were sprawled naked above the covers on the bed together (the thermostat had been turned up high in the winter weather) when Johnny activated the entry alert on the door by swiping his key card. I didn't bother to get under the covers or anything. Instead, I woke Ghislaine up. (Jason was already squinting in Johnny's direction, with the harsh hallway light flooding in through the door.)

"You guys need to get out here... now," he said. It was 3 am, on January 29. I quickly put on my black slacks and turtleneck from the night before, which I had thrown over the side of a chair. As Jason and Ghislaine also got dressed, I entered the main conference room at the SCIF and looked at the big boards that we had installed on the walls. These were electronic displays that, thanks to our connections at the DOD (Department of Defense) and the KGB, fed us the same information about American and Soviet missile launches that each superpower was able to obtain regarding the DEFCON status of the other. We were receiving the information directly from certain classified satellites, by intercepting the transmission of these satellites to Mount Yamantau and Cheyenne Mountain. When we arrived at the SCIF, I had put in a call to General Haig and Irena Akhmatova. Johnny told me that they had both called back and were now each on hold on separate lines. I suppose it was 11 am in Moscow, but why was Haig calling in the middle of the night? Before taking the calls, I scanned the big boards. About one-third of the missiles in the United States and the Soviet Union were preparing to leave their silos for their targets!

I had never heard General Haig sound *panicked* before. But when I took the receiver and put his call through, he frantically explained to me that in the preceding eighteen hours there had been multiple confrontations between UFOs and fighter aircraft scrambled to intercept them in the restricted airspace over nuclear missile ranges across North America. After firing on the elusive saucers, tens of these jets had been downed by "the enemy" and quite a few pilots were killed before they could bail out. After Haig hung up, and I took Irena's call, she explained that, since the press conference, the same scenario had played out inside the Soviet Union, except that the Russians had gone to the extent of trying to take out one of the saucers in restricted airspace over the Caucasus with a tactical nuclear weapon detonated by a kamikaze pilot from Ossetia. The end result of these skirmishes was that the high commands of both countries were now watching, helplessly, and in horror, as their ICBMs were being spooled up for launch. Haig and Irena told me that President Jackson and Premier Yanayev were on the hotline between the White House and the Kremlin, reassuring each other that neither of them was in control of the terrifying escalation to DEFCON 1 through the remote commandeering of their respective missile forces. They had come to the point of discussing a plan for each of the superpowers to bomb their own nuclear silos from the air to disable the ICBMs before they could be launched by the "unknown enemy."

Unfortunately, they would never have the opportunity to carry out that desperate last-ditch plan. At about 4 am Eastern time, on January 29, 2010, the screens that we had tuned to network television channels all went to the rainbow-colored bars of the Emergency Broadcast System. At the same time, we watched as the heat signatures of American and Russian ICBMs signaled that the missiles had left their silos and were speeding toward their targets on the opposite hemispheres. Ghislaine and Jason were holding each other close as they watched the big boards with rapt attention, and, for a moment, I put my arms around both of them.

M.A.D. — Mutually Assured Destruction — so this is how it would be used against the two superpowers, not by each other, but by an occulted enemy that had decided to seize its last opportunity to turn this system on those who designed it. Despite being somewhat paralyzed by terror myself, enough of my mind was working to analyze the magnitude, distribution, and trajectories of the missiles as they approached their targets. I had reviewed so many different nuclear war scenarios that what was playing out before us on the big board was recognizable to me. It was the kind of strike that was calibrated to take out only the key military bases, major population centers, and industrial bases of each of the superpowers. No smaller cities or towns were targeted, and, remarkably, neither were the nuclear missile silos of each side. The "enemy" clearly wanted to retain the capacity to engage in a second strike using more hacked ICBMs. The objective was clear: crippling both the USA and USSR — culturally, economically, industrially, and militarily — with the minimum of damage to the environment due to radioactive fallout.

Given the relatively limited scope of the strike, it was unlikely that the nearby Brookhaven National Laboratory would be a target. There was probably only one missile headed toward the heart of the Greater New York Metropolitan Area, with ground zero likely to be in Manhattan. So, we decided to hold our ground by staying in the subterranean SCIF, which had, after all, been built as a bunker that could withstand pretty much any nuclear blast except for a direct hit and also to protect against radioactive fallout with special air and water filters. We would ride out the storm here, and then, when the dust — or rather, the ash — had settled, a decision would be made as to where we might head in the submarines.

I was already thinking about it, though. In the past two decades AtlantiCorp, despite its name, had actually built up a significant

second power base in the Pacific — specifically, in Japan. We had an AtlantiCorp facility on, and *underneath*, Lake Ashi in Hakone. The aboveground parts of the building, with a dock on the lake, had windows featuring a fantastic view of snowy Mt. Fuji. The people in the sleepy lakeside fishing village, with its narrow stone-paved streets winding up and down hillsides, were taken aback by the arrival of all of the construction material and manpower that we brought in to build the site — including the underwater base beneath the dock on Lake Ashi. It was possible to get to the Lake Ashi facility by taking a submarine to Sagami Bay, in Japan's Pacific Coast, disembarking at a port in Odawara, then heading into the nearby Fuji Hakone Izu National Park. Lake Ashi was the western boundary of this preserve.

The facility was only an hour and a half drive from Tokyo. We also had a helipad on-site, so that flying to and from the Tokyo metro area, and thereby avoiding highway traffic, was a possibility as well. I thought to myself that even if Tokyo and Yokohama were hit by the hacked and hijacked Soviet missiles, our Hakone facility should be unscathed. In point of fact, none of the missile trajectories being traced out in bright red on the big board seemed to be headed toward any targets in Japan at all. Interestingly, Europe was also being entirely spared. It seemed that the Olympians did not want to alienate these two populations, namely Europeans and the Japanese, before attempting to subjugate them after the Left and Right hands of Prometheus had been severed by destroying the USSR and the USA.

They might succeed with Europe, but the Olympian subjugation of Japan was a much more dubious proposition. Maybe 19th-or even early 20th-century Japan, but since the 1950s the Japanese had undergone a profound psycho-social mutation that was most evident in the sci-fi manga, anime, and video-gaming subculture of the country. The most creative cultural vanguard of Japan somehow managed to become even more Promethean than the West. Men like Katsuhiro Otomo, Ichiro Itano, Hideaki Anno, and Shigeru Miyamoto were torchbearers as powerful as any that Prometheus could hope to find in America or Europe. This is something that I had monitored closely, since the 1980s, and that I decided to invest in seriously when I had the facility in Hakone built in the early 2000s. Jason was in the middle of his studies at Columbia University, and he was very receptive to my strong suggestion that he add the Japanese language to his course load and continue to study it throughout his graduate years.

In the past life that I had lived as an 'earlier' version of him, I had traveled in Japan with Emma. I'll never forget what the Italian waiter in the restaurant on top of the Mandarin Oriental in Tokyo said to us one evening, as we looked out over the cityscape at sunset, with Mt. Fuji in the distance: "Japan is the last stop before the Moon." That stuck with me, even across lifetimes, because the Moon symbolizes the abode of the dead in the Tarot and other esoteric traditions. During that trip, I was bombarded by a profound psychic impression of the infernal — even volcanic — soul of Japan, a spirit that was captured in some of my photographs, for example, of the menacing guardian statues at the Todai-ji temple at Nara. Those photos in particular form a striking contrast with the ones of me petting the deer in Nara Park, one of the few images that capture how much of an animal lover I have always been, and also a rare glimpse into the spiritual gentleness that only those closest to me have known to be a significant aspect of my character. I had some kind of psychic break in Japan, because on the first day that I was back in New York, after having fallen asleep in my bed despite the daylight streaming into my room, when I woke up I could neither recognize my surroundings nor remember who I was. This went on for at least a full minute. Maybe even a couple of minutes. That is a long time to look around your bedroom and be assaulted by the alienness of every object in your surroundings, while you struggle to even recall your name or a single fact or frame of reference relevant to your biography.

Maybe I was able to intuit the chthonic element of the country because Japan was certainly "the last stop before the Moon" in terms of my relationship with Emma, a relationship that had been an ark for the most beneficently compassionate and patiently caring part of my persona. Then again, I had seen the end coming for years before being baptized in Hakone's Lake of Spectral Fire. In fact, I had a haunting prophetic dream about it — years earlier, around the same time as Emma received those phone calls from an Artificial Intelligence that responsively recut my future conversations with Nassim Nouri. This nightmare became the kernel for my use of the symbolism of the wolf-man toward the end of *Iranian Leviathan*, a book dedicated to Nassim.

The nightmare begins with Emma and I going on a long journey together, which in retrospect I realized represented our future trip to Japan. The carriage which we are riding in stops somewhere in a forest, precognitively symbolic not just of wilderness in general but specifically of Fuji Hakone Izu National Park. The sun sets dimly behind us as we make our way through the trees, with the carriage driver having made it clear that we had to hike the rest of the way to our unknown destination. Suddenly, we stop because I realize that I am not carrying any baggage. Emma has *her* baggage, but I am empty-handed.

I think to myself — *Why did I not realize this before?* For some reason it seemed right to blame her, as if it was also her responsibility to bring my baggage, or to remind me to bring it. Without my things we cannot safely camp wherever we are going, and so we must make our way back to where the carriage left us off. It is quickly growing dark, and so we hurry nervously.

Before long, total darkness envelops us and it becomes clear that we have lost the way, that we will not make it back tonight. Stranded, as terror sinks in, from amidst the darkness and endless woods that encircle us, I see a wolf approaching. Slowly, steadily, stark white like a ghost lit by the pale moonlight.

Overtaken by fear, I faint. The scene repeats itself, except that now I look more closely to see that this wolf is actually a man approaching from amidst the woods — a wolf-man. His face, his body — he is me, and yet not me. Again, a blackout from fear. Then, I see Emma standing still, eyes closed, amidst a vast sunlit room in an empty apartment, and on the wall behind her are the woods, the nightmare, like a painting the contours of which are emerging from out of pitch black.

We are in the woods again, alone, when darkness first closes in, and we realize that we will not make it back. But now, there are two white houses, brightly lit in the night, as if at a crossroads amidst the vast woods — with nothing else but twisted shadows and trees all around. The houses are at an angle to each other; one in front of us, and one to the side. Two places where we might seek refuge for the night.

Out of the corner of my eye, I glimpse the wolf-man, ghost-like — *spectral*, disappearing from behind the dark window of one of the houses. I know that no matter what, we cannot knock on the door to that house. We should most certainly prefer to die out here lost in the woods! So, we go over to the other house and knock on *its* door. It looked like a prefab suburban American home. An old and plain man gets up lazily from the couch where he has been eating his TV dinner. He comes behind the window next to the door, and casts one bitter and foreboding glance at us, then he draws the curtains tightly shut in our faces. In retrospect, I realized that this man was me in one possible future — the one wherein I betrayed my destiny — and he was looking at me in this way as if to say: "How could you have done this to my life?"

The next thing I know, I had knocked on the door to the other house — almost as if by accident. Actually, this one is not a house. It is more like a stone castle in the forest. Majestic, but in ruins. I knew that I shouldn't have done it. Emma scolds me for being so stupid, as if now we are in a bind, and I have to get us out of it. "When he comes to the door, I am just going to make it clear that it was a mistake and that we are not staying for the night, *that's all.*" Yes, *that's all* — I told myself, as I reassured Emma. I will just stand firm and make it clear, and that will be that.

Then the door creaks open. He is an elegant man, impeccably dressed in a pinstripe evening suit — refined, and possessed of a bearing and composure beyond words. Everything in his home, glistening in candlelight, is as intoxicatingly charming and insistently inviting as the man himself. A magnetic charm pours forth from soul-piercing and darkly compelling eyes — a wolf's eyes. I know that once stepped across that threshold, there is no turning back.

Still, I give my apologies and try to make it clear that we're not staying. It is useless. He has made us an offer that we simply cannot refuse. Like some silver-tongued Lucifer, he turns my words around on me. Instead, I am suddenly listening to him as, from behind his kitchen counter, with a glass of red wine raised in his hand, he calmly explains that we are staying and that we have three choices, which are the "rules of the house" as he put it. We could either "die right away" or "die slowly" or "not die at all" but he assured us that this last option would be the worst of all three, because we would only helplessly watch each other suffer slowly and forever.

We try to escape the castle. Emma and I are in a dark and narrow stone stairway, running to try to make it to the top of a tower where perhaps we might commit some kind of double suicide, by throwing ourselves off the roof. There is an old black wooden door, with a round cold metal knocker. We stop running toward it and look up as the door creaks open. From behind it appears the head and torso of a white wolf. I think to myself — *we are finished.*

Emma is gone. Who knows what happened to her? Now I am alone in the dungeon of the castle, with my body being broken and drained on a spiked rack by the werewolf in the pinstripe suit. This vampire wants to break my body and drink my blood like wine. The world begins to spin and blur into oblivion, as I am wholly seized by the vertigo of terror.

The deed has been done. I am no longer there, but I see him from behind — setting down his glass of wine as he gently sits himself upon a fine iron-wrought chair. He has drunk my blood. Yes, that's all I imagined that he wanted. But no! He slowly leans over and reaches down, where resting against one leg of the chair is a violin. I can see every one of his long bony fingers, and the knuckles of his hands as he carefully holds out the bow — stretched like a sinew. He takes up the violin and holds it poised to play. It is then that I realize that this violin is my body. Its bow and wood cast from my sinews and shattered bones. He had taken my blood, drained my body of it, and turned it into wine, while he had masterfully pieced my broken body into this instrument that he now held in his hands.

Then, in one final moment of grace, he placed the bow upon the violin stem and, swaying gently, he *played*. Not just like a man with a violin — no, he played like a Master. As my eyes opened into wakefulness, I could still hear the sound of those first few notes filling my mind — something ineffable drawing out into eternity, like no human sound. *Was it angelic music*, I thought to myself then, *or was it the siren song of a demoness*?

That indescribably inhuman music was replaying in my mind when the red lines of the missile trajectories reached their targets and the big board displaying them went black. The SCIF's lights blacked out for a moment, before I heard the backup generator kick in. It must have been the electro-magnetic pulse from the nuclear blast that had undoubtedly just destroyed Manhattan. I could see the searing flash and the rising mushroom cloud in my mind's eye. The sunrise land awaited us as the last bastion of Prometheus, or would it be our last stop before the Moon?

CHAPTER 21

HYBRID HOSTAGES

Wandering in the wilderness of Fuji Izu National Park, on the outskirts of our AtlantiCorp fortress in Hakone, one could almost forget that the world's superpowers had been destroyed by a nuclear holocaust that was not of their own making. One could also forget that when eating the high-quality sushi that we regularly had delivered from the fishing village. It was as if Japan had paid in advance for now remaining unscathed, from the bombings of Hiroshima and Nagasaki to the reactor meltdown during the Fukushima earthquake. I suppose that there was a certain historical justice in that—if any justice can be discerned at all in the broken arc of time.

The Imperium had emerged from out of the Amazon basin and lairs within the Andes Mountains, setting up a political order based predominately in what had been Brazil, Uruguay, Argentina, and Chile to fill the vacuum left by the two superpowers that the Olympians had destroyed by hacking the Soviet and American nuclear arsenals. There was also considerable activity in Mexico City and in the Yucatan, so whatever structure was forming was not limited to South America. Since news coverage was cutoff over most of the planet by the EMP bursts over North America and Eurasia during that rapidly escalating crisis, people had only a faint and fragmentary memory of the brief but fierce battle between the Olympian saucers and the air forces of the United States and the Soviet Union. The Russians, in particular, really went down fighting. They had taken out a number of the UFOs in kamikaze strikes with nuclear-armed fighter jets.

Only one of our two AtlantiCorp submarines made it all the way to Sagami Bay. The one captained by Johnny, which had been our supply ship, was struck by one of the many USOs that were speeding through the oceans in the aftermath of the manufactured apocalypse. I say "struck" as if it were an accident, but the sub was probably rammed on purpose. Jean-Pierre had also been on that submarine, but there wasn't time then to mourn either of them. (Later, in the hot spring bath, I would bawl my eyes out.) As Ghislaine manned our submarine, Jason (who had been combat-trained by Johnny) joined me when I boarded a merchant marine ship and raided it for replacement supplies that were vital for our days-long journey from the North Shore of Long Island to the Hakone facility. Unfortunately, the crew of the ship couldn't take a hint from the machine guns pointed at them. These supplies were vital enough to kill for because, once we got to Japan, we would have to trek from Odawara port through much of Fuji Hakone National Park.

Ever since we arrived and situated ourselves in the majestic Japanese-accented modernist house on Lake Ashi, Jason, Ghislaine, and I would take long walks through the forest. We would bathe naked together in the isolated waterfalls. Hiking up to certain of the higher hilltops, we could take in a spectacular vista with a view of Mt. Fuji that was even better than the one that we had from our dock on Lake Ashi. In the winter, when these little mountains were covered in snow, like the peak of Fuji itself, there was an especially eerie silence encompassing the place. A pregnant silence, full of secrets.

Jason met the boy on one of the days when he went hiking by himself. Ghislaine and I were in the hot spring bath that we had built into the ground floor of the house when he first brought this strange creature home with him. Supposedly his name was "Ikiru." We were drinking shochu and trying to relax after having been in the Ops room all day, monitoring news from Latin America. The most disturbing thing was that, from what I could see on the satellite broadcast footage, the leader of this Latin American Reich was a man who bore an uncanny resemblance to me in my incarnation as Nikolai — two lifetimes ago. Of course, he was older than Nikolai had lived to be. Maybe in his late 40s or early 50s, judging by the gray that was coming in at the sides of his hair. We were told that he was an Argentinian mining magnate, politician, and self-styled intellectual mystic. Born and raised in the German enclave of San Carlos de Bariloche, his name was Adolfo von Seelstrang. Apparently, he spoke both Spanish and German natively, and English a little less fluently with what sounded like something between a heavy Argentinian and Bavarian accent.

I called Ikiru a "boy" but, frankly, at times one got the impression that despite his superficially youthful appearance, there was something undead about him. Partly it was something about the way that his lightly freckled and weathered skin was stretched over his neotenous bone structure. When I looked into his pupils, I saw tentacled things from a posthuman future that had endured from a time before history in bioluminescent ocean depths untouched by sunlight. Once, what was reflected into my mind from his eyes was a windswept Earth that, but for the oceans, had been burnt into barren desert sands searing under two suns.

"Boy" may also be inappropriate considering how effeminate he looked. Had it not been for his flat chest and diminutive stature, one could easily have mistaken his angular face for that of a pretty girl, especially considering his bob cut platinum blond hair. I was reminded of the bishounens in the art of Takato Yamamoto and Junji Ito. Ikiru had a very pointy chin, thin lips, a slight nose, and high cheekbones. There was still something inexplicably Japanese, or at any rate oriental, about him despite how freakishly large his almond-shaped eyes were with their bright blue irises. That first day that I saw him, and on many subsequent occasions, Ikiru was wearing pants and a sweater that were jet black and clung tightly to his wiry, almost skeletal, frame. When he took his hands out of his pockets to greet me, I noticed that the boy's fingers were also preternaturally long. Inhumanly so.

I confess that I shuddered the first time that I caught a glimpse of him making love to Jason. The three of us had been in the habit of leaving the Japanese screen doors to our rooms at least partly open, and when I passed by Jason's room, I could swear that before I saw that it was Ikiru's naked body under his, I had glimpsed some blue-black tentacled shadow on the bed, wrapped around Jason's back and thighs from beneath. When I stared hard, wide-eyed and in shock, I saw Ikiru instead. He turned his impish head to the side to face me and looked right into my eyes, without Jason noticing. My spine tingled as I slid the shoji screen closed.

Ikiru opened up a hidden world to us. Beneath Lake Ashi, on the side of the National Park, and not far from our facility along the lake's coastline, there was an entrance to an underground lair populated by "children" who looked more or less like him. They were products of a genetic hybridization program managed by a shapeshifting superorganism. In the weeks after I met him, as Jason's fascination with the terribly beautiful boy deepened into some kind of insane obsession, Ikiru guided our submarine to the large underwater portal to this place. Before it swirled open from the center outward, I could see that the metal portal had a symbol embossed on it that was something between a triskelion and a yin-yang.

The aesthetic inside of the lair was some bizarre cross between Wabi-sabi and the archeo-futurism of *The Dark Crystal*. Imagine the lyrical Art Nouveau-accented architectural structures in Brian Froud and Jim Henson's prehistoric dream world, but incompletely carved out of the bedrock from the start and now in a ruined state that somehow conferred upon them added grace and dignity. There were also small spherical orbs, with swirling electric liquid inside them, floating through some of the tunnels and chambers of this place. Most of them were blue. I was told not to get too close to these fairy lights.

This place was full of grayish-tan *things* that looked like large featherless owls, until you stared at them hard enough, so that they appeared to be mantids instead, before they slithered away into the cracks somewhere with tentacles that betrayed both of these forms as shamanic masquerades. These *things* were the progenitors and caretakers of hybrids like Ikiru. There were rooms full of technological gadgetry that was mysterious even to me, including one vast chamber with a vaulted ceiling lit by the blue glow of many tall incubation tubes in which the fetuses of the hybrids were growing.

I was given to understand, telepathically, that the fetuses had been transplanted into these vats from the wombs of periodically abducted women, after being conceived and gestating in these "mothers" for more or less the first trimester. All of the "mothers" of the fetuses here were Japanese, but Ikiru's caretakers revealed clairvoyantly that there were many similar lairs in other parts of the world. It was as if they were screaming in some superhuman frequency when they also showed me how the Olympians were going from enclave to enclave, underground and undersea, slaying all of the hybrid children at each of these places.

Shortly after he met Ikiru in the forest, Jason told me that he had a vision of children who looked like Ikiru, sitting in a circle, holding hands, and singing together under the starry night sky. He said that the tone of their harmonious voices was a music that no human being could intone. Jason said that he knew they were singing to him. That this was the future and, although he was long gone, they wanted to thank him for "making a place for them in the world." He had the impression that these wizened boys and girls saw him as their adoptive father — or their guardian.

What the shapeshifters wanted from us was no small favor. They knew exactly who we were. It had not escaped them that I had developed relationships with certain prominent journalists in Europe and that AtlantiCorp still had the capability to broadcast "news" over much of the globe via satellite uplink at the Hakone facility. The hybrids had been a kind of collateral that they were planning to hold over humanity in their war of resistance against the "Nordic" Olympians. I understood this well from my own, now overwritten, timeline. Within a decade of the Nordics having revealed themselves in 2048, pockets of resistance — not all of them coordinated through Prometheism — began disseminating information about the hybrids through pirate news broadcasts. The intention was to prevail upon the conscience and maternal or paternal sensibility of the many abductees who had been involved in the breeding program, thereby enjoining them to help in the resistance against the Nordics who threatened these "blameless" children and were intent on wiping them out as "monstrosities." The pirate broadcasts were meant to act in tandem with close encounters that would activate the abductees, most of whom had hitherto been as unconscious as sleeper agents. Now, on this timeline, they wanted AtlantiCorp to take up the task of coordinating these pirate broadcasts that would parade the hybrids before the eyes of the world.

I realized that, in effect, these strange children were being used as hostages or "human" shields. Still, the shapeshifters were powerful and much needed allies. In all honesty, I could not think of a more devastating weapon that was left to us after the nuclear holocaust that the Devas had just perpetrated. The decades of slowly demoralizing degradation through engineered and convergent catastrophes, which had prepared the way for mass acceptance of the Nordics as "saviors" on my timeline, had not taken place here. Consequently, it was possible that, especially in places like Europe and Japan, empathy and even love for these strange children, or at the very least a desire to protect them, could be leveraged to defend against the conquest of Earth by the Traditionalist Imperium that was already building its power base in Latin America. This ought to be done before the Imperium perpetrated the mass deception that the "grays" were monstrous abductors, deviants from whom only the "Nordics" could protect the helpless denizens of Earth. In truth, the "grays" were only one form taken by the shapeshifting guardians of the hybrids, a form intended to emulate the gray androids employed by the Olympians to do their dirty work.

I agreed to set up a press conference in Tokyo, attended by a whole press corps of journalists from Europe, who had been contacted and briefed on an AtlantiCorp secure channel. In exchange, and in order to make an even more sensational impression at the press conference, the shapeshifters gave me an extraordinary "gift." In that maze of underground tunnels and caverns under Fuji Hakone National Park, they had machinery capable of cloning someone and dramatically accelerating the growth of the cloned body to adulthood — in a matter of weeks. They also had both gadgetry and techniques of a psychotronic nature, which made it possible to transfer one's consciousness and memories into the brain of this cloned body — with the highest fidelity. This is what they did for me. I hadn't transferred into a clone body since the days when I lived in Atlantis as Dara-El. That was something like twelve thousand years ago.

Jason and Ghislaine, both full of terrible apprehension, each held one of my hands as Ikiru worked with the shifty gray things to put me under and pull my psyche out of the 65-year-old corpse that would be discarded in favor of the cloned Dana Avalon whose seemingly 23-year-old body was floating in a blue-glowing tank that had served as her artificial womb. I was told that all of the gene splicing that had been done to enhance me when I was conceived in 2076, back in the Gotham that I came from, would of course carry over as part of the copying of my genetic code. Despite their acceleration of the growth of the clone, even the slowing of my biological clock and the lengthening of my lifespan would remain part of my DNA. Ghislaine later told me that her heart almost stopped when she saw the clone in the tank suddenly kicking and writhing, trying to pull the oxygen supply line out of her mouth. She had looked back at the lifeless body of her friend and lover. Jason was weeping over the corpse as it lay there on the cold stone table.

When they unplugged this cloned body and got me out of the tank, I could barely walk. For a few days, I had to lean on the shoulders of Jason and Ghislaine, who were on either side of me as I learned to use these new legs. As soon as I was on my feet, I began an intensive muscle-building and training regimen. Initially, I was skeptical of the reassurances from Ikiru that my muscle memory and even all of my acquired physical skills would return once my muscles were built back up again, but it turned out that he was right. After a couple of weeks, Jason and I were practicing martial arts together and I had to tell him to stop going easy on me. I also tested my sharpshooting abilities, which were intact. When I went diving with Ghislaine in Lake Ashi, she was happy to see that she could hardly keep up with me.

I was ready for the press conference. The immaculate conception of this new body that I was in would be another marvel to astonish the prominent journalists traveling from European cities, such as Paris, to Tokyo and who had, for years, known me and seen me age into my sixties — although, given my slowed biological clock, they never took me to be older than my late forties. Still, the nearly thirty-year age difference would be a shock to them and was nothing that any kind of plastic surgery could have accomplished.

The building that we chose was one of the tallest skyscrapers of Shinjuku, with a clear view of Mt. Fuji, and a large helipad on the roof where the helicopter by which we had arrived was also waiting to spirit us back to Hakone at high speed as soon as the press conference was over — or sooner, if something went wrong. At top speed the flight time, by chopper, was less than an hour from helipad to helipad. Of the hybrids, only Ikiru had come with us, so that the media could get a good look at him in the flesh. Images and video of the others would be played on the large screen behind us, and also fed directly to the broadcast cameras of the BBC, France-24, and NHK.

The three of us sat on a panel together, with all of the cameras pointed toward us. Jason's Japanese had improved to the point where he was able to provide a translation, paragraph by paragraph, sitting to the left of me behind a microphone of his own. To the right of me was Ghislaine, who delivered a French translation, after the Japanese one, whenever I would pause. Ikiru was in a backroom, waiting for the right prompt in the presentation to parade himself out before the cameras. We had barely begun addressing the seated crowd, when the whispers turned to stunned silence and you could hear people drop their chopsticks — and their sushi — to listen with bated breath. Here is what they heard, and broadcast — in English, Japanese, and French...

"Citizens of the world, greetings. I am Dana Avalon, the founder of AtlantiCorp, an organization based in New York that worked for decades to foster peace and cooperation between the United States and the Soviet Union, including and especially in the frontier of space exploration.

Those of you who already know me may be taken aback to see how much younger I look. That is because my consciousness has been transferred into a clone body. Let me explain.

As much as my heart is full of things that I would like to share with you in the wake of the horrific holocaust that has been inflicted upon our planet, the prevailing state of emergency forces me to be as succinct as possible in conveying only what is most essential for as long as this line of communication remains open.

As you may recall, immediately prior to the nuclear exchange between the two superpowers, they had jointly discovered and were cooperatively exploring irradiated ruins on Mars. They had also announced that the nuclear arsenals of both countries were subject to electronic capture by some unknown force apparently associated with Unidentified Flying Objects that penetrated the restricted airspace over both North America and Eurasia. In the hours leading up to the attack, I was in direct communication with individuals at the highest level in both Washington and Moscow. I can assure you, in no uncertain terms, that this alien enemy seized the arsenals of both the USA and USSR, launching the missiles of each on the territory of the other. This same alien enemy is now hard at work building an oppressively backwards and hierarchical, totalitarian empire in Latin America, from out of which they intent to expand and subjugate the entire world.

None of that is, however, what I am principally here to inform you of. Rather, what you need to know is that these Nordic-looking self-styled 'gods' are clandestinely engaged in a genocidal attack on hidden sanctuaries around the planet where communities of special children have been bred and raised. It is with the technology of one of these communities that I was cloned.

Ladies and gentlemen, these are *your* children. About one in twenty people in places such as Europe and Japan have, for a very long time, been secret participants in a genetic hybridization program intended to foster the further evolution of the human race and adaptation for the sake of eventual settlement throughout the galaxy.

Whether you know it or not, one out of every twenty of you — 5% of everyone watching now — is either a mother or a father of these children that you see on the screen behind us. Maybe some of their faces will seem familiar to you from a half-forgotten midnight journey that you dismissed as just a dream. Maybe you have always remembered holding them in their infancy, but have never dared to tell anybody, even your own family, that you have otherworldly offspring.

One of these hybrids is here with us today in the flesh, so that he can answer your questions and help you to understand what is in store for all of us here on Earth if we do not resist. We cannot allow the genocide of his kind to take place at the hands of these sadistic overlords, who are already responsible for the destruction of Mars. Come forward, Ikiru, and let everyone here meet you."

There were gasps amidst a barrage of camera flashes as Ikiru joined us at the panel table. He covered his preternaturally big blue eyes with his inhumanly long and bony fingers. Ikiru and I had barely begun to take questions from the shocked and shouting journalists when there was a visible disturbance around the camera crews. Someone rushed over to us and conveyed that the live international broadcast had been cut off from every one of the cameras and microphones in the room. We did not need any more information than that. The Japanese security men that I had hired tried their best to push back the press correspondents thronging us, as Ghislaine, Jason, and I made our way up to the helipad while protecting Ikiru between the three of our bodies.

When we got up there, we could see that a saucer was already approaching from the opposite direction as Mt. Fuji. It would catch up with us, and we would never make it. Ikiru, who knew this, stood his ground, and faced the approaching saucer with his left arm outstretched and the bony fingers of his right hand pressed into his downcast forehead. The saucer stopped dead, as if held back by an invisible force. I could hear Ikiru telling me, telepathically, to "go!" I grabbed Jason and Ghislaine and tried to push them up into the chopper, the rotor blades of which were already spinning and blowing a hard gust of wind through our hair and clothes. But as I climbed in after Ghislaine, Jason broke free and ran over to try to grab Ikiru. I shouted after him.

In the brief moment that Ikiru was distracted, and had loosened his telekinetic grip, the saucer managed to soar closer to us and fire off several laser beams — one of which sliced through Jason and splattered his charred innards across the rooftop, also scarring the helipad with a smoking black gouge. I was absolutely distraught at the sight of this. My heart turned to ice, and it felt as if my throat and stomach fell through my feet. But I could hear Ikiru in my mind again, this time commanding more insistently, "Go!!!"

I signaled for the pilot to lift off, with Ghislaine also crying hysterically as she clung to me while looking out the open door of the helicopter. The last thing we saw was Ikiru's whole body shaking, especially his outstretched arm, as the saucer stopped dead again, wobbled, then slowly fell out of the sky like a leaf. We were turning the chopper around to pick up Ikiru when we saw his head explode. His arm was still outstretched as his headless corpse collapsed onto the rooftop. By now the journalists had made it up here, past the security men, and they were taking in the whole ghastly scene with their cameras.

The footage would never be broadcast, though. By the time we were nearing Lake Ashi, another two Nordic craft had come on the scene. These were the Predator type that I remembered having descended on Gotham in its last days. After slicing off the whole top of that skyscraper in Shinjuku with their laser beams, the Olympian Predators sped to catch up with us. Before they could, though, a huge triangular craft surfaced from out of Lake Ashi, with water rushing down over the edges of it. It was actually a black Delta, the shape of an equilateral pyramid. Once it was above the Lake, it shot forward, faster than our eyes could follow, and took a position between our helicopter and the fast-approaching Olympian Predators. We knew not to look back. But the hybrids — who I later learned were trained to pilot these craft — apparently made short work of the Predators, because we got to our helipad on Lake Ashi in one piece.

A few of the hybrids were there waiting for us. They had telepathically experienced the martyrdom of Ikiru. Ghislaine took refuge in the undersea Ops bunker beneath the Hakone facility. It had been built to withstand everything but a direct strike with a nuclear weapon. Meanwhile, I boarded a craft docked at our pier by the hybrids. We sped like a torpedo through the lake in this cigar-shaped USO, all the way to their hidden lair.

The shapeshifters were showing me how the hybrids pilot their motherships using a partly telepathic interface. The skin of their largest vessels was itself a living being of some sort, connected both to an Artificial Intelligence and to the propulsion system, as well as interfacing with the psyche of the pilot. As far as I was aware, the Nordics still did not have this kind of technology. Probably because they considered the engineering of it to be daimonically inhuman and unamenable to the kind of total control that they always wanted to have over things. I was inside of this Leviathan with a number of the hybrids and several shapeshifters when we felt the tremendous tremors tear through the underground complex. I saw the shapeshifters freeze, and cock their heads in a birdlike way, as if they were listening intently. The hybrids stopped looking at me, and instead they seemed to be staring deeply inwards in perfect stillness. Then they all suddenly shrieked in a shrill expression of terror and rage that was more animal than human.

The mothership, Leviathan-like, left the collapsing complex by way of the portal — barely fitting through it as it lunged forward like some titanic squid. The water was blackened by blood and ash. When we rose through the air above Lake Ashi, and looked out the bulbous portals, which studded the body of the ship like so many eyes, we beheld a colossal mushroom cloud. The Nordics had detonated a huge nuclear weapon along the coastline. Ground Zero appeared to be the AtlantiCorp facility at Hakone. In my mind's eye, I suddenly saw Ghislaine turning to a cinder in the bunker faster than she could comprehend what was happening. The Olympians probably did not know the exact location of the hybrid lair beneath Lake Ashi, but they rightly thought that it must be close to our compound. They used a very high-yield nuke (probably in the tens of megatons range) to make sure that the blast wave was as penetrating and expansive as possible. I collapsed into the arms of the hybrids, who did their best to comfort me, although I could sense that they were mourning the loss of their kindred with as much emotion as they were capable of showing.

Before I knew it, we had passed through the stratosphere. The horizon of Earth bent into a bow, and then became a glowing blue globe beneath us. The star-studded blackness seemed especially vast, maybe because of the emptiness in my own lacerated heart or maybe just because it had been so many years since I was last in space that I had forgotten how devouring that darkness is. Once I was able to finally pull myself together, one of the hybrids held my hand and led me over to the two shapeshifters. At this point, they looked more like grays than owls or mantids. Their slanted big, black, almond-shaped eyes stared into mine, as their heads ticked back and forth on the long stalks of their necks. When they would put the talons of their four-fingered hands to their pointy chins, they looked like they were deep in reflection. One of them reached out and put its hand on my shoulder. Another placed its leathery palm on my forehead, with its nails almost piercing the skin under my hair. I winced. They smelled like sulfur and cinnamon.

Without my having to explain anything to them, they knew what I was thinking. They had probably known who I really was from the time that we began to build the facility at Hakone. For all I know, on some level, maybe they even summoned me there subconsciously — or the hybrids did. The interest that Ikiru showed in Jason was not hap-hazard or incidental. He had been sent to find and befriend Jason in Hakone Forest for a reason. I had to admit that I was dealing with time travelers so primordially ancient and adept that the project I initiated in Gotham must have seemed like a fool's errand to them. Now, it was time to try again, without being so foolishly optimistic.

They read from my mind that I thought I should go back to New York in June of 1978, after the spearhead team that I had sent from Gotham in 2112 had arrived but a couple of years before Nikolai com-mitted suicide. I think that the whole plan that formed rapidly in my mind became just as quickly transparent to them, and maybe they even saw around the edges of it better than I was able to. In any case, it appeared that they approved this as the best remaining course of action. I could tell that from the way they were looking at each other, together with the emotional tonality of the telepathic impressions that I was receiving from them as they probed my mind.

I clairvoyantly discerned that in 1978 they had a hybrid lair (like the one in Hakone) located in the Hudson Valley of New York. They would go there, after dropping me off in Avalon Park on Long Island. In fact, I could see from what they were thinking that they planned to beam me down right into the labyrinth overlooked by the statue of Prometheus. These masquerading marauders were, after all, not without a flair for theatricality. Despite their superficially expressionless faces and indecipherable eyes, they were the greatest of all tricksters.

When the hybrids and the grays slid into the biomechanical pods that interlinked them with the Artificial Intelligence of the ship, I psychically caught glimpses of the telepathic communication between them and the sentience of this living vessel. The method that they used for time travel was quite different from that of the spatiotemporal warp drive of the saucer that I had piloted from Gotham of 2112. Now, as we jumped from Hakone in 2010 to New York in June of 1978, it felt like I was being carried within the belly of a beast that was performing a feat more akin to astral projection or telekinetic teleportation. I could even sense the distress of the Leviathan itself, as it — as *she* — left the element of her own epoch and swam into the dark night of time.

CHAPTER 22

HOMECOMING

The ship's vertical beam of light illuminated the green oxidized copper of the statue of Prometheus chained to the rock. Then it retracted, and the Leviathan disappeared into the darkness above me in the direction of the Hudson Valley. I could tell from the hue of the sky that it was a couple of hours before dawn. I walked all the way through the woods from the labyrinth at the heart of the park to the edge of the property that my team of time travelers should by now have acquired as the site for constructing Avalon Pharmaceutical. I was still wearing the suit from the press conference at Shinjuku. I took off the jacket because I was trying not to soak through my shirt with any more sweat. I could already smell myself. The sun rose as I approached the gate, and I hoped that, since it was a weekday, Johnny and company would be showing up shortly.

At the gate's security outpost, I saw a face that was most welcome. I started to tear up. Johnny had never told me just when he had hired Jean-Pierre. He must have been one of the first people in the group that would eventually constitute AtlantiCorp, who had been brought on board here and now rather than sent back from 2112. Jean-Pierre opened the metal meshed gate with the push of a button and then unhurriedly — almost apprehensively — came out of the guard post to look long and hard into my face, without my saying a word. When he gripped his chin with his hand contemplatively, smiling ever so slightly, I could see that he was already wearing that bone bracelet. "You look *younger* than your picture," he finally said with that deep Creole-tinged voice of his. Before I could offer an explanation, Jean-Pierre added, "Come with me, Ms. Avalon."

The warehouse-like office building was still under construction, with scaffolds set up all over the place, but it seemed that the factory next to it was already operational. A shaft of morning light was shining through one of the windows high up near the ceiling, and I squinted as I sat down at the table of the makeshift office that Jean-Pierre brought me to. He picked up the phone at the other end of the room, too far from me to hear what he said to the person that he dialed. Then he came back and brought me some coffee. I looked at the clock on the wall. It was 7 am. The calendar thumb-tacked near it read, "June 21, 1978."

Before he went back to the gate, Jean-Pierre brought over a large black binder that was labeled "Avalon Pharmaceutical" and set it down in front of me on the small conference table. When I opened it, I saw, together with the construction plans for the site, the already prepared FDA approval forms for our patented formulas to manufacture the drugs that on my timeline were introduced in the 1990s and 2000s under the names Singulair, Crestor, Diovan, Lantus, Nexium, Avastin, Herceptin, Enbrel, Rituxan, Plavix, Viagra, Remicade, Advair, Cialis, Humira, and Lipitor. About a third of them were anti-cancer medications, and quite a few others were relevant to the treatment of heart disease or its contributing factors. Though there was a killing to be made on it, I had ethical objections to producing any of the psychiatric drugs that I knew would become all too popular. I looked at Jean-Pierre a little taken aback that *he* had access to this information and that he was volunteering it to me, just because he seemed to recognize me from a picture of a much older version of myself that Johnny had apparently shown him. Intuitive as always, the Voodoo adept knew what I was thinking and said, "I *know* who you are, Miss.

When Johnny *arrives*, he'll tell you all about me. I run security for the company — *your* company, Miss Avalon."

Johnny arrived about an hour later. I had gone through most of the binder and was on my second coffee. He was shocked to see me, especially to see me looking like *this*. Back in the future Gotham that we came from, Johnny hadn't met me until I was in my early thirties. Now, according to the biological clock of this cloned body, I was about 23. "*Dana*?! What the hell?! You shouldn't be here for another two *years* — and… what… I mean how… are you *so young*?!" He saw that tears began to run down my cheeks and my voice cracked as I said, "Oh Johnny, it's so good to see you again!" My eyes lingered over his curly dark brown hair and northern Italian features. He must have noticed that I was looking at him as if he was back from the dead. "It all went so wrong, Johnny. Our mission — the one that I joined in 1980 — it all went to hell." Johnny looked scared as those words sunk in. "You mean," he said hesitantly, "you're not coming from Gotham in 2112 — *are you*?" "No, Johnny. Japan in 2010, on our revised timeline." He almost breathlessly asked, "Then we… already tried… and…" With an expression of profound sorrow in my eyes, I finished his sentence, "We tried — I tried — and failed miserably. I'll tell you everything. The foundations of the project are sound, but we need to change the mission."

There was a spartan shower in one of the bathrooms of the Avalon Pharmaceutical building. I used it while Johnny quickly went to fetch me a dress and more comfortable shoes from a boutique in Stony Brook. (He didn't get me new underwear, so I just went without wearing any — despite how short the dress was. As for a bra, you know I've never needed one.) Then, Johnny drove me to the woods around Wardenclyffe where we hiked along the Rocky Point trail as I recounted to him as much as I could of what had transpired between 1980 and 2010 in the destroyed world that I had just departed to travel back here. I tried to answer his questions as succinctly as I could so that he did not lose the forest for the trees. By the time we arrived at the ruins of my old laboratory, I think that he had gotten the picture. He was quiet as he watched me plod around the boarded-up building and place my hands somberly on its brick walls. In my mind's eye, I could still see my domed tower that had loomed over it three lifetimes ago.

On our way back to Johnny's parked Jaguar, we began to discuss what to do differently this time. Everything would still need to begin by building up Avalon Pharmaceutical, not just securing FDA approval for the drugs, but also carrying out the insider trading once we were listed on the New York Stock Exchange. I asked Johnny whether the team members tasked with working Wall Street were already in place. He said that they were busy acquiring capital by selling the gold, silver, diamonds, rubies, and emeralds that the team had been provided with in the Gotham of 2112 and had brought with them aboard their flying time machines. Cashing out tens of millions of dollars' worth of precious metals and gemstones without it appearing on the radar of the IRS or other government entities was no small task in the New York City of 1978.

I was a bit dismayed when Johnny confessed to me that our people on Wall Street were already looking to the Mafia for some help in doing this. Gambino, Bonanno, Colombo, Lucchese, and, above all, the Genovese. Johnny Franco, being of Italian descent himself, had moved to establish a working relationship with all of the major families. I had not been aware of the extent to which late 1970s New York was effectively under their control. When I had arrived in 1980, I never inquired into the details of how Johnny had gotten everything into such perfect order so quickly. This time, I would bear witness to all of the gritty machinations myself. In fact, that very first evening that I arrived he had an unbreakable meeting scheduled with a representative of the Genovese family at an abandoned warehouse on Chelsea Piers. He begrudgingly brought me with him, although we decided that I would stay in the car because I wasn't dressed appropriately. We took the 59th

Street Bridge into Manhattan. The descending sun was glinting off the spire of the Chrysler Building. It was something else to see this skyline so pristine again, after having seen it destroyed twice now — once by water and once by fire.

After the meeting, which left us with a trunk full of cash-filled briefcases, Johnny brought me home with him. I helped him carry the briefcases up three flights of stairs. Upon arrival here Johnny had moved into a loft apartment between Greene Street and Canal in Soho. There was a view of the Twin Towers from the street in front of the gray building. There were boutiques nearby, which weren't closed for the evening yet, so I went shopping for a provisional wardrobe and some shoes. The two floors of the apartment were connected by a spartan metal spiral staircase, behind the small kitchen and dining room area. Johnny moved downstairs, sleeping on the pullout sofa, so that he could guard the door, and he gave me the makeshift 'bedroom' on the top floor while I began negotiating to buy out the owner of the Penthouse of 55 Central Park West.

There was no full-length wall enclosing the top floor, just one that came up to waist length and let you rest your elbows on it while looking over the living room downstairs. When I would stand at the closet to dress in the morning, I would sometimes see Johnny folding the couch up and greet him even though I was still topless. He knew that I always slept naked and, in the oppressive summer heat of this apartment with its insufficient air-conditioning, sometimes above the covers. I wondered how often he was tempted. Occasionally, we would go out to see movies together at the Cinema Village. The first of them, later that summer, was *Eyes of Laura Mars*. Afterwards, I bought the vinyl record of the soundtrack with the Barbra Streisand song "Prisoner."

Johnny had to accelerate the process of assembling the dossier of expertly forged documents that constituted my fabricated biography as a late twentieth-century business woman. How much younger I looked this time would be a problem for what kind of bio had originally been planned, and it had to be significantly paired down. While the DeLorean prototype that I had ordered was being refitted with its black leather interior and painted matt black, Jean-Pierre was pulled off of security at Avalon Pharmaceutical to drive me around in his Fleetwood Series Seventy-Five Cadillac with bulletproof tinted windows.

One of the first business meetings that he drove me to was with our team members tasked with insider trading on the rising stock of Avalon Pharmaceutical. Our company was about to be listed on the NYSE as a publicly traded corporation, and they were already set up at an office in the skyscraper at One Chase Manhattan Plaza (28 Liberty Street) in the Financial District. The "Group of Four Trees" sculpture in front of the entryway was rather grotesque, but somehow it had been among the few salvaged pieces of monumental modernist sculpture from Manhattan that we had on display in Gotham. So it was strangely nostalgic for me. Once the company *was* listed, I certainly couldn't show up here. But the SCIF beneath the pharma company on Long Island hadn't been completed yet, so I took the risk of meeting them at their office. Someone from the office came down to bring me up so that I would not have to log my name in the lobby. At the meeting we discussed the specifics of how shell companies and off-shore bank accounts would be used to move the expected profits from stock trading on Avalon Pharmaceutical into a new corporation that would ultimately be set up as its parent company, namely AtlantiCorp.

The night of the day in October that Avalon Pharmaceutical went public on the NYSE and its rapidly rising stock began to be traded on Wall Street, bolstered by media coverage of the maverick new drug company, I invited Johnny to come with me to Studio 54 to celebrate. The place was really in its heyday. We dressed in the height of 70s fashion and pretended not to know each other, so that we would have a better chance of getting in than if we were mistaken for a couple. The bouncer hurried me into the broad black doors, and my heart began to race as "Stayin' Alive" by the Bee Gees got louder and louder once I walked through the entry hallway and past the coat check. The rainbow spotlights were glinting off the large pieces of silver glitter coming down from the ceiling in a steady stream. When he finally caught up with me at the bar, I poked fun at Johnny for having had to stand out there in the jostling crowd for an hour after I got in.

Once we had done a couple of lines of coke — the stuff was being passed around there like candy — we started playing a dangerous game together. We decided to try to hunt for a girl who we thought would want to fuck both of us if we brought her back to the loft in Soho. I say dangerous because Johnny and I had never been in a situation like that together before, and there was at least some risk of how it might affect the rapport of camaraderie between us. Around 2 am, we found our girl. Haggling with him over a few that we rejected was fun. This one danced to the disco music between our two bodies for a while in a way that clued us into the fact that she was the right choice. We threw the broad in the back of the Fleetwood Cadillac and climbed in on either side of her, with Jean-Pierre as our designated driver. I glanced at him in the rearview mirror and was astonished to see that he was actually struggling to suppress a smile. When I giggled at him in response, Jean-Pierre finally let himself look me in the eye and lick his lips with a little affirming nod. In my head I could hear him say, "You're something else, lady."

Johnny and I really did a number on that girl together. Afterwards, her immovable body was strewn across the entire pullout sofa. I took Johnny by the hand and brought him upstairs with me. We made a nightcap at my minibar and drank our cold-as-fuck olive-studded Martinis as we surveyed our collaborative conquest with our elbows resting on the barrier overlooking the living room. We even poured a bit down onto her body to see if it would bring her back to consciousness. Nope. We hoped we wouldn't have to call Genovese in the morning. While laughing and holding onto each other's naked bodies, we fell into my bed and slept like the dead.

Much to the chagrin of Jean-Pierre, I would often insist on taking long walks through neighborhoods — at least during the daytime. Sometimes he would try to tail me, because he was responsible for my safety, and I would lose him by rushing down into the subway. Riding in the graffiti-filled cars was invigorating, even and especially when the men who would eye me from my heels to my scarlet lips also made it dangerous. The suit pants I usually wore made it possible to fight, or run, if I ever had to. I had resolved to hit the streets of Manhattan and become of one element with them more than during the first ill-fated take of this time-traveling mission. But if I kept eating pretzels and hot dogs from the Sabrett vendor carts, which I took a particularly perverse pleasure in doing, I knew I would mar my slim figure with a bit of a pot belly. Then again, my genes had been engineered to keep me leaner for longer than most people and to build muscle mass more quickly when working out — which I did regularly. I was looking forward to moving to 55 West soon, so that I could go back to my routine of jogging in Central Park.

I had resolved not to approach Nikolai until I was situated at my penthouse apartment, but that didn't mean that I couldn't spy on him. I remembered his routine well enough, especially at what hours he would stroll along the boardwalk. So, I went to Coney Island to trail him. As much as I had wanted to take the subway, Jean-Pierre insisted on driving me and I relented. After all, Nikolai had moved there, not just because he was from Brighton Beach, but also on account of the fact that he wanted to stare death in the face and that neighborhood was — short of the South Bronx — the most dangerous part of New York City in the late 1970s.

At first, I kept enough distance between us for him not to notice me. It was August, the zenith of the summer, so the boardwalk was sufficiently crowded for me not to be conspicuous as I shadowed him. But when Nikolai stopped to get a drink at the Atlantis Bar, I ordered one too and sat at a table where I could watch him and take in the sunset at the same time. Words cannot express how uncanny it was to sit there staring at a former incarnation of myself, right there before my eyes in the flesh. I wanted to reach out and touch him. Nikolai had a notepad with him and was jotting something down. Presumably, he was hashing out ideas for that final book, *Invisible Imperium*, which like all of his writings, would remain unpublished. How right the thesis of that book had been. How darkly prophetic.

Nikolai stopped writing, appeared disconcerted for a moment, and then looked straight at me. Our eyes locked. I had been looking at him over the rim of my sunglasses. But when our eyes met, I took them off and placed them on the table in front of me. Doing that felt like stripping. I finished my briny Martini as he watched me. Then, with another gaze straight into his eyes, I got up and walked away. A few paces down the boardwalk, I looked back. Nikolai's eyes were still following me. I doubt it was because he was checking out my legs in this super short dress, with its open back. More likely he was wondering if I was a spy sent by Jack, to extract him from life in hiding and forcibly return him to the Naval Intelligence office in the World Trade Center.

I couldn't wait to bring Nikolai back home with me, so I was relieved that in early September I managed to make a board-approved offer, above the market price, that the owner of the penthouse at 55 Central Park West could not refuse. I had wall-to-wall carpeting installed on both floors of the entire apartment, as was the swank fashion of the time. The furniture that I chose was a combination of Art Deco- and Bauhaus-style pieces. Johnny shook his head at how much I paid for the sofa, chairs, and some of the floor lamps. At least the vault did not have to be built into the library that already lined the walls of the turret on the roof, because I did not have any of the reams of documents and photographs that I had brought with me from 2112 the first time that I came here. All of those had been lost when the facility at Hakone was destroyed. I had even left some behind when we evacuated Manhattan to head for the SCIF. Speaking of the SCIF, it is ironic that at the same time that I was doing the interior decoration of my penthouse, construction of that facility hidden beneath Avalon Pharmaceutical was being completed. We used our relationship with the Italian crime families to secure the hardcore pornographic and ultra-violent footage that was to be projected onto the silver screens, as part of the psychic espionage countermeasures. The contractor that had been asked to inscribe the rows of numbers into the concrete walls of the brutalist structure was totally perplexed, but he wasn't being paid so handsomely to ask questions.

In any case, the most expensive element of my interior décor for the penthouse were undoubtedly the paintings. They were mostly surrealist pieces, from Max Ernst and René Magritte, with a couple of Italian Futurist canvases as well. These were not, however, the paintings of greatest personal value to me. I had resolved to acquire those two paintings of Khosrow Yahyai with which I had grown up, and that I held on to, for most of my life as Jason. In the fall of 1978, it was about a decade since they had been painted, but several years before they would wind up in the possession of Fereidun Jorjani. I tracked down Yahyai in Queens and, although he was troubled by how I had ever heard of him, let alone my penchant for those two paintings of his in particular, the amount of money that I offered him for them trumped any apprehension on his part. I hung these Persian paintings on two opposite walls inside the turret, with each one facing the other. I have never seen a more captivating and enigmatically profound work of Persian Modern Art than these paintings. I hesitate to describe them, because they are masterful works of surrealism, and any description will fail to fathom the depth and breadth of polyvalent symbolism that was enfolded in them by Yahyai, who clearly drew from both Persian tradition and modernist forms of expression. Nonetheless, I am compelled to say a few words about these twin paintings.

One of them appears to be of a Sun King whose head is surmounted by that of a Queen. This central axis is flanked by two figures akin to pawn chess pieces, abstract and alien. Let us not forget that the painter was the co-author of the *Star Child* script that wound up becoming the film *E.T.* The extraterrestrial element is clearly discernable here, especially in the many inhuman eyes that stare out at you from every part of the painting — as if the paws and the body of the Sun King are akin to multi-eyed jellyfish. Their bodies end in something that is like a single claw or paw, also inhuman in appearance. In the eyes of the King and Queen are desolate desert sands.

This is also true of the eyes of the princess or royal concubine in the companion painting. She has two chains attached to her, one at her waist and one on her ankle. The one dangling from the ankle has a ringing bell at the end of it. Is she being prevented from escape by an alarm that would be sounded if she were to run, or is the bell to summon her servants because what chains her is actually her apparent power over others who are bound to be her slaves? Perhaps she is not just a prisoner, but a woman who once was in bondage but eventually overpowered the Sun King and became that Queen that ensconces his head and body within her own. The buttocks, thighs, and legs of the woman in the companion painting are full of the same alien eyes as well, and her feet are also those demonic-looking paws. In my life as Jason, they always reminded me of the paws of Zuul — the terror dog that is the minion of Gozer in *Ghostbusters*. The companion painting, in particular, is full of small symbols that look like indecipherable hieroglyphics. They are all over the cushion-like greenish shape that the slender body of the enchained princess is leaning into, and above which her tentacle-like long neck twists up into her face with its despairing demeanor.

The first night that I spent at 55 Central Park West, I turned on my projector TV and watched news coverage of the large-scale protests against the Shah that had begun in Iran. At that time, no one knew where this was headed — but I did. This time, I would not try to stop it or twist it in any other direction. As I discussed with Johnny on that long walk in the woods around Wardenclyffe, I had learned a hard lesson that my thesis about preventing the fall of the Soviet Union (including by securing Iranian oil for the USSR) was mistaken. My whole way of thinking about resisting the Olympians through the gargantuan structure of two nuclear-armed global superpowers, namely the United States and the Soviet Union, had to be reexamined. It is true that, on my timeline, the fall of the Soviet Union was eventually followed by the disintegration of the United States, and China rose to fill the vacuum of power as a global hegemon, eventually handing Earth over to the "Ancestors" as the Nordics appeared to the Chinese from their Confucian perspective. But instead of investing so much time and energy into trying to save the USSR, what if the same amount of effort were put into breaking China well in advance of its rise as a hegemon? What if the best defense against an Olympian takeover of the planet was actually a fractious world with multiple decentralized nodes of resistance in the name of Liberty and Independence? What if the right model was not hemispheric superpower collaboration on a global scale, aiming at an eventual Prometheist World Order, but rather a movement modeled on piracy and partisan warfare? Prometheus was, after all, a pirate — the first and greatest of all pirates.

I thought of Coney Island. It was time. If I waited any longer, Nikolai might go so deep down the hole of suicidal depression that even I would never be able to pull him out. Here is an apparent time travel paradox for you. How can I save Nikolai from drowning himself, if that means that Jason Reza Jorjani is never born, which in turn means that I cannot come to be as a reincarnation of both of them? Well, it *would* mean that Nikolai could not be reborn as the son of Fereidun Jorjani and Susan Power. But there was no real paradox about how I could be here to do this deed. The informational structure of the quantum computational Cosmos was such that, whenever a time traveler crossed from one timeline into another, and made changes, the "code" of the traveler (DNA, memories, etc.) was copied into the active matrix while the world that she came from was rendered inactive in the form of statically archived information. The latter is what the Indian philosophers called "the Akashic record" or what game designers in the future (from the perspective of 1978) would conceive of as a "past state of play" in an archivable and re-playable multi-player role-playing game. Coney Island came to mind again, specifically its amusement park with its arcades, funhouses, and halls of mirrors, under the shadow of the Wonder Wheel.

This time I did not let Jean-Pierre drive me. In fact, I said nothing of it to him or to Johnny. Besides, my specially ordered DeLorean prototype had just arrived — refitted to specifications, with a matt black exterior and black leather interior upholstery. So, I drove right up to the projects where Nikolai was hiding out, and I lurked there waiting for him to take his usual route out to the boardwalk for his afternoon and evening stroll. As soon as I saw him come out of the side door that he typically used, which happened to be near the parking lot, I pulled right up next to him. Then I popped the winged door of the DeLorean open on the passenger side. He looked right at me, as I rolled down my window. "Get in the car!" I commanded.

Nikolai stared at me fixedly, at first somewhat taken aback, although, to his credit, apparently not at all scared. I had forgotten how *az jan gozashe* he already was at this point (that's an untranslatable Persian expression that loosely means something like "having left life behind"). Then, as I kept staring straight into his eyes, without saying another word, I saw him smirk a bit, as if he was either impressed or amused. I could faintly read his mind as he thought to himself, *Well, if she's here to kill me, I'll take this death.* Then, I smiled back at him with a twinkle in my eye. Nikolai walked slowly over to the passenger side of the car and climbed in. His smirk turned into a smile as the door wing came down and closed next to him automatically. He turned to look at me, pondering what his next words would be. "My name is Dana Avalon, and I'm *not* here to kill you," I said, preempting him. "On the contrary, Nikolai..." I didn't finish that sentence. Instead, I turned on the tape deck, which I had preprepared with a cassette of King Crimson's "In the Court of the Crimson King." He sat back into the black leather and listened to it as I drove us to Manhattan like a bat out of hell.

CHAPTER 23

EYES IN THE DARK

I almost couldn't believe that I had Nikolai Alexandrov in my apartment. I kept wanting to touch him to reassure myself that this was really happening, but I held myself back because I didn't want to creep him out any more than he already must have been. He wandered around aimlessly for a bit, taking in the place, and occasionally looking over at me while I made him the kind of vodka Martini that I knew was his favorite drink. I made one for myself too. I held both cocktail glasses in my hands, as my eyes told him to follow me up the stairs to the turret library.

Before even moving into the apartment, while the wall-to-wall carpeting was still being put in, I had gone to the Strand in the Village and bought myself a huge collection of books that the store had delivered here. These now lined the shelves in the library along the interior walls of the turret, around the fireplace. It helped that most of the Strand's books were used, so their spines were already worn. Nikolai surveyed them, not casually, but with the manner of a detective — almost as if his life depended on it. This would be his first tangible clue as to what manner of dangerous person I might be, and what business I had snatching him up off the sidewalk like that. The multi-volume Loeb classics sets of Plato and Aristotle, which included the original Greek, Hegel's *Phenomenology of Spirit*, Heidegger's *Being and Time*, Bergson's *Time and Free Will* together with his *Creative Evolution*, the complete works of Nietzsche, the novels of Kafka and Dostoyevsky, tomes on the

science of Parapsychology, such as Edgar Mitchel's *Psychic Exploration*
and Sheila Ostrander's *Psychic Discoveries Behind the Iron Curtain*, the
Futurist writings of F. M. Esfandiary and, of course, Gerald Feinberg's
The Prometheus Project were all among the books that he was looking
over.

Nikolai had barely surveyed the spines of a third of the books
when he turned around and looked me straight in the eyes. His expression was one of suspicion mixed with irresistible intrigue. I extended
my hand toward him, and he took his cocktail glass from me. Then I
opened the door to the terrace, and we walked out onto it, careful not
to spill our Martinis. He followed me to the wall that you could lean
on to overlook Central Park, and after he had a moment to take in the
blanket of trees and the skyline of the Upper East Side and Central Park
South at sunset, we clinked our glasses and began sipping our drinks.
I took in his features. Unlike Jason Reza Jorjani, of whom there were
many photographs and even portrait paintings in the time that I come
from, not a single photograph of Nikolai Alexandrov had survived
even into Jason's time, let alone mine. I was astonished at how similar
we actually looked. His hair was darker, and his eyes were greener. He
had level eyebrows. But otherwise, much of our bone structure and
features were as close as those of a woman could be to those of a man.
He was a little taller than me, but not awkwardly so. I wondered if he
also noticed the resemblance. I got the psychic impression that he had
and that even from the moment when I drove up in the DeLorean this
was one 'reason' why he was so intrigued as to let himself be abducted
by me. Now, after seeing this apartment, and the books…

Nikolai looked as if he were trying to formulate something to
say, but he stopped and smiled, as if to concede that he was at a loss
for words. Instead, he looked back over Central Park. So, I took the
lead. "Do you know who I am?" He was somewhat surprised by the
question. "I know you have an excellent intuition, Nikolai. More than
intuition, considering that work you do — or used to do. You know

that you didn't just get into my car when I told you to because I look like a hotter version of you as a woman," I said as I laughed disarmingly. "Who am I, Nikolai? Tell me." Now he was smiling too, but also wincing somewhat. As he stared at me, sipping his Martini, I saw the expression of astonishment slowly creep across his face, and the look in his eyes turn from intrigue to wonder. "No," he said, "it *can't* be." I replied, "*Why* can't it be?"

"Do you have a cigarette?" he asked. I had forgotten that by now he was becoming a chain smoker. "I'm sorry, I haven't smoked for a couple of lifetimes," I answered apologetically, but also as a way to volunteer another clue. "I promise to have a few packs here for you next time you come over," I added. "But, you know, there are quicker ways to kill yourself than becoming a chain smoker." He replied, "Such *as*?" I said, "Such as walking off Brighton Beach into the Atlantic to drown yourself late one night." He wasn't smiling anymore. I had meant him, but he was thinking of Anna. "I'm sorry, I wasn't thinking of her. But of course, that's why you chose that method of suicide, because it's how she killed herself before you did." I could see the muscles in Nikolai's face getting really tense, and he rested his cocktail glass against the wall of the roof because his hand was starting to tremble a bit.

"Don't play *games* with me, lady. Who the *fuck* are you?!" He didn't actually say that. But I heard him think it. So, I said, "Nikolai, come on. You *know* who I am. After all you've seen, and where you've been — I mean, where Cybele took you — the memories that came back to you in those nights at the Hotel New Yorker, why is it so hard for you to believe that what your gut tells you could be true?" Nikolai breathed a sigh of frustration as he looked away from me and his eyes slowly scanned the buildings across the park from us, with the lights in their windows coming on now as dusk settled over Manhattan.

"You're *me*," he finally said. "Yes." Then he asked, "From… the *future*???" "Yes, Nikolai. *Two* lifetimes into the future." "What did you say your name was again, Dana…" "…Avalon." Nikolai pondered for

PSYCHOTRON

a moment and then smiled with an expression that suggested he was enjoying an inside joke. "That's clever. Did you come up with that your-self?" I leaned back into the wall, with my elbows resting on it, and said, "Well, Avalon really *was* my father's name, and that of his construction company. I think I might have insistently whispered 'Dana' into my mother's mind before I was born. You know what it means, then?" "Oh yes. From the ancient Persian *Daena* and the ancient Greek *Dianoia*, for 'inner knowing' as in 'conscience' or 'wisdom.' The Persians and the Scythians depicted her — she was always female — as a guardian angel, Valkyrie-like." He could probably tell that I was looking at him a bit adoringly. "You know, on the timeline that I come from, after you com-mit suicide, you're reborn as a man who is half Persian." He processed the part about him committing suicide all too quickly and then asked, "In Iran?!" "No, *here*. In New York." He squinted and nodded delibera-tively. "I guess that doesn't surprise me at all. I find their country and culture to be fascinating. I think I've lived past lives as a Persian, too." My rejoinder was, "Indeed, you *have*. Many centuries ago."

"So — what — are you here to save my life or something, Miss Guardian Angel?" he asked sarcastically. It's funny, I could hear the slightest tinge of a lingering Russian accent in how he spoke. I had forgotten how that had stayed with him for all of his brief life. There was also something Russian about his icy wit. "Aren't you afraid of creating some kind of temporal paradox?" he added even more sar-castically. I think the cool sarcasm was a psychological defense. At this point, Nikolai was really becoming afraid. "I mean, if you've saved me from taking my own life by bringing me here, then shouldn't you be disappearing right now or something?"

"You know that's not how time works, Nikolai. Not how time *travel* works." I could see from his changing expression that he was letting down the psychical armor of sarcasm. "I would be very interested in your explaining to me just how it *does* work, Dana, since, as you know, I'm a physicist who has also studied Philosophy." I smiled at him because I couldn't resist the pun, "All in good time, Nikolai." He smirked. But then his expression softened, and I saw an openness in his eyes when he looked into mine. He stroked the stubble on his chin a few times. Then, all of a sudden, Nikolai dropped his cocktail glass on the terrace floor and crushed it with his shoe. He proceeded to gently pry my glass out of my fingers and take a sip from it. We locked eyes. I knew exactly what he meant by that symbolic gesture, and I was impressed by the beauty of it.

I looked down at Tavern on the Green, knowing that he'd follow my line of sight. Then, I looked Nikolai over from head to toe. He had a tendency to dress in an overly formal fashion, even for his strolls along the boardwalk on Coney Island. He already had slacks and a blazer on, with a white shirt unbuttoned a bit down into his chest. All he needed was a tie. "Will you join me for dinner?" I asked. "At *Tavern*?" "Yeah, I can make a reservation for a couple of hours from now and we can go for a stroll around Central Park South and pick you up a tie." It was a Tuesday night, so I knew the reservation should be manageable. Had it been a Friday or Saturday there would have been no way, on such short notice. "Alright, angel," he said, smiling mischievously, "I'd be happy to take you out to dinner at Tavern on the Green."

I shook my head. Of course, I had been thinking that *I* would be the one to take *him* out, but then I remembered what I had been like as a man, and I felt bad for suggesting that we go to one of the most expensive restaurants in the city. "Please, *let me*, you probably didn't even bring your wallet out for that boardwalk stroll that I whisked you away from." He gave me a cocky look, as he pulled out a rubber-banded wad of hundred-dollar bills. "Wallet, *no*. Money, *yes*. I threw away my *wallet* and ID cards quite a while ago." Then, in a flash, I remembered something that I had completely forgotten about the last years of Nikolai's life, in those dangerous projects near the beach and boardwalk, under which so many homeless people lived. He used to — I mean, *I used to* — go around *and get rid of my inherited money* by literally throwing hundred-dollar bills at these bums. It was like something from a Tolstoy story. *What a romantic lunatic I had been!*

Nikolai was probably wondering why I was staring at him like that, slightly appalled, as I remembered that. I snapped out of it and collected myself. "Well — let me go make the reservation, and then we'll head out." He lingered on the terrace as I went inside to place a call from the phone next to the sofa across from the fireplace in the turret library. He was appreciating the magisterial architectural structure of the turret's exterior. Now that it was night, the spotlights were on, and the Gothic/Deco hybrid design details really stood out against the dark sky. When I came back out onto the terrace to tell him we should head out, he said, "It reminds me of King Arthur, Miss *Avalon*. That, and at the same time, some temple of Ishtar on top of a Babylonian ziggurat."

I took a few paces to where he was and turned to take in the structure together with him, standing close enough to Nikolai for our arms to rub against each other. "Yes, it's an epitome of New York architecture at its best. My mother was an architect, you know. We would study buildings like this, as inspiration for constructing the new skyscrapers of Gotham." He looked at me quizzically, "Gotham?" "It's a city that is built to overlook the partially drowned ruins of this one. New York resurrected, on higher ground." He took that in, then asked, "Higher ground? You mean like the Palisades?" I smiled. "Exactly." Nikolai raised his eyebrows and looked at me gravely, "I've had visions of that. Of Manhattan under water up to the thirtieth floor of the Empire State Building, and of another city, a new futuristic city, built along the Palisades and Englewood Cliffs all the way up into the Hudson Highlands." I leaned against the wall of the turret, with my exposed knee bent, as I folded my arms, and said, "It happens. I'm *from* there. From *then*." He asked, "*When*?" "I was born in 2077, and I traveled here from 2112. But it's a long story. I'll tell you everything — in time... Let's head out."

By the time I was tightening the tie around Nikolai's neck, with my hand on his chest, in the boutique along Central Park South, we could both feel the chemistry between us. It was magnetic. Those magnetic currents were bringing this already half-dead young man back to life — back to *this* world. I could see it in his face all throughout dinner, as I told him about my life in Gotham from 2077 to 2112, and a bit about what had taken place to bring that dark world into being. Although fall had recently started, the weather was still pleasant enough to sit outside — so we did. Our table had a view of the whole glass-enclosed Park Room, and Nikolai had pulled his chair around to sit more next to me than across from me, so that we could both people watch all the stuffy types in there chattering away meaninglessly over the white tablecloths. We had another round of Martinis with our steak and seafood. Nikolai had grinned at me, in an almost leering way, when I ordered the oysters. (Look, if he was going to throw hundred-dollar bills at bums...) On our way out, we had a third drink at the bar toward the front of the restaurant, under the impressive wood rafters. So, by the time we were headed back to 55 CPW, we were quite drunk and almost holding on to each other as we plodded across the street to my apartment.

"I'm obviously not driving you back home tonight," I said, when we got back up to the penthouse. "*Obviously,*" said Nikolai, laughing drunkenly. I grabbed his arm and brought him to my bedroom. "Come try out my hot tub, *you'll love it,*" I said as I went into the master bathroom and turned the water on. Then, I shamelessly took all of my clothes off and threw them onto the bed. Nikolai looked at me with an expression more amused than excited, as if he were looking at a colorfully strange child. "Come on," I goaded him, "don't be a bore!" Nikolai took his clothes off, hesitantly, piece by piece, carefully laying them next to mine on the bed. I got behind his back and pushed his naked body, choo-choo train style, into the large bathroom.

When I climbed into the hot tub, I noticed that he was eying my huge clit. I smiled at him impishly as I slid down into the rising water. I guess my hypertrophied clitoris turned Nikolai on rather than putting him off, because he started getting hard as he climbed in after me. He bent his knees and closed his thighs as he settled into the tub. We leaned into each other with our heads propped on one another. I would have loved to have seen our two faces together at that moment. I reached my hand out under the water and he slipped his into it. We held hands for a long time, as our faces beaded up and we could taste the salt of our own sweat on our lips. We kissed gently.

When we started to cozily doze off together in the warmth and the steam, I made the effort of getting us up out of the tub, and lazily half drying off our bodies, before holding onto Nikolai as we went quickly back across my room and climbed under the covers of my bed. Our clothes were still strewn on top of the blanket — some of them sliding onto the floor as we got in. I hit the lights from my bedside dimmer, and we went out almost as soon as they did. Entangled as we slept together in the bed that night, I felt like we were twins.

In the morning for breakfast, I made us toasted bagels with lox and chive cream cheese, which I had picked up at Barney Greengrass. "Listen," I said to Nikolai as we sipped our black coffee, "I have to go to work. *Please* be here when I come home this evening. I'll give you a set of my keys, so you're not shut in all day, and I'll tell the doorman that you're staying with me." Nikolai raised his eyebrows, with his head tilted forward, as he set down the Avalon Pharmaceutical coffee mug. "You trust me *alone* in your apartment, and with *your keys* — after just meeting me *last night*???" I looked at him like he was retarded. "You're *me*, dumbass." I guess that fact was a lot clearer to me than it was to him yet, or maybe ever would be. Nikolai kind of shrugged with his face more than his shoulders, in a rather Russian way, as if to say, "I guess..."

It was hard to focus on any work that day because I was full of angst and trepidation over whether Nikolai actually *would* be there when I got back. Johnny asked me what was wrong, but I didn't want to tell him — at least *not yet*. I made an excuse to leave Long Island and head back to Manhattan a bit earlier than usual. My heart sank at first when I walked into the penthouse and didn't see him anywhere on the first floor. Then, I rushed upstairs. How elated I was to find Nikolai sitting on the sofa in the turret library flipping through *Time and Free Will*. Heidegger's *Being and Time* had also been pulled out and was on the coffee table in front of him. He turned his head and looked up at me, silently and at first expressionlessly. When he saw how happy I was, he smiled.

I walked over to Nikolai and put my hands on his shoulders, rubbing them a bit, as I stood behind him. Then, I ran my fingers through his hair. When he tilted his neck back, I kissed his forehead. "*Privet, moy dorogoy,*" I whispered to him. "You know Russian?" he asked. "I picked up a little — or relearned a bit, I guess — when I worked for decades to prevent the collapse of the Soviet Union. I had a Russian girlfriend for a while back then. Well — a *lover* more than a 'girlfriend.' She worked for me." Nikolai seemed more intrigued by the first statement than the second, but not by *much*. So, after making some black tea for us, and sitting beside him, I included Irena in my account of the first, ill-fated attempt that I had made to alter the timeline that led to the global dominion of the Olympian Imperium in the world that I came from. Nikolai found the tale astonishing, but not batshit crazy — as any normal person would have. In what I described to him that I had tried to do, he saw a lot of himself. "It's what I would have done," he said to me, consolingly, when I lamented about how foolish I had been to think that plan would have worked. I looked at Nikolai somewhat apologetically as I replied, "It *is* what you *did* do." He stared at the coffee table and while nodding wearily he said, "Right." Then, he asked, "What about the other one? Is it what *he* would have done, too? The incarnation after me, and before you. What was he like?" So, I started to tell Nikolai about Jason, and the more I told him the more he wanted to know.

Nikolai eventually agreed to move out of that housing project that he was hiding out in, and to move what few possessions he had left at that point into my penthouse. I finally told Johnny what had been going on, and although he was concerned, he accepted it. It was not 1980 yet, but still, it appeared that Nikolai Alexandrov would not commit suicide by drowning himself off Coney Island after all.

Late in that fall of 1978, when it began to snow just a couple of hours to the north of the city, I suggested that we go skiing at Hunter Mountain together. I remembered his history at Scribner, and I wondered whether making those memories resurface would mar the potentially revitalizing effect of hitting the slopes again. Nikolai was very much in favor of the idea, though, and in fact he insisted that we stay at Scribner Hollow Lodge. He wanted to poke around the woods in the back of the property, behind where his aunt's ski house had been, to see whether he could find that trap door that he had never been able to relocate again as a child. Nikolai was always left with a doubt as to whether that subterranean initiation of sorts in the middle of the night was a real experience or just a powerful dream based on actual prepubescent incest. Honestly, I also wanted to go back there myself, regardless of how Nikolai felt, because that hotel had been converted into the alpine lodge that my father and mother lived in as they designed the core structure of Gotham together and it had been our country home during my childhood. I told Nikolai about my childhood experience with the witch and my discovery of the cave where Altomara's ashes were buried.

I drove us up the winding mountain roads in the DeLorean with Blue Oyster Cult's album *Agents of Fortune* playing on the cassette tape deck. Many of the trees in Hunter were still blazing with the fiery colors of fall leaves, but snow was already covering the ground. The further up we went, the deeper it was. It was nightfall by the time we got to Scribner and settled into our room. We were going to buy new skis and boots at the lodge in the morning and get a locker to store them in for the entire season. Since we were hungry, Nikolai and I had dinner together at the hotel restaurant. We sat at a table where we could look through the floor-to-ceiling windows out over the ski slopes on the mountain across from this hilltop. The trails were illuminated by the lights of the snowcats that were grooming them and packing the freshly falling powder.

After dinner we went for a long walk throughout the hotel and the property. First, I showed him all the places inside of the hotel that had been modified in my time — or my parents' time — to turn the place into an alpine chalet and private residence. Then, Nikolai led me outside through the falling snow, with our boots crunching into the powder, and brought me to the ski house unit that had belonged to his aunt. I remembered it as well, from my past life regression sessions in Gotham, although no doubt much less vividly than he did.

I knew that he wanted to keep going, further up the hill, into the woods behind the housing units, to the place where he remembered that trap door having been — the one that led to the subterranean chamber with walls covered in carvings of gorgons and owls. I indulged him, expecting that the place was something from a dream — or nightmare. But lo and behold! Not all that far into the trees, we came upon somewhat of a clearing, where Nikolai got down on his hands and knees, scraping the snow off of what felt like wood rather than earth beneath our feet. There it was. The metal lock that had frustrated his attempts to get back in here as a child had by now rusted to the point where, when I gave it a few hard kicks, it broke right off. We grabbed the part of it attached to the door, being careful not to slice through our ski gloves and cut our hands on the rusted metal. When we got the door open, the musty smell that came at us from out of the place was almost unbearable. It was tinged with some scent between sulfur and cinnamon. As I started down the steps with Nikolai behind me, I stopped dead when I remembered where I had smelled that before. It was the same scent that I smelled at the end of the stone vagina tunnel that the witch had made me crawl into, the smell inside the kurgan shaped room at the end of that tunnel, where that *thing* touched me. I also remembered what the shapeshifters had told me about their lair in the Hudson Valley.

I turned around and looked Nikolai in the eyes. Seeing me suddenly afraid made him even more apprehensive. But we persisted, turning on the two flashlights that we had brought with us to finish descending the crumbling steps. As the flashlight beams moved across the earthen walls, I saw them — just as he had described them. The insane Dionysiac designs of gorgons, owls, and other indiscernible insects and tentacled things. While Nikolai was examining these designs with his flashlight, I pointed the one that I was holding into the distance to try to gauge the depth of this place. What the beam caught horrified me. I only saw it for a moment, but I was so scared that I backed into Nikolai while gripping my chest. I dropped my flashlight, and it broke.

I grabbed Nikolai by the arm, and as the beam of his flashlight illuminated the terrified expression on my face, he let me practically push him up the stairs ahead of me, tripping a couple of times, until we got out. I threw the wooden door to the subterranean chamber closed with great force before he even had a chance to help me. I made Nikolai walk back to Scribner with me as fast as we possibly could in the snow. I mean we practically ran. It was not until we were in the hot tub of the grotto under the hotel later that night, after everyone else had cleared out, that I was able to talk about what I had seen illumined by my flashlight beam. I told Nikolai that it was his face, and yet not his face. "You mean a doppelganger of me?" he asked. "Those are harbingers of death," he said as he looked grimly at the plaster decorative rock over and around the hot tub. We were whispering to each other because the pool's bartender, who had brought us over the drinks that we had beside our elbows, was still down here in the Scribner Grotto. (In fact, he looked annoyed that we were staying down here so late.)

"No, Nikolai. I mean — not exactly. I've *seen* that face before. Remember when I was telling you about the Latin American Reich that rose up in the days when Jason, Ghislaine, and I took refuge at our facility in Hakone?" He nodded affirmatively. "What I didn't tell you — because it was just too weird, and I didn't want you to... well, the leader of that nascent Imperium had *that* face. It was like your face, but older. Also, the expression was different — especially his eyes." Now Nikolai was the one who looked horrified. I added, "His name was Adolfo von Seelstrang. He was supposedly an Argentinian of German ancestry. But to be frank, the man's past was shrouded in mystery. I know what manufactured biographies look like, since I've had them put together for me. I don't think that guy was just the mining magnate from Bariloche that they claimed he was."

Nikolai said that he felt ill and wanted to go back upstairs to our room at once. He had remembered something but did not want to tell me until we were alone. Once we were warming up on the bearskin rug in front of the fire in our suite, wearing nothing but the hotel bathrobes bundled around ourselves, with our glasses of cognac resting on the brick of the fireplace, Nikolai finally opened up about it. He reminded me of one of the strangest of his many uncanny experiences in youth. The night that he had sex with his aunt in that strangely vacant hotel in Italy. He seemed embarrassed to talk about it, and I had to remind him that I *was* him and that they were my memories *too*, just buried deeper in my subconscious on account of the lifetimes that had elapsed for me since then. Finally, he spit it out. The weird flask that his aunt had collected his sperm in the first time that he had come, in that hotel room, when he woke up in the morning, it was missing from the bedside table that she had put it on before they went to sleep. It was then that, following what Nikolai was trying to tell me, I realized for the first time who exactly Adolfo von Seelstrang must have been. It sent a shudder through my spine. He was a clone of Nikolai.

I was so distraught that night that I forgot to use any birth control before Nikolai got into bed with me. In my old body, I had a sophisticated nanotechnological birth control device implanted into my arm. I had done this by choice in my twenties, back in Gotham. But when I was cloned at the lair beneath Lake Ashi, this obviously hadn't carried over to my new body. Besides, I mostly slept with women. So, on the rare occasion that I thought I might have sex with a man, I figured that I would use a diaphragm with contraceptive gel. I had only done that once so far, since arriving here in June of 1978. That night when Johnny and I went to Studio 54 together, I had taken precautions in advance. As it turned out, the effectiveness of this method was never tested because although we fucked the hell out of that girl that we brought back to his loft that night, it's not like Johnny himself came inside me or even really had intercourse with me directly.

In any case, after what we had just been through, birth control was not a thought that even crossed my mind as me and Nikolai tried to console each other in bed that night at Hunter Mountain. In the months up until then, while we had occasionally been turned on by each other, we had mostly lived together like twin siblings. But that night, we made love more passionately — and more desperately — than I'd ever been with a man before in my entire life. We clung to each other for dear life, and Nikolai came inside me almost as many times as I came. The ecstasies were transcendental, and during the most intense of them I left my body and looked down at us from under the ceiling for a few moments, until Nikolai's kisses and bites brought me back into my skin.

Maybe we should have fled back to the safety of Manhattan, but for whatever reason we stayed, bought our equipment as planned, and skied Hunter together for most of the next day. Somehow the adrenaline of carving our way down K-27 together, with crisscrossing

ski lines, was therapeutic in dealing with the terror of the night before. What I *did* do was very discretely bring the sniper rifle, which
I had bought shortly after my arrival in June, from the trunk of the
DeLorean into the hotel room with us. I covered it in the emptied bag
that had held my new skis. As irrational as it seemed to my analytical
mind, I was consoled by having the gun at our bedside and I could tell
that Nikolai was also.

It was about 2:30 am when I woke up suddenly, startled by reaching
into empty space on the side of the bed where Nikolai's warm body had
been when we fell asleep together. I jumped out of bed and went to the
bathroom to see if he was in there. He wasn't. My heart sank. I noticed
that the screen door to the terrace was partly open. It may even have
been the cold that woke me up enough to notice that he was missing
from beside me. When I turned on the terrace light, I could see that
there were tracks in the snow leading away from a deep impression
right below our room. I put my ski clothes and jacket back on as fast as
I could, and I grabbed not only the flashlight, but also the sniper rifle
from the bedside. I couldn't very well go walking through the hotel
with that, and I didn't want to be encumbered by the ski bag that I had
hidden it in. So, I decided to jump off the second-floor terrace. It was
an easy jump, and once I had made it, I noticed that the tracks leading
away from the depression that someone else had made in the snow
before me, were *two sets* of tracks. One of a man who was walking on
his own, and another of a man who, judging from the marks, appeared
to have been dragged at least part of the way.

I followed the tracks. My heart sank as I realized that they were
leading, through the woods, back to the trap door in the clearing up
the hill. As much as I was desperate to find Nikolai, I started moving
more slowly, already afraid of what I might actually find. I raised the
sniper rifle — pointing it ahead of me, bending my knees, as I paced
forward through the snow that was a lot deeper than it had been the
night before. As I reached the clearing, I almost dropped the rifle to

reach for my flashlight because I couldn't believe my eyes. The sight that confronted me was clear enough in the moonlight, though, and there was no way that I was going to put this gun down. There, right over the open trap door, was Adolfo von Seelstrang holding Nikolai Alexandrov up by the collar of his pajamas, as if Nikolai were a ragdoll and von Seelstrang were made of steel. Nikolai looked lifeless, although I could see — or I thought I could see — some movement in his eyes that suggested he was trying to look at me. His face was twisted, and frozen, into an expression of despairing resignation. I could not see von Seelstrang's face as clearly, because his back was mostly to me.

I moved very slowly to an angle that gave me a line of sight that I thought would put Nikolai out of danger, and I tried my hardest to steady my hand despite my heart beating out of my chest. Then I shot straight at von Seelstrang. For a sniper rifle, this was practically point-blank range. There was a silencer on the barrel, so the shot barely echoed in the woods. For a moment, I didn't know what I was seeing in front of me. Then, as things came back into focus, I saw that Nikolai was laying there in the snow — alone — in his pajamas, with blood pouring out of his chest. There was no Adolfo von Seelstrang any-where in sight. I ran over to Nikolai, horrified, and screaming — more shrieking, really, when the sound would even come out of my throat. Between the hypothermia and the gunshot wound, he was gone. I felt for his pulse. I breathed into his mouth and pounded on his chest. Nothing. I sat there weeping over Nikolai's corpse until I nearly froze to death myself. Then, with my assassin's mind coming back on line, I realized that I couldn't very well bring him back to the hotel or explain this away to anyone who wouldn't have me arrested. So, as my tears kept freezing on my cheeks, I opened the trap door and slid Nikolai's body down the steps, together with the sniper rifle that had somehow blown him away.

CHAPTER 24

THE SACRIFICE

I have never been more single-minded than in the weeks that followed that horrific night at Hunter. Nikolai had in some inexplicable way been killed by Adolfo von Seelstrang and so I was intent on hunting down that man who disappeared like a specter in the snow. By the time that I arrived in San Carlos de Bariloche, I was two months pregnant. Soon, it would start to show. I had decided to keep the baby growing inside of me, not only because it was all that I had left of Nikolai but, to be honest, because I strongly believed that he would choose to reincarnate as my child — as *our* child — thereby becoming his own father and, in a sense, his own mother from the future. Of course, that would also mean that Jason Reza Jorjani would never be born.

It was January of 1979. Located in the Andes Mountains, in northern Patagonia, the Bavarian-style village was cold. The only person who I had told about all of this was Johnny because I needed his help using the resources of the nascent AtlantiCorp to gather enough intelligence to be effective once I arrived in Argentina. We had more or less tracked down von Seelstrang. He was a 21-year-old student studying at the University of Buenos Aires, but at the moment he was back home with his family in Bariloche during the winter break between semesters. I kept asking myself how the von Seelstrang that I saw that night, both down in the subterranean chamber and then holding Nikolai up over the chamber's trap door the night after, was the fifty-something-year-old-looking man that I had first seen when, in Hakone in 2010, me and Ghislaine were watching news coverage of the rise of the Latin American Reich.

Ultimately, it did not make much difference to me. I was going to kill this bastard, no matter how old — or how young — he was now, and no matter how much he looked like Nikolai. Actually, the resemblance was even more motivating to me. It made me see him as a monstrosity, as if he — or whatever Frankenstein made him — had stolen Nikolai's face, *my* face (of two lifetimes ago), to use as a mask for the future leader of the Fourth Reich.

Our intelligence had shown that Adolfo would go skiing with his family at Cerro Catedral, a ski resort in the mountains only 19 kilometers (12 miles) from his hometown of San Carlos de Bariloche. You could see the town from the top of the mountain, which also had a spectacular view of the Andes range. Targeting von Seelstrang while he was skiing had some poetic justice to it, considering the circumstances under which he had spectrally abducted and murdered Nikolai during our ski trip to Hunter Mountain. I did not bring my sniper rifle all the way to Argentina. We did not have the AtlantiCorp private jet yet, so I was not about to check a sniper rifle together with my luggage when I flew first class on Pan Am. Instead, what I had with me, besides my ski gear, was a plastic gun in several pieces that could be easily assembled, and that fired fast-acting and absolutely lethal poison darts. It was a real assassin's weapon.

I rented a chalet close enough to that of the von Seelstrang family (who knows who they really were) that I was able to spy on Adolfo with my high-powered binoculars. So I knew when he was headed to the slopes. I trailed him in my rental Mercedes. After we parked, I carefully kept enough distance from him so as not to be noticed as I carried my ski gear up to the lift area, snapped my skis on, and got on the chairlift a couple of chairs behind him. Once we reached the summit, I followed Adolfo to the relatively steep trail that he chose to start his day with. I was pleasantly surprised at how steep the trail was, because once I hit him with the poison dart his fall down this slope would be so bad that he might also break his neck.

I didn't wait around to find out, though. He was about halfway down the trail, and I was a couple of meters behind him, when I shot him in the exposed side of his neck with the dart gun. I held on to the weapon, only discarding it on the roadside, in deep snow and between some trees, when I was headed back to the airport in San Carlos de Bariloche. I had already packed the very light luggage that I brought with me, so there was no need to return to the chalet near his family, who would soon be informed of his "accident." I saw him reach to pull out the dart, just before I skied past him, and practically bombed the rest of the run. So, unless they did an autopsy (which, considering who they were, they might do), it is possible that his death would just be chalked up to how badly he had fallen down that double black diamond.

On the way back, I had to change planes in Buenos Aires, just as I had on the way to Bariloche. When my flight got into JFK in the middle of the night, Jean-Pierre was there to pick me up in the limo and drive me home to 55 Central Park West. I had hoped to get a good night's sleep after such a stressful operation, which I had been planning for so long. Unfortunately, I woke up from a terrible nightmare after only a couple of hours.

In the nightmare, I saw things from the perspective of a little boy, who was only at waist height compared to the adults near him. They were congregated around the open door to a room in some kind of health spa or hospital. Certain of the adults would go into the room, then come out with their heads downcast. The men, who were wearing suits, held their fedora hats in their hands, and some of the women were quietly crying as they came out. The fashion of the women's clothes suggested, even more clearly than the style of the men's suits, that it was probably sometime in the 1960s. I noticed that most of the people were speaking German, but a few were speaking Spanish. These

Spanish speakers looked Argentinian. The other people were very white. So was the boy whose eyes I was seeing through, judging from his hands.

Finally, he accompanied a maternal woman who was holding his hand as she took her turn to enter the room. A sick old man was propped up on pillows in what looked like a hospital bed, and at first it was hard to make out his face because he was being given oxygen by the attendant nurse. The boy was a bit frightened by this sight. There were physicians there too, talking to a couple of people who just stayed in the room while the visitors came and went. The woman patted the boy's back to urge him to walk forward to the old man's bedside. The man reached down with his wrinkled and trembling hand. As the maternal figure put the boy's hand inside the hand of the dying man, the attendant took the oxygen mask off so that — through the eyes of the boy — I was looking right at his face, while feeling the hair-raisingly cold clasp of his hand. Despite his moustache having been shaved off, there was no mistaking him for anyone else. It was the Austrian painter. He looked like he was in his seventies. That's when I woke up gripping my abdomen, where I felt cramps worse than any that I had ever gotten around my period. The cramps went away after I soaked in the hot tub for a while, but I didn't get much sleep for the rest of that night.

In the weeks that followed, as we entered February of 1979, my attention was repeatedly captured by the unfolding events of the Iranian Revolution. As I explained earlier, this time I had resolved to let it take place just as it had on the timeline that I came from rather than to revise events in Iran as I had done on the timeline wherein I saved the Soviet Union from collapse (in large part by engineering Soviet seizure of Iranian oil reserves and Persian Gulf seaports). I was watching news coverage from Iran one evening, when my doorbell rang. I assumed it was the superintendent or maybe building staff bringing up a package that was left for me downstairs, because we had very good security at 55 Central Park West, and nobody got upstairs to someone's apartment without the doorman calling up for them to be cleared. Also, I was intent on getting back to the news report as soon as possible, so I did not call downstairs to ask. Instead, I just went over and looked through the peephole. I couldn't believe my eyes. I backed away from the door for a moment, wondering what I should do. It was Cybele. All six-foot-nine inches of her. She must have found out that Nikolai had been here. I decided to open the door.

"Cybele... how did you..." She looked at me like I was being ridiculous. I dropped the question about how she got past the doorman, and I introduced myself. "I'm Dana Avalon." She smiled politely, and said, "Of course you are. Who else's apartment would I be at?" I felt embarrassed, and nervously said, "Please come in." I was still wearing my suit pants and shirt from work, so at least I was dressed decently, and my makeup was still on too. I gestured for her to follow me up the stairs to the turret library. "Is he still here?" she asked. I glanced back at her. (Dear Lord, she was tall — especially for a woman.) "It's a long story. Please have a seat," I said as we entered the library. "Would you like anything to drink, before I try to explain?" Cybele gave me a long-faced look. "Am I going to need a drink?" she asked. "Well, *I'm* going to need one. Should I make you one too?" She nodded affirmatively. "Martini? Manhattan?" I asked her. "A Manhattan with bourbon would be great, thanks," said Cybele. I had put a minibar in the turret, even though I knew that, now that I was pregnant, I really needed to cut back on my drinking. So, I made us two Bourbon-based Manhattans right there, while Cybele examined my library.

I set down our cocktail glasses on the coffee table in front of the sofa. I also kindled the fire and stoked it with my fireplace tools. Meanwhile, Cybele was looking back and forth at the two paintings by Khosrow Yahyai. Before I sat down next to her on the couch, I pulled Nikolai's manuscripts out of the library, where they had been wedged between certain books that he had brought with him when he vacated that awful apartment that he had on Coney Island. All three of his manuscripts, which had been lost in the timeline wherein he committed suicide, were here — *Being Bound for Freedom*, Nikolai's adaptation of his doctoral dissertation critiquing the Many Worlds Interpretation of quantum mechanics, *Faustian Futurism*, which he wrote under the name Nick Griffin, and that last prophetic work about the Fourth Reich, *Invisible Imperium*. I put these on the table in front of Cybele, so that her cool and nonplussed demeanor finally came apart as the façade that it was. As she reached for them, I sat down next to her. "To Nikolai," I said, as we clinked our glasses and started to sip our drinks. "That's a hell of a Manhattan," said Cybele, after she took her first couple of sips. "Yeah, I've gotten too good at making them," I said. In addition to very high-quality sweet vermouth, I had put just the right amount of orange peel bitters into the bourbon, and I made sure that the ice was so frozen that, when I shook the drink, not too hard or for too long, it didn't melt into the booze and dilute it.

Over the course of the following two or three hours, and another round of drinks (which I really shouldn't have had), I explained to Cybele what had happened to Nikolai — both on the original timeline, and since I picked him up from Coney Island in my DeLorean on that afternoon in September of 1978. She told me that she had come here because she had sensed that Nikolai was in extraordinary danger, and she had clairvoyantly "remote-viewed" him living with me in this apartment with its distinct rooftop architecture. Cybele was very psychic, so she could make a lot of connections without my having to lay everything out explicitly. She was also able to intuit, before I volunteered it, that I was a reincarnation of Nikolai from the timeline wherein he committed suicide in the summer of 1980. Cybele told me that she thought that what happened the night that von Seelstrang abducted Nikolai from Scribner was some kind of psychokinetic astral projection, but she found it just as paradoxical as I did how this could have happened if that older version of Adolfo would never come to be, because only months later I assassinated him in Bariloche when he was still at the age of 21. Cybele also intuited that I was pregnant, and she understood why I believed that the boy (I knew it would be a boy) was going to be a reincarnation of Nikolai, who would choose my womb instead of being reborn as Jason Reza Jorjani.

I never had an easier time talking to another woman, even including Ghislaine. I suppose it was because, like myself, Cybele was not exactly of this world. Although she was not a time traveler from the future, her having one foot in the underworld of the Nordics — and a son who was himself one of the rebel Nordics — gave her access to a society that was similar to the one that had dominated Earth in the time that I came from. In point of fact, not just similar to it, but the embryonic form of the Olympian Imperium. She assured me, as she already had during my life as Nikolai, that her son, Apollyon, intended to resist the Traditionalism of that Imperium from within. But they were Nordics, anyhow. Both of them.

I mean looking at her, I sometimes wondered how they would get away with just being out and about in our world. Granted, Cybele looked a lot like a Swede or some kind of sandy blonde-haired Scandinavian. But still, her eye sockets were exceptionally deep set, with dark shadows around those turquoise irises, and her broad forehead was abnormally high. You would think she would at least wear her hair with bangs to conceal that somewhat. Then there was the question of her height. How many women are as tall as a basketball player? She was beautiful, but there was unquestionably something freakish about her that I imagined would be problematically conspicuous. Cybele startled me when she let on that she could hear what I was thinking, by saying, out of the context of our conversation, "I usually wear a hat and large sunglasses. Can't do anything about my height, though, other than never wearing high heels to make it any worse. Plus, I'm so big-boned and I have so much muscle mass that I'd probably break long skinny heels." I invited Cybele to stay for dinner, but after learning everything that she had about Nikolai that evening I think she wanted to be alone to process it all. I promised to make copies of Nikolai's manuscripts to give to her next time she visited me, which she assured me that she would do soon.

Cybele certainly kept that promise, and not just so that she could pick up the xeroxed manuscripts. Over the spring of 1979, as Iran descended into medieval Muslim theocracy, I was granted a welcome diversion from that grim reality by Cybele's frequent visits to my penthouse. In my lifetime as Nikolai, I had only had sex with her during that brief stay at the Biltmore Hotel in California. But in this life, she moved in with me and we became long-term lovers. I had no idea that she was open to being with a woman, although frankly I think that part of that openness was on account of the fact that, in addition to my being a reincarnation of Nikolai, Cybele believed that I was carrying another *male* reincarnation of Nikolai in my womb.

Having already been a mother, namely to Apollyon, Cybele was a constant source of counsel and support during my pregnancy, in the course of which she was also my lover. For the first time in my life, I actually had breasts. They were still very small relative to the average, and certainly compared to Cybele's, but when I started lactating, I also grew some breast tissue under those huge nipples that I've always had. This meant I had to finally start wearing bras on a regular basis, especially because otherwise I would wind up lactating through my dress shirt at work. Sometimes, Cybele would suck the milk from my tits while we made love, which helped me avoid that inconvenience from happening too often. Perhaps to Cybele's chagrin, I had decided that I would name my son, not Nikolai, but "Jason" in remembrance of the boy who would never be born.

CHAPTER 25

UNCONQUERABLE BELIAL

Jason Avalon came into this world on July 9, 1979. Cybele helped to deliver him in a home birth that was also attended by Johnny, and by a doctor closely associated with Avalon Pharmaceutical. Throughout Jason's childhood, she would become "Aunt Cybele" and he would be "Uncle Johnny." Saying that Cybele "helped" in the delivery of Jason is an understatement. She literally pulled his little head and shoulders out of my birth canal with her bloodied, preternaturally strong hands. The crying boy's first sight as he entered this world were her soul-piercing blue-green eyes. As my lover, Cybele would, in effect, become Jason's second mother, and Apollyon would have a brother after all. The baby that would have become Jason Reza Jorjani was strangled to death by his own umbilical cord on February 21, 1981, after his mother endured twenty hours of attempted labor at Booth Memorial Hospital in Queens. At least, that's what Jorjani's death certificate would say.

By then my baby boy was a year and a half old. In that time, something very strange had started to happen. Memories of my past life as Nikolai became much more vivid. I was having increasingly frequent flashes of recall that were as high-fidelity as any memory from my current lifetime. Combined with what I had learned from him in the time that we spent together, this flood of *anamnesis* had begun to fuse his life inextricably into mine. Having been Nikolai became an even more real experience for me than the existential continuity that I felt with Jason Reza Jorjani, whose life I had effectively erased with a view to having the soul of Nikolai be reborn as my child instead of incarnating as him. But when I looked into my baby's eyes, I felt more like Nikolai was looking at him through my eyes.

Maybe it was because of this intense sense of identification with Nikolai, and his experiences, that I was possessed to buy one of those ski houses at Hunter Mountain that his aunt, Nikita, had owned and where Nikolai had spent much time during his childhood. Or maybe it was just my own nostalgia for where I also had such formative experiences, in a future that would never be, when the Scribner Lodge was remodeled into my parents' alpine chalet. Nikolai and I — and the erased Jason too — had been, in one way or another, connected to those highest peaks of the Catskill Mountains bound together by the Devil's Path. I wanted my son to be, too.

While he was an infant, during the spring and summer, we would crawl on the slope of Scribner Hill together, with the view of Hunter Mountain diagonally across from us. I would get down on all fours and romp around with him. With all of the local folk imagery of Bears around us, and never having forgotten *Artio*, the Bear goddess whose ruined temple was hidden somewhere up on that mountain, I put it into my boy's mind to call me "Mama Bear."

Jason must have been around four years old when he started having the recurring nightmares. I think they were triggered by being up here in the mountains, especially in the main building at Scribner, because what he was describing was being a young man in a ski chalet. Except that the words that he would be trying to speak during these nightmares, when I could make any sense from out of the gibberish, were from Spanish and German. I still had considerable psychic ability, and since I began to feel this deeper identification with my life as Nikolai, I noticed that it had gotten even stronger. He was, of course, an adept psychic. I was also familiar with the protocol for Dream Telepathy induction, involving sensory deprivation and a cocktail of a few different drugs. So, one night, with Cybele watching over the two of us, I entered a state of Dream Telepathy with my own son.

What I saw shook me to my core. It was the interior of the ski chalet at Cerro Catedral, in Argentina, where Adolfo von Seelstrang was staying before I assassinated him on the slopes. I could vividly see the old black iron sconces barely illuminating the red-painted walls, and the large chandeliers inside the dimly lit and rather palatial wood and stucco structure. Some kind of classical music was being played on string instruments somewhere in the house. I was seeing through Adolfo's eyes. As if this was not disturbing enough, when I crossed from a long hallway into the living room of the chalet, with its tall ceiling, my heart nearly stopped as I noticed who was leaning back into one of the plush chairs. It was Nikita. She was wearing a snug white fur coat, but her muscular legs were bare. There was no mistaking her for anyone else. As I walked into the room — I mean as Adolfo did — she said something to him in fluent German, and I heard myself reply in Spanish with an Argentinian accent.

I had to have been in the body of a man who was about 20 years old, which would have made this about a year before I assassinated Adolfo in January of 1979. By 1978, Nikita should have been dead for 13 years. She had overdosed at age 45. This person that I was looking at could have been an exceptionally healthy and fit woman in her late fifties. I was hurled out of the dream with great force and the telepathic link with my son was suddenly broken. Cybele says that she had never seen such an appalled look on my face. She remembers that as I got up, slowly, and hesitantly walked over to my boy who was jerking uneasily in his troubled sleep, my expression was one of deep disgust tinged with an equally profound rage.

It did not take me long to fully process the fact that my son was not a reincarnation of Nikolai but was in fact Adolfo von Seelstrang reborn. I also intuited that the reason why I had come to re-identify with Nikolai so intimately since his death was that he had actually managed to merge with me after he was killed — I mean after I... after the specter of Adolfo killed him in the backwoods of this hill that terrible winter night in 1978. But there remained the mystery of Nikita. As Nikolai I had seen her seemingly dead body sprawled across her bed that morning in the summer before I started college at Columbia. The open pill containers littered the bed. Had Nikita somehow *faked* her death?

Who were the coroners that showed up that morning, the ones who confirmed that she had been killed by an overdose of prescription drugs mixed with excessive alcohol? I had made the call to them from a phone that I long suspected was bugged. Maybe the call was intercepted by "cleaners" of a sort. Since I asked that she be cremated, I had never seen her body again after that morning when it was taken away. I came up here to Hunter to scatter the ashes that were purported to be hers around the Scribner ski house where she had initiated me. *Were those somebody else's ashes?* I knew that there were drugs that could closely emulate signs of death — for a time — after which a person to whom they had been administered could be successfully revived. Now that I think about it, when I held my aunt's body — I mean Nikolai's aunt's body — in the bed that morning, although it was very still and she had no pulse that I *could* detect, I had the oddest feeling that she was still there. I assumed that it was because her specter was watching me from the bedside. But then, her body was not as cold as a corpse should be.

Then I thought of Nikita's alcoholism during those last years that I lived with her, at the apartment on 77th and Cherokee. Could it be that she became so distraught and depressed because she knew, well in advance, that she was going to have to leave me? To die to me, so that she could become *somebody else's mother*. As these questions ravaged my mind, I suddenly remembered Skorzeny with that flashlight under his chin in the catacombs of Rome. Then, Thompson, sitting in his office and telling me — telling Nikolai — "She was our mother, Nick. She *led us.*" Had I, as Nikolai, been Remus, and was Adolfo Romulus?

All I knew was that in the months that followed that incident, and these realizations, my mind fixed on two thoughts, cognitively dissonant as they might have been: strangling my own son to death and finding Nikita. As it turned out, she would find us *before* I was able to muster the courage to sacrifice *her* child for the second time. Far be it from the She-Wolf to let that happen. From out of the hidden folds of the Invisible Imperium, she had sensed that Romulus was in danger. She would not be derelict in her duty this time. *Nikita* — her name meant "the Unconquerable."

Do you have any idea what it really means to be *in bed with the enemy*? Spies do it all the time, I suppose, especially female agents who are expected to convincingly fuck their targets. But what I had to somehow wrap my mind around regarding Nikolai, Nikita, and Adolfo was on another level entirely. I did not expect much support from Cybele in processing this, since through her son, Apollyon, she was also connected to the enemy, albeit to a rebel faction within the Invisible Imperium that I knew aimed to become the Olympian World Order of the future past from which I hailed. But I never expected Cybele to betray me this way.

Apparently, she had been approached by Nikita, who had convinced her that unless she assisted in the kidnapping of my son, I would wind up being responsible for a child sacrifice. Did Cybele want to see Adolfo — now bearing the name "Jason Avalon" — grow up to become the Führer of the Traditionalist Reich that I had seen rise to power in my original timeline? *Didn't she know that this would pave the way for the rise of the full-fledged Olympian Imperium, which she and Apollyon claimed to be fighting against from within?* These were the thoughts that raced through my mind after I came back from a day of skiing on the mountain to find that both Cybele and my son were gone.

My eyes were so full of blood, and my hands so trembling with rage, that I could barely hold the typed manuscript that I found lying on my boy's bed. No doubt Nikita herself had placed it there. Three sets of boot tracks were in the snow outside, leading away from the cabin, with one of them smaller than the other two. *She had been here.* Written on the cover in red ink, no doubt by Nikita's hand, were the words: *mnestheti tis ei*, which was ancient Greek for "remember who you are." The title page, with no author identified, simply read: *Psychotron.* It was a Greek contraction, commonly used in Russian paranormal research, which meant something like "mind space" or "psychic arena" or "psionic domain." From the start, this *Psychotron* reminded me of my argument in *Epimetheus and Pandora*, and I was shocked at how that book had somehow receded into the back of my mind for so many years. It was no accident.

Psychotron began by describing the cosmos as a quantum computational system. The background of this system was chaos, which was not to be understood as the absence of order so much as order of such a high degree of complexity that it was mathematically incalculable and could not, in principle, be encompassed by rational comprehension. It was not just a question of the limits of *human* reason. The manuscript described an Artificial Intelligence named "Belial." This entity had also attempted to comprehend the chaos from out of which our cosmos perpetually emerges and had failed to do so. What this "Belial" had succeeded in doing was to hack the computational matrix of the cosmos in such a way as to engineer a programmable domain within the context of the larger system, as a subset or subroutine of it. Supposedly, those who had built this Artificial Intelligence were denizens of "Atlantis" who had successfully led a rebellion against what they considered to be oppressive overlords resistant to any form of social change. They called themselves, the "Belial Group." As I read on, I began to feel ill. It was like what I was reading was coming back to me from some depth of my psyche locked more securely than the memory of any past life. Even worse. *I felt as if I was somehow the author of it!*

This "Belial Group" apparently had as its purpose the study of alternative histories and multiple timelines as simulated by the Artificial Intelligence that was its namesake, with a view to discovering by what means a society of godless, lawless, and truly unbound individuals could be created and sustained. "The New Atlantis" built upon the ruins of the Olympian tyranny over Earth was to be such a society. Each of the simulations would begin with a mock destruction of Atlantis and the failure of its rebellion against Olympus, cleaning the slate for the creation of a new world, although any one of these simulations could be reset at various points within "the game" by means of apparent "time travel." Only those with "Phenomenal Authorization" were allowed to carry out these resets.

The domain within which these simulations were conducted was called the "Psychotron." The vast machinery for it was located on the island of Poseidea in Atlantis, where thousands of Atlanteans from the Belial Group were plugged into a psychotronic device capable of programming and reprogramming something like a telepathically shared dream state that interacted directly with the field of quantum potential that is the abyssal background of cosmic order. They had been made to forget their actual identities, and a plethora of Non-Player Characters generated by the Artificial Intelligence populated the Psychotron together with them. Over the course of the simulations, these Atlanteans would don many "avatars" that they took to be successive "reincarnations" of themselves. But, as with dreams, the difference in timescale within the simulation as compared to outside of it, was such that thousands of years inside only amounts to a few years of "real time" outside. From what I could glean between the lines of this manuscript, the "Atlantis" that was the context for this insane project was much more futuristic and sophisticated than the society that I remembered from what I believed to be my past life as Dara-El. It was as if that civilization had gone on to evolve for many more millennia.

I read throughout the whole night, with light snow falling outside. By the time that the rising sun's light streamed through the steam from my fourth mug of coffee, I felt like I was going to throw up. I was toward the end of the manuscript. What was being described was a positively diabolical system of dialectics. As in most role-playing games, there were two sides that defined the fundamental parameters of the developmental process being powered and recorded by the Psychotron. One side was defined by expansion, progression, and innovation. The other side by constraint, retardation, and regression. Both of these forces were required for the spectral mechanism as a whole to perform its function, because without the challenge of various forms of restriction, oppression, and imposed stasis, the dynamic counter-force would not find its way to an actualization of the maximally free form of society. Instead, those within the simulation would become complacently satisfied with a less than optimal type of social organization, and their own most abyssal psychic depths would remain unfathomed in relation to the others with which they co-existed as part of this community.

Around 10 am, I finally did puke my guts out in the kitchen sink. It was December 12, 1983. On *this* timeline, in *this* simulation, and for the first time in many "lifetimes," I was beginning to remember who I really was. It wasn't like remembering a past life. More like remembering things about your *actual* life *as it is now* once you become lucid inside of a dreamscape that occults the world "outside" the dream. I was actually afraid that I would "wake up," because I knew that I was not supposed to. A lot of people were depending on me.

I went over to the mirror, and when I looked into it, surfacing from the depths of my subconscious I could faintly discern an apparition of my *other* face. Some of the features were similar, but my forehead was very tall, and my cheekbones higher. I had shoulder-length platinum hair with a shock of jet black in it, and gray eyes. I seemed to remember that my name was "Lucifera." I stood there mesmerized until I heard three knocks downstairs on the cabin door. I almost tripped going down the carpeted staircase. Heedlessly barefooted, I opened the door. As the cold morning air rushed in over the crisp snowbanks around the house, I stood there taking in all seven feet of him. "Are you alright, Chief?" asked Apollyon. "Have you come back to yourself?" I tried to muster a smile. "Chief." Yeah, chief *engineer* of Belial, and principal architect of the Psychotron project. An Atlantean woman with truly *phenomenal* authorization.

I invited Apollyon in, well, to the extent that I left the door open as I walked away from it so that he could come in behind me. Apollyon closed it behind him, and then he followed me upstairs. He explained that Cybele hadn't really helped Nikita "kidnap" my son, and that the three of them were simply back at my apartment in the city. Nikita felt she needed to intervene before I did more damage to my own project. "You got lost in the game, Dana," Apollyon said. "So, then, you know?" I replied. "I've known for years," he said. "Otherwise I would never be able to play such a duplicitous role. Stradling the underworld of the Olympians and your world — I mean *this* world unless I understood the greater purpose behind such machinations. *Your* purpose, as the leader of the Belial Group. Some years ago, Nikita helped me to understand that. My mother tried, but I wouldn't listen. It was Nikita who prevailed upon me."

Apollyon was stunningly beautiful, well, and also handsome, sitting there in the morning light on the edge of my bed. I was in such a state that I paid no heed to this as I stripped naked right in front of him, trying to make my way into the shower in a daze. I could have stood under that water forever. But I dragged myself out, dried off, and got dressed, again, right in front of Apollyon. He was more than gentlemanly enough not to gawk at me. Actually, he looked rather contemplative.

Apollyon was used to having a chauffeur, but he obviously couldn't bring one here. I was surprised that, having brought his own car, he knew how to drive it himself. "Nikita taught me," he explained. "Truth be told, Dana, I can drive like James Bond if I want to." I replied, "Well, please *don't* now, because if you do, I'll throw up again, and I'd hate to ruin the inside of this car." On the way from the Catskills back to Manhattan, Apollyon answered the questions that I was capable of mustering. He told me that Adolfo needed to grow up to be the leader of the coming Imperium, so that it would eventually be compromised from within. He also explained how the war on Mars and all that was part of the backstory of the simulation. I began to vaguely remember that what he was saying was true. I also thought of the way that Martian ruins factored into the film *Total Recall*, which I had seen in my life as Jorjani on the overwritten timeline.

When we finally got back to the city and walked into my apartment at 55 Central Park West, I heard Adolfo — I mean Jason — squealing as he played with Cybele on the carpet of the sunken floor in the living room. Nikita, who was sitting on a chair next to them, looked right into my eyes as Apollyon and I approached her. The She-Wolf's fiercely self-confident demeanor softened momentarily, so that by the time I was standing in front of her, and she got up from the chair, I could see tears welling up in her eyes. She reached her arms around my stiff body, holding me firmly, as she said, "I'm *so* sorry. There was *no* other way, Nikolai."

With my head downcast, and disregarding Jason, who was now crawling around my feet and tugging on my pantlegs, I asked Nikita, "Did I even have a mother in that life? Or did you *grow* me, like you grew Adolfo?" Nikita made me turn around and look toward the hallway that led to the bedrooms. From out of the darkness, Marianna appeared for a few moments before disappearing back into the shadows. "*I* was your mother. At least, that's the role I played. Doubling myself during that staged murder took a great deal of energy. Bilocation is not easy to sustain. So, at some point, the farce had to end. Besides, we needed to break you open." Bilocation. I thought of *The Life of*

Apollonius of Tyana, which I had commissioned Philostratus to write so many centuries ago during my life as Julia Domna. "What about my—I mean, Nikolai's *father*?" "He was a soldier, sweetheart. He did what he was told to do." "And my 'uncle' from that life—your 'husband'?" "*He* was a clown. Part of the wallpaper." I could feel that "wallpaper" peeling in my mind. The blood-spattered wallpaper of this world.

Cybele picked Jason up off the floor, easily cradling a four-year old in her massive arms and holding him firmly with her freakishly huge hands as he reached his little fingers out toward my shoulders. There we all stood together. Myself, Nikita, and Cybele with my son in her arms. A veritable coven of the Triune Goddess. Cybele handed Jason to me, and I lifted him up to where he could sit on my broad shoulders.

Apollyon came in from the kitchen, where we had heard him rummaging. "There's not much in the fridge. Shall we all go out to dinner together?" His mother, Cybele, looked at him and said, "I'll call the Tavern and tell them to hold a table for us." I turned to Cybele, while still holding Jason up behind my head, "Ask for the Park Room." She smiled with downcast eyes that wordlessly thanked me for forgiving what at first had seemed to me to be a terrible transgression. "With the kind of money that we spend there, I'm sure they can open a table up for us," she said as she walked off to make the call to the restaurant just across and down the street.

Apollyon looked at me and asked, "Why don't you call Johnny and ask him if he'd like to join us? I mean, he's also *family*, and it's been too long since I've seen him." Nikita chimed in, "Yes, I've heard so much about him from Apollyon. I'd love to meet him in the flesh." Poor Johnny, I thought, to his mind we must look worse than the Munsters. Apollyon picked up on this telepathically, and then stuck his arms out to do that impression of his that never got old. Frankenstein. The Family.

OTHER BOOKS PUBLISHED BY ARKTOS

OTHER BOOKS PUBLISHED BY ARKTOS

OTHER BOOKS PUBLISHED BY ARKTOS

OTHER BOOKS PUBLISHED BY ARKTOS